Carl Hiaasen  the bestselling *Nature Girl, Skinny Dip*, *You*, and three popular children's books His most recent work of nonfiction i *Hacker's Return to a Ruinous Sport*. He also writes a weekly column for *The Miami Herald*.

'His investigative journalist's eye for detail and his merciless, only-just exaggerated satire are a killer combination ... wickedly funny' *Sunday Times*

'A hilarious send up of trash celebrity culture ... a crazy, riotous, and thoroughly rib-tickling ride'
Irish Independent

'*Star Island* is a concoction worth the time of any reader who wants quality entertainment'
San Francisco Chronicle

'Hiaasen reclaims his groove in *Star Island*, a wicked, fizzy sendup of American celebrity culture ... A very funny book about life in the fast lane' *Boston Globe*

'A wild and fun Sunshine State ride' *New York Post*

'This is classic Hiaasen – demented, hilarious, and utterly over the top' *Booklist* (starred)

'An outrageous, offbeat novel ... The torrent of pop culture barbs are bound to please Hiaasen's ardent fans'
Publishers Weekly

ALSO BY CARL HIAASEN

Tourist Season
Double Whammy
Skin Tight
Native Tongue
Strip Tease
Stormy Weather
Lucky You
Sick Puppy
Basket Case
Skinny Dip
Nature Girl
Bad Monkey

For young readers

Hoot
Flush
Scat

Nonfiction

Paradise Screwed: Selected Columns
(edited by Diane Stevenson)
Kick Ass: Selected Columns (edited by Diane Stevenson)
Team Rodent: How Disney Devours the World
The Downhill Lie: A Hacker's Return to a Ruinous Sport

CARL HIAASEN

STAR ISLAND

sphere

SPHERE

Published in the United States in 2010 by Alfred A. Knopf,
a division of Random House, Inc., New York
First published in Great Britain in 2010 by Sphere
This paperback edition published in 2011 by Sphere
Reprinted 2012, 2013, 2014

A CIP catalogue record for this book
is available from the British Library.

ISBN 978-0-7515-4333-9

Typeset in Janson by M Rules
Printed and bound in Great Britain by
Clays Ltd, St Ives plc

Papers used by Sphere are from well-managed forests
and other responsible sources.

MIX
Paper from
responsible sources
FSC
www.fsc.org   FSC® C104740

Sphere
An imprint of
Little, Brown Book Group
100 Victoria Embankment
London EC4Y 0DY

An Hachette UK Company
www.hachette.co.uk

www.littlebrown.co.uk

For Sonny Mehta,
a great editor and friend

STAR ISLAND

★

1

On the fifteenth of March, two hours before sunrise, an emergency medical technician named Jimmy Campo found a sweaty stranger huddled in the back of his ambulance. It was parked in a service alley behind the Stefano Hotel, where Jimmy Campo and his partner had been summoned to treat a twenty-two-year-old white female who had swallowed an unwise mix of vodka, Red Bull, hydrocodone, birdseed and stool softener—in all respects a routine South Beach 911 call, until now.

The stranger in Jimmy Campo's ambulance had two 35-mm digital cameras hanging from his fleshy neck, and a bulky gear bag balanced on his ample lap. He wore a Dodgers cap and a Bluetooth ear set. His ripe, florid cheeks glistened damply, and his body reeked like a prison laundry bag.

"Get out of my ambulance," Jimmy Campo said.

"Is she dead?" the man asked excitedly.

"Dude, I'm callin' the cops if you don't move it."

"Who's with her up there—Colin? Shia?"

The stranger outweighed Jimmy Campo by sixty-five pounds but not an ounce of it was muscle. Jimmy Campo, who'd once been a triathlete, dragged the intruder from the vehicle and deposited him on the sticky pavement beneath a streetlight.

"Chill, for Christ's sake," the man said, examining his camera equipment for possible damage. Stray cats tangled and yowled somewhere in the shadows.

Inside the ambulance, Jimmy Campo found what he was looking for: a sealed sterile packet containing a coiled intravenous rig to replace the one that the female overdose victim had ripped from her right arm while she was thrashing on the floor.

The stranger struggled to his feet and said, "I'll give you a thousand bucks."

"For what?"

"When you bring her downstairs, lemme take a picture." The man dug into the folds of his stale trousers and produced a lump of cash. "You gotta job to do, and so do I. Here's a grand."

Jimmy Campo looked at the money in the stranger's hand. Then he glanced up at the third floor of the hotel, where his partner was almost certainly dodging vomit.

"Is she famous or somethin'?" Jimmy Campo asked.

The photographer chuckled. "Man, you don't even know?"

Jimmy Campo was thinking about the fifty-two-inch high-def that he'd seen on sale at Brands Mart. He was thinking about his girlfriend on a rampage with his maxed-out MasterCard at the Dadeland Mall. He was thinking about all those nasty letters from his credit union.

"Whoever she is, she's not dead," he told the photographer. "Not tonight."

"Cool." The man continued to hold out the wad of hundreds in the glow of the streetlight, as if teasing a mutt with raw hamburger. He said, "All you gotta do, before loading her in the wagon, just pull down the covers and step away so I can get my shot. Five seconds is all I need."

"It won't be pretty. She's a sick young lady." Jimmy Campo took the crumpled money and smoothed it into his wallet.

"Is she awake at least?" the photographer asked.

"On and off."

"But you could see her eyes in a picture, right? She's got those awesome sea-green eyes."

Jimmy Campo said, "I didn't notice."

"You really don't know who she is? Seriously?"

"Who do you work for, anyway?"

"A limited partnership," the man said. "Me, myself and I."

"And where can I see this great picture you're gonna take?"

"Everywhere. You'll see it everywhere," the stranger said.

Eighteen minutes later, Jimmy Campo and his partner emerged from the Stefano Hotel guiding a collapsible stretcher upon which lay a slender, motionless form.

The photographer was surprised at the absence of a retinue; no bodyguards or boyfriends or hangers-on. A lone Miami Beach police officer followed the stretcher down the alley. When the photographer began snapping pictures, the cop barely reacted, making no effort to shield the stricken woman from the flash bursts. That should have been a clue.

Sliding closer, the paparazzo intercepted the stretcher as it rolled with an oscillating squeak toward the open end of the ambulance. True to his word, Jimmy Campo tugged down the sheet and stepped away, leaving an opening.

"Cherry!" the photographer shouted at the slack face. "Cherry, baby, how 'bout a big smile for your fans?"

The young woman's incurious eyes were open. They were not sea-green, mint-green, pea-green or any hue of green. They were brown.

"Goddammit," the photographer growled, lowering his Nikon.

The woman on the stretcher grinned behind the oxygen mask and blew him a kiss.

Grabbing at Jimmy Campo's arm, the photographer cried, "Gimme back my money!"

"Mister, I don't know what you're talking about," said the paramedic, elbowing the sweaty creep back into the shadows.

*

Inside a chauffeured black Suburban, racing across the MacArthur Causeway toward Jackson Memorial Hospital, a performer known as Cherry Pye was retching loudly into a silver-plated ice bucket. Her real name was Cheryl Bunterman, one of many ferociously guarded secrets about her life. Since the age of fourteen, when she'd first appeared in a dubious buckskin cowgirl outfit on the Nickelodeon network, Cheryl Bunterman had been introduced to one and all as Cherry Pye.

The person who'd invented that shamelessly porny name was sitting next to Cherry Pye in the third leather bench seat of the big Suburban, stroking her daughter's crusty blond hair. "Feel better now?" Janet Bunterman inquired soothingly.

"No, Momma, I feel like shit." Cherry whimpered, hurled, and then drifted off again. Half-sitting and half-sprawled, she wore a white terry-cloth robe, courtesy of the Stefano Hotel, and nothing underneath it. Even in semi-consciousness her small red-knuckled hands remained fastened on the rim of the ice bucket.

Janet Bunterman had long ago chosen to overlook her off-spring's promiscuous fondness for drugs and alcohol, and on this particular occasion decreed that a late snack of spoiled shellfish was to blame for Cherry's current debilitation. Also riding in the vehicle were a locally recruited physician, two stone-faced publicists, a hairstylist and a chunky bodyguard named Lev, who claimed to have served with the Mossad.

"Who ordered those vile scallops from room service, anyway?" Janet Bunterman demanded.

"Cherry did," said Lev.

"Nonsense," snapped the superstar's mother.

"And also the two bottles of Grey Goose."

"Lev, how many times have I warned you about calling 911? Like she's some sort of . . . *civilian*."

The bodyguard said, "I thought she was dying."

"Oh please. We've been through so many of these gastritis scares."

The doctor looked neutrally at his new patient, but the publicists, who were identical twins, exchanged dour glances. The hairstylist yawned like a cheetah.

"This time was worse," the bodyguard said.

Janet Bunterman said, "That's enough. Don't upset her more."

"Ask the doc. It was bad."

"I said, that's enough. Lots of girls have tummy problems. Right, Dr. Blake?"

"Let's see what the tests show at the hospital." The doctor was being diplomatic, for he knew very well what would turn up in the blood and urine of Cherry Pye. Upon arriving at Room 309 of the Stefano, he'd found the starlet nude, speckled in sunflower husks and twitching like a poisoned cockroach on the carpet. The bodyguard had pulled the doctor aside and provided a list of all known substances that the girl had consumed during the night, and the approximate amounts. It was the doctor's earnest desire to be free of this crew before those three hundred milligrams of Dulcolax kicked in.

"Well, our Annie sure saved the day," Janet Bunterman said in a positive tone.

"That's her job," one of the publicists remarked coolly.

The other one said, "It was her night off. We lucked out."

"Ann's a pro," Lev agreed.

"Sometimes," added Janet Bunterman with a barbed pause, "I think she's the only one we can count on in this organization."

"What do you mean by that?" Lev asked.

Conversation was suspended when Cherry Pye awoke and burped again, stentoriously.

Afterward she wiped her mouth on a sleeve and whined, "Can't somebody please hold this freaking bucket?"

"Of course, sweetheart," her mother said. "Lev will hold your bucket."

"No, Lev will *not*," said Lev.

Cherry Pye's mother reached up and angrily punched one of the dome lights, harshly illuminating a scene that had been barely tolerable in the dark.

She said, "Lev, turn around and steady the bucket for Cherry. It's the least you can do."

"No."

"Somebody?" gurgled Cherry. "Jesus, what do I pay you assholes for?"

No one, including the woman's mother, made a move. Only the hairdresser spoke. "Come on, people, step up," he said. "Baby girl's in pain."

Janet Bunterman fixed her well-practiced glare on the stubborn bodyguard. "Lev, I swear, if you don't hold that yuck bucket for my sick child, my only child, your meal ticket, then you're fired."

"Understood."

"That's it? That's all you've got to say?"

"No, Mrs. Bunterman, that's not all. Your daughter's a fucking train wreck. Also, she sings like a frog with emphysema." The bodyguard tapped the chauffeur on the shoulder. "Pull over, François," he said. "I'm getting out of this nut wagon."

Still wielding his cameras, Bang Abbott returned to the lobby of the Stefano and took an ambush position behind a potted schefflera tree. The security goons paid no attention, which probably meant that Cherry Pye had already left the hotel.

If she'd ever been there at all.

Bang Abbott gave up and drove his rental car to a nearby McDonald's. For breakfast he ordered three McSkillet burritos, a Danish and black coffee. He was met in a corner of the restaurant by a drawn, gray-skinned man named Fremont Spores, who had come to be paid.

"For what?" Bang Abbott scoffed. "It was a bum tip."

Spores kept a bank of digital police scanners going 24/7 in the kitchen of his Collins Avenue apartment. He was considered the best in the business.

"You told me to let you know, was anything beachside with a young white female. You said to call right away, was anything at the clubs and hotels." Spores bared his stained dentures. "Don't cheap out on me, you sonofabitch."

Bang Abbott shrugged. "Your bum tip cost me a grand."

"Twenty-two-year-old OD at the Stefano—it don't get no better than that. And now you're sayin' the information ain't worth a hundred lousy bucks."

"Wrong bimbo, Fremont."

"Welcome to Miami. Now hand over the dough."

"Or what?"

Spores stood up slowly, teetering on scarecrow legs. He probed into his shirt pocket and came out with a soggy cigarette, which he dried in an armpit of his T-shirt.

"I got other clients more important than you," he said to Bang Abbott, who snickered.

"'Clients'? That's rich."

Spores lit the cigarette. "One, name of Restrepo, he's a businessman from South America. For him, I listen to the Coast Guard frequencies. Marine patrol, too. A heavy dude."

"Relax, Fremont."

"My man Restrepo, he said to call day or night, was any kind of favor I need. He's so grateful for all the good work I do, he said to let him know, was any problems in my life." Spores coughed and squinted at Bang Abbott through the cigarette smoke. "Is this a problem or not?"

Bang Abbott tossed two fifties on the table. "Thanks for nuthin."

"Blow me," said Fremont Spores. He picked up the cash and walked away.

After breakfast the photographer drove back to the Stefano. His plan was to sneak up to the third floor and knock on the door of Room 309, just to make sure. He got halfway to the elevator before one of the security guards intercepted him. Because it was early and the lobby was empty, the security guard felt free to knee Bang Abbott in the groin.

Limping back toward his parking space, Bang Abbott spied the scrawny bellman who'd assured him that Cherry Pye was partying on the third floor, a piece of apparent misinformation that had cost the photographer another fifty bucks. The bellman had just gotten off work and was standing at a bus stop, tugging off the nappy jacket of his monkey suit and yakking on a cell phone. Bang Abbott came up behind him and twisted the fuzzy flesh of his neck until the bellman whinnied.

"You screwed me over," the photographer said.

"No way!" The bellman wriggled free.

"It wasn't her, *chico*," Bang Abbott said.

"In 309, right?"

"So you said."

"Man, I seen the babe with my own eyes."

"Wrong babe. Now gimme back my fifty dollars."

The bellman backed away, fearing that the hefty photographer might actually try to mug him for the money. "Hold on, man—it was totally her. I'd know that lady anywhere. I got all her videos downloaded, you don't believe me." He held up his iPhone for effect, though he had no intention of letting the fat man put his grimy paws on it.

"Listen to me, junior," the photographer said. "I eyeballed the girl myself. It was *not* Miss Cherry Pye. I shot her picture on the goddamn stretcher when they were haulin' her to the ambulance."

The bellman cocked his head. "Whatchu talkin' 'bout, bro? She didn't go out on a stretcher, she went out in a wheelchair."

"Don't tell me this."

"Through the kitchen, man. I was the one who held the doors."

Bang Abbott kicked at the curb.

"And there wasn't no ambulance," the bellman added. "They put her in a black Suburban."

"Well, fuck me up the butthole." Bang Abbott scratched his scalp.

"I wondered where chu was, man. How chu missed her."

"They took her out through the goddamn kitchen?"

"The chick was major messed up," the bellman said. "I mean, she was pukin' into an ice bucket."

A money shot, the photographer thought ruefully. *Worldwide gold.*

The bus rumbled up, brakes hissing. The bellman made a quick move, but Bang Abbott blocked his path.

"Did you see any other shooters outside?"

"Any *whats*?"

"Photographers. Anybody get a shot of our girl blowing chunks?"

The bellman shook his head. "Swear to God, I dint see nobody."

"'Cause if that picture turns up anywhere in this universe, even the *West Fargo Weekly Foreskin*, I'm comin' after you for my fifty bucks. Understand?" Bang Abbott stepped aside, and the bellman scrambled onto the bus. The photographer returned to his car, inhaled four Advils and headed for the Standard, where Jamie Foxx was rumored to be staying.

These days a photo of the actor was worth maybe a grand or two, depending on the wardrobe and sobriety level of his dates, who were customarily gorgeous. However, a single exclusive picture of Cherry Pye in the debasing throes of a narcotics overdose would have fetched five figures, Bang Abbott figured. A very solid five.

He hoped with all his withered, calcified prune of a heart that the bellman was telling the truth. He hoped that nobody else had gotten the shot.

He also made up his mind to find out how he'd been tricked. It wasn't really a matter of honor, for Bang Abbott held no illusions about the odious station of his profession. However, he owned a fiercely competitive streak and he hated to be stymied or outwitted, whether it was by a fellow shooter or the celebrity target. He took such setbacks hard.

The dull and often lonely nature of his work—stalking people who kept no schedule—provided hour upon unhealthy hour in which Bang Abbott could work himself into a fevered snit. That is what happened as he paced the sidewalk outside the Standard Hotel, waiting for Jamie Foxx to swagger in from a wild night of clubbing.

It wasn't unusual for stars to attempt to fool the paparazzi by donning wigs or switching cars, but this time Cherry Pye's handlers had shown exceptional guile and enterprise. The more Bang Abbott thought about it, the more agitated he became.

I will get a picture of that crazy twat in all her dysfunctional glory, he vowed bitterly, no matter what it takes.

2

Ann DeLusia woke up at 4:09 a.m. in Room 409, and she couldn't go back to sleep. When the first call came, she was soaking in the bathtub.

Not a world-class marble bathtub, either, not at this lame Deco hotel. Somebody had figured it would be cool to keep the old plumbing fixtures from the thirties, a real design treasure. The tub was so short and shallow that Ann DeLusia couldn't stretch without raising her feet from the water and bracing them on the clammy wall tiles.

Although she wore noise-suppression headphones, Lenny Kravitz rocking full blast, she still heard the phone ringing. How could she not have? It was mounted on the wall right next to the damn toilet, on the notion that important people liked to chat while taking a dump. Even in her new five-star life, Ann refused to embrace this custom.

14

By the time she'd removed her iPod, climbed out of the munchkin-sized bathtub and wrapped herself in a towel, the phone had stopped ringing. She put on a terry-cloth robe that she found in the closet and sat on the bed to wait. Two minutes later, the phone rang again. Ann picked it up and said, "Yo."

"Can you get down here right away?" Janet Bunterman asked.

"It's my night off. I've got company." A harmless lie—Ann didn't wish to be taken for granted.

"We need you," said Janet Bunterman.

"What's the dress code?"

"Take the stairs. Hurry up."

"All I've got on is a robe."

"They won't care one bit at the hospital."

Here we go, thought Ann DeLusia. "Gastritis? *Again*, Janet?"

"Get your butt down here, Annie. The ambulance is coming any minute."

The mood inside Cherry Pye's suite was urgent but not panicky. Lev covered the door, conversing in hushed tones with a stranger toting a black bag. Cherry's hairdresser, Leo, was at the bar, mixing himself a Tom Collins. The publicists stood in tandem by the bay window, chain-smoking and murmuring gravely into matching cell phones. The starlet herself had already been moved to the master bedroom, where she was being tended by her mother and a Spanish-speaking nurse who'd been sent by hotel security.

Kneeling among the medicine bottles and empty Red Bull cans was a young curly-haired actor whom Ann recognized from the MTV awards, although she could not recall his name. He wore a sleeveless gym shirt and inside-out boxer shorts, and he was picking up pills from the carpet. Ann leaned over and told him, "You'd better get outta here."

"In a minute," the actor said, not looking up. He wasn't leaving without his Vicodins.

"How's our homegirl doin'?" Ann asked.

The young man shook his head. "She ate, like, a pound of fucking birdseed. She said she was coming back as a cockatoo."

"Coming back from where?"

"You know—from the other side. After she dies, she wants to come back as a cockatoo."

Ann said, "Oh, I like it."

"We went to Parrot Jungle today and got a private show, just for the two of us. There were all these cool birds doing far-out tricks, riding tricycles, dancing with umbrellas, shit like that. Cherry, she was totally blown away. On the way home we had to stop at PetSmart for a bag of seed."

"Good thing you didn't take her to a rodeo," said Ann.

"She's been listening to Shirley MacLaine's books on tapes, so she's like totally into reincarnation." The actor stood up, cupping the recovered tablets protectively. "Have you seen my jeans?" he asked.

By then they could hear the siren of the ambulance. Lev

hustled the young man out of the suite and warned him to keep his mouth shut.

"Where do you want me?" Ann asked.

"It's not my show," Lev said, nodding icily toward the twin publicists.

One of them, still glued to the phone, pointed at an uncluttered section of floor near the bar. Ann arranged herself in a convincing sprawl. Leo knelt down and mussed her hair meticulously. "Undo your robe," he whispered. "Quick, you're supposed to be sick."

"Dying sick or just party sick?"

The second twin loomed over Ann DeLusia and said, "We need you to hurl when the paramedics get up here."

"Okay." This was one of the improvisational talents that had helped Ann win the job.

Clicking her phone shut, the publicist explained, "It was called in as an overdose."

"Imagine that."

"So we'll need some vomit for verisimilitude."

"For *what*?" Ann was thinking about what she'd eaten for dinner: room-service lasagna and a small Caesar. But that was eight hours ago.

She said, "You might have to settle for dry heaves."

The publicist would have frowned were it not for the fact that her face was paralyzed from brow to chin with an exotic Brazilian bootleg strain of botulinum toxin.

She looks so shiny and new! marveled Ann, gazing up from the floor. *Like glowing ceramic.*

Leo hurried out of the suite, followed by the grim sisters. The man with the black bag was admitted to Cherry's private bedroom, and the door was locked from within. Moments later, the paramedics arrived and Lev, playing the anxious boyfriend, let them in.

Ann DeLusia flopped around impressively on the carpet and even managed to hack up some bile. The only unstaged moment of her performance occurred when she jerked the IV out of her arm; Ann was genuinely terrified of needles.

She overheard Lev tell the paramedics that he didn't know her name, much less her next of kin, because he'd met her for only the first time that night in the VIP room at the Set, where she'd been grinding on the lap of a second-string NBA power forward. Ann thought the last fictional detail was unnecessarily salacious.

"Are you sure she's over twenty-one?" one of the paramedics asked Lev.

"The bartender said he checked her ID."

"Then where's her purse?"

"How should I know?" Lev said.

So Ann DeLusia was strapped onto the stretcher as an unaccompanied Jane Doe. She was a bit disappointed that only one paparazzo—a grimy toad that she'd seen before—was lurking in the alley as she was wheeled to the ambulance. Where was the rest of the maggot mob? she wondered. Britney or Paris must be in town.

The ride to the hospital was smoother than most, though Ann had to fight off two more attempts to poke a glucose drip in her vein. At the emergency room, the paramedics informed the admitting nurse that Jane Doe's vital signs appeared to be completely normal—pulse, BP, respiration—which seemed weird considering she was supposed to be an overdose. The nurse wasn't exactly consumed with curiosity, and within minutes Ann found herself unattended in a small examining room that smelled like Pine-Sol and stale piss.

Beyond the half-open door she heard the moans and wails of real patients, and she felt a twinge of guilt for occupying a needed bed. She hopped down, tied the sash of her robe, pulled her hair into a ponytail (which she secured with an elastic examination glove that she'd fashioned into a scrunchie) and walked barefoot out of the hospital. Nobody tried to stop her. Nobody said a word.

A white Town Car was out front, idling in a handicapped spot, exactly where Lev had told her it would be. Ann got in the backseat and rolled down the window to admire what was left of the Florida sunrise.

"I got some bagels," the driver offered.

"Sounds good."

He handed the bag across the seat. "They said I'm supposed to bring you back to the hotel."

Ann DeLusia blinked up at the brightening sky. "Where else would I go?" she said.

Cheryl Gail Bunterman was born in Orlando, the youngest and most outgoing of four children. At age six she won first place at a regional talent show with a spirited off-key version of "Big Yellow Taxi," a song she'd learned from one of her mom's Joni Mitchell albums. As she grew older, Cheryl's stage poise improved far more than her singing, but her parents aggressively compensated by supplying a provocative wardrobe and dance lessons from a petite stripper recruited at a local gentlemen's club, the Central Florida equivalent of Parisian cabaret. Ned and Janet Bunterman were determined to make a superstar of their lil' punkin.

Debuting her new show-business name, Cherry Pye auditioned for, and won, a small role as a cartwheeling cowgirl in an ill-conceived after-school TV special called *Hudson River Roundup*. The story followed a group of innocent yet resourceful Wyoming teens who get lost on a school field trip to New York and are forced to pitch camp in a Bronx subway tunnel.

The former Cheryl Bunterman had only one speaking line—"Back off, buckaroos!"—but her spunky delivery enchanted a viewer named Maury Lykes, who had TiVoed the program in the Key Biscayne penthouse where he spent three months a year. Maury Lykes was a record producer, concert promoter and talent shark who addictively monitored the Nickelodeon channel in search of fresh prospects. That, and he nursed a criminal fondness for underage girls.

Cherry Pye underwent three months of expensive coaching before Maury Lykes resigned himself to the fact that she had the weakest singing voice he'd ever heard from anyone not confined to a hospice. A well-known backup vocalist was brought to the recording studio while Cherry herself was whisked away to study the valuable craft of lip-synching.

Her first single, "Touch Me Like You Mean It," was released with an accompanying video podcast on her fifteenth birthday. The ensuing uproar from offended Christian groups caused a spike in sales that vaulted Cherry Pye's inaugural effort to number nine on the *Billboard* charts. A CD with the same title was rushed out three months later, selling 975,000 copies. It proved to be the biggest hit of the year for Jailbait Records, and Maury Lykes rewarded Cherry with a contract that made her an instant millionaire though essentially a slave to him for life—and an eventful, high-maintenance life it was. These days her reckless escapades made more of a splash than her music, a situation that Maury Lykes was eager to rectify. He'd heard from reliable sources that, anticipating her final crash, one of the major tabloids had already composed Cherry's obituary.

"She goes on tour in three weeks," he reminded Janet Bunterman.

"Don't worry, Maury. She'll rebound."

They were standing at the foot of the bed, in a private room at Jackson Memorial. Cherry lay before them, fast asleep and snoring like a trucker. A bedpan had been wedged unceremoniously under her bare bottom because the laxatives had struck with magnum force.

"She's your daughter, for God's sake. Get her under control," Maury Lykes said, a replay of more conversations than he chose to remember. "Whatever it takes, I don't care. Stick a LoJack up her butt."

"Not so loud," Cherry's mother whispered.

The promoter led her outside, to the hallway. He noticed that the door to Cherry's hospital room stood unguarded. "Where the hell is Lev?" he asked.

"Oh, we had to fire him."

"What for?"

"Insubordination," Janet Bunterman replied.

"Huge mistake. Gi-mongous mistake," Maury Lykes said irritably. "Lev was sharp. He stayed on top of things."

"Yes, including my daughter."

"That was all Cherry's move. You can't blame Lev."

Janet Bunterman said, "She has a weakness for certain types of men."

Yeah, thought Maury Lykes. *Anybody with an eight ball and a nut sack.*

"So what happened last night?" the promoter asked.

"She went out clubbing with that boy from the new Tarantino project."

"The one who plays the necrophiliac surfer? What's his name—Tanner something?" Maury Lykes always liked to know whom his troubled wards were dating. He didn't wish to read it first in the tabloids, or see it on TMZ.com. "Is that the asshole who fed her all the pills?"

"It's just gastritis, Maury. Cherry ate some bad scallops."

"Right. Last time it was eggplant."

"What's your point?" said Janet Bunterman.

"And the time before that, Cobb salad."

"She has a hypersensitive stomach. Ask her doctor!"

Maury Lykes appreciated the value of occasional public misbehavior—it had prolonged the careers of several clients who would otherwise have vanished from the celebrity radar due to a manifest lack of talent. Airport tantrums, DUIs, botched shopliftings and other episodes of delamination could be useful between projects, when there was no other way for a young star to keep from being forgotten. But soon Cherry Pye would be launching a much-anticipated comeback CD (her second), and embarking on a twenty-seven-city concert tour that was (to the deepening consternation of Maury Lykes) not yet sold out. Rumors of another sloppy overdose would dampen advance ticket sales, for at this point even Cherry's most loyal fans wouldn't pay forty-two bucks to see her perform in a trashed condition. They could already watch that for free on YouTube: the infamous aborted show at the Boston Garden, a crisp spring evening two years earlier.

Before the opening number, Cherry had whimsically decided to try crystal meth—"just to see what all the buzz was about," as she later explained to *Details* magazine. She'd lasted for three songs, and at no time had the movement of her lips matched the voice track being piped through the speakers. When the crowd in the first few rows had begun to jeer, Cherry had spun around, dropped her leather mini-shorts and bent over to moon the offenders. Naturally she'd lost her balance and fallen on her head, leaving Lev to haul her offstage with a modified fireman's carry.

"Pay attention," Maury Lykes said to Janet Bunterman. "Your daughter's turning into a cliché, and I don't represent clichés."

"You do if they sell records, Maury."

"But they don't sell records. They just sell magazines," he said. "So clean her up, and keep her that way."

"She needs to watch what she eats," Janet Bunterman muttered.

"And don't let her fuck any more actors, okay? They're a bad influence."

"Now hold on—that boy she was with last night, he's done Tennessee Williams in Chicago."

"I don't care if he did Tennessee Ernie Ford in the basement of the Grand Ole Opry," Maury Lykes said, "keep the kid away from her. You got a pen?"

Janet Bunterman found a pink Sharpie in her purse. Maury Lykes grabbed it and wrote a phone number on the back of his business card. "Cherry's going to need a new bodyguard."

"Who is he? Does he work for you?"

"If you don't call him, I will." Maury Lykes pressed the card into her palm and said, "He's an expert on 'gastritis.'"

Cherry Pye's mother frowned. "I hope he's nothing like Lev."

"Oh, he's not like Lev, honey. He's not like anybody you ever met."

*

24

Bang Abbott still found pleasure in his craft, such as it was. Unlike most paparazzi, he had once worked for a serious newspaper, back in the day when newspapers mattered. For four years Claude J. Abbott had been a staff photographer for the *St. Petersburg Times*, and during most of that time he'd performed his job without controversy or distinction, shooting murder scenes, car wrecks, hurricanes, flash floods, birthday parties at nursing homes, adoption days at the Pinellas Humane Society, the Buccaneer cheerleader tryouts, the Rays dancer tryouts, the Hooters calendar-girl contest, the trial of a county commissioner who trolled the Internet for Cub Scouts, a 10k run against skin cancer, a 5k run against HIV, a one-mile walk/run against osteoporosis, the birth of a rare snow leopard cub at Busch Gardens, the death of the world's oldest circus fire-eater in Sarasota, and an Ecstasy raid that snared a prominent transsexual evangelist.

Crashing several company cars earned Bang Abbott his nickname, and he was on the verge of being fired from the *Times* when he'd stunned his editors by winning a Pulitzer Prize for spot news photography, one of the most prestigious awards in journalism. Bang Abbott's self-nominated picture of a Canadian tourist being mangled by a lemon shark would soon become a focus of dispute, but for a short while he'd been able to bask in his triumph. Anticipating trouble down the road, he'd made a point of quickly spending the ten thousand dollars that had come with the Pulitzer, selecting a superb Japanese entertainment system for his small apartment in Clearwater Beach. As it did for all its award winners, the newspaper had presented Bang Abbott with a raise, which he'd pronounced insufficient. The *Boston Globe* and *Washington Post* made better offers, but these eventually were rescinded when the distasteful circumstances surrounding the shark photograph began leaking out.

It was one night during that dark and turbulent period when the *Times* sent Bang Abbott to shoot a Hannah Montana concert in Tampa, an assignment he'd correctly perceived as punitive. Afterward he'd gone out for drinks with a group of paparazzi who were pursuing the young singer, and he had listened with hungry fascination to their lurid battle tales. It had dawned on Bang Abbott that he could make more dough with one titty shot of a wayward starlet than he would busting his hump for six months on a newspaper salary. Better still, freelance photographers were unbound by any of the snooty ethical rules against bribing tipsters, for example, or misrepresenting one's self as, say, a CSI. A paparazzo was limited only by the breadth of his imagination and the size of his balls.

Bang Abbott had left his new acquaintances roaring at the bar and driven directly to the newspaper office, where he'd furtively removed his Pulitzer certificate from a trophy case in the lobby. Five days later he was in Beverly Hills, trailing Cameron Diaz down Rodeo Drive. At first the all-night hours jarred his system, but Bang Abbott eventually came to believe it was the life he was meant for. Being punched, shoved, cursed, toe-stomped and spat upon didn't bother him at all. The waiting could be a drag, but a hot chase was always fun.

And the money . . . well, the money was excellent.

Despite his sullied exit from conventional journalism, Bang Abbott never regretted his impoverished years as a daily news photographer. In truth, the experience helped make him a more agile and resourceful paparazzo. His predaceous instincts were exceptionally keen and much admired by competitors, which is why he was so enraged about being faked out of his shoes at the Stefano.

Loath as he was to concede defeat, he knew there was no point in checking the numerous hospitals in the Miami area; Cherry Pye's handlers were skilled at smuggling her in and out of medical facilities. In every city she visited, the services of a discreet physician were arranged in advance, with an agreement that he or she would serve on call for the duration of the superstar's stay. If an emergency arose, the doctor would remain at Cherry's side throughout the ordeal until she was safely aboard a private jet, homeward-bound. The woman never flew commercial unless she was traveling overseas.

For that reason Bang Abbott didn't waste his time staking out the nonstop clusterfuck known as Miami International. Instead he raced out to the Tamiami Executive Airport, which was favored by celebs sneaking in and out of the city. He parked near the charter-jet terminals in a shady area from which he could scout for an approaching black Suburban.

At that very moment, a gaggle of Bang Abbott's ruthless cohorts was swarming the doors of a sushi bar on Lincoln Road where Jennifer Aniston was innocently sharing California rolls with Robert Downey, Jr. A waiter had called to tip off Bang Abbott and, for an extra hundred bucks, offer exclusive access through a fire exit.

Although the Jen shot would have been a slam dunk, Bang Abbott had blown it off in favor of a fading, no-talent pop bimbo who was one bumbling overdose or drunken car wreck away from Slab City. The paparazzo was convinced that when Cherry Pye finally bought the farm—either by gagging on her own puke or wrapping her Beemer around a utility pole—it would be chronicled as an American tragedy, the death of a beautiful and ruined innocence.

Marilyn redux.

Bang Abbott wanted to be the one who documented this tawdry decline in photographs, which he grandiosely imagined as one day hanging in some museum of hip modern art, next to those of Avedon or Annie Leibovitz. And of course he wanted the body-bag shot.

Now a black SUV appeared in the distance, and Bang Abbott used his binoculars to verify the make. It was a GMC Yukon, not a Suburban, but that brainless bellman could easily have confused the two wagons. Bang Abbott waited until it pulled to the curb and then lurched from his rental car, aiming a camera with the motor drive whirring.

Cherry Pye did not emerge from the SUV, but her bodyguard did.

"Hello, douche nozzle," he said to Bang Abbott.

"Give me five seconds, Lev, that's all I need," the photographer pleaded, gesturing at the tinted windows. "One pretty smile for all her fans."

"She's not in there," Lev said.

"Come on. Just one picture."

"See for yourself." Lev stepped away from the door.

Bang Abbott squeezed past the bodyguard and stuck his lumpy head inside the Yukon, which indeed was empty. "Goddammit!" he brayed. "Where is she?"

"Don't know. Don't care." Lev lifted his garment bag off the seat. "Jesus, man, when's the last time you took a shower?"

"I'll give you five hundred bucks," Bang Abbott declared. "Just tell me where she's at."

"Why not," Lev said. "But make it fast." He held out an open palm.

Bang Abbott warily counted out the bills. "How come you never let me pay you off before?"

"Because Cherry paid me more."

"Screw you, Lev. Where the hell can I find her?"

The bodyguard looked at his wristwatch. "My guess is thirty-six thousand feet, somewhere over the Gulf of Mexico."

"You're hilarious. You could be the Jewish Chris Rock, you're so damn funny."

"Seriously. Cherry's mother fired me," Lev said without rancor. He pointed to a Lear warming up on the tarmac. "That's my ride, numbnuts. It's been real."

Eyeing the waiting jet, Bang Abbott groped in his camera bag for a longer lens. "You're fucking with me again, right? My lady is on that plane."

Lev laughed. "Try Stevie Van Zandt. He's giving me a lift to Teterboro—we go way back."

Bang Abbott made a clumsy lunge for his misspent cash, but the bodyguard flattened him with a head butt.

"One more hot tip," Lev said, looking down at him, "just so you get your money's worth: That girl you shot at the hotel this morning, it wasn't Cherry."

"No shit," Bang Abbott wheezed.

"They totally faked out your fat ass."

"Like I care."

"And it wasn't the first time, either."

"What?" cried Bang Abbott.

Lev said, "I hope you get cancer of the schlong. I hope it falls off in your hand." He stepped over the sprawled photographer and disappeared through the doors of the terminal.

3

Janet Bunterman phoned the hotel room and said, "Take a few days off, Annie."

Ann DeLusia knew what that meant: Cherry Pye was heading back to rehab.

"With pay, right?" she asked Cherry's mother.

"Oh, I suppose."

"'Cause I'm sure you want me on standby."

"Just in case," said Janet Bunterman. Her daughter often fled rehab—or, as Janet Bunterman insisted on calling it, "dietary camp."

Ann DeLusia said, "How's she doing, Janet?"

"Fast asleep in her own bed. She'll be better tomorrow."

"You're already back in L.A.? That was quick."

"We chartered," Janet Bunterman said.

"Sweet." Ann reminded herself to ask for a raise when she got back to California.

"We'll need you here by next Wednesday. Usher's label is having a big party for him at the Beverly Wilshire," said Cherry's mother.

"Okay," Ann DeLusia said. There was no cause to get excited. She wouldn't actually be attending Usher's party; she would be pretending to attend. The obligatory black SUV would transport her from Cherry Pye's house in Holmby Hills to the hotel, where she would be hustled through a back entrance in plain view of the lurking shooters. She would be placed in a private room for an hour or two, and allowed to kill the time by watching Pay-per-View and ordering pizza. Then Cherry's bodyguard would escort Ann out of the hotel, through the same door, to be photographed by the same unsuspecting horde. The purpose of this exercise was to give the false impression that Cherry Pye was out and about, vibrant and carefree, when in fact she was moping through three group sessions a day at Malibu's most exclusive twelve-step clinic.

It was a peculiar gig, working as an undercover stunt double for a celebrity space case, but Ann DeLusia made more money than most of her struggling actor friends. Her plan was to bank a chunk of dough so that when a promising role finally came along, she could afford to say adios to the Buntermans. Unfortunately, there was an increasing likelihood that Janet's daughter would accidentally snuff herself before then, in which case Ann would again be waiting on line with her friends, auditioning for soap operas and sanitary-pad commercials.

Cherry's mother said, "Keep your cell phone on."

"I'll probably blow out of here tomorrow."

"Where to?"

"Key West, maybe. I don't know," Ann said. "Or Grand Bahama."

"Don't forget to go heavy on the—"

"Sunblock. Yeah, Janet, I know."

While Ann DeLusia was able to tan, Cherry Pye typically turned pink and blistered like cheap vinyl. It was necessary to Ann's function as a decoy that she resemble the pale singer, so a bronze glow would be problematic, even at a distance.

In most other ways the two women looked alike. Both stood five six. Both wore size seven shoes. Ann weighed 118 pounds, while Cherry fluctuated between 120 and 126, depending on her monthly water retention and alcohol intake. Cherry's straight blond hair was a half shade darker than Ann's, but that was an easy fix. Neither of them owned distractingly oversized breasts; while Ann's were natural, Cherry had worn out three sets of implants and was shopping for new ones. Both women had roundish faces, small unreconstructed noses and dimpled chins. These similarities were neither uncanny nor accidental; Ann DeLusia had been hired principally because of her likeness to the former Cheryl Bunterman. Her acting skills were a bonus.

The most noticeable physical difference between the two women—even more obvious than their complexions—was in the eyes; Cherry Pye's were green, while Ann's were brown. Because Ann had a phobic aversion to contact lenses, she usually donned grotesque designer sunglasses before leading the paparazzi on a chase.

"Do you have your passport?" Janet Bunterman asked.

"Shit," Ann muttered. The passport was in her apartment, back in West Hollywood. That meant she could forget about the Bahamas.

Cherry's mother said, "Key West is fun. We always stay at the Pier House."

"Sounds good to me."

"There's a topless beach, but—"

"Don't worry, Janet. I've got about a gallon of SPF 50."

The prospect of another loud night among the posers of South Beach was so depressing that Ann asked the concierge to locate a rental car. By dusk she was fed, packed and rolling fast, the toneless voice of the nav system directing her southbound on the turnpike extension. She'd never been to the Keys, but she figured anyplace had to be more interesting than Ocean Drive.

Traffic on Highway 1 was clotting up in Florida City, the last stop on the mainland, so Ann jumped off on the Card Sound Road, an unlit two-lane toll route through North Key Largo. Her GPS companion was briefly unsettled by this move, but she ignored its stern instructions to make a U-turn and instead mashed down the accelerator.

Soon a new driving map appeared that conceded Ann wasn't lost, although she was adding a few miles of swamps and mangroves to her trip. A handful of cars blew past heading the opposite way, but otherwise she was alone in what looked like a tropical twilight zone. She wondered what had happened to all the god-awful suburban sprawl; suddenly there wasn't a rooftop in sight. Eventually the road took a turn, and out of the emptiness appeared a small fishing village where hand-painted signs touted fresh blue crabs for sale. She spied a waterfront joint called Alabama Jack's, and she considered stopping for a potty break. But the place looked dark, so Ann drove ahead to the tollbooth. When she reached out of the car window to pay the dollar, she felt raindrops on her arm.

The attendant said, "There's a squall blowin' through. Take it easy on the bridge."

"Thanks," said Ann, thinking: What bridge?

Then it was rising from the lonely road ahead of her, a steep concrete arch over a broad, choppy channel. Gusts of wind shoved the rental car as it started the climb, so Ann slowed down, squinting through the rapid swipes of the windshield wipers. At the top of the span she touched the brakes just long enough to take in the view—northward, across Biscayne Bay, the spread of greater Miami glowed golden yellow through a light fuzz of clouds; the other way, under clearer skies beyond Card Sound, was the scattered twinkling of the islands. As Ann coasted down the big bridge, past the hunched fishermen and their lanterns, she imagined herself crossing some sort of cosmic seam between two diametric realms. It felt liberating and borderline adventurous to be leaving one world for the other, even if a tourist hotel was waiting at the end of the journey.

She smiled to herself, and turned up the radio. The rain softened to a drizzle, the speedometer crept to sixty, and before long she was back on emotional autoglide. Thick mangroves hugged both sides of the road, pinching the headlight beams. Ann experienced a sensation of shooting through a long slick tunnel. Two small bridges jounced the car, but the sharp bend is what caught Ann by surprise.

That, and the hoary, drenched figure crouching on the center line.

She had only milliseconds to see it was a man, and he was lifting something wet in his hands.

Ann cursed and jerked the wheel and instantly felt the car begin to fly. The crash seemed to unfold so slowly that it became dreamlike, and for that reason she wasn't quite as scared as she should have been.

Still, spinning airborne in a rented Mustang toward a wall of mangroves, Ann understood that her vacation plans were being radically altered.

Cherry Pye awoke at midnight and somehow made her way to the kitchen. Hearing ice cubes clatter on the tile, Janet Bunterman threw on a robe and hurried down the hall.

"Hey, where's Lev?" Cherry asked.

"We fired him, remember? Back in Miami?"

"Not really."

"What are you drinking, honey?"

"Cranberry juice," Cherry said.

"And what else?"

"Chill out, Mom." Cherry stepped to a window, parted the drapes and peeked outside. The street was empty—no TV crews, no photographers. "Where are they?" Cherry asked.

"Who cares."

"I miss Lev. He was cool."

Janet Bunterman said, "You want something to eat? Let me get Marissa to make us some omelettes."

"He had his you know what pierced."

"Or crepes. Would you like some crepes?" Janet Bunterman asked.

"I'm talking about Lev. He had a platinum thingie right through the tip—it looked awesome."

"Thanks for the visual," said Janet Bunterman, thinking: Maybe she *does* hate me. That would account for the raspberry thong and the T-shirt that said FIRST PRIZE.

Cherry Pye yawned and flopped down on a leather couch. "When can we go back to Florida? Tanner's leasing this amazing house on Star Island."

"We're taking you to Malibu for a week. Maury insists."

"Not Rainbow Bend again. No fucking way."

Cherry's mother said it wouldn't be so bad. "They've got a new yoga instructor from Bangladesh. Plus, one of the Poon Pilots just checked in—I saw it on the E! channel. The drummer, I think."

"Screw Maury. I'm not going to Rainbow Bend," Cherry said, "and you can't make me."

Janet Bunterman reminded her daughter that Maury Lykes had invested a humongous sum of money in Cherry's upcoming CD, which would sink like a sack of petrified cowshit if the concert tour didn't go well. And Maury Lykes was disinclined to send Cherry out on the road with a case of "gastritis."

"Honey, we can't afford another Boston," Janet Bunterman said gently.

"Do I get a new bodyguard for the tour? Because I want a black guy this time. And he has to be shiny bald, like Britney's guy. That young man looks *so* bad," Cherry said. "Fact, I want *two* big bald black dudes. And they've gotta know kung fu, or whatever that crazy shit was that Lev used on my stalker in Dallas."

"That was just a fist," Janet Bunterman said. "A good old-fashioned fist to the groin. Maury has a security man he wants us to hire. He says he's better than Lev."

Cherry leered. "Better at what?"

"Why do you say these things? Are you trying to break my heart?"

"I'll do Malibu on one condition, Mom. I get to change my name."

"Don't worry, sweetie, we always check you in as 'Sally Simpson.'"

"No, not just for rehab. I want to change my name for real."

"What?"

"For good."

Janet Bunterman was determined to stay cool in the face of her daughter's goading. She said, "The CDs have already been boxed for shipment, okay? The tickets are printed, the Web site is up and running. You're a brand, honey. An entertainment franchise."

"Whatever. Diddy changes *his* name, like, every other week." Cherry got up to refill her glass. Her mother, who followed her to the kitchen, was relieved to see her pouring straight Ocean Spray, and no vodka.

"I want a one-word name," Cherry said, toasting thin air. "Like Beyoncé and Madonna and Eminem—stop giving me that look, Mom. I hate that."

Janet Bunterman said, "You know what Maury's going to say: The whole world knows you as Cherry Pye, so don't mess with a good thing. That's how Maury thinks."

Cherry shrugged and slurped at her juice. "You want to hear it, or not? I thought you should be first."

"Sure," her mother said thinly.

"Cherish!"

"One word. You're serious."

"Yeah, just Cherish. Is that sick or what?" Cherry Pye started bobbing. "Yo, c'mon evahbuddy, put your hands together for Cher-ish! Cher-ish! Cher-ish!"

Janet Bunterman said, "We'll talk about it after the tour."

Cherry announced she was hungry, but not for omelettes or crepes. She poked her head in the refrigerator. The sharp light shone harshly on her blanched, splotchy face. "I crapped out a pile of birdseed," she said. "What's *that* all about?"

"Reincarnation," said her mother.

"Hey, you think this ceviche is still good? Here, smell it for me."

On the day Michael Jackson overdosed, igniting the most loathsome media frenzy since the O. J. Simpson trial, Bang Abbott was 2,500 miles from Los Angeles. He had flown to Nassau to check out a sketchy but enticing tip that Mitt Romney was frolicking with a pair of Italian hookers on Paradise Island. The Republican presidential contender was said to have checked in at the Atlantis resort under his own name, and the *National Eye* had already prepared a splashy double-decker headline:

MORMON BIMBO TRYST—
IT'S WETTER IN THE BAHAMAS!

Unluckily for Bang Abbott, it was a different M. Romney—Melvin, a widowed veterinarian from Joplin, Missouri—who was visiting the islands in the company of his two grown daughters. Neither of the women had ever been mistaken for a Mediterranean prostitute, and they didn't know what to make of the obnoxious fat photographer who dogged them at Cable Beach while their father was playing blackjack. As soon as Bang Abbott confronted the equally bewildered

Melvin Romney, who bore no resemblance to the former Massachusetts governor, the paparazzo rushed back to the airport and called the *Eye*.

That's when he learned that the King of Pop had expired. Bang Abbott immediately dropped to his knees and broke into a racking sob that other passengers assumed to be a cry of grief, which indeed it was. Bang Abbott knew Jackson's death was a lost once-in-a-lifetime opportunity—a photograph of the unbagged body would have fetched half a million dollars, maybe more. It would have been an epic tabloid coup, bigger than Elvis in his casket or Lennon on the autopsy slab.

Bang Abbott's pain was made worse because he'd anticipated such a squalid demise for Jacko, and had been meticulously cultivating potential sources, from entrepreneurial paramedics to disgruntled mortuary personnel. He'd even sent Dodger tickets to a 911 dispatcher who had agreed to make Bang Abbott's number the second one she dialed (after fire rescue) if there was an emergency at Jackson's rented mansion.

Yet all the photographer's preparations had been in vain. The golden window for getting a blockbuster photo comes in the first chaotic hours after a celebrity mishap; after that, the chance of scoring an exclusive is remote. Bang Abbott was helplessly, maddeningly stuck three time zones away from the scene of the Jackson cataclysm. By the time he barreled off the plane at LAX—after an excruciating delay in Atlanta—the Gloved One's corpse was safely in the custody of the coroner and the story belonged to television. The brigades of paparazzi that had descended from all corners of the earth upon Los Angeles were, in Bang Abbott's opinion, as brainless as lemmings. There was no picture worth the risk of a fatal trampling, unless the pallbearers dropped the casket and MJ himself did a horizontal moonwalk down the steps of the Staples Center.

The inability to cash in on Jackson's death had scarred Bang Abbott, and he resolved not to miss out the next time. Of all the stars who were crashing and burning, Cherry Pye seemed most likely to beat the others to the grave, and for that reason she'd become a focus of Bang Abbott's morbid scrutiny. Although she was neither as global nor as gifted as Jackson, she was a wild, hot babe and would therefore, in his view, be worth plenty of money dead.

In the meantime, he had bills to pay. As soon as he walked off the flight from Miami, he checked his Black-Berry for overnight messages. A valet from the Peninsula had called to say Katie Holmes was table-dancing in the bar. Next a dry cleaner in Westwood had phoned to say Johnny Depp had personally dropped off a cummerbund for laundering. Then a waitress at Hugo's had breathlessly reported an unpleasant encounter with Star Jones, involving a decaf triple latte.

Only the Katie sighting sparked any interest from Bang Abbott, and he suspected the tip wasn't true; the source was so hopelessly nearsighted that he'd once mistaken Lyle Lovett for Anjelica Huston.

Bang Abbott deleted the messages and headed for Holmby Hills, the manored enclave between Bel Air and Beverly Hills where Michael Jackson had taken the big sleep. Cherry Pye was renting a house with eight bedrooms, six baths, a gym with a sauna, a billiards room and a mushroom cellar. The photographer knew this because he'd called up the rental agent and pretended to be interested in buying the place.

As always, he stopped his car halfway down the block. The Mercedes sedan was an expensive lease for a paparazzo but worth every dollar, for it allowed Bang Abbott to park practically anywhere. Cops in the neighborhood were reluctant to tow an S-Class, fearing it might belong to some Hollywood big shot who'd call up the chief and raise hell.

Bang Abbott took out one of his Nikons, locked the car and strolled down to the foot of Cherry's driveway. He was alone on the hunt, which was often the case these days. So many younger starlets were unraveling in sensational ways that the tabloids had to scramble to keep up. Consequently, a picture of Cherry Pye on a party spree wasn't as valuable as it once had been, and no longer a lock for the front page. It was a fact that Bang Abbott refused to dwell upon. The new CD and concert tour would boost her back to the A-list, he was certain. When the rabid wolf pack of his peers returned to the chase, Bang Abbott would be miles ahead of it.

He squatted down to wait in the shade of a ficus hedge. Technically he was trespassing, so he kept alert for police cruisers. An hour passed with nobody coming or going, yet he remained patient. If Cherry wasn't inside the house then she was probably on her way. He wondered if Lev had been telling the truth about getting canned—if so, Cherry's handlers would be hiring a new bodyguard. With a little luck, the man would be more ethically flexible than Lev.

When a dirty white Land Cruiser pulled up in front of Cherry's house, Bang Abbott rose slowly to his feet. The driver rolled down the window and said, "You're kiddin' me, right?"

It was another shooter. His name was Teddy Loo, and his biggest score was one of the Britney beaver pics. Bang Abbott flipped him the finger and told him to get lost.

"If I wasn't such a goddamn humanitarian, I wouldn't have stopped," said Teddy Loo. "I woulda let you sit out here all day and rot like a turd in the sun."

"What're you talkin' about?"

"You missed her, dog. She checked into Rainbow Bend about an hour ago."

"Nice try," Bang Abbott said.

"I shit you not. I got the pictures."

"No way. Who tipped you off?"

Teddy Loo laughed. "Nobody, dude. I was up there chasin' some rock drummer who's discovered the joys of smack. Got a call the guy might be breakin' out of rehab, y'know, so I took a ride and parked in the usual spot. Then, who pulls up in her vanilla-cream Beemer but Cherry and her old lady! No muscle or nuthin, just the two of 'em."

Bang Abbott felt sick. "You sure it was her?" he asked, thinking of the decoy. "Lemme see the shots, Teddy."

"Dog, you got beat. It happens."

"I don't believe you."

With a pitiful sigh, Teddy Loo shook his head. He took out his camera and beckoned to Bang Abbott, who approached the Land Cruiser as if it were a rancid Dumpster. Over Teddy Loo's shoulder he watched a sequence of pictures flash across the camera's viewfinder, and he felt the iron weight of despair.

The young woman being hustled into the Rainbow Bend Hope & Wellness Center was definitely Cherry Pye, not an imposter. Teddy Loo had caught her groping in her handbag for a pair of sunglasses. Much to Bang Abbott's misery, Teddy's close-ups were sharply focused, and Cherry's stunning green eyes were unmistakable. She was wearing jeans and a black surf hoodie. As usual, her mother was dressed for a hotel tennis lesson.

"Don't hate me," said Teddy Loo, grinning. He put his camera away. "You want a lift to your car?"

Bang Abbott said no thanks. He tried to calm himself with soothing thoughts. He remembered the time that one of Michael Jackson's security goons drove a full-sized Hummer over both of Teddy Loo's feet at the gates of the Neverland Ranch. He remembered Teddy Loo crawling around the pavement and yipping like a crippled hyena while Jacko's gloved hand waved serenely from a window of the departing vehicle. It was classic.

"Teddy, I don't hate you," Bang Abbott said. "You lucked out today, is all. Some days it's better to be lucky than good."

"I feel sorry for you, dog."

"Ha! Don't."

"You know who just bought that house at the end of the street? The one with the stone gate?"

"Yeah. Kiefer Sutherland," said Bang Abbott.

Teddy Loo hooted. "See, that's what I mean, you're like two years behind. Sutherland sold the place to Sandra Bullock and then she sold to Paula Abdul."

"And that's where you're going now? To shoot *her*?"

"I got a tip she walks her pug every Wednesday at noon sharp. You wanna come?"

"That's great, Teddy, except I wouldn't waste a frame on Paula Abdul if she set her hair on fire at the goddamn Ivy. Second, it's not even Wednesday, you fucking moron."

Bang Abbott stalked back to his car. He was steaming all the way to Malibu.

4

Ann DeLusia was surprised not to wake up in a hospital. Instead she was lying in a car, which she assumed to be the crashed Mustang. Then her vision cleared and she saw that the automobile was old and rusted, and the interior had been stripped bare, and that she was in the custody of a stranger.

The man stuck his head through an open window and told her to be still.

"You had a big night," he said.

Ann nodded, staring. The stranger had to be well into his sixties, with crinkled skin as brown as cured leather. He had one gleaming eye, and a cracked fake that sat somewhat at odds with the form of its socket. On his bald pate he wore a flimsy diaphanous shower cap from which protruded two silvery braids, each strung with red and green shotgun shells. Ann noticed that the caps of the shells had been drilled out so that the hair could be threaded.

The braids weren't growing from the back of the stranger's head like regulation pigtails; rather, they appeared to sprout sideways at conflicting angles from his baked scalp. The plaited roots were visible through the shower cap, several inches above each ear. It was a nifty grunge look, although Ann doubted that was the stranger's intended effect.

"You're the guy in the middle of the road," she said through a swollen lip.

"My hip locked up." His voice was deep and rolling.

"Least I didn't hit you."

"You have superior reflexes," he said.

"How bad am I hurt?"

"No broken bones but a few bruises. I had to cut you out of the seat belt," the stranger said, making a snipping motion with his fingers. Then he disappeared from view.

When Ann sat up, she felt sore and dizzy. She wondered how the homeless man could be certain she hadn't fractured anything, unless he'd been an orthopedist back in the productive phase of his life. It was creepy to think of him examining her while she was unconscious.

He came back with a mug of hot tea. "Homemade," he said. "Local herb."

"I hurt all over."

"Understandable." With one arm the man lifted her from

the car and carried her to a blanket near a campfire. He propped her upright and helped her sip the tea. She saw that he was garbed in a crusty old trench coat and black high-top sneakers with no socks. Possibly she had the worst headache in the history of humanity.

"Is that a real race car?" she asked, looking back at the peeling hulk. The sides were plastered with faded decals, and the number 77 was still visible on the hood and sides. She said, "That's pretty cool. Where'd you get it?"

"Jiffy Lube 300," the stranger said.

"Were you a driver or something?"

The stranger seemed to think the question was quite humorous. It dawned on Ann that he was very tall, probably too tall to fit inside a racing car.

He turned away, tending to a frying pan that was sizzling over the fire.

"Have I been here all night?" she asked.

"Correct."

"Didn't you call an ambulance?"

"No phone, Ann," the stranger said.

She saw that her purse and travel bag had been placed on the rust-pocked hood of the race car. Obviously the man had gone through her belongings or he wouldn't have known her name. She wondered why he hadn't used her cell phone to call for help.

"Do you know somebody with a car that works? Can you get me to a doctor?"

"Let's have some breakfast and map out a plan."

"Okay, sure." Ann realized she was famished. "Something smells good."

"Crocodile," the stranger said.

She managed a smile, playing along. "Mmm, my favorite."

"That's what I was taking off the road last night when you almost flattened me. Just a little fella, barely four foot. A FedEx van clipped him, guy never even touched the brakes."

"Actually, I'm not all that hungry," said Ann.

The man explained that it was technically illegal to eat a North American crocodile because the species was federally protected. "But it's a goddamn sin to waste good meat," he said. "You can write that down as a natural law, young lady— never waste good meat."

"There's some aspirin in my purse," Ann said.

"Of course."

"And a phone, too."

He returned with only the bottle of Bayer, tapping three tablets into her palm. She downed them at once and said, "I should really see a doctor."

"Some call me Skink," the man said. "Or captain. All depends."

"Do you live out here?"

"Your car sunk—I take full responsibility. Here, try some."

The chunks of croc tail tasted all right, Ann discovered. Like overcooked fish.

"I thought I crashed in some trees," she said.

"Blasted straight through 'em, like a rocket ship," said the man. "Landed upside down in a crick."

"Holy shit." Ann shivered, thinking about how close she must have come to drowning. However, it seemed odd that her clothes and bags weren't damp. "Please get me to a doctor," she said.

"You're going to be fine." His smile caught her off guard. For a homeless dude he had unbelievable teeth, so white and straight; a complete set, too.

He said, "Here's the situation, Ms. Ann DeLusia. I can't let you go right now."

"What?" She thought she must have misheard him.

"I need your help with a project," he said.

She put down the plate. "Captain, stop. You're freaking me out."

"When this is over, I'll arrange speedy transit—that's a promise," he told her. "But for a while, you'll have to stay here with me."

Ann's hands were shaking. "Jesus, are you nuts? That's kidnapping!"

"Truly I regret the inconvenience," said the man called Skink. "How about some fried bananas?"

The drummer for the Poon Pilots was Methane Drudge. He refused to admit it was not his baptismal name. The group leader gently chastised him, saying, "We're not going to make much progress unless you choose the path of self-honesty."

"Yeah, well, you can choose the long hairy path up my ass. How's that?" said Methane Drudge.

Cherry Pye rolled her eyes, thinking: Another low-rent rocker, covered with cheap Venice ink. How boring. *Booorrrr-ing.*

The group leader pressed on. "Methane, you came to Rainbow Bend voluntarily, like everybody else in this room. You signed a pledge to try this our way, remember?"

Methane laughed hoarsely. "Dude, I was totally baked on China white. I woulda signed a pawn slip for my thirteen-year-old sister."

"Asshole," Cherry said. This was why she never slept with drummers or bass players.

It was a small group, only six patients and the therapist. Cherry recognized some of the other addicts from her previous rehabs. One young woman was almost as famous as she was, owing to a co-starring role on a popular cable sitcom. The woman played the perpetually horny neighbor of a beleaguered single mom who was working her way through dental school.

The group leader said, "Recovery depends on knowing ourselves completely, and we can't know who we truly are unless we shed our disguises. That's why we use only our real names here at Rainbow Bend. We'll come back to Methane later in the discussion. Cheryl, would you like to share?"

"Not really." Cherry detested being called Cheryl.

"Please," the group leader said. He was new to the clinic.

For being such a high-end nuthouse, Rainbow Bend had a serious problem with staff turnover. Apparently it was difficult finding counselors at any salary who could tolerate a clientele of spoiled show-business fuckups.

"Cheryl, please get us started," the group leader prodded again.

"Yeah, whatever." Cherry had gone through the drill dozens of times, but still she would have killed for a cigarette. "Okay, so, things are goin' supergood. I got a new CD coming out in a few weeks, which is incredibly hot. It's called *Skantily Klad*, with all *k*'s, and I'm doin', like, a hundred-city tour. Plus I had a walk-on for Kid Rock last month in Vegas, and he is so *smokin'*. And what else—okay, I've probably been partyin' a little too hard, on account of all the pressure. Tryin' to finish the album, you know, plus gettin' ready for the road. There's, like, eighteen songs to learn and they're all different. Plus I hadda fire two of the backup singers because they weren't givin' me my righteous space, y'know. They had, like, zero respect. So I had to cut those bitches loose and audition some new ones—"

"Excuse me, Cheryl," the group leader interrupted. "Can you rewind and talk a little more about the partying?"

Methane clapped his tattooed hands. "Yesssss! We wanna hear it all."

Cherry Pye fidgeted in her chair. "Same old shit. I get with certain people, y'know, then it's back to the evil old ways. You guys can relate, right?"

All the other patients nodded knowingly, except for

Methane, who was slapping his kneecaps with both hands, keeping the beat to a song that only he could hear.

The group leader said, "Does it always start with the alcohol, Cheryl?"

"Nah. Whatever's on the table."

"So you don't have a particular drug of choice."

Cherry shook her head. "I go with the flow. It's all good."

"But the results aren't so good, are they?" the group leader said. "That's how you wound up here."

"Hey. You don't know what it's like to be me."

Methane groaned. "Now she's poachin' from Tom Petty. Gimme a fuckin' break."

"Don't be such a dick," Cherry told him.

The group leader thanked her for sharing and said, "Who wants to go next?"

"But I'm not done," Cherry complained.

"We have to make time for everybody."

"Yo, she can have my goddamn turn," Methane volunteered.

"Cool," Cherry said. Then, re-addressing the group: "I just had one more thing to say: I'm gonna change my name to Cherish."

"Cherish what?" the sitcom actress asked.

"Just Cherish. One word. I picked it because it sounds, like, totally pure."

The group leader clucked disapprovingly. "Cheryl, you're just creating another façade to hide behind. That's not a path to self-honesty."

"Let's take a vote," she said. "Everybody in favor of Cherish raise your hand."

"Hold on—there's no voting in therapy!" the group leader protested.

Four of the five other patients raised their hands. Only Methane Drudge voted no. He said Cherish was bogus. He said it sounded like a brand of lame perfume. Cherry ignored the comment.

"I'm also thinking of getting bigger boobs," she told the group.

This time the vote was 4–0 against. Everybody except Methane Drudge said Cherry's current boobs were lovely. The drummer abstained, insisting he had to see them in the flesh before he made up his mind.

"Pervo," Cherry muttered, folding her arms.

The group leader rose, plainly annoyed by the shift in the discussion. "Break time," he said curtly, and walked out.

Rainbow Bend had a shady serenity garden surrounded by ivy-covered walls. Cherry found a patch of sunlight and sat down cross-legged in the soft grass. Methane walked up and offered her a Camel. The smoke irritated her throat, which was still raw from the Miami vomitfest. Methane asked how many times she'd been rehabbed and she said four, counting this one.

"It's all a bunch of horseshit," he said.

Cherry laughed acidly. "Ya think?"

"What would they do if you said fuck it and then bailed?"

"I dunno. Bill my manager for the whole week?"

Methane said, "Hell, I'm supposed to be stuck in this hog farm for thirty days. There ain't no way."

The sunlight warmed Cherry's cheeks. She closed her eyes and said, "I hear ya, dude."

"I mean, do you love it here or somethin'? 'Cause I already seen enough."

"Yeah?" Cherry opened her eyes and looked at the stringy, bleary-eyed skinhead. Why don't junkies ever brush their teeth? she wondered. Guy can afford a three-hundred-dollar-a-day smack habit but he can't afford some freaking floss?

Methane said, "Know what we should do? We should split—you and me."

"Wow."

"We could hop the damn wall, no problem." He winked and tapped his cigarette ashes into the koi pond. "Come on, what the hell are they gonna do?"

"Cheer, probably," Cherry Pye said.

She stood up and tossed her Camel into the ivy. She was thinking about Tanner what's-his-face back on Star Island, trying to remember if the sex was any good. She had a vague recollection of helping him put on a condom, but the rest was a fog.

She said, "I'm sure we could walk out the front door just as easy. It's not a prison, dude. It's just a spa for drunks and dopers."

Methane explained that he couldn't leave by the front

entrance because his bandmates, who were a bunch of self-righteous pricks, had hired a couple of Latino gorillas to hang close and make sure he didn't bolt. It had something to do with the promoter's insurance policy—Methane was supposed to test clean before he could go on the road again.

"Bummer," said Cherry.

"So, how 'bout it? Let's jump the wall and run down to the beach and get high."

"My mom would die."

"Aw, come on, *Cherish*." The drummer smiled and traced a finger along her neckline.

She smiled back at him. "Sounds nice. Say it again."

"Cherish? You like that, huh?"

She stood up, dusting the seat of her pants. "Okay, let's go. Me first."

Methane boosted her over the five-foot wall, the vines abrading her palms. She came down on all fours in some dry scrub on a high slope overlooking the Pacific Coast Highway. The drummer landed with a grunt beside her, wrenching an ankle. They followed the wall to the corner of the property and took a hiking path down the hill.

When Methane said his leg hurt too badly for him to continue, Cherry told him to man up. They couldn't call for a ride because neither of them had a cell. Rainbow Bend had confiscated the devices upon admittance, due to a problem with patients secretly phoning their drug dealers, who would dutifully drive out to Malibu and lob Baggies of pills, rocks, buds and powder over the wall. On some mornings the serenity garden looked like the Customs locker at LAX.

"Just keep walkin'," Cherry told the drummer.

"But I think my damn foot is broke," he whined.

"Don't be such a twink."

The path emerged a few hundred yards from the white gatehouse that stood at the tree-lined driveway leading up to the Rainbow Bend chalet. No members of the Poon Pilots' security detail were visible, but the gatehouse attendant appeared to have taken notice of the two unlikely hikers. Cherry was dressed in a manner that wouldn't normally arouse suspicion in Malibu—Hudson jeans, Rafe sandals and a black DK top—but Methane looked like a degenerate neo-Nazi child molester. He'd been delivered to Rainbow Bend wearing unlaced combat boots, a shredded white undershirt and baggy, low-flying board shorts that displayed not only his ass crack but the tattoo of a snake-entwined swastika.

Cherry Pye said, "Know what? Let's split up, dude."

"Shit, baby, I can barely stand. Gimme an arm."

Briskly she began walking down the street. The drummer hobbled after her, cussing under his breath.

A silver four-door sedan was idling at the downhill end of the block, facing away. A heavyset civilian sat behind the steering wheel, his capped head lolling. Cherry walked up and tapped her fingernails on the trunk, startling the driver so much that he knocked the Bluetooth out of his ear.

When he rolled down the window, she said, "Can you give me a ride?"

"Me, too," chimed Methane from behind.

The man asked where she was headed.

"Holmby Hills," Cherry replied. "Then Burbank."

"Hey, what happened to the beach?" said Methane.

The driver looked curiously at Cherry. "You mean Burbank airport?"

"If it's not too big of a hassle. I'm totally good for the gas."

"No problem."

"I got, like, a major meeting in Miami."

"Sure. Hop in."

Cherry Pye slid into the front passenger seat. "Nice wheels. Is this the new C-Class?"

"S," said the driver.

"Killer." *It's an expensive car to be stinking of french fries,* Cherry thought. The guy looked familiar, although she couldn't place the face.

Methane rapped on the side of the Mercedes and said, "Back door's locked, bro."

"Let's roll," Cherry said to the driver.

"What about your friend?"

"Mental defective, I mean big-time. Just drive."

"Absolutely."

"Hey, *Cheryl*!" Methane shouted snidely. "Tell him to open the fuckin' door!"

She didn't bother to look back as they sped away, leaving the drummer gesticulating in the middle of the street.

Laying an adorable smile on the paunchy driver, Cherry said, "Thanks. My name is Cherish."

"I know who you are."

"Yeah?" She glanced over the seat and saw among the crumpled McDonald's wrappers a large camera bag and a pair of binoculars. She said, "Oh, don't fucking tell me."

The man extended a greasy hand. "Claude Abbott. Big fan."

5

The real-estate crash couldn't have happened at a more inconvenient time for Jackie Sebago, whose privileged circle of investors collectively had sunk more than nine million dollars into Jackie's condominium project. To allay their concerns, the Sebago Isle Limited Partnership, LLC, invited the investors to a lavish retreat at the exclusive Ocean Reef Club on North Key Largo, a legendary haven for rich, fretful white guys. On the recreational agenda were tennis, golf, deep-sea fishing, Pilates classes, hot-stone massages, a private concert by Michael Bolton and—if necessary—a tour of the development site, located along County Road 905 only a few miles south of the club. The tour would be brief, as only two slabs had been poured.

It was Jackie Sebago's plan to keep the investors playing

during the day and drinking all night, thereby minimizing the opportunities for fiscal probing. Jackie had taken their money and purchased four one-acre lots upon which he'd intended to build a total of twenty-four luxury town houses, within strolling distance of the Atlantic. The property alone had cost four million; rather than deal with a nosy bank, Jackie had paid with cash from the investors' stake. He had appropriated the remaining five mil, preferring to finance the phased construction with future down payments from eager buyers. It was a classic bit of Florida smoke that worked fine when there was an abundance of flush, gullible customers; in a busted market, it was a formula for disaster.

With reluctance Jackie Sebago had dipped into his own Luxembourg stash for the 250 G's that the Ocean Reef clambake would cost. Based on experience, he felt confident that a weekend of sun-drenched excess would derail any simmering revolt. Eight of the nine investors had RSVP'd; all would be bringing either wives or mistresses. Jackie met them in baggage claim at Miami International and escorted them outside to a plush coach-style bus with satellite TV and a wet bar. He figured the sooner he got them tanked, the better.

Still, the ride to the Keys was tense. One of the partners, a young hedge-fund hawk from Providence, refused hard liquor and loudly peppered Jackie with questions that Jackie was disinclined to answer. The man, whose name was Shea, struck an accusatory tone that alarmed his host, who waited in vain for the other investors to speak up in defense of his rectitude. Instead they fell silent, except for an occasional murmur to their female companions, and listened with disturbingly sober expressions to Shea's nasal interrogation. Jackie Sebago could hear the ice cubes clink in their glasses whenever the bus took a bump.

At issue was the balance of the investors' principal, and what was being done with it. When Jackie assured Shea that the money was being safely held in California, the arrogant worm had the gall to challenge this smallish lie by demanding the name of the bank and the account number. Jackie said he was insulted and offered to return Shea's entire investment by wire transfer. He whipped out his smart phone as if to initiate the transaction, and he was rattled when Shea failed to back off. In fact, everyone on the bus was watching to see if Jackie would follow through. It was appalling—nobody spoke up to get him off the hook.

With creeping dread, Jackie stalled by pretending to be searching his contact list for his banker's private number. *What a shitty way to begin a Florida vacation*, he thought. These ungrateful swine did *not* deserve to be serenaded by Mr. Michael Bolton.

"What's the goddamn problem?" asked Shea.

Jackie continued scrolling intently. "I thought I had the number in my directory but I guess it's in my other Pearl." He made a show of checking his wristwatch. "Anyway, shit, the banks just closed in L.A."

"So do it by e-mail," Shea said.

"What exactly are you insinuating?" Jackie asked, as if he didn't know. This was a nightmare—what if all of them demanded the return of their money?

At that instant, as if by a miracle, the driver stomped the brakes. The bus swerved sharply, then shuddered to a halt. Jackie hurried up the aisle, elated to have an excuse for fleeing Shea's inquisition.

The bus driver held a death clench on the steering wheel. "Damn, I almost hit her," he gasped, pointing to a young woman who was signaling from the edge of the road, in the wash of the headlights. She wore rhinestone flip-flops and a flimsy wrap with a black-and-white checkerboard pattern.

"Everybody stay right here," Jackie Sebago said dramatically to his investors, who appeared more annoyed than concerned. Jackie regarded the injured pedestrian as a divine distraction, and bounded off the bus.

The young woman said, "Thank God you stopped."

"What happened? Are you okay?" Jackie noticed she was quite attractive, even with a puffy lip.

"It was terrible," she said. "I can't describe it. He made me put on this . . . this nasty old *thing*." She flicked disgustedly at the silky garment.

"What is that?"

"It's from some stupid NASCAR race."

"The checkered flag?"

"Yeah, he's a real sicko." The woman swiped at a cloud of gnats.

Jackie Sebago was thinking she looked pretty tasty

wrapped in a Jiffy Lube banner, but he prudently withheld the compliment. "Want me to call an ambulance?"

"First get me out of here, okay? Like right this minute."

The woman stepped toward the idling bus. Jackie intercepted her and said, "But we're going the other way, down to Ocean Reef."

"That's fine. Anywhere but here is fantastic."

"What's your name, honey?"

"Annie," the woman said.

She followed Jackie Sebago up the steps of the bus. He explained to the driver that the woman needed medical attention, and that she would be riding with them to the club.

From the rear, Shea called out, "What the hell's going on?"

"This young lady's been hurt. We're giving her a lift," Jackie announced. He felt very good about helping the woman. Her striking presence guaranteed there would be no more talk of audits or escrow accounts during the remainder of the ride.

One of the wives asked her what in the world had happened.

"It was awful, just awful," Annie said with a shiver. "I can't talk about it."

Jackie told the bus driver to get moving.

"Oh no, wait!" Annie blurted. "I forgot something."

She hopped off the bus and disappeared into the shadows of the mangroves. Jackie Sebago peered apprehensively out the window. To the impatient passengers he said, "Don't worry, she'll be right back."

The young woman returned a few moments later, but she wasn't alone. A grizzled giant with clacking red-and-green braids calmly entered the bus behind her. His eyes seemed crooked, and he was nude except for a trench coat and an ill-fitting shower cap imprinted with faded butterflies. The man had shaved his tanned body and grease-painted himself in the emphatic manner of an aboriginal.

Jackie fumbled to unholster his phone, but it was too late. When the stranger raised a sawed-off Remington to his head, Jackie was actually relieved to hear one of his investors cry out, "Don't do it, mister! He's got all our money!"

The woman named Annie took custody of Jackie's cell phone. Then she walked down the aisle with a dirty pillowcase, collecting all the other phones and saying: "I'm so sorry. He's just impossible."

In a quavering voice the bus driver begged the stranger not to shoot him. The stranger motioned for him to start driving.

"What do you want?" Jackie Sebago bleated. "Is this some kind of robbery?"

"You should be so lucky," said the man with the braids.

Janet Bunterman phoned Maury Lykes to give him the bad news: "Cherry jumped the wall at Rainbow Bend."

"Jesus."

"She chartered a G5 and flew back to Miami."

"On whose dime?" Maury Lykes asked.

"There was another passenger on the plane. We think it's the drummer from the Poon Pilots—he went missing from the clinic at the same time as Cherry."

"Beautiful. She couldn't run off with a lead singer, I suppose. Some ripped, sensitive surfer guy that every teenage girl in America wants to ball. No, your daughter goes for the scrawny no-talent scag freak with rotted teeth." Maury Lykes sighed sourly. "What a moving love story, Janet. I can't wait to read it in the tabs."

"You think Ned and I are thrilled about this?"

Maury Lykes said he would sue the Buntermans for every dollar they had if Cherry Pye took up heroin before the big concert tour.

"She would never!" said Janet Bunterman. "And even if she does, we can find a way to make it work."

"Excuse me?"

"Look at all the great musicians who've used the stuff and didn't die. Clapton, Keith Richards, David Bowie—I mean, Maury, come on! Let's not automatically assume the situation is unmanageable."

There was a long silence on the other end. Eventually Maury Lykes said, "Janet, you'd better be on the next goddamn plane to Florida. Meanwhile, I intend to track down your idiot offspring and get her on a leash."

"How?"

"That guy I told you about. The new Lev."

"But we haven't even had a chance to interview him," Janet Bunterman complained. "There's a process to be followed, Maury. He hasn't been officially hired yet."

"Consider it official," said Maury Lykes, and hung up.

Janet Bunterman was packing when her husband came in and told her that the twin publicists were waiting downstairs. Word of Cherry's admission to Rainbow Bend and subsequent escape had leaked out, and the PR team had come up with a plan.

"They're smoking in the kitchen," Ned Bunterman reported with distaste.

"Then put them outside, like we do with the cats," his wife said. "Are you coming to Miami with me, or not?"

Ned Bunterman said no. He said he was committed to play in a charity golf tournament at Palm Springs. "For lupus awareness," he added.

"I thought that was last week."

"No, honey. Colorectal was last week," he said, "at Torrey Pines."

"Fine." Janet Bunterman had no reason to believe her husband, who for several years had been carrying on a relationship with a bisexual middle-aged Danish couple who owned a consignment shop in Pasadena. Sometimes he accompanied them on long weekends to Ojai or Moab. Janet Bunterman tolerated Ned Bunterman's antics because he did a semi-competent job of managing their daughter's earnings, and because Janet herself was sweatily involved with her thirty-year-old tennis instructor.

"I've got a great idea how to kill the rumor," Ned Bunterman said.

His wife neatly stacked three bathing suits in her suitcase and said, "It's not a rumor, darling. It's reality."

"Just listen, okay? We sneak Ann DeLusia up to Rainbow Bend in the middle of the night. Then tomorrow, for like five minutes at lunchtime, she walks out on the sun terrace—the one on the second floor, remember? You can see it from the street. That way the paparazzis can shoot her with a long lens. We'll give her the big hat, the shades." Ned Bunterman smiled craftily. "The pictures go out all over the world, and everybody thinks it's Cherry, safe in the healing womb."

Janet Bunterman shook her head. "I already thought of that, Ned. There's one little problem: Annie's in Key West and she's not answering her bloody phone."

"You're kidding. Ann?"

"Yeah, and I'm seriously pissed. We've got a code blue here and she's wasting away in Tequilaville."

Ned Bunterman rarely attempted to correct his wife's mis-references; in their marriage she had long ago seized the role of pop-cultural authority. He said, "The Larks are waiting, Janet."

"Christ, I need a drink."

Lucy and Lila Lark sheathed their phones and stubbed out their cigarettes when Cherry Pye's parents came out on the patio deck. Because the twin publicists shared a gifted Brazilian surgeon and identical Botox regimens, few people could tell them apart. It wasn't actually necessary, as the

Buntermans had learned. The two Larks spoke as one. They specialized in problem celebrities, and Cherry Pye kept them hopping. Typically, Lucy and Lila were not consulted until a career was spiraling downward full bore, which was why so many of their clients ended up dead or imprisoned. Anticipating a similar fate for Cherry, the Larks billed the Buntermans by the week.

"Listen up. Rainbow Bend never happened," Lucy said.

"Fine by me," said Cherry's mother.

"Just like the Stefano never happened," Lila added.

Ned Bunterman tentatively raised his right hand, as if he were in philosophy class. "So what's our official line?"

The twins looked at each other, then Lucy said, "Cherry is visiting friends in Florida, resting up for the concert tour."

"Which starts in Miami," said Lila, "so why *wouldn't* she be there?"

Lucy nodded. "Exactly. She's been at the Stefano for a week. We'll have the manager leak it to the *Herald*."

Again Cherry's father lifted a hand. "Somebody got a photo in Malibu when Janet checked her in at the clinic. It's all over the *Globe*'s Web site, and TMZ, too."

While the Larks pondered this information, Janet Bunterman asked, "Do we really care about the scuzzy old *Globe*?"

Lucy snapped two fingers. "Cherry was visiting a friend at Rainbow Bend. A good friend who's been going through a rough time."

"Of course," Lila said. "Then she flew back to Florida to—"

"Rest and rehearse for the tour," said Lucy.

"Yes, rest and rehearse."

The Buntermans agreed it was a good story, but they were worried about the drummer. "He's a well-known heroin addict," Janet Bunterman said. "Maury says it would be death if somebody spotted him and Cherry hanging out together."

Lucy said, "You're talking about the dork from the Poon Pilots, right?"

"His name is Methane Drudge," her sister added.

Janet Bunterman nodded. "Maury says it'll murder advance ticket sales if Cherry's fans think she's on smack. Even a rumor would sink the tour, he says."

The sisters smiled. "Cherry's not 'hanging out' with Mr. Drudge," Lila said, "because Mr. Drudge is back at Rainbow Bend. They picked him up yesterday afternoon, passed out on the beach behind Kate Hudson's place."

Ned Bunterman said that was wonderful news. Janet Bunterman asked, "Then who did Cherry take on the plane with her to Miami?"

The Larks, who didn't engage in pointless speculation, advised the Buntermans to locate their reckless daughter as soon as possible and attach some serious security.

"Because there's only so much we can do at our end," Lucy said.

"That's right," said Lila. "We're only human."

*

Bang Abbott had never before flown private. It was fucking fantastic. He was on his third screwdriver by the time they were over New Mexico. He quietly snapped a picture of Cherry Pye, who was curled up with her eyes closed across the aisle. When she heard the shutter click, she came out of her seat and threw a punch at him.

"Easy, babe," Bang Abbott said, and hastily put the camera away.

"You do that again and we'll ditch your fat ass in West Texas. I'm not kiddin'."

"Sorry, okay?"

The photographer certainly didn't want to piss her off. This was the ticket of a lifetime, a one-on-one with a crashing starlet.

"They killed Princess Di, you know," Cherry said.

"Who did?"

"Your people. She was tryin' to get away when her limo wrecked in that tunnel." Cherry waved at the flight attendant. "Bring me a Jack on the rocks," she said, "and leave the bottle."

Bang Abbott said, "I'm not like those other guys."

"Really? You're not a 'stalkarazzo'? Ha!" She tapped three white pills from an envelope and swallowed them dry. "I 'member you now, dude. You're the one always asks me to smile pretty." She made a phony dumb-blonde face. "Just like that," she said.

"Look, Cherry—"

"It's *Cherish*, goddammit."

"Cherish. That's what I meant." Impossibly, Bang Abbott

was losing his vodka buzz. The temperature gauge in the jet's cabin said sixty-eight degrees, but he was sweating like a constipated sumo wrestler. He hadn't foreseen such a coherent burst of hostility from Cherry. He had counted on her to be stoned senseless—why else would she have invited a tabloid shooter to join her on the flight?

As soon as she finished the first drink, Bang Abbott poured another one.

"What's your name again?" she asked.

"Claude."

"I had a cat named Claude. He ate a poison toad." Cherry Pye shrugged. "God called him home. That's what my mom said."

Suddenly the Gulfstream felt rather small to Bang Abbott. The thought of having to converse with this woman for three more hours was dispiriting. Bang Abbott had zero interest in the childhood memories, political views or life-guiding philosophies of the celebrities he pursued; the pictures were all that mattered. He wondered how long it would be until Cherry passed out, so he could try again with his camera.

But if she didn't nod off, what then?

"You look whipped," he said.

"Thanks. You look like Jake Gyllenhaal. *Not*."

Bang Abbott was lousy at small talk. He'd been spared during the drive from Rainbow Bend to the airport because Cherry had been nattering on the phone—his phone—the whole time.

He said, "I meant it when I said I was a fan."

"Yeah? Then what was the first single off my last CD?"

"'Runaway Tongue.'" Bang Abbott could have recited her entire discography, not because he liked her music but because it was smart business to pay attention. The value of his photographs rose and fell with Cherry Pye's fortunes as a recording artist.

Predictably, she was tickled that he knew the title of the song.

"Wanna hear the new album? I got it right here." She fished an iPod out of an alligator carry bag, but the battery was dead. "Shit," she muttered, and hurled the device across the cabin.

Bang Abbott said, "I've got all your stuff, Cherish. Even the Telluride tape."

"Oh-my-God." She giggled and covered her mouth.

A couple of years earlier, during another self-inflicted lull in her career, Cherry Pye had made a sex tape and paid a publicist who specialized in such projects to spread it around the Internet. Bang Abbott, who considered himself a connoisseur of homemade pornography, purchased the DVD for seventy-seven dollars, which he wrote off on his tax return as professional research. To his disappointment, the sex scenes turned out to be even more tedious and unimaginative than Paris Hilton's. Cherry had chosen as her partner a hirsute Argentinian soccer goalie who grimaced with each thrust while Cherry stared with glazed eyes at the ceiling. Occasionally she would writhe halfheartedly and gasp in the manner of a rheumatic terrier. All this took place in nineteen minutes on a white alpaca rug beside a cheesy gas fireplace at a Colorado ski resort.

"It was way hot," Bang Abbott lied.

"Thanks, round dude."

"Was that guy on the tape your boyfriend?"

Cherry laughed. "My *what*?"

Bang Abbott perceived that she was warming to him. He fixed her another drink and said, "Can I ask you something? Were you staying at the Stefano the other night?"

"The one on South Beach? Yeah, I guess."

"You remember if there was a problem? Because somebody called in an OD."

Cherry said, "You got any cigarettes?"

"And I rushed over there, you know, to see if it was you," Bang Abbott said, "but there was some other blonde on a stretcher. They were putting her in an ambulance."

"Then it wasn't me," said Cherry with a trace of impatience. She asked the cabin attendant for a smoke but was informed that the charter company didn't stock cigarettes on their airplanes, even the Gulfstreams.

"Well, that totally sucks," said Cherry.

"But later I ran into Lev," Bang Abbott went on. "He said your mom fired him, by the way—"

"Yeah, she can be such an ice bitch."

"Anyhow, Lev told me it was, like, a body double. That girl on the stretcher," said Bang Abbott. "He made it sound like she's on the payroll, just to keep us faked out."

Cherry Pye seemed curious. "Who got faked out? You mean the maggot mob?"

"All us shooters."

"Right, the maggot mob. That's what we call you guys."

Bang Abbott hadn't heard that one before. He wasn't even slightly offended.

Cherry acted like her pills were kicking in. She sat back and said, "I'm gonna miss Lev. He rocked my world."

"But was he bullshitting me, or not? About the fake?" Bang Abbott couldn't let it slide. He was aching to know how many times he'd been played for a sucker.

Cherry put a hand on his arm and said, "Claude, I honestly don't know what the fuck you're talkin' about." She set down her drink and snatched a handful of beer nuts from a crystal dish. "Dude, I thought you'd be way more fun than this. Take off those farty old shoes."

Bang Abbott did what he was told. His travel companion looked as if she was ready for a nap, and in his mind he'd already composed the money shot: Cherry slack-jawed and snoring, the half-empty bottle of Jack Daniel's propped between her legs.

She eyed the flat-screen monitor mounted on the wall by the galley. "Hey, we can put on some porn."

"Why don't you try and get some rest?" the photographer suggested.

"Claude, I got a question. When's the last time you got laid? And tell the truth."

Bang Abbott felt his cheeks redden. "You mean where I didn't pay for it?" He tried to make it sound like a joke.

To his astonishment, Cherry Pye peeled out of her jeans and straddled him on the seat.

"Oh, you'll pay for this, too," she growled in his ear. "Nuthin good is ever free."

6

The man called Skink told Ann DeLusia she was a good sport.

He said, "I'll drop you at Alabama Jack's. There's a guy named Jim on a blue Harley, he'll take you back to the mainland. I'd be grateful if you didn't contact the authorities for a day or so."

"Let me think about that."

"Nearest hospital is Homestead."

"I feel okay," Ann said.

This was after the man had taken the people on the hijacked bus to a wide clearing near the ocean, arranged them in a circle around a bonfire of their luggage, and berated them with wild profanity for forty-five minutes. The one named Jackie had gotten the worst of it—Skink had tied him to a tree while Ann and the bus driver stood off in the shadows, listening and sharing a beer. Evidently Jackie had recruited some itinerant crackheads with machetes to shear twenty wild acres of red mangroves, an illegal enterprise designed to provide a premium view of the Atlantic from the future town houses that Jackie and his investors planned to erect. It was Ann's impression that the investors themselves were not enamored of Jackie, though for other reasons.

"How did you know they were coming?" she asked Skink.

"It was all over the bulletin boards at Ocean Reef. I stopped by one night to return some cutlery."

"And how'd you know their bus would stop for me?"

He grinned. "Because a meteor would stop for you, dear Annie."

This was after she'd changed back into her vacation clothes and Skink had fastened the checkered flag around his bare waist like a kilt. He'd returned her purse and her cell phone, and treated her abrasions from the car crash with antibiotic cream he'd found in a first-aid kit on the bus. Afterward he had taken her to see the grave of a panther that had been hit by a beer truck many years ago, or so he'd said. It was there, in a stand of old buttonwoods, that he'd sat beside her with a penlight and read aloud Baudelaire's "The Remorse of the Dead." She had expected the man to make a grab for her boobs, at least, but nothing happened. He said he'd once been the governor of Florida, and she said she was the empress of Japan.

"I need to clear the record," he said. "I sunk your rental car on purpose, so no one would see it and come looking for you."

"That sounds like a lot of work."

"Jim will tell the hospital he found you stumbling along the road."

"No problem. I can do dazed and disoriented," Ann said.

This was later, on the way to Alabama Jack's. As the bus was climbing the Card Sound Bridge, Skink's fake eye fell out and rolled down the aisle. Ann found it under the wet bar and handed it back to him. He made her promise to download Gram Parsons when she got home, and she told him to check out the new Farrelly brothers flick. He declared there was no hope for the Jackie Sebagos of the world and said it was a waste of energy, trying to make cretins like that come to Jesus. Ann DeLusia asked if he was going back to the bonfire at the construction site, and he said of course.

"What're you going to do to that guy?"

"Nothing his medical plan won't cover."

"Have you been to jail before?"

"Don't be ridiculous," he said. "But I see your point. I'm not getting any younger."

"Ever killed anyone?"

"Yes, I have."

"Me, too," said Ann.

He reacted as if he believed her. "It's damned unpleasant, isn't it?" he said.

"The worst." She had twice told him she was an actress, but he'd obviously forgotten. "Guns are too noisy. I usually use an ice pick," she said matter-of-factly.

Skink didn't seem to hear her. The bus had stopped at the tollbooth, and from there Ann could see the sign at Alabama Jack's. Skink re-inserted his glass eye while the driver waited for change.

"You need some money?" Skink whispered to Ann.

She thought he was the most unusual homeless person she'd ever encountered, not that she'd met many. "No, I'm good," she said, patting her handbag. "Is my phone in here?"

When the bus pulled into the empty parking lot of the bar, Skink pointed out the blue motorcycle. Standing nearby was a broad-shouldered figure wearing a helmet with an opaque face shield. "That's Jim," Skink said. "When you get to the mainland, he'll give you a piece of paper with a phone number. Put it in a safe place, Annie."

She laughed. "Is this your weird way of asking me out?"

He pecked her on the forehead and said, "Thirty years ago I would've chewed your panties off by now. Gently, of course, with candles in the foreground."

"Scented candles?"

"Use that number if you ever get in trouble. The one Jim gives you."

"Are you serious?" Ann said. "I'm callin' the cops on *you*, mister!"

"Sure you are," said Skink. He smacked her on the butt as she stepped off the bus.

*

Before Cherry Pye got hold of him, Bang Abbott's most memorable sexual experience had occurred the night after he'd won the Pulitzer Prize. The newspaper threw a party at a popular St. Petersburg sports bar, where a clerk named Naomi from classifieds led Bang Abbott to the ladies' room and screwed him silly while balancing upright in an unlocked stall. The lusty clerk wasn't particularly petite, and Bang Abbott was not (even in his younger days) especially limber. As a result, he snapped the anterior cruciate ligaments in both knees at the instant of climax, sending him and Naomi crashing to the tile. In the emergency room she had barely acknowledged him, and then rudely refused to accept his phone calls after she returned to work the following month. Before he could win her back, Bang Abbott had become sidetracked by ugly rumors about his prizewinning shark-attack photograph. The rumors happened to be true, which complicated Bang Abbott's defense. By the time he was off the crutches and packing for California, he'd lost interest in Naomi. Later he heard that she'd dropped twenty pounds and married a Saab dealer.

"Was that your first mile-high?" Cherry asked.

Bang Abbott nodded as he fumbled to belt his pants. He was in a peculiar daze. According to his watch, the entire act had taken only four minutes, yet he felt like he'd been floating for days on a tantric cloud. Cherry yelled for the flight attendant, who had discreetly retreated to the galley, and demanded a bucket of ice.

"That was incredible," Bang Abbott said.

"You bet." Cherry poured each of them another drink. "How 'bout a Percocet?"

"Not right now." Bang Abbott was already worried about his level of alertness. Cherry had more or less pounded his senses numb.

She pulled on her jeans and said, "I'm totally tuckered, Claude. You wore me out."

"Have a nap," he said.

"Only if you swear not to take my picture."

"On my mother's grave."

She reached for his crotch, her small hand burrowing like a hamster. "I mean it, Claude, don't be an asshole. Not if you ever want to make love with me again."

Bang Abbott said, "I promise, Cherish."

As soon as she began to snore, he uncapped a Nikon and popped off a dozen frames. Then he unbuttoned her blouse and took a few more shots, for the European tabs. The flight attendant, who was fixing coffee for the pilots, frowned disapprovingly but said nothing. When Bang Abbott pretended to snap her picture, she blushed and turned away.

The jet hit some rough air and he hastily put the camera away, in case the bumps awoke Cherry. He tried to doze off but he couldn't stop thinking about the astounding thing that had happened to him, and wondering why. Bang Abbott couldn't recall one other shooter who'd actually been balled by the celebrity he was chasing. Occasionally you heard about the deliberate flash of a nipple or a playful peek upskirt, but he knew of no paparazzo who'd received so much as a tug job from a star. The social chasm between parasite and host was considered impassable.

Even if he'd been an A-list liposuctionist or a hot-shot movie producer, Bang Abbott knew, it would not have improved the astronomical odds of him receiving a high-altitude quickie from a frisky blonde. He was well aware of his prevailing unattractiveness—the weight issue, his negligent laundry habits, his cursory attention to basic grooming and hygiene. He was in many ways a pig, and Cherry Pye's seduction of him defied explanation, even given her wild reputation.

The mystery nagged at Bang Abbott for the remainder of the flight, and he was forced to conclude that Cherry had been more wasted than he'd thought when she'd attached herself to his lap. By the time they landed at Tamiami she'd be sobering up, and he anticipated a cranky awakening and a brusque good-bye. *So what?* he thought. *At least I got some killer photos.*

But when the Gulfstream touched down, he was surprised to see Cherry wearing a smile. "Hey, big round dude," she said sleepily. "Can I see your phone?"

Happily Bang Abbott handed over his BlackBerry. Either she didn't remember what had occurred earlier, or she was down with it.

The jet was still taxiing as Bang Abbott squeezed into the lavatory, took a marathon piss and adjusted his Dodgers cap. What he saw in the mirror reinforced the extreme implausibility of the situation. It was beyond astounding that the rumpled, gamy-looking lump staring back at him had gotten vigorously humped at 35,000 feet by a major female recording artist. Bang Abbott felt recklessly exhilarated. Now anything seemed possible.

Cherry was still talking on his phone when they got off the plane. A stretch Lincoln with smoked windows sat idling on the tarmac. The driver loaded their bags and Cherry climbed into the backseat, pulling the door shut behind her. Bang Abbott hustled around to the other side of the limo, but it screeched away just as he reached for the door handle.

"Nooooo!" he bellowed, raising both arms. "My cameras!"

The Lincoln kept going. With a merry honk it exited the airport through a rolling chain-link gate.

"Not the Nikons," the photographer said desolately. "Not my goddamn Nikons."

The flight attendant had been watching from the top of the steps. Bang Abbott looked up and raised his arms. "The crazy cunt—she took everything!"

"That's terrible."

"Please, sweetie, I need a phone."

"Sorry," said the flight attendant, "we're off to Nassau." It was the same smile she'd worn when presenting the warm beer nuts. "Enjoy your stay in Florida."

"Drop dead," Bang Abbott said. He turned and walked heavily toward the terminal building.

*

Janet Bunterman took a red-eye and landed at Miami International the next morning. She waited nearly an hour for her luggage and then took a hired car to the restaurant at the Raleigh, where Maury Lykes sat amid a pile of tabloids in a banquette.

"Have you heard from our wandering nymph?" he asked.

"Not yet, but don't worry."

"Don't worry? That's a good one, Janet." Maury Lykes ran a warty tongue across his front teeth. "She's supposed to start rehearsing for the tour—you remember the tour, don't you?"

Janet Bunterman said, "What else can I do? She left her cell phone at Rainbow Bend—I've got no way of reaching her."

Maury Lykes said he had people check Cherry's usual haunts on South Beach—the Stefano, the Shore Club, the Setai—and she hadn't been seen.

The waiter brought Janet Bunterman a Bloody Mary. "I bet she's with that kid from the Tarantino picture," she said.

"You mean Vicodin Boy. That was my concern, as well." Maury Lykes whispered something to the waiter and then turned back to Cherry's mother. "I'm going to introduce you to somebody, Janet, and I don't want you to be alarmed. At least, try not to *show* you're alarmed, will you promise?"

Before Janet Bunterman could absorb the warning, a very tall man approached the table and sat down. He wore an execrable salmon-red hairpiece from which prunish ears extruded. His face appeared to have been massaged with an industrial cheese grater and then retouched with a glue gun. The thin, etiolated lips looked like crinkled parchment, and his eyes stared pink-rimmed and dull. Janet Bunterman nervously lowered her gaze and found herself contemplating the man's clublike left arm, which was cloaked from the elbow down in a zippered nylon bag that bore the logo COBRA GOLF.

Maury Lykes said, "Janet, this is the fellow I told you about—Cherry's new bodyguard."

"Dear God."

"His name is Chemo."

"Could you excuse me for a moment?" Janet Bunterman rose.

"Sit down," Maury Lykes said firmly.

The man named Chemo blinked like a drowsy iguana.

After Cherry's mother resettled herself, she cleared her throat and asked, "Do you have a résumé, Mr. Chemo?"

He looked at Maury Lykes. "Is she for real? Jesus H. Christ."

"Janet, desperate times, et cetera," the promoter said. "Look on the bright side—for once Cherry won't be banging the help." He shrugged at Chemo and added, "No offense, brother."

Chemo smiled, a fresh horror. His stained teeth were tiny and nubbed; it looked like stale rice kernels had been implanted in his gums.

Janet Bunterman paled. "Maury, can I please speak to you alone?"

"Nope."

"Then can I have another drink?"

"Make it a Cuban coffee for me," said Chemo. He reached into his water glass and plucked out the lemon rind and gnawed it to mush.

"How tall are you?" Cherry's mother inquired. She was at a loss for conversation.

"Six-nine. And don't fuckin' ask if I ever played basket-ball."

"Okay."

"It's like askin' a midget how come he's not in the circus."

"Chill," Maury Lykes interjected. "She's just curious about your background."

"You didn't tell her?" Chemo chuckled to himself.

Janet Bunterman anxiously looked around for the server.

"Chemo was a very successful mortgage broker," Maury Lykes said.

It was improbable but true. After sixteen years and nine months at the Union Correctional Institution in Raiford, Chemo had walked out of maximum security and straight into a job selling home loans in Orlando. Because it was the peak of the real-estate boom and flimsy credit was abundant, the state of Florida bigheartedly overlooked all regulatory restrictions and welcomed with open arms absolutely anyone—including thousands of convicted felons—to the mortgage-peddling racket. Swelling the motley ranks were unreformed embezzlers, bank robbers, dope smugglers, burglars, pimps, counterfeiters, carjackers, and even a few killers such as Blondell Wayne Tatum, aka Chemo.

Among his murder victims had been the doddering dermatologist who'd fried his face during a botched electrolysis procedure, and the crooked plastic surgeon who'd falsely promised to repair the damage. A plea deal reduced the crimes from first-degree to second-degree, so Chemo wound up at Raiford with relatively mild concurrent sentences. Like many inmates, he changed in prison, although in his case the Bible played no role in his conversion. It was instead a more slender tome called *A Snake's Guide to Milking the Mortgage Trade*, which preached a strictly nonviolent philosophy of fraud and subterfuge.

Once on the outside, Chemo learned quickly despite his rough edges. He became adept at embellishing the qualifications of shaky loan applicants, such as the fry cook at his neighborhood Sizzler for whom Chemo secured a note for $525,000, a fifteen-year subprime with zero down. Chemo was pleased that he could make the American dream come true—albeit temporarily—for a nineteen-year-old kid earning minimum wage, fresh off the freighter from Honduras. Chemo was even more gratified by his under-the-table skim from the deal, which he spent on a secondhand Denali with custom rims.

One doomed loan begat another, but brokers such as Chemo were rewarded for quantity, not quality. That was the beauty of the process. Eventually a local newspaper published an unflattering front-page article about the firm where Chemo was employed, and about his boss, who'd once done a nickel at Avon Park for sticking up a Wells Fargo truck. On the day the story appeared, Chemo drove to work and found the building shuttered and a TV crew snooping around, so he took off for his old stomping ground, Miami Beach.

Janet Bunterman said, "May I ask what happened to your mortgage business?"

Chemo looked perturbed. "The bubble busted—don't you watch the news? The goddamn bottom fell out."

Again, Maury Lykes cut in: "Before he went into finance, his specialty was security. That's why I offered him the job, Janet. No harm will come to Cherry as long as Chemo's around."

Janet Bunterman snuck another glance at the bodyguard's face. The damage obviously wasn't genetic; something awful had happened to the man. "So I guess it's a done deal, then," she said tightly as her second Bloody Mary arrived.

Maury Lykes reminded Cherry Pye's mother of his substantial stake in the new album and the upcoming concert tour. "I can't take any chances, Janet."

"But how are we going to find her?"

"Oh please. She doesn't exactly fly under the radar," the promoter said.

With his unsheathed hand, Chemo dropped a cube of sugar into his coffee. He said, "Don't worry, I'll hunt her skinny ass down."

Then what? wondered Janet Bunterman.

Chemo noticed she was eyeing his hidden arm. "Should I show her?" he asked Maury Lykes, and flashed his Halloween smile.

The promoter nodded. "Let's get it over with."

"Show me what?" said Cherry's mother.

Maury Lykes explained that, many years earlier, Chemo had been seriously injured while swimming in Biscayne Bay. "A barracuda nearly killed him," he said.

"That's horrible," Janet Bunterman said with a cringe.

"A big fucker, too," Chemo added.

"And it bit off your face?"

Maury Lykes shot her a blazing look. "No, Janet, his *hand*. It bit off his hand."

Without elaborating, Chemo unzipped and removed the Cobra Golf bag cover.

Cherry Pye's mother was dumbstruck. "Is that what I think?"

"With a power pack," said Maury Lykes admiringly.

Chemo lifted it to give Janet Bunterman a closer view.

"And it's for real?" she asked in a hushed voice.

"Best part is, you don't need a carry permit like you do for a pistol." He turned it on and shredded the floral centerpiece, three Singapore orchids in a vase. The noise brought two waiters running, but Maury Lykes motioned them away.

"A weed whacker," Janet Bunterman murmured incredulously.

"You're a quick one." The bodyguard re-bagged his unusual prosthesis. "She's a quick one, Mr. Lykes."

The promoter sat forward and rubbed his palms. "Let's order some brunch, okay?"

"I'm really not hungry," said Cherry's mother.

Chemo flipped open a menu. "Anything but fish," he said.

7

The state trooper introduced himself as Corporal Valdez. He wrote down the names of the hijacked bus passengers and listened to their story. It wasn't the first time he'd been called all the way to North Key Largo for such an incident, though he didn't mention that to the victims. The one named Sebago was in severe pain because a spiny sea urchin had been snugly trussed to his scrotal region. Valdez sensed that the other passengers weren't especially sympathetic to Mr. Sebago's situation. In fact, a man named Shea angrily demanded that Sebago be arrested on the spot for fraud and embezzlement, crimes beyond the authority (or interest) of a working road-patrol officer.

While waiting for the ambulance, Valdez went up in the bus to interview the driver, who was watching one of the morning news shows on the satellite TV. The driver gave a description of the hijacker that matched the one given by the passengers: a towering, naked, grease-painted cyclops wielding a sawed-off shotgun. Valdez wasn't surprised. Three months earlier the same suspect had ambushed two lobster poachers and strung them upside down from their ankles to the Carysfort lighthouse. The previous summer, the man had detained for several hours—and convicted in a mock trial—the daughter of a state senator and her frat-boy companion, who'd been drunkenly buzzing a pelican rookery on a high-powered Sea-Doo.

"He was actually an okay guy," the bus driver said of the hijacker, "for a whack job."

"What do you mean?"

"Well, he didn't rob or shoot nobody. He just cussed at 'em."

"How much did he give you?" Valdez asked.

The bus driver reddened. "Hundred bucks. How'd you know? 'Take your old lady out for stone crabs,' he told me. So what's the big deal?"

"It's not." As far as the trooper was aware, there was no law against victims accepting cash from an armed abductor. "What about the woman?" he asked. "Was she a hostage or an accomplice?"

The bus driver thought about it for a moment. "She didn't act scared of the guy, but she was banged up some."

"What was her name?"

"I didn't catch it."

"Where's she at now?" Valdez asked.

"He had me drop her up at Alabama Jack's. Some guy on a motorcycle was waiting."

"Did you get a look at the man?"

The bus driver said the cyclist had been wearing a helmet that covered his face. Valdez closed his notebook. He had a pretty good idea who the motorcycle man was. He'd trained under him when he first joined the Highway Patrol.

"Can I keep the hundred bucks or not?" the driver asked.

"Sounds like you earned it," the trooper said.

When he stepped off the bus, he felt a pleasant breeze and saw the sun rising over the ocean. An unmarked sheriff's car rolled up and a rookie detective named Reilly got out. Valdez had met him before, and he liked him all right. He remembered Reilly telling a story about catching a thirty-pound wahoo while vacationing in Islamorada, and how he went straight home to St. Louis, packed his bags and moved to the Keys. That was how much the guy loved fishing.

Now Reilly greeted Valdez and said, "You think it's him again?"

Meaning the wild man who'd strung up the poachers.

"He tied our victim to a poisonwood tree," Valdez said. "Then he put him in a diaper."

"So the answer's yes."

"Inside the diaper was a sea urchin."

The detective winced.

"I bet this never happens in Missouri," said Valdez.

"Where is he?"

The trooper led Reilly to Jackie Sebago, who was lying on a stretcher and no longer wailing at the top of his lungs. A paramedic had unknotted the improvised snuggy—a square of shiny checkered fabric—and was grimly inspecting the victim's multiple punctures and poisonwood rash. Reilly assumed that heavy pain medicine had been administered.

"Anybody else hurt?" he asked.

The paramedic shook his head. "Just this one here."

"Can I talk to him?"

"Now's probably not a great time."

"Hey, you guys catch that fuckin' psycho?" Jackie Sebago raised his head woozily off the stretcher. "Look what he did to my nuts! You find him, okay? Lock that crazy bastard up!"

"You bet," said Reilly. "We'll get him."

The trooper, who'd been around longer than Reilly, knew better.

They could use helicopters and infrared spotlights and heat sensors and bloodhounds, but the man who had hijacked the charter bus would not be caught. If half the stories were true, he was already deep in the mangroves, untouchable, sleeping among the crocodiles.

Ann DeLusia was scared of motorcycles. Clinging to the driver, she kept her eyes squeezed shut and one cheek pressed against his broad back. When they got to the hospital in Homestead, he parked outside the emergency room and helped her climb off the bike.

"Wait," she said.

The man named Jim hadn't spoken a word during the ride.

"I need to know something," she said.

When he removed the helmet, she saw that he was an African-American. He had gray hair and stern features. "What is it?" he asked.

"That man back there—"

"An old friend of mine."

Ann said, "But he's nuts, right?"

"No, ma'am." From his jacket the motorcycle driver took out a matchbook imprinted with a skull and crossbones and the words LAST CHANCE SALOON. "There's a phone number on the inside," the motorcycle man said.

"Are you for real? I never want to see that maniac again. Ever!"

"That's the sensible response."

Ann put the matchbook in her handbag. "What's wrong with him, anyway?"

"He's got a bad temper and a long memory, but he's completely sane."

"Oh my God! You didn't hear what he said to those guys from the bus—"

The Harley driver touched a gloved finger to her lips. "I didn't say he was harmless, did I? My advice: Don't call that phone number unless you're absolutely out of options."

Ann said, "Mister, what kind of life do you think I lead?"

"Let's go."

He took her into the emergency room, where he told a nurse that he'd found her wandering along the Card Sound Road, past the toll bridge. The nurse asked Ann what had happened, and Ann said she remembered renting a Mustang and driving south down the turnpike but everything after that was a blur. The nurse put her in a wheelchair and rolled her to the X-ray department and then to a private examining room, where she asked Ann who had cleaned and dressed her abrasions.

Ann said she didn't recall. "Maybe it was the bus driver," she said.

"What bus? You said you rented a car."

"Yeah, but I remember riding on a bus, too. It's all kind of weird and foggy." Ann was covering the bases, in case they somehow connected her to the hijacking.

The nurse said, "Come lie down, sweetie. You might have a concussion."

Later a young Cuban doctor came in with her X-rays, which he fastened to a flat lamp. He said there were no broken bones or skull fractures. While Ann lay on a padded table, he checked out her bruises and pressed his fingers on different places on her abdomen. He asked if she was suffering from headaches or nausea.

"No, I'm just tired."

"We can do a CAT scan, or wait and see how you feel tomorrow."

Ann said, "I'll be okay."

The doctor wrote a prescription for Tylenol with codeine and said she was free to go.

"Is there someone who can come get you?" he asked.

"First I've gotta charge my cell phone."

"You can use mine," he offered. "My name's Carlos, by the way."

"Hello, Dr. Carlos."

"Do they call you Ann or Annie?"

"'The future Mrs. Clooney' is what they call me."

"Oh."

Sometimes it was Mrs. Clooney and sometimes it was Mrs. DiCaprio and sometimes it was Mrs. Depp. Most guys got the message but didn't pick up on the joke.

Ann wiggled the bare ring finger on her left hand. "I left my rock in a vault at Harry Winston. Four-point-two carats."

"Congratulations," the doctor said tepidly, and handed her his phone.

The motorcycle driver was gone when Ann returned to the waiting room, where she tossed the Tylenol prescription in a wastebasket. A police officer stopped by and took some information about the rental car. She pressed Ann for details about the accident, which Ann said she still couldn't remember. The cop mentioned nothing about a charter bus being hijacked, and Ann said nothing about the man called Skink. She wasn't sure why she was shielding such a dangerous lunatic, but she figured she could always change her mind and drop the amnesia act—wake up one morning with total recall, like they did on the soap operas.

Ninety minutes after the officer departed, a black SUV rolled up outside the ER. Ann DeLusia got in the backseat next to Janet Bunterman, who was scrolling through her e-mails and sipping a sludge-colored smoothie. She acknowledged Ann with a grave nod and said, "Cherry's missing and Maury's hired this deformed bodyguard with a totally vile attitude to go find her. It's a nightmare, Annie. The man's got a damn weed whacker for a hand!"

"I was in a major car crash but I'm feeling better now. Thanks for asking."

"She jumped the wall at Rainbow Bend," Janet Bunterman went on, "and chartered a jet back to Miami. Now she's disappeared. Yes, *again*."

Ann said, "Did I mention I was held hostage by a hermit with a gun? He made me eat a dead crocodile."

Cherry Pye's mother leaned forward and peered critically at Ann's upper lip, which was still swollen. "That won't do," she said with a frown.

"I quit, Janet."

"What?"

"I met a fantastic guy. We're getting married," Ann said.

"Stop."

"He's a doctor. We're starting a family right away."

"You can't quit now—not before the tour."

"His name is Carlos, and he's brilliant."

Janet Bunterman said, "What are we paying you these days, Annie?"

"Eight hundred a week. Like you don't know."

"Well, how about nine?"

"Make it a thousand," Ann said.

"Oh, for heaven's sake."

"Carlos interned at Johns Hopkins and then he camped in Sierra Leone for a year, vaccinating lepers."

"You are so full of baloney," Janet Bunterman said.

"He's teaching me the mandolin."

"This isn't funny. Cherry's still my little girl."

Ann shrugged. "I'm totally serious about quitting. I want a life of my own."

"But you're an actress," Janet Bunterman said. She had finished the smoothie and was gnawing the tip of the straw. "The part about the car accident—was that true? Please tell me you didn't get beat up on a date or something."

"No, Janet. It wasn't a date." Ann suddenly felt like crying and she didn't know why.

"I'm glad you weren't hurt badly. I mean it."

"How touching," Ann said. She was trying to recall how much money she had in the bank. Six or seven grand tops; it wouldn't last long in L.A.

Cherry's mother said, "So, we've got a deal, right? Everything's cool?"

Ann reached over and pinched the twice-modified tip of her employer's nose. "I'm tired of playing your whacked-out daughter. I want my own *vida loca*."

"After the tour," Janet Bunterman quacked.

*

101

Although Bang Abbott had been blessed with a flaccid conscience, he felt an occasional prick of regret concerning his role in the unfortunate mauling of Terence Hughes, an orthodontist from Montreal who'd come to Florida on a four-day vacation with his family. Hughes was not an incautious fellow, and he'd done nothing to deserve what happened to him. There had been no shark warnings posted at Clearwater Beach that Sunday morning, no way for a visitor to know that a school of hungry lemon sharks had been lured close to shore with a bucket of rancid grouper guts.

On the rare occasions Bang Abbott talked about the incident, he would emphasize that it had never been his intention to cause bodily harm. The photograph he'd sought, and composed graphically in the viewfinder of his imagination, was a portrait of primal mayhem—pale innocents stampeding in terror from the green surf, a dark dorsal fin looming in the froth behind them. Bang Abbott was a film buff, and *Jaws* had been one of his favorites. There was nothing more compelling in photojournalism than capturing a moment of raw fear, and that was the picture that Bang Abbott had sought. At the center of his dream shot he had envisioned a young mother with grim desperation in her eyes, trying to escape from the water while clutching a toddler under each arm. However, in a pinch he would've settled for flailing teenagers, or even a couple of wobbly retirees.

To prepare for this masterpiece, Bang Abbott had hung

around the charter docks and schmoozed a few of the local captains, who told him that large schools of lemons and blacktips cruised the Gulf shallows at certain times of the year, though attacks on humans were quite rare. The sharks were usually following migrations of bait, and displayed no appetite for any prey larger than a two-pound mullet. Bang Abbott had asked if the beasts could be chummed—purely for sportfishing purposes, of course—and the charter captains had said sure, it was easy. All you had to do was dump some bloody fish.

So, one Saturday night, under the pretense of an angling expedition, Bang Abbott had obtained (in exchange for a fifth of Jim Beam) a jumbo bucket of smelly grouper heads and entrails from the mate of a boat called the *Master Baiter IV.* The following morning, shortly after dawn, Bang Abbott had gone to the beach and selected a stretch that he knew was popular with the family crowd. After a messy struggle he'd managed to transfer the fish parts to a large mesh bag, which he staked to the sandy bottom in about four feet of water. Then he had waded back to shore, fitted long lenses on two of his camera bodies, and sat down to wait as the tide fell, carrying the irresistible stench into the Gulf.

Terence Hughes had arrived at eight-thirty with his wife and three children, none of whom expressed any enthusiasm for swimming. There were perhaps a dozen other tourists cavorting off the beach when Hughes splashed in the water alone, wearing flippers and an ill-fitting mask. By that point, Bang Abbott had already mounted one of his Nikons on a tripod and aimed it toward the area offshore where he had submerged the chum bag.

For a man whose life's work was visual composition, Bang Abbott maintained an uncommon lack of wonder about the natural world. He had never photographed a sunset or a meadow of wildflowers, or even a flock of pelicans. If there wasn't a human being somewhere in the frame, Bang Abbott wasn't much interested. His knowledge of animal behavior was sparse, based on hokey films and staged television documentaries. Among his many misconceptions was a belief that sharks cruising in skinny water would automatically be easy to see because their dorsals would protrude above the surface. His plan, once he'd spotted the first fin, was to shout a warning to the swimmers and then begin shooting, so as not to miss a frame of their panicky flight.

The scheme was ill-conceived and preposterously dangerous. Bang Abbott had assumed that the sharks, following their noses, would race to the seeping chum bag and pay no attention to the thrashing tourists. When the screams broke out he'd been caught by surprise, because no telltale fins were visible from his improvised photo station. And he'd been authentically shocked when one of the tourists, a man in his thirties with a dive mask strapped crookedly to his face, cried out that he'd been bitten.

Howling, the victim had sloshed toward the beach, his legs churning frantically against the waves. As he'd watched through his clicking camera, Bang Abbott noticed that the man was advancing slowly, as if dragging a heavy weight.

Other tourists were struggling to get out of his way, yelling and shoving one another aside.

The reason had become evident when Terence Hughes neared the shore and his torso emerged above the waterline. A dusky young lemon shark weighing perhaps forty pounds had affixed itself to the poor man's ass. The apparition had been bizarre indeed, the gathered onlookers erupting in horrified cries. From a distance it had initially appeared that Terence Hughes was wagging an enormous chubby tail, but Bang Abbott's Nikon quickly brought the gruesome tableau into focus. The stricken man had held out his arms and pleaded for assistance, but nobody—not even his wife—would venture near him.

Marine biologists later theorized that a top row of the shark's teeth had become snagged in the reinforced nylon waistband of Terence Hughes's recently purchased and festively patterned board shorts. Once the stuck creature became suspended out of water, its bulk (combined with its manic exertions) had ripped the swimsuit from Terence Hughes, leaving him bleeding and exposed. The lemon shark had fallen back into the water and swum off with the torn swimsuit and a grapefruit-sized chunk of the Canadian's left buttock.

Lifeguards had cleared the beach swiftly and marine patrol officers had arrived in fast boats, one of which snagged its propeller on the mangled remnants of a freshly soiled chum bag. By then, Bang Abbott was gone. It had never occurred to him that the elderly fellow who'd been illegally walking his Jack Russell on the beach at daybreak had taken a cell-phone snapshot of Bang Abbott dragging the sack of fish into the surf, or that the old fart would download the photo and e-mail it to the *St. Petersburg Times* after reading that Bang Abbott had won a Pulitzer Prize for the *Chilling Florida Shark Ambush*.

The ensuing controversy was fueled by indignant bloggers who wanted Bang Abbott prosecuted for instigating the fateful feeding frenzy. Ultimately, the dog walker's cell-phone image was deemed too fuzzy to be conclusive, so the Pulitzer committee decided not to strip Bang Abbott of its coveted honor. Terence Hughes recovered from his wounds and went on to enjoy a brief spell of celebrity; he and his surgeon appeared on *Maury* and other popular interview shows, presenting graphic video of his butt-cheek reconstruction. Meanwhile Bang Abbott continued to insist that the disputed photo couldn't have been staged because both victim and shark obviously weren't faking it, and that furthermore there was no law against chumming up sea life near a public beach.

Glad to be free of the newspaper business and its stuffy ethics, Bang Abbott was soon thereafter thriving in his new career as a paparazzo. The provenance of his work product was never questioned, nor were his methods, which is why he was rattled to find himself being interrogated rather snippily by Peter Cartwill, managing editor of the *National Eye*.

"Claude, I must say, that's quite an adventure. I mean, really." Cartwill was smiling somewhat coldly.

"Well, it's true. Every word," Bang Abbott said.

"So, Cherry Pye brought you to Miami on a private jet."

"Yeah, that's right."

"And fucked your brains out along the way."

"Peter, would I make this up?"

Bang Abbott had gone to the *Eye*'s main newsroom in Boca Raton with a plan to sell his sex story for enough money to cover the cost of the lost cameras, now in Cherry's possession. Bang Abbott had enjoyed a solid relationship with the *Eye*, which had published a dozen of his celebrity-in-disarray photographs. Bang Abbott figured this deal would be a no-brainer—he'd just talk into a tape recorder, then one of the hacks on the copy desk would write it up with Bang Abbott's byline: "Seduced by Stoned Pop Star at 35,000 Feet!"

Or something like that.

"But you've no proof," said Cartwill, "not a single picture." He was one of those tough Aussies who'd learned the trade on Fleet Street and come to the United States during the post-Elvis tabloid boom.

"I told you, she swiped my goddamn Nikons!"

"Yes, Claude, it's all quite fantastic."

"And yours, for ten grand."

Cartwill chuckled. "I'm afraid the answer is no. The whole thing is too unbelievable."

"But that's only because you know me, Peter. Your readers, they don't have a clue what I look like."

"It's a first-person story. We'd have to run a picture," Cartwill said.

"Hell, you don't have to use *mine*." Bang Abbott pointed

across the newsroom at some good-looking kid standing at the coffee machine. "Put *his* face on the damn thing. Who cares?"

"I'm sorry, mate."

"Your loss. I'll sell it to the *Enquirer*." Bang Abbott was annoyed that Cartwill didn't acknowledge the obvious hook in the story. "How many shooters you heard of that got balled by a superstar? And then fuckin' robbed? C'mon, Peter, gimme a break."

Cartwill said, "Actually, it's good you stopped by. You remember this one?" He handed Bang Abbott a color print, an eight-by-ten. "We put it on page two."

"Sure. That's Cherry after the Grammys. Outside the Viper Room."

"And you're quite certain it's her?" Cartwill asked.

Bang Abbott felt like he'd been kicked in the nuts. Did Cartwill know about the look-alike? He said, "You guys bought the damn picture! Of course it's her."

But he was studying the photograph closely. Cherry—if it *was* Cherry—had been wearing a leather miniskirt and Chanel shades when she came out of the club and dashed across Sunset. Bang Abbott's flash had caught one side of her face, a washed-out exposure typical of night shoots. Lev was at her side . . . but what did that prove? After all, it was Lev who'd told Bang Abbott that Cherry had duped him more than once.

Cartwill said, "We got an e-mail about this one, Claude. From a nurse at Cedars, she's a faithful reader of our paper.

She said Cherry couldn't have been at any after-parties that night because she was in the emergency room, getting her stomach pumped."

Bang Abbott didn't take his eyes off the picture. The longer he studied it, the less certain he was. The woman could have been Cherry Pye, or she could have been the double he'd photographed on the stretcher behind the Stefano—in such poor light, it was impossible to say.

"It's Cherry, man. Who the hell else would it be?" Bang Abbott blustered. "The guy walking beside her, that's her bodyguard. Name's Lev. Here, look."

Cartwill took back the print without glancing at it. "We really don't ask many questions. You know that, Claude. This is a competitive business, and things happen."

"Not to me they don't."

"However, the IDs must be one thousand percent positive," Cartwill went on. "It's really the only rule we have. We run a shot of Charlize, it better damn well be Charlize. It's not their lawyers we're worried about, it's our reputation."

Bang Abbott said, "Your reputation?"

Peter Cartwill seemed dead serious. "Readers buy our paper to see photographs of fabulous people living fabulous lives. If they think we're faking our pictures, they won't buy the paper anymore. The stories themselves can be total bullshit, and often they are, but so what? The public has no way of knowing what's true and what's not. But the photographs have to be real, Claude, because that's what gives credibility to the journalism."

"You bet," said Bang Abbott, thinking: Did he just say "journalism"?

"They see a photo of Julia leaving the supermarket, they'll believe she's got two cartons of Marlboros in the bag because she's desperately trying to drop ten pounds for the new Soderbergh film. But it *must* be Julia in the picture for the story to play."

"What are you sayin', Peter?"

Cartwill tapped a forefinger on the desk. "Be careful, that's all. We don't want to get burned."

"No worries," Bang Abbott said thinly. When he stood up, he noticed that the color print from the Viper Room shoot was pinned firmly beneath the editor's left elbow.

"In the old days, there was wriggle room. You know—a wink and a nod," Cartwill said. "Not so anymore. Somebody smells a rat, it's all over the bloody Internet. Next thing you know, I'm getting phone calls. And I don't want phone calls, Claude."

Bang Abbott could no longer hold back. "Wait—you're sayin' you guys don't dick around with the pictures anymore? No Photoshop, no airbrush, nuthin? Not even those Bahamas shots of what's-her-face, that whale from Jenny Craig? The one your boss has been bangin' for two years? You're sayin' every photo your paper runs is legit? Get fucking real, Peter."

"Things are changing," Cartwill said. "Have you checked out our Web site? We're buying video clips now."

"Oh Jesus." Bang Abbott hated those TV stakeout crews. Total slugs.

"We pay pretty well," Cartwill remarked.

"But not for true stories like mine."

"Not without pictures, no. It's a shame about your cameras." The phone on the editor's desk began to ring, and he said, "I need to take this."

Bang Abbott paused at the door. "It really happened, you know. Up in the plane? She practically raped me."

"I believe you, mate," said Cartwill in a tone so merciless that it filled the photographer with rage.

8

The man called Chemo had come to the attention of Maury Lykes a year earlier during halftime of a Miami Heat basketball game. Maury Lykes, who had floor seats, spotted in the third row a former client named Presley Aaron, a pipe fitter turned country singer. Under the guidance of Maury Lykes, Presley Aaron had recorded a string of megahits, including "Unbreak This Broken Heart" and the crossover tearjerker "Daddy, What's My New Momma's Name?"

But stardom had been hard on Presley Aaron, whose room-temperature intellect was easily overwhelmed by all the money, women and media swirl. He went hurtling off the rails, and after his fourth arrest (with two Memphis call girls and a shaving kit stuffed with crystal), Maury Lykes had fired him from the label. At the time, the promoter had felt certain that Presley Aaron would wind up dead under seedy circumstances. Yet the scrappy redneck had managed to kick his dope habit and win back his ex-fashion-model wife and two young kids, a triumph of will and true love that was exhaustively chronicled on the morning shows and in the tabloids.

Intrigued by the prospect of a comeback album, Maury Lykes made his way to where Presley Aaron was sitting and they embraced warmly. The singer seemed to bear no ill will toward the promoter for cutting him loose. "Rock bottom's exactly where I needed to be," he said.

Maury Lykes couldn't conceal his amazement at Presley Aaron's transformation from pallid degenerate tweaker to buff bronze stud. The musician said he'd been saved by the good Lord and also his stepbrothers, Jake and Ernest, who had put him in rehab and then hired a special bodyguard to hang close and keep him straight. "Every time I'd fuck up, he beat the everluvin' shit outta me," Presley said fondly. "The man's an angel."

It was at that moment when Chemo appeared, looming above the crowd. In one arm he cradled two large sodas, and on the other arm, which was partially sheathed with a zippered bag, he balanced a cardboard tray of cheese-jizzed nachos. Maury Lykes had seen plenty of freaks and goons in his career, but he'd never set eyes on anyone like Chemo. When Presley Aaron introduced him, Chemo grunted a raspy response and sat down to dine. Maury Lykes pegged him as an ex-basketball player who'd been in some hideous accident involving fire or chemicals, possibly both. Maury Lykes figured the man's arm was so disfigured that he chose to keep it covered and spare others from the sight.

Presley Aaron, it had turned out, was starting his own TV ministry and had no plans to revive his country-music career. Maury Lykes wished him well and returned to his seat. Throughout the second half of the game he caught himself glancing back at Chemo, who was skimming a landscape magazine while picking at the skin tags on his face. The man was as formidable as he was repulsive.

Later, Maury Lykes called Presley Aaron to ask if Chemo ever did any freelance crisis management, and Presley Aaron was nice enough to offer the man's cell number. When Janet Bunterman fired Lev, Maury Lykes immediately knew whom he wanted as a replacement bodyguard for Cherry Pye. Presley Aaron, now solidly clean and sober, agreed to let Chemo out of his contract.

Maury Lykes made contact as soon as he learned that Cherry had gone AWOL from Rainbow Bend. Chemo instructed the promoter to meet him in the garden section of a Home Depot store in Kendall. There he unveiled the latest version of his prosthetic weed whacker and gave a brief demonstration, showing Maury Lykes how the power trimmer had been modified to fit the stump of his arm and then wired to a holstered battery pack. He said he'd once used the device to partially decorticate a meth dealer who'd been bothering Mr. Aaron.

Chemo was forthright about his criminal history, but he told Maury Lykes that prison had taught him to manage his temper. He said he hoped to go back to selling mortgages as soon as the housing market rebounded. Until then, he was working in the personal security field, and doing occasional gigs as a bouncer on South Beach.

Maury Lykes was sold. Chemo had never heard of Cherry Pye, but he agreed to take the job. The promoter said Cherry had skipped out of a detox mansion and hooked up with an actor named Tanner Dane Keefe, who was supposedly staying on Star Island. Chemo said no problem—he would track down the girl and straighten her out.

After agreeing on a fee and per diem, the two men walked out to the parking lot. In an effort to sound sociable, Maury Lykes commented on Chemo's height and inquired if he'd ever played pro hoops. Chemo replied that the last person who'd asked him that question spent four weeks recovering in a VA hospital. Maury Lykes apologized quickly, and asked Chemo to meet with him and the missing starlet's mother the next morning at the Raleigh. Chemo got into a Denali with chrome rims and roared away, leaving the promoter to reflect on the extreme measures to which Cherry Pye had pushed him.

Like anyone who dealt with talent, genuine or manufactured, Maury Lykes was a chronic worrier. Now, with Cherry still missing and Chemo unleashed, the promoter was on the brink of an anxiety attack. He was supposed to be reviewing the final mix of the lead backup singer's track, the one that Cherry would be lip-synching in concert (providing she turned up halfway sober and ambulatory). Instead he found himself pacing the studio, chugging coffee and checking his phone every twenty seconds for messages from the tracker-slash-bodyguard. Chemo was the first convicted murderer that Maury Lykes had ever put on the payroll, and he hoped the man understood the concept of boundaries.

What if he hurts Cherry? the promoter thought. *Even worse, what if he falls for her?*

At midnight he retreated to his Key Biscayne condo and, as was his habit when under stress, arranged an impromptu debauch. This time the participants were three lithe dancers who were being auditioned for Cherry's tour. Maury Lykes had spotted them in a Winnipeg theater production of *High School Musical* and flown them down to Florida, where they each signed a paper swearing they were eighteen years old and had simply misplaced their driver's licenses.

Following directions, the dancers tied down Maury Lykes and took turns thwacking him with a badminton racket while singing "We're All in This Together," which was his second-favorite number from the smash Disney play. He was just getting into the spirit of the lyrics when his phone began to vibrate on the marble nightstand. Maury Lykes hollered for somebody to answer it, as his own hands were hitched by parachute cord to the bedposts.

One of the dancers picked up the phone and said hi. She listened briefly and then nodded at Maury Lykes. "It's for you," she said. "Some guy named Chemo?"

"Untie me right this second."

"But you said not to," the dancer reminded him. "You told us to make you beg."

"For the love of Christ—then hold the damn phone to my ear!"

The voice on the other end said, "What the hell?"

"Never mind. Tell me some good news."

"Okay. I found your girl."

Maury Lykes woo-hooed in relief. "Way to go, brother."

"She's a pisser, too," Chemo said.

"Tell me about it."

"So double my pay."

"What?"

Chemo said, "You wanna see her alive, then double my pay."

"Unfuckingbelievable."

"She called me 'Waffle Face.' Normally I'd kill a person for that. Normally I'd stick a frog gig up their nostrils and yank their tongue out by the roots."

Maury Lykes groaned. "Fine, you got your raise. Now let me speak to her."

"Not now. She's passed out cold," Chemo reported.

"Lovely. Where'd you catch up with her?"

"Some tattoo shop on Washington Avenue."

"Shit!" Maury Lykes began thrashing against his bindings, which startled the young auditioneers.

"What the hell did she do now?" the promoter shouted helplessly at the phone. "How bad is it? How bad?"

Chemo said, "All depends on your taste. See you in thirty."

The visit had begun promisingly for Tanner Dane Keefe, with a vigorous hand job in the back of the limo. It was Cherry Pye's way of thanking him for dumping his date after Cherry had showed up unannounced on Star Island. Later, snorkeling Red Bull and vodka in the car, she told Tanner Dane Keefe about her escape from Rainbow Bend, an adventure that he cheered as totally sick. The young actor was flattered that Cherry had rented a Gulfstream and flown all the way from L.A. to reconnect, but he was wary about sharing his drugs. He wasn't up for another overdose scene.

So far, Cherry had been behaving herself. On the first night they'd stayed up until two, playing air hockey and taking dorky pictures with some expensive digital cameras that she had said were a gift from a famous fashion photographer. When Tanner Dane Keefe had scrolled through one of the cameras' memory cards, he'd found some jarringly unsexy shots of Cherry snoozing on a plane with her boobs hanging out. Cherry had acted like she'd never seen the photos before and deleted them one by one, chuckling the whole time.

Tonight their first stop was the VIP lounge at some superloud South Beach club called Abcess, where Cherry rocked slowly on Tanner Dane Keefe's lap and asked him to accompany her on the upcoming concert tour. He nipped one of her earlobes and whispered, "I can't, babe. Quentin needs me back in Vancouver to re-shoot the last two scenes."

"Aw, please. I really, *really* want you there, Tanny."

"I can't say no to Quentin—it's for the DVD. You know how they make, like, three different endings to pick from?"

Cherry lowered her eyes. "This really sucks."

"Tell you what. I'll fly down for your show in Seattle," the actor offered.

"I don't like screwing strangers, especially roadies. That's why I need you there the whole time."

"Yeah, but—"

"Tanny, you know how many guys would kill for this?" Now she was pressing it against him. Tanner Dane Keefe felt the soft wedge of heat yet did not succumb, a credit to the dulling effect of the pills.

"Cherry, gimme a break. It's Tarantino—the fucking *director's cut*!"

"Yeah, yeah."

He said, "Can't we talk about this later?" Thinking: Like when you're comatose?

She pushed away and pouted for a while and then pretended to flirt with some famous football player who had plaster casts on each of his thumbs. Tanner Dane Keefe distracted himself by dancing with a Thai supermodel who was five inches taller than he was in three-inch lifts. The model was about to divulge her phone number, when Cherry Pye seized Tanner Dane Keefe by the elbow and steered him outside through a small but raucous knot of paparazzi.

Inside the limo, more drinks were poured. The actor nodded off for a while and, when he awoke, the car was parked in front of a funky storefront that advertised psychic readings for fifteen dollars.

Cherry dragged him through the front door, saying, "You'll see—she's amazing."

The psychic's name was Madame Tula, and she wore a faded purple shawl, a necklace made of cowrie shells and a Swatch watch. She studied the right palm of Tanner Dane Keefe and announced his new film would do fabulous box office, especially overseas. Then she conducted a tarot reading for Cherry Pye and her expression turned somber. She said the singer's new CD was destined to bomb unless Cherry immediately got her neck tattooed.

"What kinda tatt?" Cherry asked with tipsy concern.

The psychic closed her eyes. "The head of Axl Rose," she said, "on the body of a zebra."

Tanner Dane Keefe snorted and said, "I don't think so."

"Shut up," snapped Cherry.

Madame Tula pushed a business card across the table. "Go see this man."

"Is he there now?"

"Yes, child, most certainly." Madame Tula, whose real name was Debbie Metzenbaum, felt no duty to inform Cherry Pye that the tattoo artist was her younger brother, Allan, or that he specialized in Axl Rose-headed creations, or that he gave Debbie a 15 percent cut from every drunk she sent his way; twenty if they paid in cash.

Tanner Dane Keefe tried to talk Cherry out of getting the tatt but she wouldn't listen, so he slipped her a couple of Xanaxes and sat down to watch. She removed her top and sprawled on a table and yelped at the first hot touch of the needle. Tanner Dane Keefe was too young to remember Guns N' Roses, so he had no idea if the tattoo guy was any good. The screaming florid face that was emerging on the milky slope of Cherry Pye's neck reminded Tanner Dane Keefe of no one so much as his Aunt Christine, who'd been banished from holiday gatherings after assaulting the family Airedale.

The actor held up a mirror to show Cherry the ink work, which she pronounced freaking awesome. "I dunno, babe," Tanner Dane Keefe said doubtfully. He was hesitant to criticize, as the tattoo artist seemed touchy and also outweighed him by probably a hundred pounds.

A bell tinkled merrily as the front door opened. Tanner Dane Keefe turned in his chair and beheld an extremely tall figure with a clubbed arm, a sorry toupee and a totally fucked-up face. The man directed the tattoo artist to stop drawing on Cherry and, without bothering to evaluate the intruder, the tattoo artist responded crudely in the negative. At that point, the tall, damaged man uncovered his bad limb to reveal a rotary weed cutter, which he started with the touch of a button.

The din captured the full attention of the tattoo artist. He set down his needle and reassessed the visitor, who was eyeing a wall upon which the tattooist had displayed two dozen intricate patterns on rice paper. Not wishing to see his artwork reduced to confetti, the tattooist politely asked the intruder what he wanted.

"Just her."

The stranger pointed his garden implement at Cherry, who screeched, "Get outta here, you fuckin' waffle-faced freakazoid!"

"Thing is," said the tattoo artist, "I ain't done yet."

"You sure about that?" the visitor asked.

"Dude, I gotta finish the zebra part."

"So you're, like, the next Picasso?"

"Okay, take her," said the tattoo artist, with the sweep of a luridly illustrated arm. The waffle-faced lawn man handed him a hundred-dollar bill and hoisted Cherry Pye over one shoulder.

The notion to intercede on his date's behalf briefly entered the mind of Tanner Dane Keefe and then exited just as swiftly when the intruder threatened to scalp him if he tried to be a hero. "No problem," said the actor. Then, to Cherry: "Catch ya later, babe."

"You pussy!" she yelled at him as she disappeared through the doorway, squirming in the clutch of her storklike abductor. Once they were out of sight, Tanner Dane Keefe dashed from the tattoo parlor and hurled himself into the back of the limousine and curled up panting on the floorboard. He whispered for the driver to take him home to Star Island.

*

The next morning, a damaged late-model Mustang belonging to the Hertz Corp. was found at the bottom of a creek along the Card Sound Road. A helicopter pilot from the Monroe Sheriff's Office had spotted the vehicle during a brief but unfruitful manhunt for the nude hijacker of a private charter bus. The suspect himself was still safely at large, submerged to his chin among the twisted red roots of a mangrove stand deep in the Crocodile Lake National Wildlife Refuge.

From the air, Skink was practically invisible, his shorn head as brown and featureless as a floating coconut. He could rest for hours like that in a salty marsh, his mind drifting into a meditative zone that was useful on those occasions when he was being pursued. Yet on this day his thoughts returned again and again to the young woman whom he'd pulled from the car, Annie being her name. Annie the actress.

She hadn't believed it when he'd said he was once the governor of Florida, but that was to be expected. Sometimes he hardly believed it himself. He couldn't recall the last time anyone had recognized him as Clinton Tyree, so many years had passed since he'd fled Tallahassee and that savage realm. The mystery of his disappearance, which had consumed the political press for some time, was no longer of widespread interest. That was fine with the runaway governor, who was happier being an odd historical footnote than he ever was as a headline.

His approximate whereabouts were known but to a single

person, Jim Tile, an old friend with whom Skink maintained sporadic contact by marine radio or a cellular telephone, when he had one. Long retired from the state Highway Patrol, and newly widowed, Tile spent his time traveling the length of the peninsula by motorcycle, a continuous lonely circuit from the Panhandle to the Keys and back. Whenever the man he still called governor needed him, Tile went without delay. Better than anyone, he knew how swiftly events could spin out of hand when Skink slipped a gear. His nomadic exile had been eventful—inspired vandalism, snipings, spectacular arsons, abductions, even killings, Tile was sure, although in each suspected instance the victim could hardly be portrayed as undeserving. As Skink grew older, Tile looked in vain for signs of mellowing, but so far the governor's only act of moderation had been to discard his AK-47 in favor of a chopped-down Remington bird gun.

Tile had asked few questions about Annie before agreeing to take her to the hospital. Skink figured she must be all right; otherwise Jim would have called from the emergency room. Still, he felt a nagging concern that bordered on fatherly, which he didn't understand. Young Annie owned a lovely self-confidence, though perhaps it was part of her act. He'd been fooled by sure-footed women in the past.

After nightfall Skink floated out of the trees and emerged dripping like a bull otter on a dry wedge of land. Cautiously he picked his way through dense hammocks until he reached his campsite, which he was pleased to find undisturbed. As before, the searchers hadn't made it that far into the swamp.

The presence of crocodiles always dampened their enthusiasm, fine bloodhounds being too pricey to risk on some unhinged old drifter with a shotgun.

A cold front was blowing through the islands, and Skink knew the police helicopter was back on the pad in Marathon. He made a small fire and then hiked to the road in hopes of scavenging supper. He returned with a fresh raccoon and a yellow rat snake, both struck by the same vehicle. Skink figured the coon was probably chasing the reptile when it got thumped.

He fried up all the meat with pepper and Tabasco, and washed it down with three Michelobs that he'd swiped from the refrigerator on the charter bus. Briefly he thought of Jackie Sebago, the turd merchant, and wondered if the doctors had kept count of all the sea urchin quills they'd pulled from his necrotic ball sack. The photos must have been glorious, Skink mused. Maybe they'll show up in a surgical textbook.

After dinner he hurled a stump of dead buttonwood on the fire and fitted one of his prized cassettes into an old battery-powered boom box. Then he pulled on his plastic bath cap and lay down naked in the leaves and sang along to Buffalo Springfield, wondering in spite of himself about Ann DeLusia—what her real story was, and if he'd ever see her again.

9

 The former Cheryl Bunterman had never met her paid imposter, and was in fact unaware that Ann DeLusia existed. She'd been completely truthful when she told Bang Abbott that she didn't know what he was talking about.

Janet Bunterman believed it would upset her daughter to know that a full-time decoy had been retained for public-relations purposes due to the episodic frequency of Cherry's "gastritis." There was little danger of the star's learning about the ruse, because she never read the tabloids and seldom watched the celebrity TV shows. On the occasions when she came across a photograph or video clip of herself ducking into a glamorous soirée that she couldn't recall, Cherry assumed that she'd been fried at the time and had blacked out the whole evening.

As an actress, Ann DeLusia was naturally curious about the woman whom she portrayed. Yet the only opportunities she had to observe Cherry in person were when the singer was being hustled out of vomit-smelling hotel rooms while Ann was being hustled in. Invariably Cherry was either unconscious or delirious, and strapped to a stretcher. Such scenes didn't give Ann much to work with, Method-wise. Dutifully she had studied all of Cherry's music videos, and even watched a stultifying reel of red-carpet interviews, in case she ever had to actually speak during one of her nocturnal masquerades.

So far, Ann had seen nothing to suggest that the former Cheryl Bunterman was complicated, misunderstood or even slightly exploited. Rather, the woman appeared spoiled, vain and empty-headed. The tattoo did not change Ann's opinion.

"Very classy," she said when Janet Bunterman showed her a Polaroid. "It looks like gonorrhea through a microscope."

"That's Axl Rose."

"Get out!"

"See, he's like a centaur," Cherry's mother explained, pointing at the picture. "It's supposed to be a zebra's body."

"I see the cock, Janet, but where's the tail? I mean, the thing has no rear end."

"The tattoo man didn't have time to finish."

Ann said, "Lemme guess. Visitation was over."

Janet Bunterman dourly snatched a cup of coffee from the room-service tray. The entourage was back at the Stefano, regrouping. Ann sat cross-legged on the bed in her room, eating a sesame bagel and poking through the *Miami Herald*.

Cherry's mother said, "The tatt's in a bad spot."

"What about makeup?"

"She's so pale and the darn thing's so loud—it's impossible to hide it unless we dress her in turtlenecks."

"Or a cool scarf."

"The Larks know a doctor in Santa Monica who specializes in laser removal. He's the one who burned Billy Bob off Angelina's arm," said Janet Bunterman, "and most of Johnny's Winona. Unfortunately, Cherry's being difficult. She says she wants to keep it. Maury's going to speak with her, but in the meantime—"

"No way!" Ann bounced off the bed, scattering the newspaper. "Do *not* even go there."

"Take it easy. We'll do it in henna," Cherry's mom said. "I got the name of a Pakistani lady in the Gables who's supposed to be amazing. You can scrub it off as soon as this nonsense is over."

"But I don't want that gross thing on my neck," Ann protested. "People are gonna think it's an infected hickey."

The door of the hotel room opened and a tall man entered holding a key card. He approached Janet Bunterman and grumbled something about breakfast. Ann DeLusia wasn't listening; she was gawking at the man's face. It was the worst chemical peel she'd ever seen.

Cherry's mother said, "Annie, this is Chemo. He's the new bodyguard."

"Hullo," said Ann, her voice barely above a whisper.

The man leaned over. "The fuck are you starin' at?"

"I'm sorry, guy, but . . . I mean, holy shit."

Janet Bunterman broke in: "Annie, please."

"No offense, but somebody did that to me? I'd get a lawyer."

Chemo blinked coldly. "I took care of it a different way."

"What's the deal with your arm?" Ann asked.

He turned to Cherry's mother and said, "Don't tell me she's part of this goddamned circus, too."

"Annie is my daughter's, uh, stand-in. Sometimes you'll be accompanying her in public, as if she were Cherry. It's a little game we have to play to deal with the media."

Chemo grunted. "I smell another raise."

As soon as the man went downstairs, Ann asked Janet Bunterman what planet he was from.

"Maury hired the monster. We had no choice."

"What does Cherry say?"

"Cherry's not happy. She had her heart set on an African-American martial-arts master, because she thinks that's what Britney's got—although I don't believe it's true. I think Britney's main guy is from Fiji." Janet Bunterman seemed to be talking to the coffee cup. "So now Cherry's locked herself in the bathroom. Do you have your little black dress?"

"Why?" Ann asked warily. "It's at the bottom of the swamp, with the rest of my stuff."

Cherry's mother looked puzzled.

"The car crash, remember?" Ann said.

"Oh, right. Well, then, you should go to Bal Harbour this

afternoon and get some new clothes, after your trip to the Pakistani. The Olsens are giving a major party tonight at Pubes—it would look good for Cherry to show up."

"But she'll be busy."

Janet Bunterman nodded. "Getting fitted for her act, God willing. This designer charges something like three grand a day, and he's such a pain. But Maury says he did Celine's show in Vegas."

Ann DeLusia wasn't opposed to the idea of a new dress, even though no one would see her in it except the paparazzi outside the club and the wait staff inside. Maybe someday she'd actually get to hang out at one of these events and have a few laughs, instead of being hidden away in a back room until it was time to split.

"Is he coming along, too—the new bodyguard?" Ann asked.

Cherry's mother sighed. "Don't piss him off, okay? He's not like Lev."

"No sense of humor, huh?"

"Zero. I mean, look at the man."

Ann said, "So, what's that big thingie on his arm?"

Janet Bunterman told her.

"Wow." Ann found herself intrigued by the concept.

"I don't know what Maury was thinking," Cherry's mother muttered.

Ann suspected that the man named Chemo had a colorful story to tell. "I'm gonna ask him to show it to me," she said mischievously, "that crazy rig."

"Only if you want a new haircut," warned Janet Bunterman. From her wallet she removed five one-hundred-dollar bills and counted them out. "Here—and don't forget to save the receipts."

With a doubtful smile, Ann eyed the money. "So I guess I'm not shopping at Tory Burch."

"Lord, you're worse than my daughter."

"Not even close," Ann sang out, and went to call for a cab.

Bang Abbott parked on the street, two blocks from the hotel. He had armed himself with a secondhand Pentax, which he'd bought at an all-night pawnshop in Hialeah. The camera was digital and the motor drive still worked, so what the hell. With any luck he'd soon recover his Nikons, and more.

Although he hadn't slept since arriving in Florida, he didn't feel tired. This was typical of stalkers, although Bang Abbott would never acknowledge that was what he'd become. He left the camera in the car and scouted the lobby, where he spotted the scrawny bellman and pulled him outside.

"She's here, bro! Room 602. I called chu like five times, why the fuck chu don't call me back?" the bellman whined.

"Somebody stole my goddamn phone," Bang Abbott said. *And the numbers of all my sources*, he thought bitterly. The cameras were replaceable, but losing the BlackBerry was a major hassle. He hoped Cherry Pye hadn't lost it, or thrown it away.

"She's up there now," the bellman whispered. "I heard the concierge calling for a locksmith."

"For Christ's sake. Is she toasted again?"

The bellman said he'd try to find out. Bang Abbott gave him fifty bucks and the number of his new cell, another pawnshop bargain.

"Let me know when she's on the move," the photographer said. "There's another hundred in it for you—and tell those other monkeys, too." Bang Abbott had gone to an ATM and gotten a fat wad. "I won't be far," he said, pointing down the street.

The rental car was a blue Buick compact. Roomy it was not, especially for a person of Bang Abbott's circumference. The morning air was chilly, so he rolled up the windows and kept the engine running and tried not to think about the sex with Cherry. Soon he had a rubbery hard-on, which he would have tended discreetly if only the snug steering wheel hadn't impeded his frontal access. *With design flaws like this*, Bang Abbott thought, *it's no wonder GM is going tits-up*.

He slid his untoned mass to the passenger side and, using a discarded wax wrapper from a Quarter Pounder, took care of Claude Jr. Yet even afterward he couldn't stop wondering about Cherry. Why on earth had she jumped his bones? Like most successful paparazzi, Bang Abbott seldom wrestled with issues of self-esteem; he knew his lowly place in the carnal order. What Cherry had done to him, pleasurable as it might have been, was a breach of natural law, like a butterfly humping a cockroach.

Most men of Bang Abbott's worldliness would have understood the futility of ruminating over the airplane romp, and fondly filed the memory for future fantasies. It was a measure of the photographer's deepening obsession that he was able to twist a frivolously empty act of intercourse into something calculated and diabolical. At times he was close to convincing himself that Cherry had hatched a dark plan, that she was using him in some cynical way.

Bang Abbott reached under the seat to make certain that the pistol was still there—a Colt .38 Special, with a plastic shoulder holster and three bullets. He'd gotten it for eighty dollars from the same upright vendor who'd sold him the Pentax. Although it was the first gun he had ever handled, Bang Abbott wasn't nervous. Mechanically the Colt looked simple compared to a camera, and the operative fundamentals were the same: Point and shoot.

Ostensibly he'd gotten the weapon to protect himself from South Florida's well-known criminal element, but in his daydreams he imagined flashing it casually in Cherry's presence. Like countless fools before him, Bang Abbott believed that carrying a firearm would make certain persons take him more seriously.

At half-past nine, the bellman called to say that Cherry's security man was leaving the hotel lobby alone. "What's he look like?" Bang Abbott asked.

"A motherfuckin' ay-leen."

"A what?"

"Chu know—a ay-leen. Like from a UFO."

Bang Abbott chuckled. "So he's got, what, antennas coming out of his head?"

"Chu'll see, bro. He be cruisin' your way."

The photographer shrank low in the Buick and peeked over the dashboard. When Cherry's new bodyguard—and who else could it be?—appeared on the sidewalk, Bang Abbott saw that the bellman hadn't been exaggerating. The guy was a geek on stilts.

Bang Abbott waited until the man was a full block past him before squeezing out of the Buick and taking pursuit. Because of his height, and the coral iridescence of his toupee, the bodyguard was easy to follow. On Alton Road he entered an organic diner, where he grabbed a breakfast menu and chose a table away from the window. He said nothing when Bang Abbott boldly sat down across from him.

"You don't know me," the photographer began. "I'm a shooter for the tabloids. Strictly freelance. Your client stole my gear."

The bodyguard didn't glance up from the menu.

"We took a plane ride together, then she bolts with my camera bag. I couldn't fuckin' believe it."

The bodyguard stifled a yawn.

"I'm talkin' about Miss Cherry Pye," Bang Abbott went on, trying not to stare. Up close, the man was a fright show. "Two Nikons and a BlackBerry—I need to get 'em back, the phone especially. And here's what else: I'll pay good money."

Slowly, the man raised his oozy eyes. The sockets appeared to be inflamed, and the hooded lids were mapped with bluish veins. To Bang Abbott he looked like a mutant gecko. And that clunky thing on his arm—was it a cast, or was he packing an Uzi under there?

The paparazzo introduced himself and gamely attempted a handshake. The bodyguard responded by baring his teeth, which were discolored and nubby.

"How much?" he asked Bang Abbott.

"What?"

"To get your shit back. How much'll you pay?"

"I dunno. Five hundred?" Bang Abbott said. "But that's only if the crazy bitch hasn't trashed the equipment."

The bodyguard said, "Make it eight, unconditional. Shit's broke, you get it fixed."

"Six fifty."

"Go away, Slim." He went to the counter and returned shortly with a glass of grapefruit juice. "Look at all the fuckin' pulp," he remarked with a frown.

Bang Abbott said, "Okay, eight hundred." He wrote his new cell number on a napkin and passed it to the bodyguard. "The BlackBerry is tangerine-colored. You can't miss it." He had custom-ordered a bright one so he could locate it easily in his cluttered camera bag.

"What's your name, dude?" he asked the bodyguard.

"Chemo."

"Is that, like, French or somethin'?"

"You ever call me 'dude' again, I'll peel your fat head like a goddamn apple." The bodyguard blinked and sipped his juice.

Bang Abbott was determined to make a personal connection. The man wasn't particularly sociable but, unlike Lev, he seemed open to cash incentives. The photographer was thinking ahead to future services beyond the retrieval of his camera bag. Cherry Pye could become his exclusive celebrity property, if Chemo could be bought off.

But the guy was an authentic hardass, possibly even an ex-con, so Bang Abbott knew he must be patient—and extremely careful—with his approach. "What's Cobra Golf?" he inquired innocently, nodding toward the bulky zippered bag on the bodyguard's left arm.

Chemo sniffed the air. "Jesus, what died?"

The photographer pressed on, searching for common ground. "When I was a kid, I fractured my ulna in two places—fell out of a tree house. Had to wear a cast for three months."

"This ain't a cast." Chemo raised his bagged limb.

"Oh," said Bang Abbott. "Man, I'm sorry."

"What for? It wasn't *your* arm that got ate." With his good one, the bodyguard signaled to a waitress, who came over and took his order: four eggs, sunny-side up, and a stack of multigrain toast.

When the waitress turned to Bang Abbott and asked what he wanted, Chemo cut in: "Don't bring him nuthin. He's hittin' the bricks."

The photographer smiled wanly and stood up. "I guess I am. Give me a call when you find my stuff—"

"That was the deal."

"—then we can meet up . . . wherever."

"Right," said Chemo. "You know, they got this slick new invention."

"Oh yeah?"

"Called soap. Maybe you heard of it."

Bang Abbott felt his neck turn hot. "Later," he said, and shuffled out of the restaurant.

The former Cheryl Bunterman sat on the toilet seat in the bathroom of Suite 602 with her bare feet propped on the paparazzo's camera bag. Her mother was rapping on the other side of the door, warning that the hotel locksmith was on the way.

"Cherry, we can do this the hard way or the easy way."

"It's *Cherish*. And I'm not comin' out till you fire that disgusting A-hole and get me a black super-karate dude like Britney's."

Janet Bunterman said, "Sweetie, I checked with her people. The bodyguard's from Samoa."

"That bald guy? No way, Mom. He was on the Raiders."

"Samoans play football, too," Cherry's mother pointed out.

"Just get rid of that freak, okay? He scares the pee out of me." Cherry and her molten hangover had been locked in the john for more than an hour. She'd passed the time by toying with the photographer's fruity-colored cell phone, reading his text messages and listening to his voice mails.

"Hey, Mom, guess what? The Olsens are having a thing at Pubes tonight."

"Yes, I know."

"Kanye might be there!"

"Where'd you hear that?" Cherry's mother demanded through the door.

"And David Spade's staying at the Standard—he checked in as 'Bubba Gump.' What else . . . Oh, Ellen and Portia canceled their reservations at the Forge . . . Uma's having brunch at the News Café with some dude in a cowboy hat . . . This is *so* cool."

Janet Bunterman pounded harder. "What are you doing in there?"

"Hush up, Mom!" Cherry Pye was checking a fresh voice mail on the photographer's phone. It was about her—some guy with a squeaky Cuban accent saying she was at the Stefano. He even knew the room number.

Cherry was positively tickled. Balancing on the porcelain lip of the claw-footed tub, she peeped out the window, which offered a partial view of the pool. Sunbathing couples could be seen snuggling heedlessly, indicating to Cherry that no cameramen or video crews were lurking among the cabanas. *Maybe they're waiting out front*, she thought, *near the lobby*.

"Cherry, honey?" A man's voice at the door.

"Oh shit," she whispered to herself. Then: "Maury, leave me alone!"

He said, "I'm counting to nine."

She shoved the BlackBerry into the camera bag. "Go away! I've got the runs!"

"Tell me—do you enjoy this pampered life of yours?"

What was that *supposed to mean?*

She unlocked the door. The promoter came in and closed it behind him. His calm demeanor was intimidating.

"Where's my mom?" Cherry asked.

"Let's see the tatt." Maury Lykes put on his wire-rimmed glasses and skeptically examined her neck. "Yeah, that's gorgeous—and just in time for the *Us Weekly* cover shot I got lined up for tomorrow."

"Well, I don't care what you say—I totally love this tattoo. It's a zebra-man Axl!"

"Who is . . .?"

Cherry knew Maury was testing her.

He said, "Come on. Hundred bucks if you can name the band."

"Blood, Sweat and Roses?"

The promoter removed his glasses and hooked them through an open buttonhole of his polo shirt. "*Skantily* is your last big shot, honey. You blow this tour, say adios to the good stuff. Because Cherry Pye as a brand is over, understand? Done."

"Awesome!" she cried defiantly. "'Cause from now on I'm gonna be called Cherish."

"How about 'Bankrupt'? You like that name? The Artist Formerly Known as Solvent." Maury Lykes wore a heartless smile. "Because, honey, I'll sue your thong off."

"For what?" Cherry asked in a wounded voice.

"Breach of contract. Misappropriation of funds. Whatever else my sharks come up with." Maury Lykes stood at the mirror and picked a sesame seed out of his teeth. "You skipped out of Malibu rehab, so now it's time for Maury rehab. You're grounded from all parties until further notice," he said. "Rehearsals start next week—I'll e-mail the song tracks from the show so you can start practicing your legendary lip magic. The lyric sheets are on the way."

"So now I'm, like, a prisoner? This is *not* happening."

"Friend Chemo will accompany you wherever you need to go."

"No, Maury! He's horrible!"

"A nightmare," the promoter agreed. "And don't think you can fellate your way to his heart—he doesn't have the same weaknesses as Lev."

Cherry raised her eyebrows. "You mean he's gay?"

"No, I mean he's cold. Maybe the coldest sonofabitch I ever met."

Janet Bunterman tapped on the bathroom door and asked if everything was all right. Maury Lykes called out, "Just peachy!"

Cherry lowered her voice. "But he knows who I am, right?"

"Chemo? Oh, he couldn't care less." Maury Lykes turned away from the mirror. "Honey, don't take it personal. Middle-aged psychopaths, they don't keep up with the music scene."

It was eating at Cherry, the idea of being seen in public with such an unattractive and possibly unfuckable bodyguard. "So, how'd he find me and Tanner last night?" she asked in a sulk.

Maury Lykes told her that Chemo had called all the beachside limousine companies and pretended to be the young actor's personal pharmacist, late with an urgent delivery. One of the dispatchers remembered a Star Island pickup and radioed the driver, who reported that he was parked outside a tattoo parlor on Washington.

"That's so freaking scummy!" Cherry exclaimed.

"More like brilliant." The promoter kissed her on the chin. "Don't forget what I said—if you fuck up this project, all major fun in your life is over. Be a good girl, we'll make you 'Cherish' on the next album."

She threw her arms around his neck and pulled him extra close. "Don't ever leave me, Maury. You gotta promise."

10

 Bang Abbott would never starve. Even with a used Pentax he could always make money.

A few years earlier, a particularly lean streak on the L.A. club circuit had forced him to the beaches of Malibu, where every afternoon he would prowl for sunbathing celebrities. Bang Abbott referred to that summer as his "Cellulite Period," because the tabloids were paying ludicrous sums for close-ups of famous asses, the flabbier the better. He'd made seventeen grand with one sensationally embarrassing photo of Jessica Simpson, and another six thousand for a wide-load sequence of Tom Hanks, who'd put on thirty pounds for a film about Theodore Roosevelt.

But beaches weren't Bang Abbott's favorite place to work. Concealment was difficult, and the lighting conditions were often bright and harsh. Worse, beaches were usually hot, and Bang Abbott was miserable in the heat. He perspired in unnatural spumes, soaking rapidly through his shirt, cap, even his pants. The odor didn't bother him so much as the stares; it was impossible to be inconspicuous while dripping like a Nile hippo.

But a man had to make a living, so here he was, scouting the famous topless stretch of South Beach, near Lummus Park. A woman he'd met in line at a Subway shop had claimed to be a maid at the Clevelander and for twenty bucks she'd informed Bang Abbott that Lindsay Lohan and her latest girlfriend were catching some rays at Fifth Street. He figured what the hell, maybe he could earn some extra coin while awaiting Cherry Pye's next ambulance ride.

So far, though, Bang Abbott hadn't spied Lindsay's bare breasts among the oiled, upright domes that glistened before him as far as the eye could see. The shore was clotted with male and female gawkers, many of them snapping pictures, so Bang Abbott saw no need for stealth as he plodded along the sand. Eventually he recognized a German supermodel and snapped a dozen shots before her swarthy male companion ran him off. A hundred yards down the beach, the photographer spied a woman who looked like Sienna Miller but turned out to be a licensed respiratory therapist from Louisville whose gym-rat husband had no sense of humor. Bang Abbott was in full flight when his cell phone began ringing. He didn't stop to answer until he made it to Collins Avenue.

"You want your cameras, or not?" It was Cherry's new bodyguard.

"Fuck yes. Where are you?" Bang Abbott panted.

"The hotel. Meet me in the john by the lobby."

"I'll be there in twenty."

"And bring the goddamn money, Slim."

Bang Abbott arrived with the cash and also the pistol, in case he was being set up. When he entered the rest room he saw Chemo standing before one of the mirrors, scrutinizing his feral hairpiece. The camera bag was on the floor.

"As promised," Chemo said, holding out his hand to be paid.

"Hang on." Bang Abbott hurriedly dug through the bag and found both Nikons and all the lenses—but no BlackBerry.

"Where's the damn phone?" he asked.

"Don't ask me." Chemo's scabrous features arranged themselves into a scowl. "Now gimme the money so I can get outta here."

"But I need my phone!"

"Buy a new one."

"All my numbers, my sources—I'm dead in the water without 'em."

Chemo shrugged. "My people are waitin' on me upstairs."

Bang Abbott was infuriated. Why would Cherry return the expensive cameras and keep the BlackBerry? She seemed determined to mess with his head. He counted out four one-hundred-dollar bills and handed them to the bodyguard.

"You get the other half when I get my fucking phone," he said adventurously.

"Oh really?" The man called Chemo bolted the rest room door and unzipped his stumped limb, revealing what appeared to be a regulation-sized mechanical weed trimmer. When he turned on the motor, the noise echoed harshly off the tiles.

Bang Abbott retreated into a stall, where he lifted his sodden shirttail to expose the butt of the Colt revolver in his belt. Chemo seemed amused. With a septic grin, he said, "That's a good one, Slim. Now hand over the rest of my goddamn money."

The photographer complied. Chemo put away the weed whacker, kicked the camera bag into the stall and slammed the door. "Don't come out for fifteen minutes," he said.

Bang Abbott stayed for nearly an hour. The toilet seat was a high-end fixture with a generous circumference, and he fit upon it comfortably. Upon inspection, both Nikons appeared to be undamaged, which was a relief, although one was missing its lens cap. When Bang Abbott scrolled through the contents of the memory file, he saw that Cherry had taken a sequence of photographs, apparently in the bathroom of her suite. In the opening frames she was topless except for a white towel draped around her neck. With one hand she was holding the Nikon over her head, aiming into the mirror while making sultry expressions with her sea-green eyes. Bang Abbott assumed the shots were meant to be private self-portraits, and he felt himself becoming aroused.

Then he advanced to a frame in which she had shed the towel, uncovering a garish tribal tattoo: the face of what appeared to be a yodeling baboon, affixed to a truncated zebra body. In the final shot Cherry was crossing her eyes and sticking out her tongue, and Bang Abbott's lust turned to fury. He thought: *The little whore is making fun of me!*

Instantly, and without a crumb of evidence, he concluded that Cherry had staged the teasing photographs specifically for him, leaving the images filed on his camera with acid mockery. He studied each picture over and over, his anger swelling, and by the time he emerged from the toilet stall he was irrationally, and fatefully, propelled.

Ann DeLusia was born in Ames, Iowa, and never met her real father. She was raised alone by her mom, a vegan grocer who became a slavering fundamentalist and wed a professional bowler when Ann was a sophomore at Michigan State. In protest Ann dropped out of school and moved to Southern California, where she planned to become a screenwriter until the night she accidentally slept with one. The conversation was even more tedious than the sex, leading Ann to conclude that the golden days of Elaine May and William Goldman were over.

At a friend's urging she decided to try acting, and because of her looks—which her insipid agent billed as "wholesomely sensual"—she landed nonspeaking parts in TV commercials for an assortment of feminine hygiene products, including a recyclable contraceptive ring. Finally Ann won the role of lawyer Joanne Jefferson in a road production of *Rent*, and although the pay was disappointing her reviews were good. She had no problem portraying a lesbian, and in light of her rotten experiences with Los Angeles men she began pondering a real-life reorientation.

Then she met Lawrence, a flutist with a dwindling trust fund and a beach house in San Clemente and a singular talent in the sack. Ann DeLusia grew unaccountably comfortable with Lawrence and found herself overlooking multiple character deficits, such as his habit of showering with his springer spaniels and tipping only 9 percent in restaurants. Every night, before bed, Ann would carefully massage Rogaine foam on her new boyfriend's flapjack-sized bald spot, a gesture that Lawrence's mother asserted was proof of true love.

After not quite a year, Ann was surprised to find out that her flutist was seeing a woman fifteen years his senior who owned a chain of dry-cleaning shops in Marin County, and would fly him up for orgies and Renaissance fairs. Ann dumped Lawrence on the same day her agency called about an unusual acting opportunity that offered good pay and frequent travel, along with a sworn confidentiality agreement. The "audition" was a ten-minute meeting in the lounge of the Four Seasons with Janet Bunterman, who fingered Ann's blond locks and examined her complexion and inquired about her bust size before sending her out the door. The next morning, Ann got the call. She said yes because she needed the money, and also because she liked the idea of not playing a stage character but rather a whole other woman, one who wouldn't be fooled by priapic show-offs wielding wind instruments.

Although she wasn't an avid follower of Cherry Pye's career, Ann was aware from tabloid television of the singer's rollicking demons and sketchy reputation. She imagined that working as Cherry's secret double would never be dull—and possibly the closest she'd ever get to living a star's existence.

"Why?" asked the henna artist, who turned out to be Lebanese, not Pakistani. "Why you do to your body such a thing?"

Ann DeLusia said it was a long story. The woman peered at the Polaroid of Cherry Pye's tattoo and huffed in disapproval. "What is supposed to be this picture?"

"A man's face on a zebra. Actually, half a zebra."

"No, no," objected the henna artist. "It is for you not right."

"Please, Sasha. I don't have much time."

"Is a penis, that thing?" The henna artist pointed distastefully. "Penis of zebra?"

"Possibly," Ann conceded.

"This is sickness, young lady! Let me instead do pretty bamboo moth."

Ann told her that the disturbing tattoo was needed for a party. "I'll scrub it off first thing tomorrow," she lied.

The henna artist said, "Salt water and loofah, hokay? Soak for twenty minutes."

"Gotcha."

Ann removed her blouse and pinned up her hair and sat down under the lamp. Afterward Cherry's driver took her to Bal Harbour, where she bought a short black dress and pumps at Max Mara. Even though everything was marked down 30 percent, Ann ended up using some of her own cash because Janet Bunterman hadn't given her enough, as usual.

Upon returning to the Stefano, Ann went straight to her room and scoped out the ink on her neck. *Catastrophic*, she thought. *Thank God it's only South Beach.*

Cherry's mother stopped by and took a look. "She did a nice job, no?"

"You owe me, big-time," Ann muttered.

"Yes, well, we made the right move. Cherry's posted a picture on her MySpace page. Now I suppose the whole bloody world knows."

"She took a picture of her tatt?"

Janet Bunterman nodded. "While she was locked in the bathroom. I told the Larks to take it down but they said it had already gone viral. They said for us to stay cool and roll with it."

"Yeah, let me know how that works out." Ann frowned at the henna replica in the mirror.

"What they did do, the Larks, they went on the site and cropped Cherry's breasts out of the frame."

"Absolutely. We wouldn't want her to embarrass herself." Ann stretched out on the bed. Listening to Cherry's mom almost made her appreciate her own.

Janet Bunterman said, "I wish I knew what was going on in her head."

"Can't help you there. What time's the prom?"

"Chemo will come get you at eleven. Did you find a dress?"

Ann DeLusia laughed. "We'll make a stunning couple, don't you think? Me and Señor Chemo."

"Don't get cute with him, Annie. He doesn't do cute."

The costume fittings took several hours, but the designer kept Cherry Pye entertained with anecdotes about famously unbearable divas. As soon as he was gone, Cherry vectored for the minibar, only to discover that all the beer and liquor had been removed. "What the fuck!" she exclaimed.

Chemo, who was reading a *National Geographic*, looked up and said, "Doctor's orders."

"Did you do this?"

"Keep your goddamn voice down," he told her.

Never before had Cherry been addressed so rudely by the help. She announced that she was firing Chemo on the spot.

He said, "I don't work for you, child. I work for Mr. Lykes." Then he went back to his magazine.

Cherry ran into the bedroom, slamming the door. In the dregs of her handbag she found a single yellow pill, furry with lint, and swallowed it. She had no idea what she was taking; she assumed it was a leftover goody from her night with Tanner Dane Keefe. Speaking of whom, she had texted the actor, like, twenty-five times on the new iPhone her mother had bought to replace the one Cherry had left at Rainbow Bend. Young Tanner hadn't responded, indicating to Cherry that their dreamy relationship had been damaged by the incident at the tattoo parlor. She thought: *What if that big waffle-faced freak scared my new boyfriend away?*

When Cherry emerged from the bedroom, she was wearing only a flesh-tone thong and a lace push-up bra. Chemo gave her an amused glance but said nothing. She sat down beside him on the sofa and scissored her legs languidly across the glass coffee table.

"Can't we be buddies?" she asked.

"That ain't what they pay me for. Jesus, what's that smell?"

"Me," Cherry said with a smoky laugh. "I got my own perfume."

It was called Fizz, a scent hastily formulated during a previous downswing in her career. Fewer than four thousand bottles had been sold, the remaining units now occupying a climate-controlled warehouse in Queens.

Frowning, Chemo sniffed the air. "Lemme guess—guava rind and horse piss."

"Real funny. What're you reading, tall dude?"

"All about penguins. They mate for life."

Cherry tittered. "How boring is *that*? I mate for fun."

She slid closer, pressing against him. Chemo said, "You can't be serious."

"My last bodyguard, he got his pecker pierced."

"Big deal. I had mine fiberglassed." He slapped shut the *National Geographic* and stood up. "Go put on some damn clothes." Her mother was coming soon and it wouldn't look good, the girl sprawling in her underwear beside him.

Cherry raised one leg and wiggled her toes. "So, boyfriend, there's a hot party at Pubes. Wanna hit it?"

"You're in lockdown." He went to the minibar and popped open a V-8.

She said, "Aw, don't be such a d-bag."

Chemo watched her adjust one of her bra cups to expose a dark crescent of nipple. Maury Lykes had warned that something like this might happen. It was kind of pathetic.

"I want a picture of us together," Cherry said. "Where's that black bag with the cameras?"

"What black bag?" Chemo noisily sucked down the vegetable juice. In prison the authorities had rewarded his good behavior by returning his dynamic prosthesis and letting him clear a small garden in the yard behind the kitchen. Over time, Chemo had developed a taste for fresh produce, although not to the exclusion of jerked pork or pot roast.

"Yo, show me your thing," Cherry said playfully. "The fake arm, I mean."

It wasn't often that Chemo got to deploy his appliance twice in the same day. "I'll let you see it," he said, "but only if you put on a robe."

"Cool!"

As soon as Cherry came out of the bathroom, he

unsheathed the weed trimmer. Her eyes widened, which is when Chemo noticed that her pupils were dilated.

She said, "Holy shit. Turn it on, dude!"

"Are you high?"

"Come on, slash away. Please?"

He touched the starter button and went to work on the wallpaper, an off-ivory damask. Cherry was hopping around like a kangaroo, she was so jazzed. Chemo silenced the device when Janet Bunterman walked in.

Drily she said, "I'm glad you two are hitting it off."

"Can I go now?" Chemo asked.

"You expect me to pay for that wall?"

"I bet you can swing it," he said.

"Go where?" Cherry demanded.

Janet Bunterman said, "Chemo's got a date, sweetie. I'm staying over, to keep you company."

"He's got a *date*? Yeah, right." Cherry let the robe fall open, just to give her mother a jolt. "So you know, Mom— the guy's, like, all over me. It's so gross."

Janet Bunterman thought Cherry was probably lying, but she didn't wish to appear to be taking sides against her own child. Adopting an air of maternal concern, she turned to address Chemo, who seemed unfazed by the sordid accusation.

"Did something happen here?" she asked.

With his forefinger Chemo was casually excavating a sore on his chin. He said, "No offense, but I wouldn't bone your daughter with someone else's dick."

Janet Bunterman reddened, while Cherry angrily cried, "Mom, I want you to fire that awful pervert right this minute!"

"Everybody just settle down," Janet Bunterman said, as much to calm herself as Cherry. The new bodyguard was outrageously crude, not to mention spooky, but Maury wouldn't cave and Maury was running the show.

Chemo asked what time it was.

"Late," said Cherry's mother. "You'd better go."

He re-cloaked the weed whacker and went next door to his room, where he put on a beret, some wraparound Ray-Bans and a black leather jacket with extra-wide sleeves. Then he took the stairs two flights down and knocked on the door of Room 409, where the woman named Ann had been waiting. Chemo was interested to see that she had a tattoo exactly like Janet Bunterman's spacey daughter, on the same part of her neck. When she noticed him looking, she tried to cover it with a swoop of hair.

As they waited for the elevator, she asked, "Does my dress look okay?"

"Okay for what?"

Ann had used a tan concealer to cover the scrapes on her legs left over from the car accident. She said, "Never mind. You know the drill, right?"

Chemo nodded. "I get out first, then you follow while I clear the way. Hang on to the back of my jacket and holler if somebody touches you. We stop for a few seconds at the door, so the assholes out front can get some pictures—"

She shook her head. "I'm not talking about that. I mean the party. You understand we won't be hanging with Kanye or Justin tonight, due to the fact that I'm not the real Cherry Pye, I'm just a civilian. This is all a dumb act, a PR scam—you're aware of that, right?"

Chemo said, "Is the question, do I give a fuck? Because the answer's no, long as I get paid."

After they entered the elevator, he said, "They got us set up in the club manager's office with Chinese takeout and a flat-screen TV. Maybe an hour, then we're back in the car."

The woman named Ann raised her eyes to the smoked-mirror ceiling and checked her makeup. Chemo saw the resemblance to Janet Bunterman's daughter, although he thought Ann was actually prettier.

"One of these nights, I'm gonna get up and dance my ass off," she said. "Screw the Buntermans."

"Some other time," Chemo grunted.

She smiled ruefully. "Right, it's your first gig. Don't worry, I won't get you in trouble."

He said, "I never worry."

As the elevator door opened, Ann put on her shades. She had to walk quickly to keep up with Chemo's long stride, the heels of her new shoes clicking on the buffed terrazzo. A few tourists paused to watch her pass, while a lone paparazzo whom Ann recognized from prior encounters trailed her across the lobby.

"Nice tatt, Cherry!" he called out. "How about a big smile

for your fans?" Ann let him snap a few shots, then she picked up the pace.

A black Suburban from the limo service was idling in front of the hotel. Chemo opened the back door and helped Ann get seated. At that moment, a bellman crossing in front of the SUV lost his footing and spilled a trolley full of Louis Vuitton suitcases, blocking the driveway. The chauffeur jumped out of the Suburban and began swearing in Creole at the bellman, who swore back in Spanish.

Chemo said, "Can you fucking believe these two?"

He closed Ann's door and went to resolve the issue by kicking the loose luggage, piece by piece, into the taxi lane. It took no more than half a minute, which was why he was surprised to see the Suburban pull away without him. Wedged behind the wheel was the photographer who'd been skulking in the hotel lobby, the same fat nimrod whose precious camera bag Chemo had retrieved and returned for a very fair fee.

"Jesus H. Christ," Chemo said.

The bereft chauffeur took off running in pursuit of the SUV, a scene that Chemo would have found funny if he weren't so annoyed. Losing a stand-in wasn't nearly as serious as losing the star, but it was still a rookie mistake that could cost him his job.

Before heading upstairs to break the news to Janet Bunterman, he stopped in the bar and leveled himself with a stiff martini. Obviously he'd misjudged the photographer as harmless; thinking back to their meeting in the hotel men's room, the bodyguard realized he should have trusted his instincts. He should have taken away the idiot's gun and then fractured every chubby finger.

There you have it, Chemo thought sourly. *No good deed goes unpunished.*

11

 In the mid-1970s a man named D. T. Maltby became lieutenant governor of Florida as the running mate of a charismatic newcomer named Clinton Tyree. Maltby had been selected for the ticket because he was from rural DeSoto County, and it was believed he could deliver the ultraconservative Panhandle vote, which he did.

Maltby couldn't have been more different from the man who had chosen him. Clinton Tyree was a towering presence, a chiseled ex-college football star and authentic Vietnam War hero. By contrast Maltby was a lumpy, marble-mouthed pharmacist whose only battle wounds were paper cuts received while tearing open his annual draft deferments. He'd spent a decade in the state house of representatives, honing larcenous skills that became known to

Clinton Tyree only after they'd won the election. The lieutenant governor was as crooked as the governor was honest, so Maltby privately squirmed as Tyree launched what was literally a one-man crusade against corruption in Tallahassee. Of course the mission was doomed, but the imposing and eloquent governor managed briefly to disrupt the bountiful flow of gratuities that for years had enriched Maltby and his colleagues. Maltby had never before met a Florida politician who refused to accept *some* form of kickback—not even a stack of Bahamian gambling chips—and he soon came to believe that Clinton Tyree was as crazy as a shithouse rat.

That view became broadly embraced after the governor suddenly vanished. It happened the day after the cabinet decided to close down a waterfront wildlife haven called Sparrow Beach, and sell the land for peanuts to a development firm that planned to bulldoze the dunes and throw up a palisade of high rises. Naturally, Clinton Tyree cast the only dissenting vote. Just as naturally, D. T. Maltby sided with the majority—the only speck of actual authority to come with the title of lieutenant governor was a voting seat in the cabinet, and Maltby used every opportunity to faithfully advance the interests of the wealthy and powerful. More often than not, his fealty was well rewarded.

During the debate over closing the Sparrow Beach Wildlife Preserve, Maltby was careful not to advertise that he happened to be a major shareholder in the Sparrow Beach Development Corporation, which was acquiring the pristine tract. The lopsided vote pushed Clinton Tyree off an emotional ledge upon which he had been teetering for months. On the following morning, he despondently folded himself into the backseat of his state car and ordered his driver, a Highway Patrol trooper named Jim Tile, to step on the gas. Six hours later Tyree was dropped at a Greyhound terminal in Orlando, and from then on his whereabouts became a mystery. A manhunt was suspended after a resignation letter arrived in Tallahassee, and FBI handwriting experts authenticated the signature.

By constitutional directive, D. T. Maltby ascended to the governorship and held the office for the remainder of Tyree's term, a wildly profitable spree that restored a climate of carefree venality to the state capitol. As the next election cycle approached, Maltby was preparing to launch his own gubernatorial candidacy when his wife caught him screwing a female crop duster and threatened to provide the Internal Revenue Service with a stack of bank statements from Curaçao. Citing unspecified health problems, Maltby abruptly retired from government service and joined a consulting firm that charged exorbitant sums to assist land developers in subverting state building regulations.

In time Maltby grew wealthy enough to purchase a spacious vacation home at the Ocean Reef Club, which was the last place he expected to encounter Clinton Tyree after thirty years of weird rumors and silence. Maltby had long ago assumed the runaway governor was dead. At first he didn't even recognize the bastard, for Tyree's appearance had changed shockingly. But the moment the intruder smiled, Maltby knew.

"Clint?"

"I shed that name a long time ago." The governor was seated in the laundry room adjoining Maltby's kitchen.

"Holy Jesus, what happened? Where the hell have you been all these years?"

"Now they call me Skink," the governor advised.

Maltby was extremely nervous. Tyree wore moldy high-top sneakers and a putrid trench coat. His head was shaved, and strings of spent shotgun shells hung on two long silver braids. He had lost an eye, undoubtedly through violence, and his skin looked baked and weathered.

"What are you doing here, Clint?"

"Stop calling me that."

"Wait—are you taking a goddamn dump in my washing machine?"

Skink rose and calmly rebuttoned his coat. "We have a mutual acquaintance named Jackie Sebago."

Maltby was reeling. What did this maniac want?

"I didn't break in. You left the sliders open," Skink explained. "I brought my own music, by the way."

Maltby worriedly followed him to the family room, where the governor inserted a disc in the CD deck and said, "Joe Walsh." He turned up the volume.

"How'd you find me?" Maltby asked.

"Vanity, you schmuck." From a pocket Skink whipped out a bright yellow sheet of paper announcing that D. T. Maltby had scored a hole in one on the Hammock Course. "It was posted on the corkboard at the clubhouse," Skink said. "Nice shot."

"Are you a member here?" Maltby asked incredulously.

The governor's laughter boomed. "No, I live down the road," he said. "I hike the grounds at night, when all you trolls are asleep." He shoved Maltby toward the living room and sat him down on the Mexican tile. "Now tell me about Sebago."

Shakily, Maltby said, "Never heard of him."

"That's not what Jackie Boy told me. He said he paid you to fix the permits for his town house project, which is quite the abomination. Have you seen the plans? We had a long heart-to-heart, the two of us."

Maltby turned pale. News of the bus hijacking had swept like a flash fire through the Ocean Reef community. "Don't tell me you're the one who—"

"Sebago Isle—does that ring a bell?" Skink lifted the mounted head of a mule deer off the wall and, using a thumb, pried out the glass eyes and tucked them in his side pocket. Then he began whipping the buck's head back and forth as he twirled in mad circles, slashing at air with the antlers.

Maltby helplessly wet himself in fear, crying, "What the hell do you want from me?"

The governor halted his primitive jig and sat down on the arm of the chair. "Those favors you arranged for Jackie? I want you to unarrange them—and don't say it's impossible." He probed Maltby's earlobes with the sharp tips of the deer antlers. "The scumsuckers you paid off to get those construction permits, you pay 'em off again to red-tag the site and shut it down. These things are very doable, D.T."

Maltby thought about what had happened to Sebago—thirty-three sea urchin spines removed from his scrotum, according to the president of the home owners' association.

"Look, Jackie's project is in the shitter anyway," Maltby said. "I think he's sold maybe two units, and the investors are ready to gut him."

Skink beamed. "Then let's finish the job." He stood up and centered the deer head on a coffee table. "Tell me something, D.T. Did you buy this place with the money you got from Sparrow Beach?"

Maltby felt himself shrivel inside his silk pee-stained boxers. So Tyree knew about his secret stake in the company.

He murmured, "No, Governor. That all went to wife number one."

"Well, it appears you bounced back just fine." Skink slapped him on the shoulder. "You've put on a few pounds since the old days. Let me guess: Third marriage?"

Maltby shook his head glumly and held up four fingers. The governor whistled. "You went one way, I went the other," he said. "Eons pass, and now here we are, bonding again!"

"Yeah. Unbelievable," Maltby said hoarsely.

"Tell the truth—did you ever think our paths would

cross?" Skink hooted and clapped his hands. "Of *course* you didn't. Where's the newest Mrs. M., by the way?"

"Sag Harbor."

"Spending your life savings, I hope. Excuse me." The governor groped into his trench coat and came out with a phone that was vibrating. He covered his fake eye and with the other he squinted at the tiny screen, trying to make out the name on the caller ID.

"I'll be damned," he said quietly. Then, to Maltby: "It's been fun catching up, but don't make me come find you again. *Comprehende?*"

Then he was gone. Maltby hurried to the window and watched Clinton Tyree jog across the backyard into the darkness—braids flapping, coat billowing, his face half-lit with the violet glow from the cell phone, which he held to one ear.

Maltby's first thought was: *For an old fart, that fucker can move.*

His second thought was: *No cops.*

Bang Abbott was halfway across the MacArthur Causeway before he realized he'd snatched the wrong blonde.

"Nice work," said Ann DeLusia.

"But, the tattoo!"

"It's henna," she said. "Cherry's is the real deal."

The photographer was trying to scope her out and watch the road at the same time. "Lose the shades," he said.

"Don't be a jackass. Take me back to the hotel."

Bang Abbott turned off on Watson Island and parked near the children's museum, where he had left his rented Buick. He put on the dome light inside the Suburban and pulled out the pistol, just to show her that he meant business.

"You must be the phantom double. The one Lev told me about," he said.

When the woman removed her sunglasses, Bang Abbott swore heatedly.

"The Viper Room, right? After the Grammys?" he said.

"Big night. I saw Ashlee Simpson choke on a prawn."

"Shit."

It was the same brown-eyed nobody whom he'd photographed on the stretcher behind the Stefano, the one who had mockingly blown him a kiss.

"I'm just an actress," she said. "My name's Ann."

"Cherry stole my stuff."

"What?"

"She balled me, then she jacked my cameras and my BlackBerry," the photographer said. "I got the Nikons back, but not the phone."

Ann nodded. "So you decided to kidnap her. Well, at least it's not over something stupid and childish."

"Get out," he snapped. "We're switching cars."

She seemed relieved when he began navigating back toward South Beach. "Just drop me at the Strand—I'll call a cab."

Bang Abbott shook his head. "You don't understand."

He'd had the whole thing worked out in his head, before the fuckup. Now he needed a plan B.

"I paid off the bellman to spill those suitcases," he bragged.

Ann told him he had a bright future as a carjacker. "It's definitely a step up, career-wise."

Bang Abbott was too preoccupied to catch the insult. All he could think about was Cherry Pye.

He said, "She's gotta pay for what she did. Let's agree on that."

"What if I could get my hands on your precious Black-Berry? Would you go back on your medication like a good boy?"

The photographer smiled to himself. How could this girl be so dim?

Ann said, "You wouldn't do well in prison. For one thing, they make you shower every week."

This time Bang Abbott reddened. "You saw the fucking gun, right? Did I also mention it's loaded?"

"Where are you taking me?"

"She needs me and she doesn't even know it."

"Cherry? You gotta be kidding."

Bang Abbott perceived that he was sweating like a pack mule.

"She'll be dead before she's thirty," he went on, "and forgotten in five years . . ."

"Less," said Ann.

The photographer stuck his face out of the window to

suck some fresh air. His skull was ringing like a gong. They were on Washington Avenue, mired in club traffic.

He said, "Marilyn Monroe's been gone for what—fifty years? But everybody over the age of sixteen still knows who she is. Why? Not because of her movies. She couldn't act her way out of a goddamn speeding ticket!"

Ann DeLusia said, "Take it easy, guy."

"It's because of all those fantastic photos—that's why Marilyn will never *ever* die. She was fuckin' amazing in front of a still camera. The swimming pool shoot—you ever see that? Serious whack-off treasure, to this day."

"What's your name?" Ann asked.

"Claude."

"So your aim, Claude, is to keep Cherry Pye alive for eternity with your photographs."

"Yup."

Ann's involvement presented a large complication, but Bang Abbott hoped that a good night's sleep would bring clarity to the situation. He cut over to Collins Avenue and turned north, in search of an affordable hotel.

She said, "Maybe I'm just slow, but could you explain to me how abducting this woman would advance your grand artistic ambition? By the way, you might want to stash that gun under the seat."

"One day with Cherry is all I need. Once she sees the pictures, she'll be so blown away that she won't press charges. Hell, she'll put me on the payroll." Bang Abbott had never done any studio work in his entire life, though in the grip of fantasy he cast himself as a natural auteur. "Besides," he said, "she owes me."

"The sex wasn't so hot, huh?"

"Ha! Off the charts."

Ann repositioned her Jackie O. shades and leaned back against the headrest.

"Don't underestimate me," the photographer warned, patting the Colt on his lap.

"Let me out of the car. Come on."

"Forget it."

"But I can't help you, Claude. I've never even met her."

"Yeah, right."

Ann said, "Seriously. She doesn't know I'm alive."

The photographer sagged. So Cherry hadn't just been playing dumb on the plane ride when he'd asked about her double—she'd truly had no idea what he was talking about.

"Fuck me," he said.

Ann clapped her hands. "Exactly. So this whole operation, all the drama and gunplay, it's pointless, okay? Now, please pull over."

Bang Abbott was sickened with indecision. "Shut up and let me think."

"Anything but that," Ann said.

He spotted a Comfort Inn and stopped near the lobby entrance. It was excruciating to know that he'd been suckered once again—the lengths these people went to! The actress's henna tattoo was identical to the one in the photos of Cherry Pye that Bang Abbott had found in his camera. He told Ann to lift the hair away from her neck so he could have another look.

"What the hell's it supposed to be?" he grumbled.

"A centaur. Half Axl Rose, half zebra."

"No kidding? She likes Guns N' Roses?"

"I wouldn't know, Claude. This is all according to her mom," Ann said. "And, FYI, I really need to pee."

Bang Abbott was angry at himself but even angrier at Cherry for heaping one more crushing humiliation upon him. He said, "That's the ugliest ink I've ever seen on a woman who wasn't screwing a motorcycle gang. What the hell were you thinking? Your boyfriend must be thrilled."

Ann said, "It's a paycheck, is what I was thinking."

The photographer cocked his moist, globular head. "Listen—no sirens. That's weird," he remarked. "I figured they must've called the cops by now."

Ann agreed that it was odd. After what had happened in front of the Stefano, police cars should've been wailing all over South Beach.

Unless Janet Bunterman had done something low and unforgivable—such as neglecting to inform the cops that Ann had been inside the Suburban. In that case, the crime would be treated as a routine auto theft instead of a kidnapping.

"I'll break her neck," Ann mumbled.

"What?"

"Nothing."

Bang Abbott reached into the backseat for his camera bag.

"I can't believe you've never even met her. That's fucked up."

"Her handlers believe she'd react badly if she knew." Ann shrugged. "I'm okay with it. I don't need another BFF."

"But when she ODs for good, you're out of a job."

"Well, there's always Broadway. What do you need with me, Claude?"

"You'll see," he said. "Let's go check in."

"God, they're gonna think I'm a hooker."

"No way. Porn star? Possibly."

The pistol was well concealed in Bang Abbott's belt, beneath abundant folds of belly, as they entered the motel lobby as a couple. As soon as they got to their room, Ann headed for the bathroom, shut the door and turned on the water spigots, to create some background noise.

She sat down and hurried to retrieve her phone from the tiny black handbag that sort of matched her tiny black dress. Accidentally she must have pressed the redial button, because she could hear ringing on the other end. A man picked up, and she felt a hitch in her breathing when he said, "What is it, fair Annie?"

At that instant she recalled what she had done the night before, alone in her junior suite at the Stefano, when she couldn't stop thinking about her big adventure on the road to Key West. After a hot bath and three glasses of cabernet she'd found the matchbook that the motorcycle driver had given her at the hospital, the matchbook from the Last Chance Saloon. In a half-tipsy moment of boredom she'd dialed the phone number written on the inside flap—and then, startled by her own boldness, hung up before he could answer.

And now he was on the line.

"Are you there?" he asked in that volcanic rumble of a voice.

"I need some help," she whispered.

"Tell me where."

To Ann it sounded like he was running in the wind.

She said, "A Comfort Inn on Miami Beach."

"Sounds cozy."

"His name's Claude. He's got a gun."

"Ah."

"But I can handle him," she said, "for now."

"Hang up and call 911."

"Okay—"

The door burst open and there was Bang Abbott, crouched and florid, aiming the pistol shakily at her head. "You think you're so damn smart?" he yelled. "Gimme that thing!"

"Do what he says," said the voice at Ann DeLusia's ear.

"Okay."

"Don't worry, Annie. I'll find you."

"Excellent," she whispered, and dropped the phone between her knees, into the toilet bowl.

12

The Larks were fraternal twins, and for the first thirty-three years of their lives it had been easy to tell them apart. Lila was a natural ash blonde with light cinnamon freckles and a thin nose; Lucy had auburn hair and an unmarked complexion and a slightly squared-off chin. They stood the same height and had the same lupine smile, due to oversized incisors inherited from their father, yet the twins were taken for cousins more often than sisters.

Ever since they were toddlers, the two Larks had longed to be identical. As they grew up it became an obsession that greatly worried close friends and family members. Lila and Lucy were continually on the hunt for a cutting-edge surgeon, and over the years they interviewed scores of candidates. Being perfectionists, the Larks never failed to find a disqualifying weakness. However, there was one doctor who had eluded their dragnet—a Brazilian with fabled flesh-sculpting skills, brilliant and fearless. The sisters tracked him down at a polo match in Wellington, Florida, where he listened to their extraordinary request and examined them side by side in a stable, behind a curtain fashioned from pony blankets. He then quoted them a fee so preposterously out of reach that they simultaneously burst into tears and fell to their knees, splatting horse dung.

Eventually the Larks' childhood dream was made possible because of Presley Aaron, the troubled country-western star. It was his public tailspin into a haze of dope haunts and riotous whores that ultimately financed the comprehensive transformations of Lucy and Lila, who'd been called in to salvage what remained of the singer's image. At the time, the Larks had not yet achieved the status of legends in the show-biz firmament, although they'd been hired, fired and re-hired by some of Hollywood's A-list flakes and substance abusers. Even as young publicists, the twins had become known as cold-blooded, discreet and impossible to impress. Lucy once made the gossip blogs by walking out on a patio lunch with Tom Cruise because he wouldn't let her light up a smoke.

The day the Larks first met Presley Aaron was the same day he'd lost his record deal with Maury Lykes. Lucy and Lila listened without judgment to the strung-out musician's tale of woe, and then knocked out a boilerplate press release announcing he had quit drugs and found Jesus Christ.

Presley Aaron actually wound up doing both, so the sisters set aside their skepticism and went to work publicizing his heartrending climb from the depths. Their efforts culminated with an interview on *60 Minutes* in which even the hard-bitten Steve Kroft was moved to a sniffle.

Presley Aaron was a bit of a bumpkin, but Lucy and Lila liked the guy enough not to sue him for their fee, which was hefty and three months in arrears. After a lengthy Caribbean rehab, Presley Aaron self-attached the title of "Reverend" and soon thereafter was given his own Sunday television show on the Holy Word Network. The day he inked the contract (a three-year deal providing a cathedral and the use of a Falcon 900), he FedExed to the Larks his outstanding balance, plus a six-figure bonus. He included a note: "Dear L and L, thank you for believing in me. Praise the Lord!"

As a matter of policy, the twins never believed in any of their clients. They'd always assumed that Presley Aaron, like so many others, would end up jailed, deceased, or featured on a cable reality show for junkie has-beens. The generosity of the singer's payment check was quite startling, and right away the Larks knew how they would spend their windfall. After five fuzzy weeks in Rio de Janeiro, they stepped off the plane at LAX as shining mirror images of each other. Practically every feature was new: noses, cheeks, chins, teeth, breasts, tummies, buttocks and thighs. Their own mother didn't recognize them.

From then on the sisters were unstoppable, the go-to team for celebrities in mid-flameout. When Cherry Pye's high-paid publicist jumped ship—after accompanying her to an NPR interview in which she pretended to deep-throat the microphone—the rocket ship was already on fire. It was Maury Lykes himself who called the Larks, asking for help. When he sullenly agreed to their outlandish fee, Lila and Lucy put on hold their current project—a fifty-four-year-old actor who'd recently become a sex addict in order to revive his career—and dedicated themselves to stabilizing the nose-first descent of the former Cheryl Bunterman.

"What now?" asked Cherry's mother, minutes after the car-jacking.

She sat pondering a watery Bloody Mary while the Larks paced the suite and chain-smoked brazenly, the latter to underscore the seriousness of the situation.

"This one has the potential for ruination," Lila declared.

"It's beyond the pale," Lucy agreed, which was code for "Wait until you get our next bill."

Janet Bunterman coughed glumly. She was still grappling with the notion that a paparazzo had snatched Annie DeLusia. The new bodyguard had recognized the chubby maggot from a previous encounter. Undoubtedly, the intended quarry was Cherry.

"We'll have to call the police soon," Janet Bunterman said. "The limo company will be missing their Suburban."

As they passed each other on the carpet, the Larks pivoted and sniffed at the unseemly task confronting them. Lucy said, "First thing we do is pay off the driver."

Cherry's mother frowned. "For what?"

Lila impatiently swirled one hand in the air. "To lie to the cops, of course. To say there was no passenger on board when the SUV was jacked."

"But what about Annie?"

Lucy tapped her cigarette ash into a dish of stale cashews. "Annie who?" she said.

Janet Bunterman sipped her drink and fell silent. The Larks had a point. If it became known that Cherry Pye's organization employed a full-time look-alike to help cover for her skanky romps, the publicity would be disastrous. The new CD would immediately become suspect, and the concert tour would turn into a media smackdown. Maury Lykes, ever true to his word, would cut Cherry loose and then sue the piss out of the Buntermans.

Lila said, "If this psycho lets Annie go—and let's pray he does—we'll pay her off and put a muzzle on her. But if he should kill her, well—"

"Then there's only the chauffeur left to dispute your story," said Lucy.

Cherry's mother could hardly believe what she was hearing, although she had to admit it made sense. As soon as the deranged photographer figured out that he'd grabbed the wrong blonde, he would either free Ann DeLusia or murder her and dump the body. She wasn't the least bit famous or important, and therefore had no value as a hostage.

"This sucks," Janet Bunterman said. "I really like Annie. She's a good kid."

The Larks agreed in unison, although their Botoxified

features made it difficult to gauge the depth of their sincerity. Sometimes Janet Bunterman felt like reaching out and tapping their faces, to find out if they felt as laminated as they appeared.

She said, "Here's another idea—we could put out a release saying a 'valued employee' of Cherry Pye was abducted, and then we post a reward. Nobody knows that Annie works as Cherry's double—she could be a PA, or a dresser."

Lucy crossed her arms as she turned away, and in profile Janet Bunterman noticed the carved resemblance to a sphinx. From the other side of the room, Lila said, "And what happens if the police catch the bad guy and rescue Ann? Think of the downside, Janet."

"Downside?"

"Annie becomes famous overnight is what happens," Lila went on. "The morning shows, *Access Hollywood*, *ET*, you name it. It would be a distraction that your daughter definitely doesn't need, not while she's out promoting a new CD."

Lucy said, "Not to put too fine a point on it, but there's no room on this ark for two hot babes. Annie's an actress, Janet. She gets a whiff of the limelight, it's game over."

They're brilliant, these twins, Janet Bunterman thought. *Sneaky, but brilliant.*

"All right, how much do we pay the driver?" she asked.

Lucy held up one finger. "A grand, tops."

"Not a dollar more," her sister agreed. "Go too high, he'll get wise and put the squeeze on you."

Janet Bunterman took a thousand in hundreds out of the room safe, and sent one of the Larks downstairs to take care of the frantic chauffeur. Then she tried to call Ann on her cell phone, but nobody answered.

"Know what's super-scary?" Janet Bunterman said to the remaining twin, who happened to be Lila. "This maniac was after Cherry tonight. What if he comes back?"

"Maybe you need more than one bodyguard—Carrie Underwood's got two, you know."

True, thought Janet Bunterman, but Carrie Underwood could afford it. Carrie Underwood could sell out the Hard Rock for a year, if she wanted.

"Have you met the new muscle?" Janet Bunterman asked Lila.

"Not yet. Is he bigger than Lev?"

Cherry's mother polished off the Bloody Mary and said, "You should ask him for a demo."

"A demo of what?"

"The man could seriously prune your trees," Janet Bunterman said. "Listen, I'm not up for chatting with the police. Do you mind calling in about the Suburban?"

Lila Lark almost smiled. "No problem. You go on to bed."

They went out through the Stefano's kitchen exit and climbed in a charcoal-black minivan. The chauffeur spoke with a Brooklyn accent—a young guy, smooth-shaven and thin.

Said his name was Thad.

Said he was into modeling.

"Who besides your mother gives a flying fuck?" Chemo growled.

Cherry Pye jabbed an elbow into his ribs. "What crawled up your ass and died?"

Chemo said nobody in Brooklyn would ever name their kid Thad.

The driver raised a hand, seeking permission to speak. "He's right. My real name's Lou. The modeling agency, they made me change it."

Cherry leaned forward. "Well, I like Thad. It's very sexy."

"Yeah?"

"My name's Cherish," she said.

Chemo grimaced. "Stop now," he told her.

It had been a bad night. Maury Lykes himself had called to chew Chemo out for losing the actress, and to warn him to keep quiet about it.

"Hey, what happened to your hot date?" Cherry needled. "Is that why you're in a crappy mood—she was a no-show?"

"Yeah. That's it," Chemo said. Maury had told him to get Cherry out of the hotel until the cops were gone, but now what?

"My tatt's sore," she complained. Leaning forward, she spoke to the back of the driver's head. "Hey, Thad, where can I score some X?"

"For real?" he asked.

"No, not for real," Chemo cut in.

"Because I know a guy—"

"No thanks, dickwad. Keep your eyes on the road." With his only hand, which was exceptionally strong, Chemo squeezed one of Cherry's arms. "You've got no fucking idea who you're dealing with," he said.

"Ow! You're hurting me!"

"One time, lady called me a name and I drowned her. This was the middle of Biscayne Bay," Chemo said. "I still got the clipping from the newspaper."

Cherry shook free. "Stop! I didn't call you a name!"

"Yeah, you did. 'Waffle Face.'"

"The other night? Omigod, are you serious? I was, like, totally wasted—"

"And I cut you a break," Chemo said. "Doesn't mean I forgot about it. Then tonight you go and tell your mother I copped a feel. Trying to get me canned, remember?"

Cherry struck a sulky pose; he could see it in the light cast by oncoming cars. She said, "Sorry, 'kay? I'll never do it again. Geez."

Chemo noticed that the driver was listening in and cuffed the side of his head.

"You want one?" Cherry whispered.

"One *what*?"

"A feel, man." She nudged Chemo with a breast. "Go on. Then we're even."

He didn't take his oozy eyes off her face, nor did he move to touch her. He said, "This lady, we were on a boat together. Just me and her."

"Was it, like, a date?"

He sneered. "We were out lookin' for her ex. Anyway, she calls me this nasty name so I toss the anchor on her lap and over the side she goes. Bubble, bubble, bubble—yakkin' the whole way down."

"Dude, that's *so* not funny."

"Point is, don't push your goddamn luck."

From the front seat, Thad spoke up in an apologetic tone. "I gotta turn either left or right at this light. Does it matter to you guys which way?"

"Go right," Cherry said, "to the causeway."

Chemo shot her a look. "What's right?"

"Star Island," she replied. "Where Tanner lives."

"Who?"

"My boyfriend, remember? God!"

Thad eyed them anxiously in the rearview. "Light's green," he said.

"What the hell. Hang a right," said Chemo. It was better than riding around in circles all night long with this ditz. He was hungry, too, and he figured that anybody living on Star Island was sure to have decent food in the house.

The guard at the gatehouse was gabbing on the phone, and he waved the minivan past with barely a glance. Cherry immediately began pointing out the mansions of celebrities—P. Diddy, Julio Iglesias, A-Rod, the Estefans, Shaq's ex.

Chemo yawned and said, "I am *so* excited."

"Know what? Screw you."

Tanner Dane Keefe was renting a house once owned by

either Rosie O'Donnell or Al Capone, depending on which real-estate agent was showing it. Cherry knocked for a while before a young woman wearing red Sarah Palin-style eyeglasses opened the door. She identified herself as Tanner Dane Keefe's personal assistant, and said he was asleep upstairs.

"Tell him I'm here for a playdate," Cherry bubbled.

"But it's two in the morning."

"Really?" Cherry slipped past the woman and entered the foyer, calling Tanner's name.

Chemo made his way to the kitchen and piled some smoked turkey on rye bread with tomatoes and buffalo mozzarella. He was slathering the mustard when he heard yelling. He hurried up a marble stairwell and found Cherry in a high-ceilinged bedroom overlooking the bay. She was hopping up and down, shrieking at a young man whom Chemo recognized as her wimpy companion at the tattoo parlor. The man was sitting in bed with a sheet pulled up to his armpits. Beside him, motionless under the covers, was an elongated form.

The woman in the Palin frames pleaded with Cherry to go downstairs, but Cherry grabbed the sheet and furiously tried to yank it off the bed. The unidentified shape next to Tanner Dane Keefe drew itself into the protective shape of a comma.

"Quit hiding, you slut!" Cherry hollered.

Chemo slung his good arm around her waist and pulled her away. She was thrashing and spitting like a cat.

Tanner Dane Keefe had a policy of avoiding violence, which he saw as a threat to his handsomeness and therefore his future in film. He urged Cherry's bodyguard to stay cool.

"It's not as bad as it looks," the actor insisted, though the form huddling next to him convulsed in alarm. Moments later, a sweaty feline head popped out of the covers. It belonged to Tanner Dane Keefe's personal trainer, a female high jumper on loan from the Syrian national track-and-field squad.

Cherry emitted a whoop of outrage. The woman jackknifed nude from the bed and disappeared out the doorway.

"She was working on my hamstrings," Tanner Dane Keefe declared.

His personal assistant quickly excused herself.

Cherry Pye shook a fist. "Tanny, I can't freaking *believe* you'd do this to me!"

"Come here. Lemme see the new tatt."

"No way," Cherry said. "How come you didn't text me back?"

The actor patted the covers. "C'mon, *Cherish*. Don't be like this."

At the sound of that name, her anger melted. She leapt to the bed and crawled in beside him.

"See, I even wore a rubber," he said, lifting the sheet.

"Aw, baby. I love you."

While the two morons snuggled, Chemo confiscated a prescription bottle of pills from the nightstand and another from the bathroom. Then he walked downstairs, where the actor's personal assistant brought him a cold Miller Lite.

"Your friend 'Cherish' dropped this on the floor. It's ringing." She held up a brightly tinted BlackBerry.

Chemo peered. "What do you call that color?"

"Melon?"

"Nah, I don't think so."

The woman shrugged. "Tangerine?"

"Lemme have it."

When he pressed the Connect button, a gravelly voice on the line said, "Abbott?"

"Yeah."

"Timberlake just checked in at the Mandarin. You want the room?"

"Sure."

"Fifty bucks?"

"Not a problem."

"He's in 710. And Taylor Swift, she's in 714. I shit you not, brother."

"Nice." Chemo hung up. At least he had a name for the kidnapper: Abbott. Somewhere he had a number, too, left over from the camera transaction.

The BlackBerry chimed twice. Chemo held it up and saw a text: kanye just split from pubes. alone. plum bentley.

Now he understood why Cherry had hung on to the photographer's smart phone—to someone like her it was golden, a streaming voice-guide to the party circuit.

Tanner Dane Keefe's personal assistant asked, "Are you her bodyguard, or what?"

"More like a life coach," Chemo said.

"She needs one. You think they're screwing? Even after what happened?"

Chemo said it wouldn't surprise him. "Unless your boy's too stoned to get it up. I could go for an éclair."

The personal assistant smiled. "In the fridge, top shelf. How'd you know?"

"This house, it looks like a place where they'd eat éclairs."

She was doing a poor job of trying not to stare. "Can I ask you something?"

"The answer is six foot nine," Chemo said tersely.

"Wow. Did you ever play—"

"No."

"Not even in college?"

In a bladed voice, Chemo said, "Not even in prison."

Tanner Dane Keefe's personal assistant seemed unfazed by the information. "How come no hoops? Because of the accident?"

Chemo wondered if she was referring to his arm or his face. It amazed him that people could be so tactless. Being a disfigured felon carried weight in certain social circles, though apparently not on South Beach.

He found himself thinking, for some reason, about the kidnapped actress, Annie. He recalled when they were in the hotel elevator together, and she'd asked him how she looked in her new dress. It had caught him completely off guard, her caring what he thought. Now she was gone and it was his fault. Chemo had long been immune to normal feelings of guilt, but he was angry at himself.

"Was it a car crash?" she asked.

"What?"

"Where you got so messed up. I'm just curious."

"Unbelievable."

"You don't wanna talk about it, that's cool."

"Let me try those." Chemo lifted the thin rectangular glasses from her nose. When he put them on, he noticed that his vision was unaltered. Everything looked the same.

She said, "It's okay. They're non-prescriptions."

"Then why the hell do you wear them?"

"Are you kidding?" She laughed. "Because they're smokin' hot, that's why."

"I see," said Chemo.

He locked the personal assistant in the kitchen pantry and helped himself to two chocolate éclairs from the refrigerator. Then he went upstairs and extricated Cherry Pye from beneath Tanner Dane Keefe, who was grinding away with an expression of grim duty but no discernible lust. The actor seemed almost relieved when Cherry was whisked from the bed, and he floated facedown into the sheets.

As Cherry bleated in protest, Chemo stuffed her mouth with a pair of dirty gym shorts that he'd grabbed off the floor. Then he inserted her into a baggy Dolphins sweatshirt, slung her over one shoulder and trudged downstairs, out the foyer door.

The minivan sat idling at the bottom of the driveway. Chemo slid open a side door and shoved the former Cheryl Bunterman onto one of the bench seats. He squeezed himself upright beside her and told the driver/model to take them back to the hotel.

Thad gave him a thumbs-up. "Nice frames, man."

"Yeah," said Chemo. "They smoke."

13

Bang Abbott decided to flee the Comfort Inn after catching Ann on the phone in the bathroom. He assumed that she'd blabbed their location to some interested party, if not the cops.

Before leaving, the paparazzo actually took a shower. He and the actress would be keeping company for a while, and he wanted no more wisecracks about body odor. He wasn't opposed to bathing; he simply had other priorities. Life as a tracker of celebrities was hectic and highly competitive—an hour spent grooming was an hour lost off the streets.

It didn't improve Bang Abbott's sporadic relationship with soap that he had no one to clean up for; no wife or girlfriend, not even a dog waiting to greet him after those long nights chasing stars through the streets of Hollywood. He interacted almost exclusively with other paparazzi, whom he didn't mind offending. In fact, his humid cloud of reek often proved useful on the hunt, clearing a pathway through competing shooters to the front of the pack.

Ann DeLusia said, "Claude, this is so wrong."

He was making her wait on the toilet lid while he scrubbed himself behind the shower curtain, which was not sufficiently opaque. In one hand he clutched a sudsy washcloth, and in the other he brandished the Colt revolver, draped with a towel to shield it from the shower spray. He told Ann that he'd shoot her dead if she tried to run from the bathroom.

She said, "Then can you please hurry it up?"

"Hey, you don't have to look."

"God, Claude. You ever heard of the Geneva Convention?"

Even with water in his ears, Bang Abbott could tell he was being dissed. It was exasperating that Ann was so snarky in the presence of a loaded gun. As he struggled to dry himself off in the small tub, she buried her face in her hands and said, "Gimme a break."

The photographer testily reminded her that Cherry Pye had voiced no complaints while jumping his bones on the Gulfstream.

"She was high," said Ann.

"How would you know?"

"Because she's *always* high. That's why they hired me."

"I need another towel," Bang Abbott snapped.

"Also, she's a ho. Let's be honest." Ann tossed him two towels.

"You weren't there. You don't know how it was."

"Wild guess: Quick and sloppy?"

Bang Abbott elected to drop the subject. Unlike snotty Peter Cartwill at the *Eye*, the actress at least seemed to accept that the tryst with Cherry had really occurred.

Modestly swathed, the photographer stepped from the tub. For the first time he noticed some scrapes and bruises on the otherwise-attractive legs of his captive. When he asked what had happened, Ann said she'd been in a car accident.

"I had Pam Anderson lips for about a day and a half. You should've seen me." She stood up, self-consciously tugging the hem of the little black dress. "I'll be needing some privacy, Claude."

"What for?" He didn't trust her for a second, not after he'd caught her making that phone call.

"To take a bath," she said.

"I don't think so."

She rolled her eyes and pointed to the Axl-headed zebra on her neck. "I wanna soak off this stupid ink."

"No, don't touch it!" he said, waving the gun. "Not yet."

"Does this mean you've got a plan?"

The photographer said, "Put your shoes on. We're outta here."

Later, in the car, he secured the pistol beneath one thigh while he dialed information, trying to track down some of his contacts. Ann DeLusia watched with curiosity as he grew increasingly aggravated. When she asked what was wrong, Bang Abbott said he had tipsters all over Miami who were texting and calling his old number with star sightings, only he wasn't receiving any of the messages because you-know-who still had his you-know-what.

Ann said, "Ah. The mystic BlackBerry."

"Now all these shitheads, they'll expect to get paid."

"Your tipsters."

"They got no fucking loyalty," Bang Abbott complained. "Won't be long, they'll freeze me out and start selling to other shooters. Here." He handed the phone to Ann. "Your turn," he said. "Talk to Cherry's old lady—she's the one in charge of the circus, right?"

"And tell her what?"

"That you're a hostage."

"And?"

"And I want a straight-up trade—you for her daughter."

Ann said, "It's almost a shame to spoil this moment by asking, but: Or else *what*, Claude? You gonna kill me?"

He sniggered. "Hell, that's what they probably want."

"Get out."

"I'm serious. You're a big-time problem for them now."

Ann fell silent, wondering if the photographer might be right. He wasn't quite loony enough that she could automatically discount everything he said.

She asked, "So what's the big 'or else'?"

"If they won't do a trade, then I go on the Internet and

post some slutty topless pictures of Cherry that she took of herself at the Stefano—on *my* camera, the dumb flake."

He was driving back toward Ocean Drive, and catching every red light.

Ann said, "Cherry's people don't care about topless. A crotch shot, maybe, but her titties are already out there, Claude, all over the Web."

Bang Abbott frowned, remembering Cherry's trip two years earlier to the Greek island of Santorini. Judging from the photos filed by the European paparazzi, Cherry hadn't bothered to put on a shirt for two weeks. Bang Abbott himself had missed that trip because he'd been at Aspen, staking out a house in which a famous NFL quarterback was rumored to have re-injured an ACL while cavorting on a defective futon with his supermodel girlfriend.

"I've got a backup, don't worry," the photographer said.

Ann sighed. "Gee, I wonder if it involves me."

"You'll finally get to do some real acting."

She said, "It won't work. Her fans'll figure out I'm not her."

"Hey, you fooled me. You can fool the rest of the world," Bang Abbott said, "especially with that wicked tatt."

Ann wasn't sure what he had in mind, and she didn't want to ask. It was her intention to escape from this loser as soon as possible, then reboot her life. In the meantime, she had her own reasons to call Janet Bunterman, who picked up on the seventh ring. Ann first explained the situation with Cherry's topless self-portraits, and laid out the paparazzo's peculiar demands.

"Is he there now?" Janet Bunterman asked.

"Yes indeed. And he has some sort of gun."

"I better talk to Maury."

Ann said, "You do that."

"And the Larks."

"Cherry, too. She's got the man's BlackBerry and he wants it back."

In the driver's seat, Bang Abbott nodded somberly. "Tell her I'm serious as a heart attack," he whispered.

"He's as serious as a heart attack," Ann repeated.

Janet Bunterman said, "You lost me. How'd Cherry get this guy's phone?"

"She stole it after she banged him on the airplane." Ann wasn't one to sugarcoat bad news. "Anyhow, he needs it back ASAP. She can bring it when she shows up for the shoot."

Cherry's mother lowered her voice. "Not gonna happen, Annie."

"He says one day with her is all he needs."

"You may tell him the answer is no."

"Janet, you did call the cops, right? About what happened tonight?"

"Of course we called the cops."

"So they're looking everywhere for me," Ann said, "scouring the county."

There was a pause on the other end, then a muffled noise that sounded like a cap being twisted off a water bottle. Janet Bunterman said, "They found the Suburban about an hour ago on Watson Island."

"That's great, but I'm pretty sure they didn't find *me*."

"Annie, it's a complicated scenario. Cherry's got the new CD coming out, not to mention the tour—I don't have to tell you how huge that is. What I'm trying to say is, we're still working out a strategy to get you back . . ."

With the heel of her free hand, Ann pounded the dashboard. Bang Abbott poked her in the ribs with the barrel of the pistol and gave a querulous shrug.

"Now take it easy," Cherry's mother was saying.

"Nobody told the police I was in the Suburban? So, now what—case closed?" Ann was outraged, although she should have seen it coming. She was a secret that needed to be kept.

Janet Bunterman said, "We'll put our heads together and figure things out."

"You're really pissing me off," said Ann.

"Has he hurt you?"

"Thanks for asking. Really."

Now fuming, Bang Abbott pulled to the side of the road and said, "What'd I tell ya? They'd cut you loose in a heartbeat."

The photographer snatched the cell phone and got out of the car. He could hear Cherry's mother on the other end of the line, saying, "Annie? Are you still there? Annie?"

He held the phone near the gun, aimed the barrel toward the sky and fired off a round that blew out a streetlight. "Fuck me!" he cried, and clambered back into the Buick. His ears rang and his hands trembled on the steering wheel as he sped west toward Alton. "That was so fucking loud!" he said excitedly. "Ask did I get her attention! Go ahead. Tell her it was a real bullet."

Ann took the phone. "Janet, that was the gun. The dude is serious."

But the line had gone dead.

"Shit," Ann said.

Bang Abbott stuffed the Colt under the front seat. "Those are some real slimeballs you work for," he remarked.

"And you, sir, would be an expert."

She kept glancing at the side-door mirror, hoping to see the flashing lights of a squad car, but the street behind them was empty. Evidently, random gunfire was no longer a top priority for police in Miami Beach. Bang Abbott permitted Ann to roll down her window halfway, so she could listen in vain for the sound of sirens.

Detective Reilly stayed late again, surfing the databases, trying to learn more about Jackie Sebago. The man had no criminal record, though a Nexis search turned up newspaper articles about a bankrupt ski-in condo village in Montana, where disgruntled business partners had sued Jackie Sebago over missing funds and a no-show "executive assistant" who'd turned out to be his mistress. Jackie's name also popped up as a principal in a Maryland golf resort that was fined $37,000 for poisoning a flock of mallard ducks that kept crapping all over the thirteenth green.

The information shed enough light on Sebago's character to bolster Reilly's belief that the developer had been the choice target of the raving bus hijacker in North Key Largo. How an unbalanced vagabond managed to plan and execute a crime of such precision intrigued the detective, but he was no closer to identifying the culprit, much less finding him.

The detective would have been intrigued to know that among the hulking nomad's unlikely talents was marine navigation, and that as Reilly was heading home from the office his suspect was racing through ocean darkness in a striped Donzi speedboat, somewhere off the coast of Elliott Key.

As it turned out, the boat—which Skink took from a slip at Ocean Reef—hadn't been run wide open for months. The owners, who spent their summers on Cape Cod and their autumns in the Berkshires, paid a mechanic to come service the big twin Mercury outboards only twice a year. The mechanic never took the Donzi from the dock, just kicked back in the cockpit with a six-pack of Land Shark and let the engines idle. Sometimes he brought along a girlfriend or a spinning rod. Because the boat didn't go anywhere, there was no need for the mechanic to top off the gas tanks, which is why Skink found the gauge nearing empty as he passed to the east of Fowey Rocks.

By good fortune he came across a twenty-eight-foot Aquasport waylaid by fouled spark plugs, which the governor was pleased to fix in exchange for six gallons of fuel. The snapper fishermen aboard the Aquasport were alarmed by his tattered appearance and also the shotgun, but they remained calm. He dismissed them with a rousing quote from Melville, and they motored with relief back to Black Point, where their wives had been stewing since sunset.

A mile off the shoreline of Miami Beach, Skink shut down the Donzi and opened a bottle of beer he'd found in a refrigerator beside the fish box. Peering out at the flickering neon filament of Ocean Drive, he felt a clenching in his gut that had nothing to do with the roll of the sea swells. City life derailed him; the crowds, the noise, the walls, the lights. And this particular city was a minefield of incivilities and pretension. Surely there would be incidents, moments of vertiginous risk, but what choice did he have?

Annie was there.

Skink drank another beer and yowled at the sky. Decades of hermitage had kept him barely on keel but his turbulent aversions never waned. He'd fled the governor's mansion with his values intact but his idealism extinguished, his patience smashed to dust. Politics had scrambled his soul much worse than the war, and he left behind in Tallahassee not only his name but the discredited strategy of forbearance and compromise. The cherished wild places of his childhood had vanished under cinder blocks and asphalt, and so, too, had the rest of the state been transformed—hijacked by greedy suckworms disguised as upright citizens. From swampy lairs Skink would strike back whenever an opportunity arose, and the message was never ambiguous. Even schmucks like Jackie Sebago got the point.

The governor rocked back and looked up at the stars and began to sing in a papery falsetto. It was a Celtic lullaby he'd learned from his mother, long gone, but he remembered every verse. When he was done, he sang it again.

Then he turned the ignition and aimed the stolen boat full throttle toward South Beach.

14

The next morning, while the former Cheryl Bunterman was posing for the cover of *Us Weekly*, Maury Lykes convened a meeting of concerned parties and ordered two dozen sesame bagels with lox and cream cheese. Chemo's late arrival seemed to affect the usually unflappable Larks, whose surgically fixed expressions seemed to grow more taut and goggle-eyed.

Maury Lykes began by stating the obvious. "This situation with Ann is a huge fucking problem." He waggled a bent finger at the bodyguard. "You first. What's our next move?"

"Depends," said Chemo, "whether you want this shithead dead or you just want the girl back. Or maybe both."

"Both," said the promoter.

"Not so fast," interjected one of the Larks.

Maury Lykes laughed hollowly. "I was just kidding. We're not killin' anybody."

Chemo shrugged and reached for a bagel. "Suit yourself."

Janet Bunterman recounted the late-night call from Ann DeLusia, and the alarming way it ended—gunfire, and a dead phone line.

"Jesus, you think he really shot her?" Maury Lykes asked.

"Get serious," Chemo said, chilling the proceedings with his smile.

An uneasy silence took hold. The promoter cocked his head. "What'm I missing here?"

"The big picture," Lila Lark said. "That's what you pay us for."

Taking turns, the sisters enumerated the public-relations perils facing Team Cherry if Annie's role in the organization became known, which was certain to happen if she became the subject of a police search.

"Which is why we didn't tell them she was in the Suburban," Cherry's mother said.

Maury Lykes nodded impatiently. "Yeah, yeah, I get all that."

"So let's say this guy went bonkers and shot Annie," Lucy Lark continued, trying not to glance at Chemo, "or for some other reason, she doesn't come back. Yes, it's horrible. Yes, it's a heinous tragedy. But, on the other hand . . ."

Janet Bunterman picked up the ball. "Look, Maury, it would be one thing if money was all he wanted. That's a controllable situation. We could pay a ransom and bring Annie home ourselves. But he wants to do a trade—Annie's life for one day with Cherry!"

"One day? To do what?" Maury Lykes asked.

"Take her picture, is what he says. But come on."

Like her sister, Lila Lark was conscious of her pulse skipping in Chemo's presence. She composed herself and said, "People, can we backtrack for just a moment? Even if there was a straight ransom demand, the odds of us pulling this off without somebody leaking *something* to the media are about a billion to one. Once Annie's name gets out, once the tabloids dig up the whole story, there's no keeping her on the reservation. When *People* magazine calls, Maury, you seriously think she'll say 'No thanks'?"

"Shit," the promoter muttered. He wondered if this was what they called a "moral quandary."

Not to be outdone in the dire-scenario department, Lucy Lark said, "Imagine what our sensitive young client's reaction would be, she turns on *TMZ* and here's some hot chick named Ann DeLusia talking about how she got paid to dress up and go out as Cherry, talking about all those times Cherry pulled a Winehouse and got shipped off to rehab—"

"Dietary camp," implored Janet Bunterman.

"—some girl Cherry's never even seen before, talking about how she was kidnapped and held hostage by a gun-toting stalker who mistakenly thought he was snatching a superstar. It would be an ultra-humongous story," Lucy Lark pressed on, "way bigger than Cherry's new album, Maury. Bigger than the tour."

Maury Lykes held up his hands in the shape of a T. "Thanks for that rousing pep talk," he said. "Now, just out of curiosity, can anybody please tell me how the hell we got caught in this particular shitstorm—like, for instance, what's the connection between our self-destructive starlet and this psychotic photographer?"

The Larks turned to Cherry's mother, who tightly said, "Apparently, he's the person she brought with her to Miami."

Maury Lykes winced in disgust. "On the Gulfstream? Good Christ."

"She screwed him, too," added Lila Lark.

"Naturally." The promoter took out a toothpick and dealt with more sesame seeds in his bridgework. "Janet, it sounds like you're doing your usual stellar job of parenting."

"The man's obviously hallucinating. It never happened," Cherry's mother insisted.

Maury Lykes reflected upon the many emergencies that had sprung up during his long association with Cherry Pye—the meltdowns, disappearances, drug binges and sex sprees. All those potentially career-smothering incidents had proved manageable, and in a few cases had even served to rekindle the public's waning interest in his minimally talented ward.

This new crisis, though, was different. Cherry was not at large; she was more or less in custody. What worried Maury Lykes was the decoy, this missing Ann person, whose reliability under duress was an unknown variable. An actress, for

God's sake! As for the deranged paparazzo, Maury Lykes felt confident in assuming the worst. It wasn't hard to imagine the lurid kind of photo session he had in mind for Cherry, and how much money he would demand in exchange for keeping the pictures out of circulation.

That Cherry herself was oblivious to the mayhem she'd caused was ironic, though hardly surprising. *What kind of drooling half-wit fucks a freelance photographer?* Maury Lykes wondered.

"Our professional advice," one of the Larks was saying, "is to sit tight for now. See what this madman tries next."

"And no cops," the other sister added, "unless you want it smeared all over the news."

Maury Lykes asked if the kidnapped actress had any immediate family, but nobody could give him an answer.

"Boyfriend? Ex-husband?" The promoter caustically raised his palms. "Anybody close, who might be aware that she's working for us?"

In her most assuring tone, Janet Bunterman said, "Annie signed a confidentiality agreement."

"Which might be a useful document," said Maury Lykes, "if we happen to run out of toilet paper. My concern, *people*, is that someone will come looking for Ms. Ann DeLusia, even if we don't. Did that not occur to anybody else in this room?" He drilled the Larks with a glare. "Young women don't just disappear without a ripple, especially young women with SAG cards. Sooner or later, her absence will be noticed."

Chastened, the sisters sucked in their cheeks and went rigid. Janet Bunterman nervously tore off half a bagel and smeared it with cream cheese.

Chemo spoke up. "It's like a tickin' bomb."

Maury Lykes sagged with exaggerated relief. "Oh Lord, let there be light."

"I think I know the dickwad's name," Chemo said, peeking over the rims of his Sarah Palins.

"Yeah? Who is he?"

"I got a cell number. Lemme take a shot."

"Can't hurt," Maury Lykes said. "Go for it."

Chemo stood up and stretched. His gummy red eyes settled on Janet Bunterman. "I can't believe you were gonna cut the girl loose," he said. "Weren't for her, your dumbass daughter would be the one who got grabbed."

As he walked out of the room, Chemo shrugged at the breathless Larks.

The first single from *Skantily Klad* was a cut called "Jealous Bone," which was chosen as the visual theme of Cherry Pye's cover shoot for *Us Weekly*. The photo director proposed that she be costumed as a sultry cannibal.

"What's a freakin' cannibal wear for clothes?" Cherry asked.

Her hairdresser, Leo, was also perplexed. "The song is about boning someone else's man," he pointed out, "not *barbecuing* him."

The photo director presented a leopard-print loincloth with a matching halter that barely covered Cherry's augmentation scars. She emerged from the dressing room wearing a broad smile and reeking of weed. The photographer, a young Belgian with numerous magazine covers to his credit, said she looked totally fabulous. But when the makeup artist attempted to conceal her new tattoo beneath a spray-on tan, Cherry slugged him in the sternum. After a thirty-minute break, during which she bummed a Kool and two Valiums off the catering guy, the shoot resumed.

At Cherry's insistence, the tatt on her neck became a focal point of the photographs, and Leo dutifully styled her locks in a fashion that gave generous display to the Axl-faced, half-assed zebra. At noon, Tanner Dane Keefe showed up on the set with a DVD containing all his scenes from the upcoming Tarantino film in which he portrayed a corpse-diddling longboarder with the soul of a poet. He and Cherry disappeared into her dressing room for nearly two hours, emerging only when the photo director banged on the door and threatened to give away her cover slot to Christina Aguilera, who also had a red-hot new CD on the way.

After Tanner Dane Keefe departed, Cherry was coaxed back to the set, where she was positioned suggestively astride a skeleton, in keeping with the kinky cannibalism motif. She lasted only a few minutes before emitting wails that pierced the studio, something about a "death vibe" choking the breath from her body. At that point, Janet Bunterman was contacted and a substitute security man was sent, Chemo having been assigned to deal with Ann DeLusia's abductor. The new guy's name was Kurt, an immense, gym-ripped African-American who had once played right tackle for the Atlanta Falcons.

At the sight of him, Cherry brightened. "This is more like it," she said, "but he's supposed to be bald." She turned to Leo. "You take care of it, 'kay?"

The hairdresser picked up his electric clippers and took a tentative step toward Kurt, who raised a large hand and said, "Back off, little bug."

Cherry staged a tantrum and fled to her dressing room. Leo brought Kurt a hot Cuban press, which was delicious. Over lunch, the security man offered a bit of history: "Lady Gaga didn't make me shave my damn head. Anne Hathaway didn't make me. Tara Reid, okay, she tried—the girl had a thing for Ving Rhames, and you know I like Ving personally, but that just ain't my best look. Bald, I'm talkin' about."

"It's been overdone," Leo agreed.

"Now, the lady here, she needs to quit this foolishness and get her ass back to work," Kurt said sternly.

"Do what you have to, brother."

The security man went to the dressing room, where Cherry had splayed herself immodestly on a couch. She was drinking a Red Bull while listening to the album cut of "Jealous Bone" on her iPod, attempting without success to nail the lip synch. Kurt plucked out her ear buds and said she had exactly three minutes to return to the set before the photo director canceled the cover.

"You believe in reincarnation?" Cherry asked.

The dressing room smelled like grass; Kurt glanced around and spotted a half-smoked doobie balanced on the rim of a veggie platter.

"I wanna come back as, like, a bird-of-paradise, or maybe a seashell," Cherry said. "What about you?"

"I want to come back as Beyoncé's bicycle seat," said the security man. "Now let's go."

The shoot slogged on for another hour, until the Belgian photographer signaled with a mimed self-strangulation that he'd had enough. On the ride back to the Stefano, Cherry became upset when she learned that Kurt was only on loan, and that he wouldn't be replacing Chemo full-time.

"That fuckin' freakazoid, he's not even human!" she cried.

Kurt said he didn't know the man. "But I already got a job," he added.

"With who?" Cherry slid closer and touched his arm.

"I can't tell ya."

"What's she pay? I'll give you more."

Kurt said, "The pay's damn good, but thanks just the same."

Cherry pressed a cheek against his shoulder. "Ever heard of fringe benefits?"

"Those I already got." Kurt smiled.

"No way!"

"Every night, girl. But I appreciate the thought."

Livid, Cherry pushed herself away. "It's totally not fair.

My mom *promised* me a big black dude," she said bitterly, "just like you."

"Yeah, well, get in line."

"Is she a singer, or a movie star, or what?"

Kurt said, "She's in film."

"Then you're a stone liar, man, 'cause movie actresses won't do the help," Cherry said. "That's a known fact." She was digging through her purse, searching for something. "I hate this goddamn bag!" she exclaimed.

"Whassa problem now?"

"I lost my BlackBerry."

"And what's that?" Kurt pointed. "You blind, girl?"

"No, that's an *iPhone*. God!" Cherry got down and groped the floorboard of the SUV. "I really, really, *really* need the BlackBerry—it's, like, bright orange. C'mon, dude, help me look."

But the missing smart phone wasn't in the vehicle. Cherry punched the seat and shouted, "This is the worst fucking day of my whole fucking life!"

The driver glanced uneasily over his shoulder. "Don't worry about her," Kurt advised.

"You shut up," Cherry said. "Maybe I need somebody to worry about me, for a change. Maybe that's what's, like—hello?—wrong with this picture? Too many people aren't worrying about *me*!"

The security man checked the time on his Rolex. He felt sorry for the poor sucker who was stuck with the job of bodyguarding this bitch.

"Hey!" Cherry barked at him. "Are you even listening?" Kurt leaned forward and told the driver to step on it.

After their hurried departure from the Comfort Inn, they spent the rest of the night in the rental car on the third floor of a covered parking garage, not far from Lummus Park. Ann DeLusia dozed on and off. She considered trying to escape but the photographer managed to remain awake, watching her like a hawk. As a visual warning he left the barrel of the handgun protruding from under the front seat, between his feet. Based on what she'd seen, Ann had no reason to believe he was an expert marksman, but even a putz could get lucky. She decided to sit tight.

By sunrise, the deodorizing effects of the photographer's shower had worn off and the interior of the Buick smelled like a wrestling mat. Ann herself felt sticky and vile. Diving into the ocean seemed like a grand idea, but Claude the kidnapper said no way. He stepped out of the car to take a "super important" phone call, carelessly leaving his hostage alone with the pistol. Ann lifted it off the floor and fitted her right hand around the grip, her forefinger resting as lightly as a spider on the trigger. For a while she had dated a Los Angeles robbery detective who would take her to the shooting range on weekends. She'd gotten pretty good with a Glock 19 before the cop broke up with her and married his Korean manicurist.

Ann was still holding the photographer's gun when he sat down in the front seat and took it away from her.

"So that's how things are," he said with a raw laugh.

"What are you talkin' about?"

"You're not goin' anywhere, are you?"

"Claude, you're so full of shit." She felt herself redden.

He laughed again. "No, you're dying to see how all this plays out. I like that."

Ann began to cry. It was a ridiculous thing to do, but she wasn't acting. Could this A-hole possibly be right?

"You think I'm enjoying this?" she said. Exhaustion was to blame; obviously she wasn't thinking straight. For God's sake, she'd had the damn pistol in her hand.

He said, "You're as smart as I think, it won't be long before the paparazzi will be chasing *you*. Trust me, I know the game."

"I don't want to be famous," Ann sniffled, "not like that."

"Of course you don't. What an awful life. Who wants to be rich and beautiful and desired?" He waggled the Colt at her. "Now, I've gotta go meet with a guy, so be a good girl and hop in the trunk."

"I'll do no such thing. You'll have to shoot me first."

"Oh, for Christ's sake."

"Take me along. I'll behave."

"You want some breakfast?" Bang Abbott asked.

"Sure. Absolutely." Ann was as hungry as she was tired.

The photographer drove to a spiffy new McDonald's, where Ann was one of two breakfast customers wearing a short black party dress. The other was a muscular transvestite in a Fanta-colored wig. Bang Abbott ordered three pungent burritos, while Ann asked for an Egg McMuffin. Bang Abbott told her she had exactly four minutes to use the bathroom, during which time he crushed two Ambiens and stirred them into her orange juice.

After she returned, he said, "Now this is important— who's gonna freak the most, they don't hear from you for a couple days. You got a boyfriend?"

"Nope," Ann said through a dainty mouthful of food.

"Mom and Dad?"

She shook her head. "Negative."

"Are they both dead or something?"

"You missed your calling, Claude. You should've been a grief counselor," Ann said. "No, they're not dead. I never met my father, and Mom and I are what you call 'estranged.' She wanted me to be a teacher."

The paparazzo grunted. He had effortlessly fit an entire burrito into his cheeks.

"A Sunday school teacher," Ann added. "Her religion treats the theatrical arts as pagan foolery. That includes television."

Bang Abbott wiped his fingers on his shirt.

"Everything was more or less okay until one of my mother's so-called friends called her up after she saw me on a Maxipad commercial," Ann went on, "and ever since that day, proper Rachel DeLusia has not spoken to her wayward daughter. I guess I should have taken that Duncan Hines booking instead—Mom can seriously pack away the brownies."

"So, what you're sayin' is, nobody's gonna miss you for a little while if you don't answer your phone—"

"Which fell in the motel toilet—"

"What about your friends?" Bang Abbott asked.

"They've pretty much given up on me."

"How come?"

"'Cause I don't tweet and I don't text."

The photographer raised an eyebrow. "Oh, you're one of *those*."

"So the answer is no, nobody's going to miss me."

"Okay, then, good."

"Yeah, fantastic. Twenty-four years old and I could fall off the planet without a soul noticing." She didn't mention the crazed homeless dude from Key Largo who'd promised to come rescue her—a noble offer, but really . . .

"Claude, I'm getting awful tired."

"Finish your juice," he said.

She was snoring like a bear by the time Bang Abbott got back to the parking garage. He drove up to an empty floor and put the Buick at the far end. After locking Ann in the trunk, he huffed to the elevator where he finished his last McSkillet on the ride down, crumpling the empty wrapper and tossing it on the floor. The sunlight blasted him in the face when he walked out of the garage, so he pulled down his brand-new Miami Marlins cap and aimed himself for the park.

The man called Chemo was waiting by the volleyball nets. He was wearing a loose black warm-up suit with one sleeve cut off, and gay squared-off eyeglasses. "Let's take a walk," he said.

They headed down the beach—the dumpy, shuffling paparazzo and the gangly, lopsided bodyguard—drawing stares from even the jaded South Beach regulars. Chemo seemed oblivious to the attention, but Bang Abbott felt uncomfortable. He was accustomed to being the peeper, not the peeped at, and he felt naked without his cameras.

"I found that item you were lookin' for," Chemo said.

Bang Abbott tried to conceal his elation. "Yeah?"

"You're a busy beaver, Slim. Damn thing rings 24/7."

"How much you want for it? I'll give you five hundred."

Chemo stopped to admire a topless Latin woman who was playing Kadima with a small boy. It was a nice scene, a long damn way from the prison yard at Raiford.

The Kadima ball landed in the sand at Chemo's size-fourteen feet, and the youngster ran up to fetch it.

Oh Jesus, the photographer thought. *That poor kid'll be sleeping with the lights on for the rest of his life.*

Yet when Chemo handed him the ball, the boy looked up, waved his paddle and said, *"Gracias."* He didn't appear even slightly traumatized. Bang Abbott was amazed—the little gerbil must be farsighted.

Chemo resumed walking. "I been authorized to negotiate for the girl," he said over his shoulder.

The bodyguard had a large stride, and Bang Abbott hustled to keep up. "Negotiate *what*? I get an all-day shoot with Cherry, they get their cute little imposter back, safe and sound."

"No deal. Twenty-five large—the money for the actress chick, straight up."

"You crazy?" Bang Abbott blurted.

"Plus, maybe I'll throw in the BlackBerry."

"Do I look that stupid?"

Chemo's cheerless smile exposed the dingy nibs of his front teeth. "A fat perv is what you look like to me," he said.

Bang Abbott was steaming. "Twenty-five grand is a joke. Do you have any fucking idea what this girl Ann knows about Cherry Pye? The damage she can do?"

"I can probably jack 'em up to fifty if maybe you slide five my way," said Chemo. "Also, I strongly advise you don't hurt the actress unless you want to die extra slow, and skinned out like a damn trout." Ominously he hoisted the vinyl-cloaked weed whacker.

Bang Abbott dropped back a step. "Christ, I'm not a killer!"

"Well, I am. Where's she at now?"

"She's safe, swear to God. Asleep in the car."

Chemo had stopped walking again, due to the unexpected presence among the power tanners and Frisbee tossers of at least a dozen uniformed law-enforcement personnel. Some were Miami Beach cops and some were Customs and some were Border Patrol. The photographer turned clammy with fear, the Colt feeling like an anchor on the frayed waistband of his trousers.

Cool as ice, Chemo said, "Hey, Slim, check this out."

The object of the officers' interest was a blue-over-white

Donzi speedboat that somebody had beached at high speed during the night. Tourists were clustered around, snapping pictures with their cell phones. The boat had trenched across the sand and now lay canted to its port side, thirty yards from the waterline, a row of empty Land Shark bottles aligned neatly on the transom. Nobody was on board, and the cops seemed eager to locate the driver and/or passengers.

"Talk about drunk," Bang Abbott said.

Chemo surmised it was a smuggling operation. "They bring Haitians over from Bimini," he explained.

"And just leave the damn boat?"

"All the time."

"Crazy," said Bang Abbott.

Chemo turned and headed back in the opposite direction, the photographer at his heels.

"Go back and tell your people I don't want their money, I want Cherry."

"Or what?" the bodyguard asked.

"Don't worry. I got a plan."

"Shit for brains is all you got."

A seagull had caught sight of Chemo's exotic hairpiece and began dive-bombing for nest material. As Bang Abbott tried in vain to shoo away the bird, Chemo smoothly unveiled the yard trimmer attached to his stumped left elbow joint. He touched the switch and, with one sweeping motion, he annihilated the gull in mid-swoop. Clumps of mulched feathers fell like sticky snow upon a group of lotion-drenched French models, who began to squeal disharmoniously.

To Bang Abbott, Chemo said, "Fifty grand's a lot of money, Slim."

"No can do," said the shaken photographer, and started running as fast as his gelatinous legs would push him toward Ocean Drive.

15

The assistant day manager of the Comfort Inn was named Vincent. He liked his job. The speed was just right, leaving him plenty of energy at night for cruising the clubs, where he dealt Ecstasy, roofies and bootleg Cialis. Somehow the money was always gone by dawn, so Vincent was grateful for his gig at the motel.

He was slouched in front of his laptop, downloading some particularly extreme porn, when a street person appeared at the check-in desk. The man was quite tall and he had a fake eye that looked like it came from a stuffed moose. He was dressed in a crusty trench coat and wore two ratty gray braids growing at odd measures from his shaved scalp. The braids were garnished with colored plastic cylinders.

"Good morning," the man said.

Vincent smiled neutrally. "I'm sorry. We have no rooms available."

"I don't need a room. I need information."

"We're not hiring at the moment," Vincent said, at which point the street person reached over and confiscated Vincent's laptop, which was by far the most valuable thing he owned. Vincent hopped to his feet and said, "Give it back or I'll call the cops!"

The man asked Vincent if his boss was aware that he was jerking off to gang-bang videos on company time.

"Gimme that back!" Vincent cried and lunged across the check-in desk, but the street person was surprisingly agile.

"Isn't this supposed to be a family establishment?" the man said. He snapped the laptop shut. "I'll give this to the police when they show up. They'll want to see all the filth."

Vincent believed that his boss—the manager, who was due to arrive any minute—would react poorly if the lobby was full of cops, and even more poorly if the cops were gathered around Vincent's laptop watching Jenna Jameson do a frat-house pledge class.

"What do you want, dude?" he asked.

The street person said, "Man named Claude checked in late last night. What's the room number? He had a young woman with him."

Vincent logged on to the motel's desktop. "Here it is— Claude Abbott. They're in 432."

"How'd he pay?"

"AmEx," Vincent said.

"You're kidding."

"We don't take cash after midnight. You want me to call up to the room and tell 'em you're here?"

"Just give me a key, son. It's a surprise."

"Okay, what about my laptop?"

"When I'm done," said the street person.

"Done with what, dude?"

"Socializing." The man took the key card and went to the elevator. He kept Vincent's laptop pinned under one arm.

As soon as Vincent was alone, he darted from behind the desk and hurried toward the parking lot to intercept his boss, if necessary. He had no desire to call the police, who would inevitably run his name in their database and learn he was on probation for grand theft, a drunken transgression involving a golf cart, a tow chain and an ATM machine. Vincent had neglected to mention the episode on his employment application.

Seeing no sign of the boss's car, he hustled back to the lobby and assumed his duty position at the check-in counter. Moments later, the street person stepped off the elevator and informed him that Room 432 had been vacated; Mr. Abbott and his companion were gone.

"I never even saw 'em," Vincent said, "and I got here at seven-fifteen."

"There was a phone in the toilet bowl."

"Don't look at me!"

"I'll need his credit card slip." The stranger motioned with two fingers.

"Man, you know I can't do that."

The street person said, "Okay." He sat on the floor and tugged off one of his rancid sneakers and started pummeling the shell of the laptop until Vincent surrendered the paper invoice upon which Claude Abbott's American Express information was imprinted.

"Thank you, son," the man said. He returned the dented computer to Vincent, who with both arms clinched it to his chest.

"What's your problem?" he hissed angrily at the stranger.

The man took a beer bottle from an inside pocket of his coat, sucked down the dregs and placed the empty on the counter. "I hope you recycle," he said.

Cherry Pye's mother and father weren't the only Bunter-mans who were counting on *Skantily Klad* to be a megahit. Each of Cherry's deadbeat brothers held a bogus high-paying position with her personal management company, and none was intellectually equipped to go out and find a real job. Leonard, the eldest, lived in Steamboat Springs and spoke to his famous sister maybe once or twice a year, whenever his stash of autographed swag ran out. The middle brother, Adam, divided his time between Barbados and Cabo, and communicated with the family mainly through bank transfer notices. The youngest of the boys, twenty-three-year-old Joshua, had a gallery in La Jolla dedicated to homoerotic sculpture and watercolors on butcher paper, painted with the tail of his deaf Persian cat.

The former Cheryl Bunterman had no idea what level of cash flow was necessary to keep herself and her moocher siblings afloat. However, Ned Bunterman, who managed the books, was keenly aware that the family's lifestyle would change immoderately if *Skantily Klad* bombed. The money—all that money from the other albums!—finally had dried up, and the Buntermans were rapidly burning through Cherry's seven-figure advance for *Skantily*.

Janet Bunterman told him to quit worrying. "The record's going to be huge. Where are you, by the way?"

"Palm Springs, remember? My tee time's in twenty minutes. The lupus fund-raiser?"

Janet Bunterman thought: *Right. Whatever.*

"The tour hasn't sold out," her husband noted gravely, "not even the Garden. I spoke to Maury."

"Why do you have to be so negative, Ned? It's not Cherry, it's the economy. I heard Springsteen was down seven percent."

Ned Bunterman said, "You heard wrong, darling. The Jonas Brothers were up, too. Coldplay, way up. And Britney's still selling out arenas, even after those gross beach pictures." A British paparazzo using a sniper-grade scope had spotted the singer sunbathing in an ill-chosen tank suit in the Maldives.

"Just wait till the CD comes out," Janet Bunterman said. "We'll sell out the Garden and everyplace else. They'll be adding shows, you watch."

Her husband didn't bring up *Spin* magazine's ugly advance review, which rechristened the record *"Skankily Klad."* It was a blessing that Cherry didn't like to read.

He said, "A publicity bump would really help."

"The tattoo photos are getting tons of Web hits," reported Janet Bunterman. "I mean, sure, the stupid thing looks like a cattle brand, and I'm absolutely furious with her for messing up her beautiful neckline, but the Google hits are off the chart."

"If only all those people were buying tickets to the show," Ned Bunterman said, "but they're not, Janet. We need something to move the needle." He noted disapprovingly that the Larks were several days behind on Cherry's blog, which they took turns writing.

"They've been tied up on this Annie thing," his wife explained.

"Speaking of which, Maury expects *us* to pay the so-called ransom. Were you aware of that? When I suggested that the money could come from the label's promotion budget, he went ballistic. He said Jailbait Records doesn't negotiate with criminals."

"That's ridiculous—the music industry would collapse if it weren't for the criminals!"

"Exactly," Ned Bunterman said. "But Maury won't budge. He said this one's all on the family."

Cherry's mother was aggravated. "This security guy, Chemo, he says he can persuade the kidnapper—stalker, whatever—to take fifty grand. Seventy-five for sure."

"That's too much," Ned Bunterman declared. He was thinking about his long wine-tasting weekends with the kinky Danish couple, and how grateful they always were when he picked up the tab for dinners and spas.

"I agree. Way too much," said Janet Bunterman. She was thinking about her thrice-weekly tennis lessons and what usually followed, and how accustomed her pro had become to those thousand-dollar tips she tucked in his jock.

Ned Bunterman said he had to go find his golf shoes. "Tell Mr. Chemo that fifty is our limit. End of story."

"Problem is, we can't afford to make Annie mad. We seriously can't."

Janet Bunterman didn't need to spell it out. On the other end of the line, her husband cleared his throat. "You're certain she's still alive? You said you heard a gunshot during the last phone call—"

"No, she's alive. She called again today." Janet Bunterman tried not to sound disappointed. She'd been telling herself that she wasn't as coldhearted as the Larks, that she'd never truly wished for something awful to happen to Ann DeLusia. On the other hand, the photographer who had abducted her was obviously hinky and unpredictable. There was no guarantee that he would uphold his end of the deal, regardless of how much money he was paid. The Buntermans were compelled to be cautious.

"The ransom thing," Ned Bunterman said, "wasn't that our idea?"

"Correct. He never asked for any money."

"Just for Cherry, right? A private shoot."

"Ned, what are you thinking? Don't even say it."

"Worst-case scenario—"

"No!"

"Hear me out," said Cherry's father.

Hostage keeping was hard work, and Bang Abbott felt exhausted. Watching his captive sleep off the Ambiens didn't help. He tried to rouse himself by recounting—as he did many times each day—the tryst with Cherry Pye aboard the private jet. It was a pleasant exercise that usually buoyed Bang Abbott's spirits, but not in his current state of fatigue and self-doubt.

The scheme to exchange Ann for Cherry appeared to be in tatters, and the more he thought about the ransom offer transmitted by the ghoulish one-armed bodyguard, the less insulting it seemed. He could skate away from this mess with fifty grand, tax-free, and no chance of going to prison. Cherry's handlers would take the necessary steps to ensure that the actress wouldn't press charges or peddle her kidnapping story to the media. They'd make it up to her, big-time, because they would have no choice.

Meanwhile, Bang Abbott would rejoin the maggot mob and get back in the hunt for Lindsay, Paris, Nicole, Kim, Katie, Kate, Katy, Posh, Star, Mischa, Penelope, Jen, Julia, Jessica, Reese, Winona, Gisele, Heidi, Miley . . . *No!*

He didn't want to go back to the street.

Cherry Pye was his destiny; the definitive portfolio.

Her final days, in pictures.

The photographer felt something brush against his leg and he kicked at it, eliciting a wounded cry. He opened his eyes—Christ, had he dozed off?—and saw Ann recoiling beside him in the car, her nose bloodied.

"Way to go," she snuffled.

He looked down and saw the Colt lying where she had dropped it near the brake pedal, after he'd accidentally booted her in the schnoz. She must have been stretching across from the passenger side, trying to swipe the gun from beneath his seat.

The sneaky little twat! He should've left her in the trunk.

Ann flipped down the visor and examined her injury in the vanity mirror. She sighed. "This is lovely. Goes with the tatt."

"Hey, I didn't do it on purpose." Bang Abbott rummaged through his camera bag for a box of lens tissues, which he handed to her.

Packing both nostrils, she said, "I never understood you guys. What a scuzzy way to make a living."

"Babe, we're just feedin' the beast. Soon as nobody cares about Hollywood anymore, we're all out of business." He started the car and steered down the ramp. "They all bitch about the paparazzi, but guess what? They'd totally freak if just one night they came out of a club and we weren't there. Because then they'd know they were done. Over."

Ann said, "So you see yourself as an affirmative presence, not a low-down bloodsucker."

Bang Abbott barked a scornful laugh. "You don't get it. They need us more than we need them."

"Keep telling yourself that." Ann spoke like she had a clothespin on her nose. "I saw a clip on TV, some movie star—I forget who, some bottle blonde—she's picking up her little boy from school and there's, like, twenty of you A-holes waiting in the bushes. I mean seriously, Claude, that's your *life*? The poor kid was maybe seven years old."

The photographer knew it was a useless debate; for an actress, Ann was incredibly naïve. He himself was a veteran of many day-care stakeouts. One time he'd barely escaped arrest after an encounter with a well-known nanny who took a vicious swing at him, causing her to lose her grip on the young daughter of either Jamie Lynn Spears or Jennifer Garner. The little bugger landed in a sandbox, smack on her noggin, and immediately started squealing like a pig in a wood chipper. The nanny dialed 911 and Bang Abbott ran off; he didn't shoot a single frame, and he never found out whose kid he'd been surveilling.

"Everybody's fair game. No rules," he said. Some people couldn't fathom how he did what he did, but he'd never lost a minute of sleep. His was a legitimate industry, trafficking in the vulgarities of fame.

Ann shook her head. "It's not your pits that stink, Claude, it's your soul."

"Harsh."

"Yeah, well."

He passed his cell phone to her. "Call Cherry's old lady again. Tell her no more dicking around."

The conversation was brief and unproductive. It was Ann's impression that Janet Bunterman was trying hard to sound concerned.

"Does he at least let you pee?" she inquired.

"In a supervised setting."

"What about the gun?"

"Five bullets left," Ann said. "He wants an answer right now."

"We're still working up some options."

"Janet, I swear to God."

"Stall him," Cherry's mother suggested.

"Right. We'll play some Scrabble. Take your sweet goddamn time."

"Annie, please—I mean *please*—this is our A-number one top priority. Call back a little later, okay?"

Ann tossed the phone into Bang Abbott's lap. She said, "I'm so over these people."

"Nothing?"

"She says they're still working up an offer. Unbelievable."

The photographer said, "Well, screw that."

He found another parking garage, chose another empty floor and again locked his hostage in the trunk of the rental. This time she wasn't sedated, so there was plenty of complaining.

Afterward Bang Abbott walked to Pubes, which wouldn't

open for hours. He poked around the Dumpster in the back alley, near the rear entrance to the VIP room, and soon spotted what he was looking for. Gingerly he placed it in a plastic bag.

Next he went shopping. Handcuffs were easy to find; there was a sex boutique on Fifth Street. However, the clothes were a problem—he didn't know Ann's size, and the clerk at the consignment shop was useless. Later, in a second-floor room at a Marriott, Bang Abbott showed Ann the new ensemble.

She said, "Great. I'll look like a Mennonite bridesmaid."

After a hot shower—he allowed her five full minutes alone—she tried on the cotton dress, which hung down to her shins and fit like a tent. It was mousy gray with a pale crosshatch pattern, and buttoned primly up the front. For footwear Bang Abbott had selected a pair of plain brown flats that were two sizes too large.

"How much did all this set you back, Claude? Thirty, forty bucks?"

He said, "Maybe you want to sleep in that nasty black rag for a few more days."

She eyed the gamy cocktail dress on the floor and shook her head.

"I didn't think so," he said.

The sight of the handcuffs drew sarcastic commentary, which Bang Abbott ignored. He led Ann to the bathroom, which was still steamy from the shower, and told her to sit on the floor. After rolling up the right sleeve of her dress, he cuffed her wrist to the bare pipe behind the toilet bowl.

She said, "I'm not wild about this look."

"Shit, I almost forgot." He went to the bedroom and got her Jackie O. shades, to hide the brown color of her eyes. Cherry's fans would definitely have noticed.

From behind the glasses, Ann asked, "Are you done?" Sitting on the hard tile was uncomfortable; her neck and joints were still sore from the car crash.

"Let's see some sloppy cleavage," Bang Abbott said.

"Claude, I know where you're heading."

"You want *me* to undo the buttons? Because I will."

"No thanks." Ann was good at disheveling herself; it was an important part of her role as Cherry's double.

"More," said the photographer.

"I don't think so."

"One loose boob. Come on."

"No!"

"You wanna get out of this alive?"

"Hurry up and take your stupid picture." By now she was fairly certain he wouldn't shoot her, at least not intentionally.

"Don't move." He knelt beside her and removed the belt from his trousers and cinched it around her handcuffed arm, above the elbow joint, causing her veins to bulge.

"Nice touch," Ann remarked, although she was feeling anxious.

"Just you wait."

Bang Abbott went to get the plastic bag. Ann turned white when he took out the dirty syringe that he'd found next to the Dumpster behind the nightclub.

As she watched him draw it a quarter-full with water, all she could say was, "Please don't."

"Here. Hold it just like this." He placed the barrel of the hypodermic in her left hand, between the forefinger and middle finger, and moved her thumb to the plunger. "Jesus, what happened to your knuckles?"

"Nothing," Ann said. While locked in the trunk, she'd banged both fists against the lid, trying to get somebody's attention. "Where'd you find the harpoon?"

"Behind Pubes."

"Lovely." She was thinking meth, or possibly heroin.

The photographer stood back and studied her pose. "Turn your head sideways and stare at your arm, like you're about to shoot up."

"I get it, okay?" Her hand was trembling because she was terrified of accidentally sticking herself with the used needle. She could see a bead of somebody's dried blood on the tip.

Bang Abbott stepped closer and mussed Ann's wet hair in a way that obscured her swollen nose while exposing the absurd but distinctive neck tattoo. "That'll work," he said.

Through the second-rate lens of his secondhand cell phone, the girl was a ringer for Cherry Pye. The paparazzo snapped several shots—grainy, voyeuristic, amateurish. It was purely the look he wanted.

"Now they'll know I'm fucking serious!" he crowed.

Ann threw the syringe into the bathtub and quickly loosened the belt from her other arm. She said, "Where's the damn key to these handcuffs?"

"All we need is her e-mail," said Bang Abbott.

"Cherry's?"

"No, her mother's. That's your job—call back and get her private e-mail."

"Then unhook me from the commode, all right?"

"First I gotta take a major whiz."

"That's so not funny," she said.

"What—like I'm gonna trust you not to run?"

He pocketed the phone and from his waistband removed the bulky pistol, which he wedged in his right armpit.

"Claude, are you seriously going to unzip?" Ann asked.

Bang Abbott pressed his pudgy knees together as he fumbled with his pants. "Just look the other way and be quiet, okay? I got prostate issues."

With her unshackled hand, Ann shielded her eyes.

"I love show business," she said.

16

The former Cheryl Bunterman was in a toxic mood because she was confined to her suite on a Saturday night with an unsavory bodyguard, watching TV instead of hitting the clubs on South Beach. When she whined about being treated like a prisoner, the goon named Chemo switched channels from a Seth Rogan flick to a cage fight, and cranked up the volume.

Cherry Pye was dead sober and miserable. Lev would have been boning her brains out with his platinum-studded wand and then escorting her to Opium or the Cameo. This new guy, he was a total ice monster—his expression never changed when she told him to hold the mirror while she took a razor and touched up her wax job. He looked no more aroused than if he were watching a poodle being groomed.

"What the hell's your problem?" she snapped at him finally.

"You missed a spot," he said, pointing with his unusual prosthesis.

Adding to Cherry's gloom was the fact that she'd run out of drugs. Tanner Dane Keefe was once again ducking her calls, and Cherry was nearly levitating with self-pity by the time her mother showed up to give Chemo a break.

"Mom, you gotta fire that maniac!" Cherry demanded. "I caught him peeping up my robe."

Janet Bunterman told her to settle down and listen. "Your father thinks it would be helpful to have a splash of public-ity before you go on tour."

"I'm sick of interviews. They always ask about Boston."

"This would be something different, honey. It's a very tough market this year, ticket-wise. We need to raise your profile a little bit." Although Janet Bunterman didn't wish to worry her daughter, she felt it was helpful for Cherry to possess at least a vague awareness that the global economy was in the shitter, and that music fans were being selective about how they spent their concert dollars.

Cherry said, "Okay, I'll adopt a kid—that would be huge. No, *three* kids! Tell Maury to get all over it."

"Honey, no," Janet Bunterman said. She endeavored to squelch the idea without stating the obvious—that her daughter was unfit to care for a goldfish, much less a child. "The whole adoption thing, it's been overcooked. Angelina and Madge, they ruined it for everybody."

Cherry frowned and crossed her legs. "Fine. How about we could say I was knocked up with Tanner's baby?"

"Are you?"

"I don't think so," Cherry said, "but Tanny's megahot right now."

"We had something better in mind," Janet Bunterman said. "Something bigger."

Cherry twirled the sash of her robe. "Like what—another sex tape?"

It would have been understandable for a mother at that moment to stare at her spoiled, hapless offspring and doubt herself, or at least feel hobbled with remorse. Yet, long ago, Janet Bunterman had willingly accepted the role of her daughter's primary enabler, exploiter and apologist, reasoning that such duties were better handled within the family. The fact that the whole pathetic clan was financially reliant on Cherry was the galvanizing force behind her mother's devotion, although Janet Bunterman preferred a more noble rationalization. Even though Cherry didn't write her own lyrics and the vocals were shamelessly overdubbed, her music still brought happiness to millions of loyal young fans. It was them for whom Janet Bunterman imagined herself sacrificing so tirelessly.

"First, I have a question," she said to Cherry. "When you flew back here from L.A., you brought a tabloid photographer with you?"

"Yeah. Some round dude that gave me a ride to the airport in his Mercedes."

"Did anything happen on the plane?"

"No!" Cherry said. Then: "I dunno. Maybe."

"For heaven's sake."

"I felt sorry for him, Mom."

"You felt sorry," Janet Bunterman said, "for a paparazzo."

"Plus, he had the hottest orange BlackBerry. Which now I can't even find!"

Cherry's mother got up and went to the minibar, only to see that Chemo, as ordered, had removed all the liquor products. "Shit," she said, and reached for a Schweppes.

"Jesus, it's no biggie," Cherry was saying. "Haven't you ever done a mercy fuck?"

"That's enough, young lady."

Janet Bunterman sat down across from her daughter and considered reminding her what had happened to her previous comeback album, *Down and Dirty*, which had been savagely reviewed and nearly extinguished her career. That was the tour that had been canceled after the messy incident at the Boston Garden, now immortalized on YouTube. At that point, Cherry could have easily faded from the scene, but her celebrity was kept afloat mainly by her mother's drive and determination. It helped that Janet Bunterman was blessed with a boundless capacity for denial—*Cherry's still so young*, she'd say. *Don't they all act out?*

"This photographer who was on the jet—did he seem dangerous?"

Cherry threw back her head and laughed. "Only if

you're a box of doughnuts. I told you, the guy's a load and a half."

"So, if you were to meet him again, you wouldn't be afraid?" Janet Bunterman asked. "You could stay in control?"

Cherry shrugged. "Sure, I could stay in control. What's there to be scared of?"

"I'm just saying."

"But why in the world would I ever want to see that loser again?"

"We'll talk about that," Janet Bunterman said.

"Is that you beeping, or me?"

"Me. Just a second, honey." Her hand shook slightly as she removed the phone from her handbag and clicked on the e-mail she'd been expecting. She was careful to cup the device close so that her daughter wouldn't catch a glimpse of the display screen.

"Oh boy," murmured Janet Bunterman when she saw the photographs of Ann DeLusia manacled to a toilet.

"What is it, Mom?"

"Nothing."

"Aw, come on."

Janet Bunterman was forced to improvise. "We just sold out the Staples Center."

"Awesome," Cherry said, and gave herself a high five.

The governor, seeking quiet on a raucous Saturday night, hunkered beneath an empty lifeguard tower, not far from the stretch where he'd beached the speedboat. Along the dim shore a few couples could be seen, some strolling at the water's edge, some lying entwined on the sand. They didn't notice the man called Skink, who'd dug himself a sleeping pit and was speaking low into his phone.

On the other end of the line was Jim Tile, who was alarmed to learn that his volatile friend was roaming South Beach.

"Nothing good can come of this," he warned.

"What have you got for me?" Skink asked.

During his years with the state Highway Patrol, Jim Tile had made many useful contacts in local law enforcement. As a favor, one of them had agreed to call American Express and say that he was working on a possible missing-persons case, and that he needed a printout of recent activity on the account of one Claude Abbott. The name and card number had been provided to Jim Tile by Skink after his productive chat with the day clerk at the Comfort Inn.

"Your boy spent twenty-six and change at some adult novelty shop," Jim Tile said, reading from his notes.

The governor belched.

"Then there's forty-two dollars at a place called Oldies But Goldies. Apparel, it says. Next there's a charge at a Marriott."

"Here on the beach?" Skink asked.

"1530 Washington. Looks like a room deposit."

"When?"

"Today. This stuff is all from today."

"Good work, my brother. We'll talk later."

"Don't hang up. Tell me what's going on," Jim Tile said. "This is all about that girl, right?"

"I need to see her again. She enriched my outlook on humanity."

Jim Tile pointed out that Ann DeLusia was young enough to be his daughter. "Or even granddaughter," he added archly.

Skink said, "You dirty old goat. Don't you believe in platonic enchantment?"

"Actually, I do." Jim Tile had observed his friend behaving like this before, after he'd been touched by some unlikely encounter with what he termed "a pure true soul." Clearly the woman was important to him or he wouldn't have traveled all that way to find her; almost nothing could make him leave his encampment in the Keys, not even a hurricane.

"Governor, where's the shotgun?" Jim Tile asked.

"Relax, gramps. I stashed it."

Being retired, there were limits to how much assistance Jim Tile could provide if Clinton Tyree got himself arrested for shooting up a city. The man was psychologically unsuited for a setting as loud and preposterous as South Beach; he might snap at any moment.

"Please go home," Jim Tile urged.

"When Annie is safe. I fear she's in a fix."

"But nobody's reported her missing. I checked with the Beach cops."

Skink said, "She called me for help. You think I dreamed that?"

"It wouldn't be the first time."

"Jim, you've become quite a grump in your old age. For your information, I fished her cell phone from a toilet at the Comfort Inn."

"Oh."

"Apology accepted. I'll be in touch."

Skink hung up and directed his attention to two men with dishonorable intent who had brought a drunken young woman down to the beach. She was now protesting and struggling to get free, but the men, emboldened by the darkness and seclusion, pushed her backward to the sand. They didn't know someone was watching from beneath the lifeguard stand, and they never saw him coming. Later, one of the attending paramedics would comment that he'd never seen so many compound fractures per victim, one for every limb.

During the hunt for the bus hijacker, a helicopter spotter had located what appeared to be an abandoned vehicle deep in a hardwood hammock near the boundary of the crocodile preserve. Searchers who were directed by radio to the site were surprised to see the husk of a stock car, number 77, still covered with decals from Purolator, Firestone, Autolite, Delco and Kellogg's Rice Krispies. The rusting NASCAR relic sat near an ash-filled fire pit at the edge of a sparse campsite, where the searchers also found two blankets, several water bottles, a coffeepot, three fresh raccoon hides, a collection of polished buzzard skulls, an eighties-era boom box, a bag of eight-track cassettes, a moleskin satchel containing several glass eyes and a warped steamer trunk packed with books, mostly hardback novels.

Detective Reilly had hiked out to the camp that afternoon. It looked like a place where a crazed homeless marauder could be comfortable, if he didn't mind scorpions, snakes and poisonwood. The personal items stashed at the site offered no clues to the identity of the person who owned them but clear insight into his tastes. From the tape collection Reilly noted that the camp's inhabitant was a fan of hard rock going back to the sixties; among his treasures was a bootleg import of Jimi Hendrix performing at the Albert Hall. Inside the old trunk of books, the detective found pristine editions of Kurt Vonnegut, Jack London, Ken Kesey, Jim Harrison and John D. MacDonald, each wrapped protectively in clear plastic. The only perplexing find was the vagrant's stash of glass eyes, which appeared to have been pried from taxidermied animals.

Reilly left everything undisturbed except for one empty water bottle, which he confiscated in the hope of isolating a fingerprint or salivary DNA. Yet later, upon returning to headquarters, the detective sensed among his superiors a lack of enthusiasm for the strange case in North Key Largo. He was told instead to concentrate on a string of trailer-park burglaries down in Marathon, where a group of brazen teenagers had been making off with iPods, custom bongs and fishing tackle. One of the lieutenant's nephews had apparently lost three Penn deep-sea rigs and an antique kill gaff, and the lieutenant articulated a strong interest in catching the perpetrators and retrieving the valuable property through whatever means necessary, such as tazing the little shitbirds in the nads.

Reilly had no choice except to set the Sebago file aside, but he kept it on a corner of his small metal desk and thought about the suspect constantly.

While awaiting a response from Cherry Pye's handlers to the junkie-in-the-john photographs, Bang Abbott remembered he was running low on money. Without the tangerine BlackBerry, which contained his encyclopedic source list, the paparazzo was forced to rely on his memory for phone numbers of South Beach tipsters. Eventually he connected with a bouncer at Ortho, who for a promised fee of fifty bucks laconically reported that one of the new Idols was getting ripped on Cuervo at the pool bar.

"You mean from *American Idol*?" Ann DeLusia asked Bang Abbott.

"No, from *Bulgarian Idol*. Jesus."

While preparing his camera bag, he texted Peter Cartwill at the *Eye*. Cartwill wouldn't be in the office on a Saturday night but he might have his phone on. The man was a sucker for anything *Idol*, and Bang Abbott figured a sloppy-drunk shot could sell for five to seven grand, depending on which contestant it was and the degree to which he or she was hammered.

Ann said, "Can I come with you?"

"Ha!"

"Have a heart, Claude."

Bang Abbott reconsidered, and changed his mind. He didn't trust Ann alone in the hotel room; even attached to the toilet pipes, she could make plenty of noise. Somebody was bound to call security.

So he led her out to the rental car and sat her on the passenger side and handcuffed one of her very lovely ankles to the underframe of the front seat. She didn't complain. It was better than being locked in the trunk. Moreover, she was curious about her captor's occupation. Watching him in action might be instructive.

On the way to the club, she said, "It's like you're hunting big game."

"I guess," Bang Abbott said.

"Except they can't hurt you."

"The hell they can't. Queen Latifah? She gave me a concussion."

Ann was delighted. "How'd she do that?"

"Hit me with her fucking Ferragamo. You know, one of those big mothers."

"Yeah, it's like a bowling bag."

"Exactly!" said Bang Abbott. "I sued her gi-mongous ass, too."

"What a wimp move."

Ann's reaction surprised him. "What? I spent two days at Cedars-Sinai!"

"How much money did you get from her?"

"Don't you worry," he said with an inflated smirk.

Exactly zero is what he'd gotten from the lawsuit. In Century City he had found an oily stump of a lawyer who specialized in representing aggrieved paparazzi. The dirtbag had guaranteed Bang Abbott that Queen Latifah would settle out of court for six figures to avoid a trial, but he was wrong. A judge tossed out the whole case, saying the actress had been legitimately in fear for her safety when Bang Abbott accosted her outside a Beverly Hills yoga studio and she'd left him cross-eyed and groaning on the sidewalk.

Ann DeLusia said, "Tell me some more war stories."

"Woody Harrelson spit on me."

"Big deal."

"Twice in the same night," Bang Abbott said.

"So, wear a raincoat."

"The job ain't easy—some of these people, they're full-on psychos. One of Tiger's bimbos came after me with a manure rake."

"Tell the truth. You don't ever feel like a vampire?"

"Grow up," he said.

When they arrived at Ortho, he parked the Buick between a pair of stretch Hummers. Outside the club lurked three or four freelance video shooters.

"Slugs," Bang Abbott grunted contemptuously. "A fucking chimp could do what they do, only better." He hung the Nikons around his neck and called the bouncer's cell phone to make sure that the drunken Idol was still inside. The man said she was.

"Which one is it?" Bang Abbott asked.

"I don't know her name. Some Latin chick in white jeans."

"That's real helpful. How did you not get hired by the CIA?"

The bouncer said, "Dude, she's wearing one of them big Mexican hats. What else do you need?"

Bang Abbott put down the phone. "Now we wait," he said to Ann.

She wondered if the pistol was underneath his seat, and if she'd get another chance to grab it. The photographer hadn't slept a wink since he'd kidnapped her; surely he was running on fumes.

Ann said, "Maybe you're in love with her and you don't even know it."

"Cherry? That's the stupidest thing you've said so far."

He showed her a couple of the trampy self-portraits that the singer had left on the memory card of one of the cameras. Ann couldn't help but smile at the frame in which Cherry was sticking out her tongue.

"I believe she's teasing you, Claude."

"Just shut up."

Club Ortho was owned by a group of Colorado bone surgeons who thought it would be a cool gimmick if every patron had to wear a cast. Snap-on replicas painted in citrus hues were given out to a lucky few waiting in the long line behind the velvet rope. Those selected for admission yelped with joy or knuckle-bumped each other before squeezing a chosen limb into one of the sweaty neoprene sleeves.

"How do they dance in those things?" Ann asked.

Bang Abbott wasn't paying attention. He was observing a commotion near an unmarked doorway at the far end of the building. The video buzzards had cornered somebody.

"Don't even *think* about trying anything crazy," the paparazzo warned Ann before he hopped out of the car.

She watched him hustle across the street—he was spry for being such a pudge muffin. The flash unit on his camera popped several times, followed by shouting and curses. Then a flying wedge of beef delivered the fleeing entourage to one of the waiting Hummers. Ann couldn't see who it was, but she was familiar with the escape drill.

As the limo pulled out, she spotted Claude running alongside. His lens was aimed point-blank at the tinted rear window, and the white-blue strobe from his Nikon lit up the road. When he returned to the Buick, he was flush and gulping like a spent grouper.

"Demi and Ashton. That's for real," he panted.

"What happened to your nose?"

"Slyke—one of the TMZ assholes. Nailed me with an elbow, accidentally on purpose." Bang Abbott scowled at the sight of himself in the visor mirror.

Ann pointed to her own puffy nose and said, "Now we match."

The photographer bribed one of the club's valets to fetch

two cups of ice, one of which he gave to his captive. They wrapped the cubes in bar napkins and placed the cold compresses on their respective wounds, with heads tilted up.

To Bang Abbott's annoyance, Ann began laughing. She said, "This is the most ridiculous kidnapping in history."

"You'll thank me someday."

"For what?"

"Making you a household word," he said. "Just wait."

"Claude, come off it already."

"This part'll be over soon."

"Not soon enough," Ann said.

She was now confident that she'd survive the abduction. The paparazzo was squirrelly but not homicidal. Either the Buntermans would pay him off with a nice chunk of change or he'd screw up the deal and get himself busted by the cops. Regardless of how it ended, Ann would be freed—and then what? She couldn't possibly continue doubling for Cherry Pye, not after this fiasco.

Bang Abbott said, "All those video dorks took off after the Kutchers."

"So, it's just you and the Idol."

"Looks that way." He removed the ice pack from his nose and tossed it out the window.

Ann said, "I wasn't always an actress. At first I wanted to write."

"With legs like yours? That's sad."

"Don't be such a dog."

Bang Abbott said that in all his years of tracking celebrities, he'd never purposely photographed a writer. By way of a disclaimer, he added, "When you're doing a red carpet, you shoot *everybody* in a tux, just in case. But, swear to God, name the five hottest screenwriters in L.A. and I wouldn't know those fuckers if they hanged themselves over the 405."

"I'd look pretty good in a tux," Ann said sportively. She set her ice bag on the floor.

"You don't get it, do you?"

"Don't get it. Don't want it." She found herself thinking about her puny apartment in West Hollywood, trying to recall what she'd left in the refrigerator. She hoped there was no sashimi, unlike last time. The place had stunk like a fish dock when she got home.

Bang Abbott was now studiously hunched over the camera while viewing the shaky sequence of Demi-Ashton shots. When Ann leaned over for a peek, the handcuff on her ankle rattled against the springs of the car seat.

She asked, "How much can you get for those two?"

"A lot more if they were bombed," he griped.

"They're holding hands. They look happy."

"Yeah. Just my fucking luck."

"Cheer up, Claude. Maybe your Idol will pass out in the street."

"Or at least puke in her sombrero."

"Where's the gun?" Ann said lightly. "It really isn't necessary, you know."

"Maybe not for you, but Cherry's people—that's another story."

The phone thrummed in his pocket. Bang Abbott took it out and saw a text message from Janet Bunterman. He gave a jubilant hoot and cried, "Yes! The needle shots freaked 'em out!"

Ann felt excited, too. Before long, she'd be soaking in a hot bath back at the Stefano. She couldn't wait to confront Cherry's mother about the indifferent tone of the ransom negotiations.

"How much are they gonna pay to get me back?" she asked.

The paparazzo chortled. "Not a dime, honey."

"Excuse me?"

"It's a trade, just like I wanted. You for her, straight up."

Ann could scarcely believe it. Perhaps she had underestimated the Buntermans.

"Wow," she said.

"Fucking wow is right."

17

 Janet Bunterman summoned the twins to her suite for a meeting. Because it was almost 1:00 a.m., they assumed that Cherry Pye had snuck out of the hotel and done something outrageous, the usual Saturday-night crack-up.

When they got to the room, the Larks saw Maury Lykes pacing in front of the big window that overlooked the Atlantic. "Let's have the bad news," Lila said.

Janet Bunterman took out her cell phone and showed them the pictures of Ann DeLusia handcuffed to the john. "The paparazzo e-mailed me these beauties," she said.

Lucy remarked that the hypodermic looked real. "That could be a problem."

"Ya think?" Maury Lykes said acidly. "The way he's got

her posed, she's a goddamn scag-shooting clone of Cherry. Especially with that god-awful tattoo."

Lila clicked her teeth. "The tatt's not a plus."

Maury Lykes said it would be disastrous for sales of the new CD if the photographs got posted on the Internet. The Larks concurred.

"The handcuffs we can deal with. The handcuffs sort of work," Lucy said. "But not the needle."

"And forget about the tour," said Maury Lykes. "Most of Cherry's fans buy their tickets with daddy and mommy's money, and I'm guessing daddy and mommy won't want to piss away fifty-five bucks on a junkie pop tart. Any brilliant ideas?"

The Larks glanced at each other. This was a tough one.

"How much did you offer this character?" Lucy asked.

"Fifty," Janet Bunterman said.

"Only fifty? Are you shitting me?" Maury Lykes was stupefied.

"We were prepared to go to seventy-five."

"Wooo-hooo. *Seventy-five grand!*" The promoter threw up his hands. "Jesus Christ, this is your daughter's career we're talking about! The whole damn gravy train."

"I told you our funds are limited," Cherry's mother said tightly. "Considering your stake in all this, Maury, you could have kicked in a couple hundred to help us out."

He folded his arms. "Really. So it's not enough that I pay for the album production, the concert tours, the lawyers, the rehabs. Just out of curiosity, all those millions that Cherry made, thanks to *moi*—where did they go?"

Janet Bunterman reddened. "How much we offered the man didn't matter, Maury. He doesn't want money. You know what he wants."

"Which brings us to the point of this cozy gathering." The promoter motioned for the Larks to sit down. He said, "Janet and Ned are proposing that we actually give this loser a private photo shoot with Cherry."

"But why?" Lucy's distress was sufficient to corrugate her Botoxed brow.

"So he'll destroy the fake photos, that's number one," Cherry's mother said. "Reason number two is Annie—we need to get her away from him, for obvious reasons."

Maury Lykes asked how long until the henna ink faded away. Nobody seemed to know. He said, "I don't want to see any more shots like these. The next bunch could be worse."

"He promises to free Annie the minute Cherry shows up," Janet Bunterman said.

Lila shook her head. "Too risky. The guy's a nut job."

"The situation would be totally controlled. No surprises," Cherry's mother said.

"What kind of pictures does he want—straight porn?" Lucy asked.

"Hard or soft?" Lila followed up. "And who would decide how the shots were used? It would have to be us, Maury. That's a deal breaker."

Maury Lykes said the terms would be rigorously negotiated. "Nobody's looking forward to dealing with this hairball, but there's another reason to keep the idea in play.

Janet and Ned believe you wizards can somehow spin this monumental goatfuck into a 'lightning bolt' of positive publicity, and by 'positive' we're talking concert sellouts and the *Billboard* Top Ten."

A tremor passed simultaneously through the twins.

"This is not a game," one of them said.

The promoter chuckled. "Well, it sure as shit ain't the real world."

He fixed himself a vodka tonic and sat down near the window and said, "Janet, you take it from here."

By the time Cherry Pye's mother finished laying out the plan, the Larks were on the edge of the sofa. They were thinking the same thing: It just might work.

"I'll text him now," Janet Bunterman said.

Chemo wore a weed trimmer as a prosthesis because a large barracuda had mistaken his shiny Swiss wristwatch for a pinfish and chomped off his left hand. This had occurred many years earlier, on a day when Chemo had plunged from a stilt house in Biscayne Bay to avoid being shot by a man whom he'd been recruited to kill. It was the intended victim's obnoxious ex-wife whom Chemo had drowned with an anchor on the same ill-fated assignment. The numbnuts who'd hired Chemo to murder the guy in the stilt house was a scurrilous plastic surgeon who himself had ended up messily deceased, and shortly thereafter Chemo was shipped off to prison.

The whole experience had soured him on contract killings. Working with celebrities, it turned out, wasn't much better. Presley Aaron, the country singer, was only slightly more tolerable as a TV preacher than he'd been as a gabbling meth freak. And spoiled, spacey Cherry Pye was practically unbearable. Chemo couldn't wait for the economic recovery to reach Florida, so he could go back to piping mortgage applications.

"A barracuda!" Cherry said. "That's epic."

"What?"

"Did it hurt, like, more than a shark?"

"Jesus H. Christ." Chemo decided to start keeping count of how often she used the word *like*. It was driving him crazy. He was thinking of imposing a punishment.

She said, "I'm super hungry, dude."

"It's two in the morning. Go to sleep."

"Nuh-uh." Sprawled on the floor, Cherry was watching a DVD of a professional choreographer performing the stage numbers from the upcoming *Skantily Klad* tour. Maury Lykes had sent the disc up to the suite so that Cherry would work on her moves. She couldn't sing a lick, but on a good night she could dance.

"Let's go somewhere and eat," she said to Chemo.

He advised her to call room service.

"Why are you such a dick?" she whined.

"Careful," he said. "Glug-glug-glug."

A few minutes later, Tanner Dane Keefe appeared. Chemo put him up against the wall and, over Cherry's indignant protests, frisked him thoroughly. The kid had brought Vicodins, weed, X and some lumpy white powder. Chemo flushed everything down the john as Cherry dragged the forlorn actor into her room and slammed the door.

The bodyguard turned his attention to the paparazzo's tangerine BlackBerry, which had been thrumming all night.

"This is Fremont Spores," announced a scratchy voice on the other end.

"Yo," Chemo said.

"They just nailed Larissa for a DUI on the Tuttle."

"Who?"

"Larissa, man."

"Oh. Right." Chemo didn't know who the fuck he was talking about.

"Just came over the scanner," said the man named Fremont. "The Highway Patrol stopped her on the causeway and she blew point-one-nine on the Breathalyzer. They're takin' her out to county lockup right now."

"Thanks," Chemo said.

"This time it's two hundred even. Because she's an Idol and all."

"That'll work," said the bodyguard. It wasn't his money.

"You sound different, Claudius. You sick or what?"

"Pig flu," Chemo said, and ended the call.

He dialed the photographer's new cell and asked if he was ready to accept the offer of fifty grand in exchange for the safe return of the actress. Bang Abbott let out an odd laugh.

"Then ask for seventy-five. They'll go for it," Chemo said.

"Where have you been, bro? The deal's done."

"For how much?" Chemo wondered how he'd lost his role as the middleman. He had counted on raking a juicy commission from the ransom payoff.

Bang Abbott said, "It's not a cash transaction."

"Get outta here."

"I'm serious. Straight trade—the look-alike in exchange for Cherry Pye."

"And you get to keep her?"

"For one day," the photographer said, "which is all I need."

His smug tone set poorly with Chemo.

"You want your phone back? Now it's gonna cost two grand."

"Keep it," said Bang Abbott.

"You lost me."

"I don't need the damn thing anymore. With Cherry I'm golden."

The bodyguard didn't like being cut out of the deal. He viewed it as an unforgivable shafting.

"You know some chick named Larissa?" he asked Bang Abbott.

"*The* Larissa? From *Idol*?"

"Whatever."

"You watch the show, right? She's the one wears those super-tight jeans that ride up her snatch."

"If you say so," said Chemo. "Some guy called your phone and said she got popped for a DUI."

The paparazzo gave another strange cackle. "Ha! Was it Fremont you talked to?"

"Am I your goddamn secretary?"

"Guess what—I don't care about Larissa anymore. I don't care about any of 'em."

"Too bad," Chemo said. "The guy who called, you owe him two hundred for the tip."

"You promised that rodent two hundred bucks?"

"But, hey, before you take care of Freeman—"

"It's Fremont," Bang Abbott said irritably.

"Yeah, before you take care of him, you better take care of me."

This time the photographer wasn't laughing. "I don't get it. Take care of you because . . .?"

"Because now you're golden," Chemo said. "Remember?"

When Bang Abbott got off the phone, Ann DeLusia saw he was bothered.

"Is Larissa the one we were stalking at Ortho?" she asked.

He nodded. "She just got busted for drunk driving."

"Bummer. She must've slipped out the back door."

"No big deal."

"Then why the gloomy face?" Ann asked.

"Cherry's new bodyguard wants a payoff."

"What for?"

Bang Abbott shook his head. "Unbelievable. I might have to shoot the fucker."

"That's a fine idea, Claude. Play to your strong suit."

They'd just left a joint called Cheeseburger Baby, where the paparazzo had gorged himself in a premature celebration of the Cherry Pye coup. His fleshy cheeks glistened with french fry grease, and poppy seeds speckled his stained teeth.

Ann said, "On a happier note, when will I be a free woman?"

"Not sure. Probably Monday or Tuesday."

"Then I'll need fresh clothes."

"Here we go," Bang Abbott grumbled.

Returning to the Marriott, they saw three Miami Beach police cars parked by the entrance. Bang Abbott drove to the other side of the building and hurriedly took Ann up a stairwell to their room. After handcuffing her to the bathroom plumbing, he stuffed his Colt pistol under one of the mattresses and went downstairs to investigate.

The lobby was in disarray. Clothing and toiletry items were strewn about, and a rectangular scorch mark was visible on the pale marble floor. The photographer positioned himself behind a cluster of other curious guests; some wore hotel bathrobes and were bleary-eyed, as if roused from sleep. From their conversations Bang Abbott learned that a man had walked out of the elevator and gone off on a woman who was checking into the hotel. He set fire to her suitcase, snatched a Maltese from her arms and then dashed out the front door. Nobody seemed to know what triggered the bizarre confrontation, or whether the man and woman knew each other. The missing dog's name was either Bubba or Barbara.

Bang Abbott edged closer to eavesdrop on one of the cops, who was interviewing a lanky desk clerk with a peculiar accent. Evidently the assailant wasn't staying at the hotel, because the clerk said nobody on the night shift remembered seeing him before. The cop wanted to know if the intruder appeared drunk or drugged-out, and the desk clerk said no, not really. It was his opinion that the woman must have done something to light the guy's fuse.

"Did he say anything when he grabbed her dog?" the officer asked.

"Just that he was hungry," the desk clerk reported.

Bang Abbott had heard enough; the police activity had nothing to do with his captive. So far, no one seemed to be looking for the missing so-called actress.

Stepping back into the elevator, he spotted a small green cylinder on the floor and picked it up. Ann noticed the item in Bang Abbott's hand after he came in the door and started telling her about the weird scene in the lobby.

"Can I see that thing?" she asked.

He tossed the plastic cylinder to her and told her where he'd found it.

"Just now?" Ann said.

This was after he'd unlocked her from the toilet pipes and re-cuffed her to one of the beds.

He said, "It's a damn shotgun shell."

"I know, Claude."

"With the brass cap punched out. What's *that* all about?"

Ann peered through the little green tube at Bang Abbott. "You could always string it on a braid," she said, smiling.

The one-eyed homeless dude from Key Largo had found her, just as he'd promised. Finally Ann had met a man who kept his word, only now she didn't need him. She wondered how he would take the news.

18

The name of the loud woman in the lobby was Marian DeGregorio. Her Maltese was Bubba, not Barbara. They had flown down to Miami nonstop from White Plains; Bubba got his own seat and one-third of an Ambien, to shut him up. Marian DeGregorio was on a mission to scatter the ashes of her late husband, Victor, in the Atlantic Ocean. Victor had been dead going on seven years and Marian DeGregorio's boyfriend was sick of looking at the urn, which was kept in the same kitchen cupboard with the Sanka.

Victor DeGregorio had spent nearly seven months dying, during which time he repeatedly made his wife swear on her communion Bible that she would scatter his ashes off the coast of southern Florida. It was there, aboard a charter boat called the *Happy Hooker IX*, that Victor DeGregorio had once reeled in a hammerhead shark. He considered this the foremost masculine achievement of his life, and kept a jar filled with the shark's pointy teeth on his desk at the John Deere outlet where he worked as an inventory manager. Sometimes Victor DeGregorio would present one of the teeth to a customer or a visiting big shot from Deere headquarters, and the recipients were always impressed. Also on display was a framed nine-by-twelve of Victor posing on a dock beside the gaping stiff behemoth, which had been chained up by its tail and chalked with the number 193 to proclaim the weight. Victor's friends eventually forbade him from mentioning the hammerhead—even toward the end—because he'd told the goddamn story about a thousand times.

Marian DeGregorio had been retelling the story herself, to a desk clerk, when the trouble erupted. She'd just gotten to the part where Victor and his fishing buddies set upon the gaffed shark with aluminum ball bats to—in the widow's words—"finish off the vicious bastard," when she was overheard by a tall, scruffy man coming off the elevator. He interrupted to express his disgust, and in a harsh tone went on at length about the imminent collapse of world shark populations. Except for his flawless dentition, the man looked like a street person, so Marian DeGregorio somewhat caustically challenged his expertise on the topic of marine ecosystems. At that point he seized her soft-sided suitcase, sprung the locks and set the contents ablaze with a can of paint thinner he'd swiped from the vacation home of D. T. Maltby, his former running mate. As soon as the Marriott's fire alarm went off, he snatched Marian DeGregorio's dog and fled to the streets, leaving the widow honking and flapping like an addled goose in the smoky lobby.

Skink jogged to the beach and lay down beneath the stars and thought about Annie the actress. He had prowled every floor of the hotel, listening at the doors, but he'd made no formal inquiries due to the lateness of the hour and his disordered appearance. Based on Jim Tile's information, he was certain that Annie was being held in one of the rooms. Later he would try again to find her.

Meanwhile the Maltese was fidgeting and snuffling in his grasp. Skink did not respond solicitously. Occasionally he'd dined on the pets of intolerable people, but he preferred roadkill. Bubba didn't look particularly tasty and the over-groomed pelt would be useless except as a shammy cloth for the shotgun. Moreover, Skink suspected that barbecuing a purebred would attract unwanted attention even on South Beach.

As the sun leaked over the horizon, he was approached by two disheveled but attractive women who were strolling shoeless and hungover. One was twirling a wine-stained bra and the other carried a crumpled pack of French cigarettes. The women cooed and clucked and commented upon Bubba's cuteness, which was not evident to Skink. After removing the tags and rhinestone collar, he gave them the dog and said its previous owner had been tragically beheaded on the teacup ride at Disney World, which the women seemed eager to believe. They promised that the adorable pup would have a fantastic new life in Cedar Rapids, where they would be returning that afternoon.

When the governor walked back to the Marriott, he was irked to see a police car and a bright red van from the arson unit of the Miami Beach Fire Department. He went another few blocks until he found a taxi idling illegally beside a hydrant. He got in and directed the driver to take him to the Bath Club, saying he was being interviewed for a membership. The taxi driver chose not to question the absurd yarn, and for that mistake he wound up bound and gagged in a cabana strewn with moldy flip-flops.

Skink took the man's cab and made his way back to the hotel, where he circled the block until a parking space on Washington became available. His thoughts turned for no reason to an old Scottish poem by Robert Burns called "Ode to a Haggis," which he recited several times aloud, experimenting with inflections. He remembered that Mr. Burns died at the preposterous age of thirty-seven, on the very same day Mrs. Burns gave birth to their last child.

Such depressing trivia served to fortify Skink's view that irony was overrated. He slid down low in the seat, waiting for Annie and her captor to emerge from the Marriott.

*

"You still haven't caught that crazy fucker?" Jackie Sebago asked.

"Not yet," said Detective Reilly. He had never before interviewed a man with a nut sack the size of a rugby ball.

"Unfuckingbelievable," Jackie Sebago muttered.

"We found a suspicious campsite. He wasn't there."

Sunday was Reilly's weekend day off, but his fiancée had gone shopping in Miami and it was too windy for offshore fishing. On an impulse he'd called Jackie Sebago, who was still in Key Largo recuperating from the assault by the bus hijacker.

"Why can't you guys find him? I don't get it." Jackie Sebago spread his bare legs and, with a groan, adjusted the ice pack.

Reilly turned away. It was his opinion that forcibly attaching a sea urchin to another person's scrotum was a serious crime, not a fraternity prank, and that the vagrant should be prosecuted to the full measure of the law.

"Tell me again why this man singled you out," the detective said.

"Because of the town houses, is what he said. Obviously he's some kind of enviro-nut."

"It's your project?"

"Absolutely. That's why it's called Sebago Isle."

"I figured," said Reilly.

"Hey, you were on-site. You know what I'm talkin' about," Jackie Sebago said. "It's gonna be phenomenal. It's gonna be paradise."

"Great location," the detective agreed.

"This guy, he was a big mother, had these funky braids made from shotgun shells. He yelled and cussed and called me names. Said I was killing the mangrove trees, raping the islands, whatever," Jackie Sebago recounted. "How does a whack job like that get his hands on a gun?"

"Are you kidding?"

Cops in Florida were trained to assume that everyone, crazy or not, carried a firearm. Reilly was more concerned about the suspect's sadistic tendencies and radical political agenda. No cash, credit cards or valuables (except for cell phones) had been taken from the bus passengers, and nobody besides Jackie Sebago had been harmed.

"It's definitely a buyer's market," the developer was saying. "Our units start in the mid six hundreds—those are the two-bedrooms, of course, and that's a pre-construction quote."

Reilly smiled politely. "Still too rich for my blood."

"Man, it's a steal. Trust me."

The young detective, whose entire annual salary wouldn't cover the down payment, remained determined to treat Jackie Sebago the same as any innocent victim of violence. It wasn't going to be easy.

"Did the attacker say anything about himself?" Reilly asked. "Did he give any clues about who he was, or where he came from?"

"No, but he sang a song. I forgot to tell you that."

"A made-up song or a real song?"

Jackie Sebago said he hadn't recognized the number, although some of the other passengers told him it was a well-known hit by the Allman Brothers.

"Something about a whipping post," he said.

Reilly jotted down the information, which was probably useless. "What about the young woman who flagged down the bus—you think she was in on it?"

"Hard to say. She seemed awful damn calm about the whole thing."

"The man did have a weapon."

"Yeah, but still," said Jackie Sebago.

From speaking to the investors who'd been on the hijacked bus, the detective knew they were unhappy with the slow progress of Sebago Isle, and also with Jackie Sebago's slippery account of the finances.

"Is it possible somebody hired this individual just to frighten you?" Reilly asked.

"No way," the developer said, though he privately wondered about Shea, the most vocal and disgruntled of the group.

Would the hot-tempered hedge funder go to all the trouble of setting up an elaborate highway abduction? Jackie Sebago was doubtful. Likewise, arranging the exotic perforation of a business partner's privates seemed conceptually beyond the reach of Shea's imagination. He was more the type to sue.

"A man in your position is bound to have enemies," the detective suggested carefully.

Pointing at his swollen, pustular genitalia, Jackie Sebago declared, "Nobody hates me *this* bad."

He would be reconsidering that possibility twenty-four hours later, after the Sebago Isle construction site was inexplicably red-tagged and D. T. Maltby refused to take his phone calls and Shea was texting hourly from Providence with ugly threats.

Driving out of Ocean Reef, where Jackie Sebago lay convalescing in a borrowed villa, Reilly wondered if the elusive busjacker was truly a menace to the public, or just a cagey vigilante who was careful to select repugnant targets. Prosecutors would have a hard time finding a Florida jury that would be sympathetic to a real-estate viper like Sebago.

Still, Reilly wasn't discouraged, and had no intention of backing off from the investigation. He was eager to track down the suspect and find out what made him tick.

Tanner Dane Keefe was afraid of Cherry Pye's new bodyguard.

"He's a stone psycho," the actor whispered. "What happened to his face?"

"No duh," Cherry said.

The two of them were lying in bed. He was using her bare bottom as a pillow.

"The man flushed all my dope. You believe that?"

"I asked for a black martial-arts dude," she said petulantly. "A big bald one."

"So get the scar dude fired. Tell Maury he tried to pork you or somethin'."

"Uh, I did. It totally didn't work."

Tanner Dane Keefe shifted his head restlessly on her butt cheeks. "He's, like, a serial killer. Swear to God."

She laughed. "Yeah, like freakin' Jason without the mask."

The door opened and Chemo strolled in. The actor groped for the sheet to cover himself. Cherry raised up and said, "Can you, like, knock? What's your problem?"

Chemo told Tanner Dane Keefe that it was time to leave. Cherry said she didn't want him to go.

"That's okay. I got my lava-rock massage at eleven," the actor said.

She grabbed for his arm. "Tanny, don't you dare move!"

Chemo had no patience for fuckwits. "Make me ask twice," he said, "and I'll shave your ass to the bone." He raised the weed whacker to instill motivation.

Tanner Dane Keefe managed a nod.

"You A-hole!" Cherry cried at Chemo, and hurled a chrome vibrator that flew past his head and dinged the wall.

The actor said, "Later, babe." He pecked Cherry on her Axl-zebra tatt and scrambled to collect his clothes. He was out the door in sixty seconds.

Chemo ordered Cherry to get dressed. A person named Laurel was waiting.

"Tell her to come back later." Cherry buried her face in the covers.

"Maury says now."

"I hate you!"

Chemo winked. "My heart's in tatters. Now get out of bed."

Laurel was the new lip-synching coach. She had downloaded Cherry's set list onto an MP3 player, which she plugged into a player dock in the sitting area of the suite. As a rehearsal aid she'd even brought a headset of the type Cherry would be wearing as a prop onstage.

"I already know, like, every song by heart," Cherry insisted, although soon it became clear that she didn't.

Chemo almost felt sorry for Laurel. The lyrics were brainless and repetitive yet Cherry kept getting lost, even on the refrains. Chemo made her chug a Red Bull, with no improvement. Eventually he had to leave the room. It was the most monotonous crap he'd ever heard, and he had once worked the door at a white rap club.

The Larks showed up and hovered curiously. Since leaving prison, Chemo had come to understand the power of his uncommon attraction; some women got turned on when they were creeped out. But his mind was strictly fixed on business; he was mulling what Abbott had told him about trading Cherry Pye for her double, wondering why the paparazzo had turned down a cash ransom. Obviously the douche bag was hot for Cherry, a condition that Chemo predicted would be cured after a short dose of her company.

But there also had to be more money involved—big money, Chemo reasoned, for a snake like Abbott to risk his own neck. One way or another, Chemo intended to grab a piece of the action. He felt he'd earned it. Every minute with Cherry was like a month at Raiford.

Lucy Lark said, "Tell her we're here. And we haven't got forever."

"She's busy practicing," Chemo said.

"In there? Practicing what?" Lila asked.

"Moving her lips." Chemo steered the twins outside to the hall and demanded to know what in the name of Jesus Harvey Christ had happened with the kidnap negotiation.

"When Janet and Maury get here," Lucy said, "they'll bring you up to speed."

"So it's a done deal?"

Lila nodded. "Ninety-nine-point-nine for certain."

"Goddamn." He kicked over a potted palm, causing the Larks to back away and reconsider their interest in him.

The elevator opened and out walked Maury Lykes and Janet Bunterman. At the same moment, angry shouts and yips erupted from the suite. Cherry's mother bolted inside to rescue Laurel. She was followed by the twins, who were heading for the balcony to check their text messages and sneak a smoke.

Finding himself alone in the hallway with Maury Lykes, Chemo used the opportunity to jam the startled promoter against the wall and demand a full briefing.

"So, how's this gonna go down?" he asked.

Maury Lykes had difficulty responding because the body-guard was compressing his larynx.

"After he lets the girl go—the actress—then what?" Chemo said. "He just rides off into the sunset with your star client? I don't get it. You trust this jerkoff?"

"Not for a minute," the promoter wheezed. "That's why you're goin' along on the shoot."

Chemo released his grip. "Good call."

"Oh, it gets better," said Maury Lykes, rubbing his neck.

Bang Abbott wanted to use Ann DeLusia as the intermediary but she'd copped a major attitude toward Janet Bunterman, so he was forced to pick up the phone himself. Back and forth it went—Cherry's old lady was obviously getting coached from the sidelines—but eventually the rules of the photo shoot were hammered out.

The session would go exactly six hours, including a lunch break, and take place at the big house being rented by Tanner Dane Keefe on Star Island. Cherry would be accompanied only by her bodyguard. If the goon laid a finger (or his hedge-trimming tool) on Bang Abbott, or if he interfered in any way with the photography, the deal was off and Cherry Pye as an entertainment franchise was history.

Bang Abbott's leverage was the portfolio of crude needle shots featuring Ann, posed as Cherry, in the hotel bathroom. If the Star Island meeting went well, he would—in Chemo's presence—delete the shocking images from his cell phone. He wouldn't mention that he'd already sent a duplicate photo file marked "Toilet Art" to his desktop back in Los Angeles.

And if either the singer or her cheese-faced security man started any hassles, Bang Abbott would touch a button on his cell that would e-mail the ruinous JPEGs to every tabloid in the United States and Europe, with captions in English, Spanish and French.

"What about me?" Ann asked.

"As soon as Cherry gets there, you slip out the kitchen door. A car will be waiting."

"Because they still don't want her to know I exist. Nice."

"Get over it." Bang Abbott said he'd promised Janet Bunterman that he wouldn't say a word to Cherry about her having a double, or about the trade.

"What's she supposed to think when she shows up for the shoot?"

"They're gonna tell her I'm working for *Vanity Fair*."

Ann had to chuckle. "No offense, Claude, but *Hustler* would be a reach."

He flipped her off and attacked his room-service pancakes.

"Getting back to me," she said, "what happens if—"

"Relax, for Christ's sake. You're the last person they want to piss off, okay, because you know *everything*." As he spoke, Bang Abbott spewed syrupy crumbs. "Cherry's people, if they've got half a brain, they're gonna take real good care of you when this is over."

Ann picked listlessly at a plate of scrambled eggs. "So, overall, you'd say it was a smooth career move—getting kidnapped and chained to a commode and all."

"What I'm sayin' is, you're a smart girl. Use your imagination."

There was a knock on the door and Ann thought: *Here we go.*

But it was a maid, not the homeless guy with the shotgunshell braids. Ann wondered where he was, and how he would make himself known. Having seen him in action against the busload of real-estate guys, she anticipated another memorable entrance.

After Bang Abbott sent the maid away, Ann lifted a handcuffed wrist and said, "Claude, here's a thought. Why don't you let me go now?"

"No can do."

"How come? The deal's a lock, right? They don't care about me—all they want is those stupid pictures."

He said, "They want you, too, missy. Most definitely."

"Did Janet actually say that?"

"More than once. She can't wait to see your smiling face."

"Then I'll grab a cab to the hotel."

Bang Abbott shook his head. "It's all set, so chill. One more day won't kill you."

"But I think I'm getting cramps."

"That's weak."

"Claude, please?"

He forked a rubbery strip of bacon into his mouth. "Eat your breakfast," he said.

Ann considered not warning him, just letting it play out. He was nothing but a low-rent parasite with a camera, and he probably deserved whatever fearsome shit was about to fly his way.

On the other hand, he hadn't tried to rape her, which was what she'd feared the most. And he had sort of apologized for drugging her and locking her in the cramped car trunk ("I should've rented a midsize" were his exact words). As charmless and revolting as Claude could be, Ann wasn't looking forward to watching him suffer, which was a likely scenario if he was ambushed by the man known as Skink.

"Here's a news flash," she said. "Somebody's looking for me."

"It's about time."

"I'm not bullshitting. This is nobody you want to meet."

Bang Abbott fluttered his hands theatrically. "Oooooh. Then maybe I'll just call the cops and give myself up." He reached under the mattress, took out the secondhand Colt and, in a lame Austin Powers accent, said, "Bring it on, baby."

Ann pushed away the cold eggs. "Fine. My conscience is clear."

"So who's your knight in shining armor?"

"Never mind."

"And how the hell would he know where to find you? I mean, really." Bang Abbott chuckled acidly. "Nice try, sugar pie."

His phone rang. It was Peter Cartwill from the *Eye*. He needed someone to go to an impound lot in Medley and take a photo of the Range Rover that Larissa, the drunken Idol, was driving when she got busted. Bang Abbott told Cartwill to find himself another errand boy.

"Those days are over for me," he said, and clicked off.

"What's the worst thing you've ever done to get a picture?" Ann asked him. "The lowest of your low moves."

The paparazzo thought about it for several moments. "I was on the Farrah death watch for a couple weeks. Sent her a humongous bunch of flowers and bribed the delivery guy to sneak some shots with his cell. She was asleep in the bed so you couldn't really see her face, but I still made eleven grand off the worldwide rights."

Ann said, "Okay, Claude, that's pretty fucking awful."

"She never knew it happened." He shrugged. "No harm, no foul."

"Wow."

"But here's the other side."

"Regale me," Ann said.

"One time I got a tip that Charlie Sheen was taking his kids to the doctor, okay—the twins? For their vaccines? So I get there early and pay one of these Brentwood moms two hundred bills to let me sit with her and her runny-nosed brat in the waiting room. She tells the nurse I'm an uncle or a godfather or some asinine thing." Bang Abbott smiled ruefully, remembering how it had ended.

"So Charlie and his wife roll in with the babies—he recognizes me, obviously—and he goes totally ballistic. Drags me out the door, decks me with a sucker punch, steps on my head and then proceeds to open his fly and piss in my ear! You believe that?"

Ann thought it was marvelous. "Right in your ear hole?"

"His aim was amazing," Bang Abbott said. "He must've chugged a gallon of coffee before he left the house—I had pee dripping down the side of my neck all day."

"Okay, that's gross."

"Worst part was, I never got a picture. Which means I never got paid."

"Poor Claude."

"I'm just sayin'. Every dime I make, I earn."

He believed it, too. Ann coolly reached over and lifted the pistol from his lap. She pointed the barrel at his shiny forehead and said, "Give me the key to the handcuffs."

Bang Abbott was surprised by her boldness, but he wasn't scared. He was thinking what a smokin' photograph it would make—a hot babe with one hand chained to a bed, the other hand aiming a gun at the camera.

"Like you're really gonna shoot me," he said.

"Oh, I totally will," Ann asserted, though she didn't believe it, either. If the guy was beating her up or trying to rip off her clothes, that would be different; she wouldn't hesitate to drill him between the eyes.

But not when he was just sitting there, being his usual sweaty lump. No way.

She said, "I'm dead serious."

"Ann, give me the damn gun."

"Take off the handcuffs, or I swear to God . . ."

It was humiliating that Claude displayed no fear, not even a twitch. *Some actress I am*, Ann thought.

"I'm counting to five," she announced.

"Make it a thousand."

The Colt was heavy and Ann's hand was starting to quiver. Bang Abbott noticed right away.

"Look at you," he said with a smirk.

With her thumb she retracted the hammer, just like they did in the Westerns. She pictured herself as Christian Bale's character in *3:10 to Yuma*.

"Claude, it's time."

"Oh, for Christ's sake," he said.

Bang Abbott's experience handling cocked firearms was comparable to that of his hostage, who had none whatsoever. He grabbed the barrel and yanked, with unsatisfactory results. The paparazzo's hand was so slick with perspiration that his grip slipped, which produced through simple physics a jarring effect upon the weapon and Ann DeLusia's grasp thereof.

Bang Abbott was jarred by the loudness of the shot, and the fact that the crazy girl had actually pulled the trigger. For a moment he didn't know he'd been hit.

His first clue was the bloody thing stuck to the ceiling of

the hotel room. He peered up at it with a grim curiosity, the force of the pistol blast having flattened him to a supine position. Soon the object on the ceiling came into focus, and Bang Abbott realized he was gazing at a small gooey piece of his physical self.

An important piece, it turned out.

19

Ned Bunterman wasn't one of those domineering stage fathers. It was his wife who had guided Cheryl from talent-show cutie to pop megastar, Ned Bunterman watching from the wings with a sense of marvel. To say his daughter was tonally challenged was being kind; she couldn't yodel her way out of a broom closet.

Yet it hadn't mattered, her flat and anemic cheeping, because Janet Bunterman and Maury Lykes had done a clever job of marketing a look and pose that required no special vocal skills. "The BLS brand," Maury called it—barely legal slut, the essential ingredient being an aura of insouciant fuckability. Such a sell job was made easier by the advanced technology of modern music making; on her recordings, the former Cheryl Bunterman possessed perfect pitch, and pipes worthy of a

Baptist choirgirl. The voice, angelically enhanced by computer programs and backup singers, was utterly unrecognizable to her father, who was content to stay behind the scenes, stacking the money.

Before Cheryl became Cherry Pye, Ned Bunterman managed the books for a Cadillac/Saturn/Hummer dealership outside of Houston. He was not a Texan by birth but had moved there from Shreveport in his early twenties, fleeing a pregnant girlfriend whose father owned the largest collection of Kalashnikov assault rifles in Caddo Parish. He met Janet Wingo in a faux cowboy bar, where she worked the pool room serving drinks and selling knockoff Cuban cigars. They dated for a few months, got married and in six years produced three dull sons. Cheryl was an accident, Ned and Janet having mostly lost interest in each other by then.

Their listless marriage was sustained by bipartisan philandering until Cheryl's first talent contest at age four, when she delivered a plangent but perky rendition of "You Are My Sunshine," in memory of JonBenét Ramsey. The ghastly tastelessness of the tribute had worried Ned Bunterman, who'd made his doubts known at rehearsal. Janet overruled him, and by the end of the song the judges were sniffling and Cheryl had the second-place trophy, along with a one-year modeling contract. It would be the last time Ned Bunterman questioned his wife's judgment.

Cheryl's ascendant career became the glue of Ned and Janet Bunterman's relationship, each of them being patient and single-minded when it came to their daughter's prospects. On the day she was offered her first recording contract, he quit the car dealership and began devoting all his energy to the business of star making. He had preferred the more suggestive "Cherry Pop" over "Cherry Pye," but he deferred to Maury Lykes, who was experienced at manufacturing show-business personas.

It paid off. Before long, the former Cheryl Gail Bunterman was a bona fide celebrity making millions of dollars. Unfortunately, she was also flying off the rails on a nightly basis. Like his wife, Ned Bunterman initially chose to believe that Cherry's spinout was just a phase, a young person's natural reaction to sudden fame and wealth. Yet it soon became clear that she had a genuine and indiscriminate taste for drugs and alcohol, and no common sense. While Ned Bunterman was fond of his daughter, he didn't cling to any parental illusions; she was a simpleton, shallow as a thimble. Having worked in a Hummer showroom, he considered himself an authority on the species.

Janet Bunterman maintained a protective stance of denial, but in private she shared her husband's concern for Cherry's well-being and also that of the family's cash flow. The impact of the Boston fiasco had been instant and precipitous, income-wise. "Look what happened to Amy Winehouse," Ned Bunterman had warned Janet, "and that girl can actually carry a tune."

It was imperative that *Skantily Klad* be a smash hit, and for that to happen the tour had to do huge business. Cherry needed to generate some buzz, but not in the usual tawdry way. She had to get the fans back on her side; be a victim, for a change, not a fuckup.

So Ned Bunterman was pleased when Janet, Maury and even the chilly Lark twins endorsed his audacious suggestion to let Cherry do the shoot with the demented paparazzo. Later, after paying Ann DeLusia to go away, they would roll out a story saying it was Cherry herself who'd been kidnapped, abused and made to pose for degrading pictures (the cream of which would be leaked to the tabs).

According to Ned Bunterman's plan, the photographer would be given a choice: He could go along with the family's ruse or face criminal prosecution, followed by a civil lawsuit that would leave him pauperized for life. The man who would present these harsh terms was now seated in Cherry's suite at the Stefano, spritzing WD-40 on the rotor stem of a mechanical weed-trimming device that was rigged to the nub of one arm.

"Ned, this is Mr. Chemo," said Janet Bunterman.

Her husband stepped forward and offered a locker-room smile. "Nice to meet you, sir." When he held out his hand, it was twitchy. He'd never laid eyes on anyone like this bodyguard, and he had no desire to hear the full story.

"Hello," said Chemo, without looking up.

Ned Bunterman aborted the handshake. "I'm Cherry's dad."

"Swell. Pay the brother."

"What?"

Chemo jerked his only thumb toward a bellman waiting

at the doorway with Ned Bunterman's suitcase and a room key card.

"Right," Ned Bunterman said, and gave the guy a ten.

Maury Lykes and the Larks were already there, talking in low voices on cell phones. After finishing their conversations they all sat down to review what Cherry Pye would be told about the photo session. One of the Lark sisters wondered if the paparazzo should pretend to be from *Maxim* instead of *Vanity Fair*. The other Lark said it wouldn't matter.

"She's really not into magazines," Janet Bunterman agreed.

"Or periodicals in general," Cherry's father added. "Kids her age don't read much."

Chemo peeked over his Sarah Palins. "She can damn sure read a pill bottle."

"There's no need to be mean," Ned Bunterman said, though no one backed him up.

Maury Lykes said it would be nice to pick a publication that Cherry had actually heard of.

"Oh, she's heard of *Vanity Fair*," her mother asserted. "The Lindsay Lohan spread? Oh my God."

The Larks nodded. "Cherry went postal," one of them said. "She bit herself on the foot and wouldn't let go."

"Six stitches," recalled Janet Bunterman.

Maury Lykes smiled. "Perfect. Tell her she's getting the cover, same as Lindsay."

"She can chew on her own feet?" Chemo asked.

One part of the scheme was troubling Ned Bunterman.

He said, "At some point, she'll figure out this whole thing wasn't what she was led to believe."

"You mean like when she turns on the tube and there's Billy Bush talkin' about how she was snatched at gunpoint and held hostage?" Maury Lykes sniffed. "Yeah, she might put two and two together. But you and the missus are gonna have a chat with her before we float the story, okay? Tell her everything's cool. Make sure she plays along."

Ned Bunterman said, "Of course. But sometimes she—"

"Goes off-message? Yes, we know," one of the Larks said. "That's why she's only doing one media sit-down before the tour. We're thinking Larry King."

"Or possibly Mario Lopez," the other twin interjected.

Ned Bunterman said it sounded like a plan. He and Janet would leave the coaching of their daughter to the Larks, who specialized in loose cannons. "Where is she?" he asked.

"I'll fetch her," said Chemo, and stood up.

Ned Bunterman stifled a gasp; the man was a giraffe.

"The fuck are you lookin' at?" the bodyguard snapped, and stalked toward the bedroom.

Moments later he emerged, Cherry Pye lagging behind. She wore an inside-out tube top, plaid pajama bottoms and black shearling Uggs that were freckled with rug lint. Her hair was tied in a lank ponytail, exposing the misbegotten tattoo on her neck. Her father struggled to mask his dismay; the ink work looked much worse in person than on the Internet.

"Punkin, you are a vision," he crooned.

"Hi, Daddy." She let him peck her on the cheek before slumping on the couch.

Maury Lykes turned to Janet Bunterman and said, "You do the honors."

Cherry scowled. "What now? Am I, like, in trouble again?"

"Not at all," said her mother. "We've got something major planned for tomorrow."

"But Tanny and I are doing the Seaquarium."

Ned Bunterman asked, "Who's Tanny?"

"The actor she's balling," explained Maury Lykes. "He's in the new Tarantino. Plays the necro surfer."

"I'm gonna swim with the killer whales," Cherry went on. "Tanny's gonna make a video and post it on YouTube."

Cherry's mother clucked. "Not tomorrow, sweetie. You've got a photo shoot with *Vanity Fair*."

"But it's a protest video," said Cherry, "to call out the Japanese."

One of the Larks twirled an unlit cigarette, while Maury Lykes planted the heels of his crocodile boots on the teak coffee table.

"'Cause they're, like, wipin' out all the whales," Cherry continued. "Tanny and I saw it on Animal Planet. With rocket-powered harpoons!"

Chemo said, "Jesus H. Christ."

"What's *your* problem?"

"It's not the killer whales the Japs are after. It's the humpbacks," he said. The Animal Planet station was quite popular in the Florida penal system. "The killer whale, it's not even a goddamn whale. They're in the dolphin family, for fuck's sake."

Cherry looked perplexed.

Janet Bunterman pressed forward. "You'll be doing the shoot at Tanner's house."

"On Star Island? Awesome."

"They promised us the cover, just like Lindsay."

"She is *so* gross. God!"

"Only your name will be in bigger letters," Cherry's mother added brightly.

"So who's the photographer?"

"Well, that's the thing."

Cherry jackknifed out of her slouch. "Not the same guy who did Lindsay! Forget it, Mom, there's no freaking way."

"Not him, baby. Remember the fellow who gave you the ride at Rainbow Bend—the one who flew with you to Miami?"

Maury Lykes leaned close to Ned Bunterman and whispered, "She humped him on the G5."

Cherry's father nodded somberly. He wished he'd been shocked to hear it.

"That gnarly load?" Cherry exclaimed. "He *cannot* be workin' for *Vanity Fair*!"

One of the Larks—Ned Bunterman guessed it was Lucy—said, "His name is Claude Abbott and, FYI, he's got a Pulitzer Prize."

"No way!"

"Way," said the other Lark.

Cherry grew thoughtful. "So that's how come he could afford the Mercedes."

"There you go," said her mother.

Maury Lykes snuck a glance at Chemo, who wore an expression of weary disgust.

"The Pulitzer thingie," Cherry said, "is that like a People's Choice?"

Ned Bunterman scouted the room for a minibar. He wondered if it was possible that Cherry had tumbled from her crib as an infant and dented her frontal lobe. There'd been several unreliable-looking baby-sitters that he recalled.

"The shoot starts at ten," Janet Bunterman said.

"Ten in the morning? Yuk."

"Mr. Chemo will stay with you the whole day."

Cherry said, "On the set? I don't think so," and poked out her tongue at the bodyguard.

"It's non-negotiable," said Maury Lykes.

Turning to her father, Cherry said, "Da-ad! You really want me to get all, like, naked in front of that superfr—" She caught herself just in time, recalling the bodyguard's story about drowning the woman with a boat anchor, some woman who'd called him a rude name. He was probably bullshitting, but what if he wasn't?

Ned Bunterman said, "No worries, punkin. You won't have to pose nude."

"And even if you do," one of the Larks cut in, "Mr.

Chemo wouldn't be standing around slobbering like some school-yard perv. He's a professional."

Cherry's father wished he were back in California, poring over the bills and brokerage statements, or having a spa day with the Jorgensens, his beloved Danes. Once the current crisis passed and Cherry's concert tour began, he could return to a soothing routine of golf, vineyard tours and three-way sex; his wife usually phoned once a day from the road to get the latest numbers, but otherwise Ned Bunterman was not much in demand.

Cherry said, "Who's doing hair and makeup? I don't want Leo anymore, I want Chloe."

"Chloe's in Vancouver," Janet Bunterman said.

"Then send the jet."

"She's on a movie with Hilary Duff."

"God! Not that skank!" Cherry looked around for something to throw, and settled on a sun-dried fig from the fruit platter. "Then what about wardrobe? How can you *not* wear Versace in Miami? Seriously, Mom."

Janet Bunterman adopted a gentle schooling tone. "Sweetie, this isn't going to be like any other photo shoot you've done. The man's a bit eccentric—he demands total control."

"But he's brilliant," chimed one of the twins.

"Claude?" Cherry made a sour face. "He didn't *smell* brilliant."

"Plus he's a huge fan," the other Lark said.

"True. He knew, like, every song I ever did."

Maury Lykes looked pleased. "So then we're good to go, right?"

"Then when can I do the Seaquarium?" Cherry scratched an itch under one of her arms.

"Another day," said her mother.

"But I need to get a new thong, 'kay? For our save-the-whales video."

"Of course, sweetie."

"After I die, see, I really wanted to come back as a whale? But now I don't, 'cause who wants to get, like, stabbed with a harpoon?"

Cherry misread the dead silence in the room as empathy.

Chemo coughed sharply. "I got a question," he said, eyeing Ned Bunterman.

"Yes?"

"All these years, you never had her tested? Hell, she was my kid . . ."

"That's enough," Maury Lykes said.

"Tested for what?" Cherry asked.

Ned Bunterman felt a paternal duty to inform the bodyguard that he wasn't very funny. The man's response was a soul-chilling leer.

"Does he mean HIV?" said Cherry.

"No."

"'Cause I already been tested, like, a hundred times."

Chemo tweaked an inflamed pock on his jawline. "I was talkin' about the test that tells if you're a retard or not."

Maury Lykes signaled time-out and said, "I've got a

meeting with the turds from Ticketmaster in five minutes."
Then, to Chemo: "You and I will talk later."

"Damn right we will."

The meeting broke up, and Ned Bunterman rolled his suitcase down the hallway to his room. He had a terrace with an ocean view, but it was the wrong ocean.

Instead of unpacking, he fixed himself a bourbon.

20

It had been a long time since he'd seen that particular De Niro film—or any film—but the governor understood the reference when the tourist called him "Travis Bickle." This happened while he was waiting in the stolen taxi near the Marriott, after he'd politely informed the man that he was off duty and couldn't drive him to the basketball game. The Heat was playing the Nets.

The tourist, a middle-aged knob in a distressed-leather jacket, had turned to his female friend and said, "Travis Bickle here says he's off duty."

"Sorry," Skink had said.

"Those are the worst fuckin' hair plugs I ever saw. You should sue."

"I changed my mind. Get in."

Skink took the Julia Tuttle Causeway toward the mainland. The man worked for an airline that hubbed in Newark—supervising the night baggage crew, the weight of the entire free world on his shoulders, to hear him tell it. The girlfriend, she did temp work in Brooklyn.

"How much farther?" she asked. "We're gonna miss the tip-off."

The governor asked if it was their first trip to Miami and paid no attention to their reply. He was irked at himself for buckling to a reckless impulse; he should have remained in stakeout position across from the hotel, in case Annie and her kidnapper came out.

But the guy in the leather jacket was such an ass that Skink felt compelled to impart a lesson. It was a chronic weakness; he couldn't let anything slide. Never had. *Why waste your time on these jerks?* Jim Tile always said. *People don't change, Clint.*

And his standard response: *Who cares. It feels right.*

"Are you wasted?" asked the knob from the backseat.

It was then the woman pointed out that their driver bore no resemblance to Mr. Henri Juste-Toussaint, the Haitian gentleman whose face was pictured on the taxi license. The male passenger ordered Skink to pull over and let them out.

"Hang tight. We're almost there," Skink said.

"Stop this cab or I'll kick your fuckin' ass."

"Not likely."

He pulled into the James Scott housing project and parked by a basketball court where a lively pickup game was under way. The court had a sun-bleached concrete surface and chain nets on the hoops and three-point lines that had been spray-painted freehand.

The governor's passengers bolted from the taxi, the woman whipping out her phone to call the cops. Instantly the pickup game came to a halt, as it was not a neighborhood frequented by tourists. Now the only sound was a rhythmic thump of the basketball being bounced by a rangy young brother wearing a Cavs jersey and a pair of old Air Jordans.

To the man in the leather jacket, Skink said: "You're in for a treat. These guys can play."

"This is funny to you?"

"Try to behave and everything will be fine."

"Those fuckin' Heat seats, they cost me a hundred each!"

"Right you are. It's a sin to waste them." The governor snatched the tickets from the guy's fingers and hollered out the window: "Yo! Who wants to go see D-Wade dunk?"

He picked the two smallest dudes on the court and drove them to the downtown arena, where in addition to the asswipe's tickets he gave them some cash to take a real cab home after the game. Waylaid by a massive traffic jam, he crept and crawled back to South Beach and began cruising around the Marriott, searching for a parking spot with a view.

On his third pass he spied young Ann, the actress. She wore a starchy ill-fitting dress but otherwise seemed to be all right. The man at her side was shortish and stout; he had an aqua baseball cap on his head, and a wrap of bright white bandages on one hand. His other hand was concealed in a dark carry bag that he hugged to his chest.

The bad news was, they were entering—not leaving—the hotel. The governor cursed and howled like a gut-shot wolf. It wasn't safe to follow Annie inside, not after the suitcase-burning incident; the Marriott management would almost certainly have beefed up the security crew.

Skink was jolted by a long blast from an air horn, and in the rearview mirror he saw a city bus on his bumper. He lifted his sandy shoe off the brake pedal and eased on down the road, trying to figure out a new move.

Ann DeLusia was amazed that a person could fire a revolver inside a hotel room and not one single guest would call the desk to complain about the noise. But crank up Radiohead for twenty lousy minutes while you're zoning in the tub, and they bring out the damn SWAT team.

"There's no justice," she said, balancing in bare feet on a chair. Bang Abbott was holding her ankles while she used a wad of toilet tissue to pluck the bloody remnant of his fore-finger off the ceiling.

"My trigger finger!" he kept mewling.

Immediately after the gunshot he'd gone pale and wobbly, on the verge of hurling, but he had gathered himself and grabbed the Colt away from her. He'd tried to retrieve the fingertip himself but chair number one had collapsed in pieces under his heft.

"What should I do with this?" Ann asked after hopping down with the mangled chunk.

"For Christ's sake, keep it warm!"

"*You* keep it warm, Claude."

So he wedged the seeping wad into the second-most-humid crevice on his body until they located a Cuban clinic that was open on Sundays. There a young physician's assistant informed him that what remained of the severed forefinger was too damaged to be surgically reattached.

"Don't tell me that," said Bang Abbott, sagging.

"How did this happen?"

"An iguana attacked me." The photographer couldn't reveal the truth, because in Florida medical caregivers were required by law to report all bullet wounds to the police.

"That's quite unusual," the physician's assistant remarked. "It just ran up and bit you for no reason?"

"Well, it was a big-ass iguana." Bang Abbott looked sharply at Ann for backup.

She said, "Do they carry rabies? Because this one was foaming at the mouth."

"I'm not sure," said the physician's assistant, "but I can check online." He deposited the sodden tissue containing Bang Abbott's nub into a red bin marked BIOHAZARDOUS WASTE.

Glaring at Ann, the paparazzo said, "Lizards don't have rabies."

To straighten her up, he pointed at the camera bag, which

was strapped over his left shoulder. That was where he'd put the gun.

"Darling, you should get the shots," she carried on sweetly, "just in case. I know they're dreadfully painful, but still—"

"Let's not waste the man's time," said Bang Abbott. Then, to the physician's assistant: "Just patch up my damn hand, okay?"

Back at the hotel, he cuffed Ann to a leg of the bed and hunkered down with a Nikon to practice pressing the shutter button with his middle finger. It was awkward, the weight of the camera feeling off center in his bulky new grip. The guy at the clinic had gone overboard with the tape and gauze.

Ann said, "You're uptight about tomorrow. I can tell."

"No, I'm in pain." He held up his bandaged paw. "You shot me, remember?"

"It was an accident, Claude. I said I was sorry."

"Just shut up."

"I'm the one who should be pissed, after all the shitty things you've done."

Bang Abbott didn't respond. He was trying to take pictures of a lamp.

"You're lucky I didn't pop you in the nuts," she said.

It wasn't a prudent way to address an armed, emotionally unstable individual, but Ann was mad and hungry, and she needed a bath. "I can't wait for tomorrow," she said.

"Me, neither."

"Oh, yes, you can. You're scared."

"Try psyched." The photographer waggled his untested digit. "This'll work. I'll *make* it work."

In truth, Ann herself was anxious about the meeting at Star Island. Would he really just let her walk away, free as a bird, after Cherry showed up? How could he be sure that she wouldn't run straight to the police?

Cherry's people will take good care of you. That's what Claude had said. So there would be some money offered, which was only fair—getting kidnapped was definitely not part of the job description. Ann intended to raise that issue, and others, with Janet Bunterman.

"You said they're sending a car for me."

"That's right," Bang Abbott said.

"To take me where?"

He peered up from the camera. "How the hell should I know? Back to the Stefano, I guess."

"Maybe I prefer the Setai," Ann said.

"Honey, I don't give a shit if you end up at a Motel 6. I'm tryin' to work here, so shut the hell up or I'll have to gag you."

"You already gag me, Claude."

Ann knew she'd have to call her agent once it was over. Months had passed since she and Marcus had spoken. His last gem of an offer was a leg-modeling gig for a depilatory made with Jamaican mango rind; Ann had declined. Marcus probably would want 15 percent of the payoff from the Buntermans, but in Ann's view that was victim's compensation and therefore exempt from his commission. She, not sockless Marcus in his Bally loafers, was the one held captive at gunpoint. Even by Hollywood standards his agency would appear slimy, trying to gouge a client who'd been abducted and abused. It was not an item you'd want to see in *Variety*. Ann would point that out to young Marcus if he decided to get pissy.

She said, "Maybe I'll go back to L.A. and write a screenplay."

Bang Abbott snickered.

"What?"

"You," he said. "You kill me." He put the camera down and started wiping his lenses. "When this is over, what you should write is your own ticket, understand? They'll give you whatever you want because they got no choice. And if they're too dumb or too cheap to pay up, then you turn the screws. How? Figure it out—somebody tips off somebody, and all of a sudden it's viral: 'Cherry Pye uses a double!' You got a blog, right?"

Ann snapped her fingers. "*That's* what's been missing from my life!"

"Start a blog," Bang Abbott advised. "Go easy at first, but get their attention. And leave me out of it, for sure."

She smiled. "But why, Claude?"

He knelt down heavily and seized her chin and placed his moist round face inches from hers. Ann was startled.

"'Cause nobody will believe that part of the story," he said, "and nobody—not a single human soul—will back you up.

Don't you get it? It'll be your word against mine, and by then Cherry will have seen my pictures and creamed all over herself because she never looked so hot. I'll be golden, princess, and the Larks will put out a statement saying you're just another—"

"Disgruntled ex-employee," Ann murmured through her teeth.

"Bingo. With emotional problems." His breath felt hot and rank on her cheeks. "They'll say you made up the kidnap story just to get attention and advance your own lame career. It'll be so ugly, you'll never recover."

With a grunt he arose. "But, see, the whole look-alike gig," he said, "all these months you've spent behind the scenes, that's a real problem for them. You know certain dates and places, details that could be nailed down by the tabs—like what happened at the Stefano last week. One of the bellhops saw them wheeling Cherry out the kitchen exit, puking in a bucket—you think that mangy little monkey wouldn't sell his story for party money? And he ain't the only one, either. The dam breaks, Cherry and her crew would be *muy* screwed-o. Think about it."

Ann was reluctantly impressed that the paparazzo seemed to have pondered all the angles. She herself had never been good at smelling the blood in the water. Deep at heart, however, she had no appetite for orchestrating a seedy shakedown.

"All I wanna do is go home and start over."

Bang Abbott sneered. "That's what they all say."

"Know what, Claude?"

299

"Spare me. I gotta go unhitch the train." He shuffled into the bathroom and shut the door.

Ann lay down on her back, the handcuffs clinking against the metal leg of the bed. She wondered if the photographer had kept her little black dress, and if there was a chance in hell of getting it dry-cleaned before tomorrow.

Cherry Pye asked, "What's that?"

"Cattle prod," Chemo said. He'd bought it at a farm-supply store in Kissimmee, the same week he was paroled from prison. It was a Sabre-Six Hot-Shot, with a fiberglass shaft and nickel-plated contacts. He used it for jobs that were too dainty for the weed whacker.

"Looks sorta kinky. How's it work?" She was slurping another Red Bull, painting her toenails.

"I've been making a list in my head," Chemo said.

They were outside, on the balcony terrace of her suite, Cherry wearing a DOG THE BOUNTY HUNTER T-shirt and a sky-blue string bikini bottom. The sun was intense so Chemo had smeared his face with SPF 70 sunblock, which made him look like a seven-foot mime. He was waiting for his meeting with Maury Lykes.

"Like, what kinda list?" Cherry asked, and he touched the end of the cattle prod to her bare thigh. She made a noise like a chicken going under the wheels of a truck, and pitched over sideways in the patio chair.

"Every time you say *like*, I prod your ass," he explained.

"Also on the list: *awesome*, *sweet*, *sick*, *totally*, and *hot*. Those are for starters."

She stopped writhing after a minute or so. Her first breathless words were: "What the fuck, dude?"

"That's another one—*dude*. Consider yourself warned."

"It's, like, electric or somethin'?"

He shocked her again. "Hell, yes, it's electric. They use 'em on rodeo bulls."

"But this is how I always talk," she cried. "I can't just stop all of a sudden!"

Chemo figured her brain functioned at the same simple level as livestock's. "Some of the prison guards upstate used to pack these bad boys," he said.

Cherry hopped to her feet and called him a monster and ordered him to throw the cattle prod away.

"Relax. It won't leave a mark," he said.

"How the fuck would *you* like it?" she shouted, then recoiled with a flinch.

The bodyguard smiled. "See, it's already working."

"But how come you didn't zap me?"

"'Cause you used the word the right way—as a verb, not an interjection. 'I like good weed' instead of 'I want some, like, good weed.'"

A Carmelite nun with whom Chemo corresponded in prison once sent him a book of basic grammar, which he practically memorized. His own speech wasn't flawless, yet he tried not to butcher the language.

"No volts for acceptable usage," he said to Cherry.

"I hate you!"

"That's better. Stick with simple sentences."

"I'm tellin' my mother. Maury, too."

Chemo said, "Go ahead. They won't believe you."

He pulled from his pocket the tangerine BlackBerry, which had been trilling all day.

"Hey, my phone!" Cherry exclaimed. "Give it here."

"It's not yours. You stole it from Abbott."

"That is soooo totally bogus."

"Look out," Chemo said, and stung her twice with the cattle prod—once for *totally* and another for *bogus*, although it wasn't officially on the list.

He left her flopping on the terrace and went inside to call Maury Lykes, who'd promised to return after his sit-down with the Ticketmaster people. The promoter answered on the first ring and said he was riding up in the elevator. As soon as he walked into the suite, Chemo looked him over and said, "Ticketmaster, my ass."

Maury Lykes turned crimson. "Mind your own damn business." Cirque de Soleil was auditioning in town, and he'd hooked up with a pair of Czech spinners whose combined age was at least thirty-five. "Where's our girl?" he asked.

"Pilates on the patio," Chemo said.

"What's that thing you got there?"

"Cow motivator."

Maury Lykes exhaled. "Oh Jesus."

"Don't worry. It won't leave a mark."

"Honestly? Anything I don't need to know, I don't wanna know." Hurriedly he led Chemo into one of the bedrooms and shut the door. "Okay," he said, "about Star Island."

"Lay it out."

"Between you and me, I can't afford any more surprises. All this fuckin' drama."

Chemo said, "Exactly."

"Loose ends, whatever. I'm tryin' to run a business here."

"You got enough headaches," the bodyguard agreed.

They briefly discussed the particulars. "But nobody else can know," Maury Lykes said.

"I wasn't gonna send out invitations."

"How's fifty sound?"

"Like you're jerkin' my chain."

"Seventy-five," Maury Lykes countered. "Best I can do."

Chemo's smile belonged in a Gahan Wilson cartoon. The promoter didn't know whether to laugh or crap his pants.

"Maury, you're a goddamn liar. Eighty grand, with forty up front."

"Deal. Now tell me the truth—how's she doing?"

"Cherry?" Chemo's lips curled in distaste. "She's a pain in the ass, but I'm keepin' her straight. Why do you think she hates my guts?"

Maury Lykes turned away. He was standing at a window that overlooked Biscayne Bay. The sun was in his eyes, so he slipped into his blue-mirrored Oakleys.

"When Michael died," he said, "his backlist shot through

the roof. Every album he ever made went back on the charts. Same for Elvis, same for Lennon. But Cherry Pye is no Jacko, and she's no Beatle. She ODs and there'll be a decent retail bump for maybe a month, mainly iTunes, depending on how long they drag out the toxicology. But after that, she's basically finished. Her catalog ain't exactly timeless, okay?"

Chemo was twirling the cattle prod like a baton. "Is this my problem?" he said.

The promoter wheeled around, nervously rubbing his hands together. Chemo thought the shiny sunglasses made him look like a giant deerfly.

"We've sold seventeen, maybe eighteen mil in tickets for the *Skantily* tour," Maury Lykes said, "but, unfortunately, the show's not insured. Nobody would touch her because of all the rehabs, so I had to start my own company and write the fucking coverage myself—which leaves yours truly on the hook in a semi-disastrous way if Cherry's inconsiderate enough to pull a Heath Ledger. So what I'm sayin', my brother, is this: I need you to keep this airhead alive for as long as possible, because she's got no goddamn shelf life once she croaks."

Chemo said, "Can't help you there. Sorry."

"What do you mean?"

"After tomorrow, I'll be movin' on."

"To do what?"

"High-end evictions. The banks, they're hard up for muscle."

"Please," Maury Lykes said, "I'm begging you, don't go."

"No, it's the smart play. Once this thing's done, you won't want me around."

The promoter paused to think about it, and he had to agree.

"Besides," said Chemo, "one more day, I'll end up killin' her myself."

Maury Lykes manufactured a lighthearted laugh, in hopes that the man was joking.

21

As his nickname suggested, Ruben "Whaddup" Coyle was not a man of broad vocabulary. He nevertheless was popular with a particular kind of woman, owing to his stature as a player in the National Basketball Association. Whaddup Coyle currently was listed as a point guard on the roster of the first-place Miami Heat, though he'd been sidelined indefinitely with a groin pull. The injury had occurred not on the basketball court but rather on a three-meter diving board at a private estate in Coconut Grove, while Whaddup Coyle was being ridden reverse cowgirl-style by his real-estate agent, a natural redhead who seemed intent on moving the property.

It was a nice place, six bedrooms and a basement gym, but Whaddup Coyle was looking to rent, not buy. He got traded on average every nineteen months, so he never stayed with one team long enough to flip a house and come out ahead on the deal. And, as even Whaddup Coyle knew, the market in South Florida was especially suck-ass. He made his modest housing intentions known shortly after he and his realtor fell off the diving board, while he was dog-paddling with groin afire toward the marble steps of the pool. The real-estate agent toweled off, wrung out her contraceptive sponge and frostily referred Whaddup Coyle to some rental firm in the Gables. She never called again, yet he soldiered on.

Within a week he'd found a two-story on Venetian Isle that featured not only a lap pool but a billiard room. Best of all, it was only fifteen minutes from South Beach, where Whaddup Coyle was doing most of his rehabilitating, usually into the wee hours. During his journeyman NBA career, Whaddup Coyle had earned a reputation for ragged off-court behavior. Consequently, the coaching staff of the Miami Heat had asked him to please employ a car service whenever he went clubbing. They felt entitled to such a request, since they were paying Whaddup Coyle the profane sum of five million dollars a year and he was scoring—before his injury—a measly seven points a game. The least he could do was hire a driver and stay out of trouble.

But Whaddup Coyle said no thanks. He leased a liquid-silver supercharged XKR convertible, which he soon thereafter wrapped around a pine tree after leaving the Forge (fatigue, he told the state troopers). The second Jaguar he drove off the Rickenbacker into Biscayne Bay (the cop who found him was a hoops fan, and gave a friendly read on the Breathalyzer). A third convertible rolled off the Fisher Island ferry into Government Cut, the vehicle carelessly left in Drive while Whaddup Coyle was distracted by a young heiress to an Italian shoe-polish fortune (swimming, fortunately, was among her myriad talents).

Now Whaddup Coyle was on his fourth Jag, and the leasing company had warned it would be his last. He'd also received a stern phone call from his coach, who'd gotten wind of the other mishaps and now wanted Whaddup Coyle to come in for a physical, which was league code for a urine test and drug screen. Because of the contractual repercussions attached to proof of substance abuse, Whaddup Coyle contrived to forestall the medical exam as long as possible and allow his six-foot-six system to repurify itself. He swore off marijuana, cocaine and opiates, heroically limiting himself to alcohol, which was not only legal but disappeared from the bloodstream within hours after intake.

Sunday nights being relatively quiet on South Beach, Whaddup Coyle had difficulty finding a party after the Heat–Nets game. His favorite hangouts were dead, so he tried the Shore Club, where he traded phone numbers with a Finnish model who promised to meet him later at the Rose Bar in the Delano. She showed up with a utility infielder for the Arizona Diamondbacks and proposed they all get a room. At first Whaddup Coyle was cold to the idea, but eventually his curiosity about Scandinavian poon outweighed his disdain for baseball players. He thought it actually might be fun to show off in front of the little runt.

So he charged the room to his Platinum Card, and up the elevator they went. The last thing Whaddup Coyle remembered with clarity was chugging the dregs from a magnum of unpronounceable champagne while the model and the infielder grappled on the carpet, snorting like goats. One of them would pause every so often to suck on Whaddup Coyle's toes, which failed to make him feel like an equal participant.

Now, he gradually came to perceive that he was back in the Jag, slumped over the steering wheel. The top was up, the engine was running, his feet were bare and dawn was breaking. A man was rapping on the windshield, and Whaddup Coyle assumed he was a cop—with any luck, a reader of the sports pages. Whaddup Coyle aimed a sheepish smile at the broad silhouette.

"Whaddup, Officer?"

"You're in no shape to drive."

"Big fun last night."

"Out," the man said.

Emerging from the car, Whaddup Coyle saw that his visitor was most definitely not a police officer. The man's skin was baked brown, like an Indian's, and one eye was messed up. He wore a funky trench coat and his scalp was shaved bald, except for two mismatched sprouts that rattled with red and green attachments.

Whaddup Coyle labored to steady himself. He was distressed to observe that the Jaguar's rear end was crumpled;

apparently he'd backed into the concrete wall of a kosher bakery and nodded off. A flattened tin garbage can protruded from beneath one of the rear wheels.

"Aw shit," he said.

The stranger got into the XKR and revved the engine.

"Say, whaddup?" re-inquired Whaddup Coyle.

"It's drivable," the man said.

"Are you for real jackin' this bitch?"

"Call it a loan."

"Fuck that," Whaddup Coyle said. "This is *my* ride, old man."

When he seized the guy by the shoulder, something metallic and heavy came down upon his hand. It was the barrel of a shotgun, and Whaddup Coyle wondered why he hadn't noticed it earlier. He thought: *I must be totally trashed.*

"Here's the deal," the man said.

"Naw, we're cool." Whaddup Coyle backpedaled until he found himself braced against the bakery wall. He felt woozy and nauseated.

"Where are your shoes?" the stranger asked.

"Fuck if I know."

The man pointed. "Collins is thataway. It's your best shot at a taxi." Then he drove off in the imported convertible.

As drunk as Whaddup Coyle was, he realized it would be counterproductive at that moment to summon the authorities. The police report would likely make mention of his polluted condition and then a story would wind up in the *Herald*, which wouldn't improve his standing with the coach.

So he decided to go home and sleep it off. Later he would phone the leasing company and say the Jaguar had been stolen from his driveway during the night. That way, if the car turned up, they wouldn't blame him for the damage. Had to be the thief who wrecked it, right? So please send over a new one right away—that's what Ruben "Whaddup" Coyle would say. Liquid silver, same as the others.

It was a sweet plan, and he congratulated himself for stitching it together so swiftly. Then he doubled over and keeled unconscious into a box of stale pumpernickel.

Had D. T. Maltby not been such a cheapskate, he wouldn't have found himself in the sticky position of being interviewed by an overly diligent Monroe County detective.

"It's no big deal," he insisted.

"A break-in is always a big deal," Detective Reilly said, not bothering to add: Especially at the Ocean Reef Club.

"What did the intruder look like, Mr. Maltby?"

"Just a bum. You know, some pathetic crackhead."

The former lieutenant governor had no intention of identifying Clinton Tyree or steering law enforcement in the direction of that vengeful degenerate. Maltby had called the police only because the insurance company required a report and a case number.

"Was he tall or short?" Reilly asked.

"I really couldn't say. See, he was sittin' down."

"Defecating in your dryer."

"Washer," Maltby said tightly.

"You're absolutely sure he didn't say anything?"

"Look, I already told you what happened—he took a shit and ran off. Could you please just write up the report?"

The detective asked Maltby why he'd waited days before reporting the break-in.

"Because I didn't want to bother you folks over somethin' this dumb—it's the damn insurance people who made me call."

Reilly said, "It's not dumb, Mr. Maltby, it's a felony home invasion. You say nothing was stolen."

"No, sir."

"That's pretty weird to think this person broke in just for the purpose of—"

"Hey, people are nuts," Maltby interjected uselessly.

"—emptying his bowels in your washing machine, even though there was a perfectly comfortable bathroom down the hall."

"Obviously the guy's a sicko." Maltby was becoming exasperated. "But, come on, it's not the crime of the century."

"A speedboat was stolen from one of your neighbors on the same night."

"So I heard." Maltby was hoping Tyree had taken off for the Bahamas. Maybe he would capsize in the Gulf Stream and drown.

The detective said a wandering vagrant had been

implicated in some recent bizarre incidents on North Key Largo. "Do you know a man named Jackie Sebago?"

Maltby's tongue turned to chalk. He never should have bothered with the insurance. He should have bitten the bullet and paid for a new goddamn washer out of his own pocket. Now here he was, lying through his teeth to a cop.

"The name doesn't ring a bell," he said.

Reilly related that Mr. Sebago and several associates had been hijacked on Card Sound Road by a deranged-looking street person carrying a sawed-off shotgun. "He described the man as tall with a partially bald head and one bad eye. The suspect also had a young woman with him. Mr. Sebago was personally assaulted in an unusual way."

"That's awful," Maltby said with a false wince.

He preferred that the detective remain unaware he had illegally fixed the building permits for Jackie Sebago's townhouse project, and then unfixed them after being threatened by the ex-governor, his former partner in politics, who shat in his Whirlpool. After the break-in, Maltby had jammed the tracks of all the sliding doors with broom handles. Still he hadn't slept a wink.

Reilly said, "What I'm thinking—you're a well-known person in Florida."

"Not really. Not anymore."

"But what happened to you is so . . ."

"Warped?"

"Personal," said Reilly. "It seems almost like a grudge thing."

Maltby stiffened up to scoff. "That's ridiculous. I never saw that jerk before in my life. And he didn't have a gun, or a girlfriend."

"Maybe somebody paid him to throw a scare in you," the detective speculated. It was the same theory he'd floated past Jackie Sebago the day before. "Are you involved in any unpleasant business situations?"

"None."

"Personal disputes?"

"Nope."

"What about your wife, Mr. Maltby? Are there any family circumstances that could stir up this kind of hostility?"

"Hell no!" Maltby was beside himself. "Holy Jesus, it's just some wingnut happened to pick my house to pinch a loaf in. He's probably halfway to Key West and meanwhile my laundry's piling up, okay? All I need is for you to write up a damn report so I can put in for a new washing machine."

"Of course," said Reilly, reaching for his clipboard. "But this time you might consider one of those front-loading models."

"Not funny."

"In case the guy comes back."

If the Star Island session unfolded as Bang Abbott anticipated, he would finish the day with enough stark portraits for a lavish coffee-table volume, to be rushed into print within weeks of Cherry's final breath.

Such were the heights of his delusion.

"You're a silly man," Ann DeLusia said.

"Hold still." He snapped half a dozen more frames.

"Let's see 'em," she said.

He was studying the images of Ann in the viewfinder. "The tatt's fading," he remarked.

"Not fast enough."

"Have you put on some weight? Check out your little jelly roll in this one."

"Drop dead, Claude."

Actually, the photos looked pretty good—Ann cuffed to the bed, sitting cross-legged on the floor of the motel room. Bang Abbott was pleased with himself; shooting with a different trigger finger wasn't so hard, once he'd gotten used to it.

"Where's my little black dress?" she asked.

"Forget it. You shot me."

"That was your own fault. Don't be such a wuss-boy."

He said, "The dress is a filthy rag. Besides, I need it for Star Island."

"Tell me you're not giving it to *her*!"

"Absolutely. It'll look like she wore it to a gang bang."

"You, sir," Ann said, "are all class. Here, let me see."

He handed over the camera and she scrolled critically through the frames. "I told you I don't do well in captivity," she said. "Where's the damn delete button?"

Bang Abbott took back the Nikon and erased the pictures click-click-click. "They made you look real, and that's the whole idea. To come across as human."

"As opposed to what—a werewolf?" said Ann.

Breakfast was a prehistoric granola bar that he dug out of his camera bag. He ate nothing himself, which was unprecedented. She could see he was jumpy and wired, suggesting at least a residual connection to reality. *There's no way*, thought Ann, *that today will go exactly as planned.* It was about time Claude got nervous.

"How old are you?" she asked.

"Forty-four."

"Ever been married?"

"What for?"

"Oh yeah, I forgot. You paparazzi studs get laid all the time. On Learjets, no less."

"It was a Gulfstream."

Ann said, "Fifty bucks says she won't even remember."

He winked. "A hundred says she'll never forget."

"Silly man."

"Rich man," said Bang Abbott. He unlocked the cuffs and told her to put on some clothes, which meant the frumpy cotton dress he'd bought at the secondhand shop.

"Is it time, Claude?"

"Yup," he said. "Get your cute little bum in gear."

The kid from room service was quavering in the coat closet. Chemo reached in and administered another zing with the cattle prod.

"Tell me again," he said. "Don't leave anything out."

When the kid stopped thrashing, he wheezed through the list of what he'd brought to Cherry's suite: Xanax, tramadol, Ecstasy, Bayer gelcaps, Ex-Lax, banana nut Cheerios and a bottle of Stoli.

"But she didn't do it all!" he cried.

Chemo was ticked off at himself for making another bush-league mistake. Cherry had only been pretending to sleep when he snuck downstairs for a steak. He couldn't have been gone more than an hour, but he returned to the suite just as the kid from room service was creeping out. The wiry little ape sported a fresh hickey on his sternum, which was visible only because Cherry had peeled off his tuxedo jacket and shirt. The suck mark bore a signature—"Cherish"—scrawled with a pink Sharpie.

After Chemo shoved the kid in the closet, he called a number that one of the Larks had provided his first day on the job. The line belonged to a doctor who'd previously treated Cherry's "gastritis," and was known to be prompt.

"Is she breathing?" he had asked.

"Like a snot fountain."

"I'll be there in twenty minutes."

After further prodding, the kid from room service informed Chemo that Cherry had paid him six hundred bucks, the fee negotiated during an afternoon delivery of pomegranate juice and toast points. It had taken a while to scrounge up all the drugs, which the kid had stashed in the kitchen's pastry locker until Cherry had called to say the coast was clear. And although she'd welshed on her promise of a blow job, she had granted him permission to post a snapshot of the autographed hickey on his Facebook page.

Chemo booted the kid and stalked to Cherry's bedroom. She was outstretched on the floor, humming "Yellow Submarine" and blinking up at the ceiling while snapping the waistband on a pair of silk boxers, which was all she wore. The carpet was mined with mucky puddles of Cheerio-filled vomit. It was a bad scene; worse, it made Chemo look bad. He had been hired to prevent such reckless nonsense.

With his intact arm he scooped her up and stood her under a cold shower. For balance, she dug her fingernails into his cloaked prosthesis.

"What time izzit?" she asked.

"Four-thirty."

"In the mornin'?"

"Wash your face," he said.

"Don't tell Mom about the dope, 'kay? And I promise not to tell her 'bout the cattle taze, so we're, like, even."

"Jesus H. Christ." Chemo plucked a white oblong pill from her hair and flicked it into the toilet.

Cherry laughed. "What really happened to your face? C'mon, tall dude. Whisper in baby's ear."

She started to wobble, so he gave her a slap. "Get your act together. We got a big day."

"I don't wanna go back to rehab," she drooled. "I wanna stay naughty."

Chemo dried her off and wrapped her in a robe. The

doctor arrived, stinking of cigar-bar cologne. He wore jogging shoes and a shiny track suit and a colored rubber bracelet on one wrist. Chemo wouldn't have allowed the man to treat a guinea pig.

After a cursory examination, the doctor said he could either send Cherry to the hospital for observation or keep her under bed rest at the Stefano for a day. "We'll pump some fluids. Get a nurse to stay close."

Chemo wasn't keen on either option as they would interfere with the Star Island photo appointment and therefore his pay-day. Based on experience—and he'd seen many overdoses during his bouncer days—Cherry wasn't on the verge of death, or even a mild coma. The bodyguard phoned the Larks and described the situation.

"No hospital," they decreed, in unison.

"What about calling mom and dad?"

On that question the sisters were split, so Chemo made an executive decision. He was in no mood to deal with the Buntermans. After dismissing the doctor, he hauled Cherry to the other bedroom and buzzed the housekeeping department, which was accustomed to mopping superstar barf from the master suites. By nine o'clock, when Ned and Janet Bunterman showed up, the carpet was dry and the stink was gone. Most importantly, Cherry had made it through the night without fatally aspirating.

"She's still asleep," Chemo reported.

"No tummy problems?" her mother asked lightly.

"Nuthin serious."

While Janet Bunterman went to check on her daughter, Ned Bunterman bungled an attempt at small talk.

"Can I ask what happened to your arm?" he inquired, provoking Chemo to unharness the weed whacker and lay waste to a bouquet of Chinese peonies that had been thoughtfully placed by the hotel staff upon the walnut cabinet of the entertainment center. From that response Ned Bunterman discerned that the bodyguard was overly sensitive and likely a sociopath, and spoke to him no further.

Cherry's mother emerged from the bedroom looking fretful.

"The poor thing's exhausted," she said.

Chemo said Cherry was up half the night watching pornos on Pay-per-View. Her parents seemed almost relieved to hear it.

"But no visitors, right?" Janet Bunterman said.

"Just room service."

Ned Bunterman looked at his watch, a signal to his wife that Cherry should be roused. "I'm sure she'll feel good as new after breakfast," he said. "I'll call down for some oatmeal and honeydew."

"Yuk!" It was his daughter, listing in the doorway of the bedroom. She didn't look dazzling but at least had managed to dress herself—jeans, flip-flops and a UCLA sweatshirt. "I am *so* not hungry for oatmeal," she snapped at her father.

"Then how about a smoothie?"

When Cherry spotted her bodyguard, she glowered and took a shaky step forward. "That guy, Mom, that perv over there—he electrocuted me with a thingie they use on cows!"

Chemo affected an expression of wry bewilderment.

"He belongs in freaking jail!" she screamed at her parents.

"Now, honey, stop . . ." said Ned Bunterman fearfully.

But Cherry's mother looked elated.

"That's our girl! All pumped up for *Vanity Fair*!"

22

Tanner Dane Keefe was informed by his personal assistant that he would be leaving the island for the day.

"Where'm I going?" he asked.

"Wherever you like."

"But I wanna stay here."

"Your friend Cherry needs the place for a photo shoot."

The estate had been on the market for three years, despite the listing agent's dogged efforts. On Star Island the principal selling point for property was the celebrity of its previous owners, so realtors were skilled at strategic name-dropping. Every house that came up for sale was presented as the former residence of Capone, Sly, Shaq, Cher, Johnny, Rosie, Julio, Diddy or Madonna. Occasionally an inexperienced agent would toss in Mickey Rourke or one of the Bee Gees.

Prospective buyers seldom checked the veracity of these glamorous claims because they preferred not to deflate a good story.

The home being rented by Tanner Dane Keefe had in fact been built and occupied for many years by a wholesale distributor of three-way Foley catheters. He wasn't famous but he was very wealthy. The present owner, a Venezuelan bauxite tycoon, had soured on the house after his young wife dumped him for a deejay at Crobar and skipped off to San Juan.

Now, with the economy in the crapper, not many rich people seemed eager to fork out seventeen million for six bedrooms, two pools, a dock, a cheese cellar and a wet bar upon which Cindy Crawford might or might not have simulated a pole dance. Having dropped his price twice already, the Venezuelan was hoping that a photo spread in an upscale American magazine might chum up some prospects. He had no qualms about displacing his tenant for a day.

"But this is *my* crib," Tanner Dane Keefe protested.

His personal assistant yanked off the covers and saw, to her relief, that he was alone in bed.

After wiping his nose on the pillow, the actor sat up. "Hey, what about the whale video? You were supposed to call the Seaquarium."

"Your breakfast is ready. Scrambled eggs, runny."

"From free-range quail, right? Otherwise I won't touch 'em."

"Of course." The personal assistant, who'd purchased new Palin frames after losing hers to Cherry Pye's bodyguard, steered Tanner Dane Keefe toward the bathroom.

"And the Tabasco sauce—"

"Organic," she lied.

"Cool."

"Don't forget to brush your tongue."

The actor was groomed, fed and dressed by the time the photographer and his female helper arrived. They didn't bring much equipment: a couple of cameras and two kinky props—a handgun and a pair of handcuffs.

"Why can't I stay and watch?" Tanner Dane Keefe asked.

The photographer's helper, whose name was Annie, said, "Sorry, sport. Mr. Abbott runs a closed set."

Tanner Dane Keefe had briefly met the woman before—the night that Cherry had gotten into the birdseed—though he didn't remember.

"But I wanna see her pictures," he said.

"Absolutely—when they come out in *Vanity Fair*. We'll send you a pre-pub copy."

"*Vanity Fair*? Are you shitting me?"

"She'll be the August cover," said the helper.

Tanner Dane Keefe's personal assistant led the crestfallen young man outside to his leased Lexus coupe and settled him in the passenger seat. He'd been trying to get the cover of a major magazine in advance of his new film, but so far no solid offers had materialized. Even the surfer mags were balking, owing to the necrophilia angle.

"That fucking Tarantino," fumed Tanner Dane Keefe, "he's gonna hog all the media."

"You need a new publicist," the personal assistant asserted loyally, sliding behind the wheel.

"Can't I at least hang around till Cherry gets here?"

"Be a luv and fasten your seat belt."

Coming out of the circular driveway, they saw two cars parked on Star Island Drive in front of the estate. One was a black sedan, and the other was a Jaguar with a crimped rear fender.

The actor instantly perked up, thinking the silver convertible belonged to his Vicodin connection.

"No, Tanner," said his personal assistant. "Doctor Angie drives a Vette."

"Your Town Car's here," Bang Abbott told Ann DeLusia.

The chauffeur had called when he arrived. He hadn't bothered to mention the Jag that rolled up behind him.

"When is Princess Red Bull due?" Ann asked.

"Any minute," Bang Abbott said.

"You're gonna miss me, Claude. I'm good company."

The paparazzo huffed snidely. "We'll meet again."

"Hope not," said Ann.

"Remember, soon as they get here—"

"I know, I know. Stay in the kitchen."

"Don't fuck this up," Bang Abbott warned.

On one point the Buntermans had been adamant: If Ann

showed her face in front of their daughter, the photo session was off. The psycho bodyguard would rush Cherry back to the Stefano.

"Where are you going to set up?" Ann asked.

"Not sure." They'd made a hasty tour of the house, Bang Abbott checking out the hues and the layout and the lighting. Cherry's portraits would come off stark and artsy in black and white, but the publisher could charge more money for the book if Bang Abbott shot in full color. Digital made it easy to try both ways.

Ann said, "I vote for the bedroom with the red drapes. It screams skank."

When the doorbell chimed, Bang Abbott pushed Ann down a hallway toward the kitchen. His jowls were flushed and his expression was feral.

"Beast mode," she whispered.

"Get lost!"

"Tell Janet I'll be waiting."

Ann located some cream cheese in the cavernous Sub-Zero and lathered up a stale bagel. To settle her nerves she nuked a mug of chamomile tea, which made her stomach gurgle. Soon she had to pee, but she was afraid to venture out. Edging closer to the door, she could hear voices, a muted rhythm of civil conversation. Nobody was shouting or arguing. Soon came a clicking of footsteps on the hardwood floor, and Cherry's mother whisked into the kitchen. She fixed Ann with a gaze of elated relief, her eyes welling as she scampered forward with open arms. Ann figured she'd been practicing the sappy overture on one of the Larks.

After a smothering hug, Janet Bunterman stepped back and looked her up and down, as if beholding the sight of long-lost kin. "Oh, Annie, thank God you're all right!"

"I'm not all right. Check out the dress, Janet—I look like the hostess at a polygamist barn dance."

"You look just fine," Cherry's mother said.

"We need to talk."

"I know."

"Right now," Ann said.

"Not a good time." Janet Bunterman cut her eyes toward the door and in a hushed voice said, "Cherry's here."

"Yes. Such a delicate creature."

"It's scary dealing with a reckless criminal like Abbott. I'm sure you appreciate the risk we're taking—it's all for you, Annie."

"What a crock. You're just scared he'll send out those needle pictures."

Cherry's mother began to look uncomfortable. "Well, there's that."

Ann repositioned to block her exit. "The night I got snatched," she said, "you reported the car missing—but not me?"

"The Larks had some concerns."

"I'm sure they did."

"Sometimes these situations are best handled without the police. It works out better for everybody," Janet Bunterman said.

"I could be dead right now."

"Oh, Annie."

She said it with a frothy, condescending laugh. Ann's reaction was to pin her somewhat roughly against the refrigerator. "What if that asshole had shot me, Janet? Did you guys have a story ready? If my bullet-riddled body floated up in Biscayne Bay?"

Cherry's mother was startled by Ann's muscle, not to mention her testy attitude. "You're safe and sound, aren't you? For heaven's sake, let go of me."

"Claude was right. I'm just another loose end."

Ann had thought she'd prepared herself for the dirty truth, but she was shaking with anger. After releasing her grip on Janet Bunterman, she levered herself up on the glossy granite countertop and planted her chin in her hands.

"You people are incredible," she said.

"Go back to the hotel and get some sleep. That's what you need." Janet Bunterman was well practiced at affecting sympathy. "Ned and I know you've been through hell, Annie, and we're gonna do whatever we can to make it all better. But first we've gotta deal with this lunatic paparazzo."

On the stove was a teakettle, in which Ann could see the reflection of the henna tattoo on her neck. There was, she had to concede, a comic aspect to her misadventure.

"Tell me," Cherry's mother said, "is he violent?"

"You mean Claude? That's an interesting question."

The hallway door opened and Ned Bunterman came in, dressed for either golf or happy hour at a strip joint.

Immediately he began fawning on Ann, saying what a trouper she was; a champ, an ace, a team player.

"Do you mind?" she said irritably.

"Annie's not feeling well," Janet Bunterman told her husband.

"I am *so* sorry. Why don't you go back to the Stefano and get some breakfast in your tummy?" Ned Bunterman suggested. "They make a killer mimosa."

Ann removed a spatula from the brass utensil rack and smacked Cherry's father smartly on one ear. All she said was, "Mimosa, my ass."

Janet Bunterman looked stunned, yet she was slow to move to her husband's side. It was clear that she'd misjudged the depth of Ann's discontent, a greater cause of concern than Ned's whimpering.

"Just go away," Ann said to Cherry's parents.

"Of course, honey." Janet Bunterman motioned for Ned to man up. "So, Annie, we'll see you back at the hotel?"

"No chance."

The Buntermans spun around and saw a large man with loud braids and a shotgun cradled in one arm. He filled the doorway that led from the kitchen to the courtyard, the passage through which Ann DeLusia was supposed to discreetly exit the premises.

Ann brightened at the sight of him, thinking: *So* there *you are!*

Cherry's mother and father were clutching each other for the first time in years. The fearsome intruder had broad shoulders, a gleaming pate and a bum eye. He wore a soiled trench coat but no shirt, and strung from a belt loop was some poor dead creature, possibly a bunny.

"Who are these bumblefucks?" he asked Ann.

Hopping off the counter, she said, "They call themselves Ned and Janet."

He raised the gun. "I loaded up with rat shot."

"No, captain, don't."

"Fine, then. You come with me."

Ann said, "All I want is a hot bath."

The man she knew as Skink threw back his head and laughed, a rolling quake that discouraged Ned Bunterman from intervening. Meanwhile, his wife was poleaxed by the stranger's smile, which was telegenic and appealing.

"Get your stuff," the man said to Ann.

"This is it. I am stuff-less."

"Magnificent!"

Then they were gone, out the back door, leaving the Buntermans to wonder what were the odds of Ann DeLusia, a nobody, being kidnapped twice in the same week.

Although she'd had sex on a Gulfstream jet probably a dozen times, Cherry Pye could recall the details of only one airborne encounter—with Lev, her pierced-cock, Mossad-trained former bodyguard. She'd been cold sober that night, which accounted for the uncharacteristically vivid memory. Lev had talked her into trying some exotic position called a "modified Turkish drill press" and, by the time they were done, Cherry was gasping into one of those Dixie-cup oxygen masks. For weeks afterward she'd worn a cervical collar, which she saved as a memento of Lev's gallant pounding.

By contrast, the only thing Cherry recalled from her high-flying shag with the pudgy paparazzo was that he had the same name as her dead cat.

"'Sup, Claude?" she said.

"We finally meet again."

They were in the vaulted living room of Tanner's place. Cherry noticed that the Persian rug was rolled up and the furniture had been pushed in a cluster to one side. A lone straight-backed chair stood in the middle of the bare hardwood floor.

"So, what's the look you're after?" she asked.

"Raw," Bang Abbott said.

"And this is going in *Vanity Fair*? For real."

"It's the cover, sugar—didn't they tell you?"

He wore a baseball cap, baggy khakis and a rumpled brown bowling shirt that covered his gut. Although Cherry was not usually perceptive, especially after a night of heavy drugging, she felt something about the shoot wasn't right. The photographer seemed jumpy, and the room didn't look like a serious set. There were no assistants scurrying around; no lights or backdrops or wardrobe racks. And no bottled spring water on ice!

"How come you only got two cameras?" she asked.

"That's all I need."

"What about my makeup?"

"I told you, we're going raw." Bang Abbott turned to Chemo, who'd been standing sullenly by the double doors. The bodyguard's beret and fruity little eyeglasses failed to soften his malignant presence. Still, Bang Abbott screwed up the nerve to say: "You can wait outside, bro."

"And you can kiss my balls, fat boy."

"Now, wait—"

"I got orders," Chemo said, thinking: *The dumbass, he doesn't know the half of it.*

"Then I'm gonna have to frisk you," said Bang Abbott.

The bodyguard simultaneously raised his good arm and his prosthesis. The shadow he cast on the white wall looked like a crane with a bum wing. As the paparazzo nervously patted him down, Chemo whispered, "We'll talk later, just you and me."

Bang Abbott had been awaiting the threatened shakedown, the thug expecting money for some imagined service or favor. "Sure. Whatever," Bang Abbott said.

"Where's the actress?"

"On her way back to the hotel."

"In one piece?" Chemo asked. He wasn't sure why he cared.

Bang Abbott nodded. "Bitchy as ever. They sent a car to pick her up."

The Buntermans came in, clearly rattled.

"Now what's wrong?" Chemo said.

Cherry's mother waved him off. "Nothing. It's all good."

"The fuck happened to your ear?" Chemo asked Ned Bunterman, who shrugged peevishly and looked away.

Cherry told her parents that she couldn't possibly start the photo shoot without chilled Pellegrinos and a bowl of blue M&Ms. Janet Bunterman hurried to the kitchen and returned with two bottles of Aquafina and a box of Triscuits. Cherry made a face and pretended to gag herself with two fingers.

Bang Abbott said, "Nothing until lunch! I want her looking lean and hungry."

"But Mom!" Cherry protested.

"Sweetie, please? Do what the man says. He's the pro."

Ned Bunterman said, "Cherry, come on, it's the cover of *VF.* This is huge."

"But I feel like crapola."

"Well, you certainly don't *look* like crapola. Does she, Mr. Abbott?"

The paparazzo held out his arms and framed her face with his fingers. "She looks golden to me," he said.

Cherry snorted, but Bang Abbott could tell she was pleased by the compliment. He told her parents it was time for them to go. When they reached the marble foyer he dropped his voice: "You think I'm Ted Bundy, Jr., but wait'll you see how these shots turn out. It's gonna be legend."

Ned Bunterman was still grappling with the idea that his famously hot daughter had humped such a homely wanker. Was this her way of rebelling, he wondered, or was she just a tramp at heart?

"Don't try anything porny," he told the photographer, "or the deal's off. Mr. Chemo knows what to do."

"No worries, Pop." Bang Abbott chucked him on the shoulder.

Chemo gave a sober nod to indicate the situation was under control, so Ned Bunterman turned and followed his wife out the front door.

Back in the living room, Cherry was pitching a minor snit. "What'm I supposed to wear? I hate this!"

Bang Abbott presented Ann's little black dress. She held it up, sneering at the label.

"It's all wrinkled and funky," she complained.

"That's the concept, honey."

"Gross!"

"Put it on. You will positively rule."

"But I want Versace, goddammit. We're in freaking Miami!"

The paparazzo placed both hands over his heart. "Trust me, Cherish. Please?"

She smiled at the sound of her future name. "I can't believe you, like, totally remembered."

From across the room, Chemo barked, "What'd you say, girl?"

Although the bodyguard had left the livestock prod in his car, Cherry reflexively amended her grammar. "I said I can't believe he remembered."

Bang Abbott winked. "Hey, I remember *everything*."

"Me, too," Cherry said, with a sly wink of her own.

"Seriously?"

"What happened on the G5? Dude, I haven't stopped thinkin' about it."

It was purely idiotic to believe her, but Bang Abbott was nudged in that direction by a stirring in his flab-shaded loins. He did not often hear unpaid women remark favorably upon his sexual prowess.

"Did I hear *dude*?" It was the bestumped bodyguard, calling out Cherry again.

"I said 'Claude,' 'kay? God, would you lighten up!" She rolled her eyes and whispered to Bang Abbott: "Superfreak. Major."

"Tell me about it."

She reached for his wrist and held up his hand, studying the bandaged finger. "Who bit ya, dude?"

"Shakira," he said. "Let's put on some music."

"I was in a Nickelback video. You ever see it? The one where I'm a astronaut?"

"Duh. I only got it saved on my iPod."

"Get outta town!"

There was a Jack Johnson CD in the sound deck and Bang Abbott turned it on. He would have preferred something raunchy but he didn't want to waste time rummaging through the stereo cabinet.

"Go get dressed," he said to Cherry.

"Hey, round dude, you got any homegrown?"

"Sorry, babe."

"Medicinal?"

"Nope," he said. "Powder room's down the hall. You can change there."

She grinned, and right there began stripping out of her sweatshirt and jeans. Bang Abbott was so flustered that he forgot to remove the lens cover from his camera. By the time he collected himself, Cherry had wriggled into Ann DeLusia's black cocktail dress. It fit her fabulously.

She said, "Tanny's got some Lortabs stashed under his bed."

"Breakfast of champions," said Bang Abbott. "Maybe later."

He positioned her in the chair and snapped a handcuff on one wrist, letting the open cuff dangle like bling. Cherry giggled and said, "I likey."

Chemo put down his magazine and moved closer to supervise. Bang Abbott showed him the Colt, spinning the cylinder like they did in old Westerns. "Don't worry," he said, "it's empty."

The bodyguard uncloaked his motorized lawn trimmer and let the cover drop to the floor. Bang Abbott twitched. "Listen, man, you gotta chill or I can't work my magic."

"I invented chill," said Chemo, and ambled toward the kitchen in search of pastries.

Bang Abbott found himself alone, completely alone, with Cherry. Overcome by a swirl of clashing emotions, he started panting like a Saint Bernard. A flush of perspiration dampened his shirt as he plopped to his knees beside her chair.

"I've got somethin' to show you," he said.

"'Kay."

He struggled to steady the Nikon so that she could see the photograph displayed on the viewfinder. She chirped, "Oh, yeah, I 'member that day!"

It was one of the self-portraits she'd taken with his camera at the Stefano, the shot in which she was crossing her eyes and sticking out her tongue.

"Why?" Bang Abbott demanded.

"Why what? You mean the tatt?" Her uncuffed hand went to her neck.

"No, I mean that face," he said. "The face you're making! Where do you get off?"

The former Cheryl Bunterman stared at him with crystal perplexity. Claude seemed really upset.

"It was *my* camera," he went on, red-faced. "You knew I'd find this awful picture, right? You had to know! So this was some kind of snotty little joke, correct? 'Even though we screwed our brains out on the airplane, here's what I really think of you, asshole.'"

"Whoa" was all she could say.

Among the benefits of undeserved wealth and fame was never having to deal with the hurt feelings of others. Those duties were always handled by someone else, in order to spare the star from distracting outbursts of tears or recriminations. Consequently, Cherry Pye was left adrift by the photographer's mystifying reaction to her cross-eyed pose, which had been nothing more than a hoot. She had no idea why it upset him, how it was remotely connected to their forgettable speed fuck on the Gulfstream, or what to say.

"The picture wasn't for you," she told him. "It was for, like, nobody."

"Bullshit."

"Jesus, Claude, I was probably toasted."

He rose up, sucking in a deep, raspy breath. His heart was pounding so hard that his moobs were jiggling beneath the bowling shirt. He thought: *What the hell's happening to me?*

Cherry said, "How trashed I was? I even put one of those stupid photos up on MySpace."

Bang Abbott grunted. "Yeah, I saw it. Least you kept your tongue in your mouth."

"You went on my page?"

"I told you I was a fan." He used the baseball cap to mop his brow. "Why'd you crop out your boobs?" he asked.

Cherry sighed crossly. "Wasn't my idea. It was Mom's."

Bang Abbott heard himself say: "The truth? The one you posted, that was a pretty sexy shot."

She glowed. "I was just goofin' in the bathroom mirror."

"We can do way better."

"Seriously?"

The paparazzo didn't like anything that reminded him of a beach, but the ultra-mellow surf music coming out of the speakers seemed to have a leveling effect. He felt his pulse begin to quiet and his focus return.

"I can make you look so damn hot," he said to Cherry, "they'll all be blown away. I mean speechless."

"Yeah?"

"We're talkin' *iconic*."

She wasn't sure what the word meant, but she tossed her hair, licked her lips and said, "All right, baby, let's do it."

"That's my girl." Bang Abbott raised the camera and took aim.

23

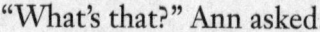"What's that?" Ann asked.

"Lunch."

"Yes, but *what*?"

"Southern cottontail," said Skink.

Ann remarked that he was probably the only person driving a Jaguar convertible around South Beach who had a roadkill rabbit strung to his trousers.

He said, "Could be worse."

"How'd you find me? You're a long way from home."

"The question is why."

"I suppose," Ann said.

"Because you give me hope for the species."

"Then you're in rough shape."

"I have some bad days," Skink conceded.

"Can we get one thing out of the way? I'm grateful for the ballsy rescue and all, but—"

"No nookie."

"'Fraid not."

He grinned. "Annie, I'm old enough to be your grandpa."

"Men are men." She was thinking of Lawrence, the philandering flutist, and others. "Captain, where's your shower cap? It definitely made a statement."

"Lost at sea," he said.

The cloudless sky was pearly blue, and a cool breeze riffled in from the Atlantic. He had the top down, so they were drawing plenty of attention, even on Ocean Drive. On impulse he recited the haggis poem in his best Scottish accent, which wasn't great. Ann listened politely, then suggested they ditch the Jag and walk to the Stefano. He drove back to the kosher bakery where he'd taken the car from the drunken basketball player and parked in the same spot and wiped off the fingerprints. Then he concealed the sawed-off shotgun in the downspout of a rain gutter. Because he refused to part with the rabbit, Ann buttoned his trench coat to conceal the limp little corpse.

Upon entering the hotel they were accosted by a security man with piggish eyes and a bad buzz cut.

"I have a room here. I'm an actress," Ann said.

The security man, who seemed skeptical of the woman's stodgy attire, turned his attention to her unkempt one-eyed companion.

"And you, sir?"

"I'm a child of the tide," Skink said.

"A what?"

"Cuka-luka-choo."

Ann quickly cut in, "He's with me. We just came from an audition at the Gleason."

She talked one of the desk clerks into giving her a duplicate key card, even though her ID was upstairs. They rode the elevator with Ivanka Trump, whose well-dressed posse shielded her with glowering resolve from the tall bum with ammunition shells dangling from his shorn head. Management would hear about this.

Upon entering the room Ann was pleased to see that her clothes and personal belongings, including her handbag, had not been removed. An enormous basket of fruit, cheeses and wine beckoned from the coffee table, with a chipper card from the Buntermans: "Welcome home, Annie!"

Skink went to a window and looked down with despair at the crowded shore and the crowded water. "It's the second day of spring," he said in a dead voice.

Then he walked into the nearest closet and shut the door behind him.

Ann knocked gently. "Don't worry. We're getting out of here."

She took a four-minute shower, brushed her teeth, pulled her hair into a ponytail, and put on a blouse and slacks. When she came out of the bathroom, Skink was on the balcony, hurling Bartlett pears and Gouda wedges from the gift basket. He had a strong arm, and it appeared that he beaned a volleyball player on the beach twelve stories below. A small crowd was clustered around the Speedo-clad victim while one onlooker pointed upward at the facade of the hotel, in the direction of Ann's room. She tugged Skink inside and moments later they were in the service elevator, a form of covert egress with which Ann was familiar in her role as Cherry Pye.

Once on the street, they merged, more or less, into the throngs of tourists. It could not be said that Skink blended in, but he wasn't the only outrageous figure attracting notice. Although past its heyday, South Beach remained a sun-soaked runway for preening grotesques and needy narcissists.

Ann, on the other hand, seemed to be the only one rolling a travel bag. She grabbed Skink's arm and said, "This isn't going to work."

"I'll be heading south, though not until I have a word with Mr. Abbott."

"Oh, forget about him."

"Too late," Skink said.

"He didn't hurt me."

"Did he—"

"No, captain. I swear."

"Nonetheless."

Ann said, "What are you going to do to a guy like that? He's already pathetic."

"In a herd, his sort would be culled."

"For heaven's sake."

At that moment, the dead rabbit came unhitched from Skink's belt loop and dropped to the sidewalk between his shoes.

"Damn," he said, stooping to retrieve it.

Ann yanked sharply on his coat. "Don't. I'm begging you."

He paused and took note of the surroundings. The air smelled heavily of corned beef because they were standing in front of a busy deli, bursts of customers going in and out the door. A small girl who'd spied the furry brown form on the ground was reaching down to stroke it when she was jerked clear by her mother.

"That's what I'm talking about," Ann whispered anxiously to Skink.

"But it's sinful—"

"To waste good meat. Yeah, I get that." She clamped onto one of his thick wrists and led him away. After a few blocks his gait slowed and his breathing came in gulps. They turned up an alley, where he sat down clutching his head.

"What's wrong?" she asked.

"I need a still, dark place."

"Or?"

"Bedlam. Bloodletting. Who can say?"

"Just 'cause I made you lose the bunny?"

"Once all this was mangrove swamp." Skink made a weary sweeping motion with one arm. "Annie, there was no Miami Beach—they dredged up all the sand from the ocean bottom. It's entirely unnatural, an obscene façade. And every few years they've gotta dump more sand, thousands of tons, or else the whole goddamn place would disappear into the sea."

He was whirlybirding his braids, the shotgun shells clicking like dice.

"I'm far out of my element," he added.

"Thanks for the insight." Ann sat down in front of him and with a fingertip lifted his unshaven chin. "Where's your phone, captain?"

Absently he patted the trench coat. "It's here somewhere."

When the call came, Marcus Mink was in a meeting with an actress who had recently changed her name to Tessa Cloud-feather in hopes of landing the plum role of Sacagawea in an upcoming biopic about the Lewis and Clark expedition. Marcus Mink faced the sad task of informing his lissome young client that she'd lost the part to a genuine Native American, and that she should probably go back to being Tessa Grunwald, as casting calls for Indian maidens were relatively few and far between. Tessa had absorbed the news stoically; a quick puke, two rails of blow and she was solid. Marcus Mink told her she had a world-class attitude—good things were bound to happen.

Then he excused himself to take the call from Ann DeLusia, one of his low-maintenance favorites, whom she hadn't heard from in months.

"How's our gorgeous pop stunt double?" he asked.

"Tapped out. I just spent three days being held prisoner by a paparazzo. What else have you got for me?"

"You mean in the way of work?"

"No, Marcus, in the way of lasagna recipes. Don't be a schmuck."

"Girl, I haven't heard that sweet voice in ages."

Ann said, "Gosh, was *I* supposed to call *you*? I thought it was the other way around—the agents call the clients."

"Word is, the new album is way lame. *Skantily Klad* with all *k*'s? I don't think so." Marcus Mink had an ironclad policy against getting to the point, unless there was wonderful news to pass along. "Don't forget to phone me from the road. I want to hear stories."

"I'm not going on the tour. I'm done being Cherry Pye," Ann said.

"The Buntermans fired you? They can't do that!"

"I didn't get canned, Marcus. I'm quitting."

"What happened?"

She said, "Never mind. Tell me what's available."

Marcus Mink spun in his chair and gazed out the window at a verdant sliver of Westwood Village Memorial Park. The lone celebrity grave that he could see from his desk was that of Don Knotts; only the senior agents got a view of Marilyn's crypt. Someday Marcus Mink would have one of those offices.

"Sugar, I'm afraid there's not a whole lot happening," he said to Ann DeLusia. "Some commercial work, maybe a soap opera. You still speak Spanish, right? It's brutal out there."

"No movies?"

"Oh, the usual." Marcus Mink riffled through some call sheets. "Pert but clueless receptionist. Third hooker on bar stool. Pregnant hitchhiking vampire."

"Would I have lines?" Ann asked.

"Just a few. The hooker gets torched in a tanning bed, so they'll want a big scream."

"I smell a Golden Globe."

"Look, I know this Cherry gig isn't megastellar. But it's steady work, Annie, and you're pulling down eight bills a week. Most young actors, be honest, they'd ride that train for as long as they could."

"Which I did," said Ann. "By the way? Janet bumped me up to a thousand, but I'm bailing anyway."

"No, no, no!" Marcus Mink grieved for his lost commissions. He wondered what had happened that pushed her to the breaking point. "You mentioned a paparazzo?"

"Just do your damn job," she snapped, and hung up.

After leaving the mansion they gathered three estates away, beneath a banyan tree on the manicured emerald-green lawn of Julio Iglesias. The Larks had a connection, having represented a friend of a friend of the Latin heartthrob during a routine paternity scandal. Julio's Star Island mansion was being renovated, but his people sent word that Cherry Pye's parents could hang out as long as they wished in the backyard, which overlooked Biscayne Bay. The cabana, however, was off-limits.

"I've seen that fellow before," said Janet Bunterman, referring to Abbott, "lurking in the maggot mob."

"He didn't look so scary. Mr. Chemo can handle him, no problem," her husband asserted. "Cherry will do fine."

The Larks, who met the Buntermans there, took advantage of the outdoor setting by lighting up. They were less worried about Cherry's photo shoot than about the latest disappearance of Ann DeLusia. The twins weren't convinced it was an abduction.

"Why would she call him 'captain' unless she knew him?" Lucy wondered aloud.

"I thought the same thing," Janet Bunterman said, "but that's how she talks to everyone—you know, saucy, unflappable Annie."

Ned Bunterman's scornful appraisal: "No way that guy is captain of *anything*. He's a stone derelict."

Lila shook her head. "Lucy's right. The whole thing smells."

It was crucial to their media strategy that Ann be safely under wraps. The plan was to pay her off and then threaten to sabotage her future career if she ever blabbed. In the twins' view, an ambitious actress posed a much greater threat than a devious street photographer, who was basically a single-cell organism motivated by greed and/or lust. Ann DeLusia was more complex and unpredictable.

"What did the new kidnapper look like?" Lucy Lark asked.

"Big, dirty, shiny bald head with braids," Cherry's father said. "And one eye was screwed up."

"You've never seen him before?"

"I would've definitely remembered. His smile was outstanding," said Janet Bunterman. Realizing how that might have sounded, she added quickly, "The dental work, I mean. For a homeless person? Off the charts."

Tautly, Ned said, "I didn't notice his smile. I *did* notice the shotgun."

Lila took another drag and blew the smoke sideways. As usual, she and her sister were thinking the same thing: Annie could sink the whole damn boat.

The night before, the Larks had stayed up late to polish the draft of Cherry's future blog entry about her abduction and sordid humiliation at the hands of a demented fan, identity unknown. To improve the story, the twins described the singer's abductor as tall and hooded, with rippling muscles and a Middle Eastern accent. He carried a camera, and forced her to pose for degrading photographs under threat of death. On the third night, Cherry boldly escaped through a window and found herself alone in a snake-infested wilderness, possibly the Everglades, where she wandered for hours before collapsing.

I woke up in a Miami hospital—bruised, thirsty, but happy to be alive, the blog continued, Lucy at the keyboard. *I have no clue how I got there, but I'll always be grateful to the person who rescued me from that swamp, wherever it was, and also to the doctors and nurses who looked after me.*

As for the vicious dude who kidnapped me and hassled me for all those days and nights, I've got, like, one thing to say: You can't hurt me anymore!

At that point, Lila took over: *As jazzed as I am to be free, I know my nightmare isn't really over. I wish I could forget some of those things he did to me—and I'm sure there's other stuff that our Lord and Savior doesn't want me to remember. I can't even imagine what that monster plans to do with all the awful pictures he took, but they could totally show up anytime on the Internet.*

So I want to prepare all of you—friends and loyal fans—for the shock. I did what I had to do to save my own life.

Then Lucy finished it off: *But I refuse to let this coward, like, haunt me. That's why I'm going ahead full throttle with the big concert tour to promote my hot new CD,* Skantily Klad. *Even though I'm pretty wiped out from the hostage thing, I'm still rehearsing every single day, determined to put on a super-awesome show that you'll never, ever forget!*

Love, hugs, and kisses . . . CP.

For the Larks, ghostwriting as an airhead had turned out to be fun. Neither of them doubted that lowly Claude Abbott could be persuaded to shut up and disappear. The specter of being prosecuted and concurrently sued into destitution would be a powerful incentive to cooperate. The twins suspected, however, that Ann DeLusia would not be so easily corralled.

"Let's say it wasn't another kidnapping," Lila said. "Let's say it was a getaway. Maybe she was friends with the shotgun guy and—"

"She wasn't escaping from Abbott," Lucy broke in. "She was escaping from all of us."

The Buntermans looked muddled and distressed. Ned

swatted awkwardly at a bug and wished he were on a plane heading home. Florida was a callous, uncultured place; it brought out the worst in people. Ann was the last person he would have expected to cut and run.

Fumbling with a tube of French sunblock, Cherry's mother said, "Annie's upset because we didn't tell the police she was in the Suburban when Abbott swiped it. This is understandable."

The Larks were frowning, although an outsider would have been hard-pressed to notice.

"How do we reach her?" Lila asked.

Janet Bunterman said she had no idea. "She drowned her phone."

"Suppose she doesn't call," Ned Bunterman said.

"That would be bad." Lucy palmed her iPhone, skimming through e-mails. "Unless she's dead. Otherwise it's best to keep an open dialogue."

Cherry's mother said she didn't think the gun-toting vagrant intended to kill Ann. "I really didn't get that vibe."

"Me, neither," Ned Bunterman said. "And Annie didn't look all that scared."

"Because she knew the guy. That's our working theory," said Lila.

"Which means you should probably expect a call," Lucy said to Cherry's parents. "Be prepared to open the checkbook."

Janet Bunterman sighed in resignation. "So, what would be fair?"

The twins snickered bleakly. Fairness had nothing to do with it. "She can slaughter us, that's the problem," said Lila. "Think of what would happen, Annie goes to the cops and spills everything. Sure, we can say she's disgruntled, bitter, whacked-out, whatever. They've still got to investigate—and then the story's all over the media. We're talking a Cat 5 shitstorm."

"Ten thousand dollars. Twenty?" Janet Bunterman scowled at her husband and raised her hands. "Little help, Ned?"

He said, "Maybe we should talk to Maury."

A sleek hundred-foot yacht idled past, a red-and-white flag fluttering on the stern. A tallish middle-aged couple, dressed in matching white linens, stood hatless on the upper deck. They were listening to a piece of classical music, which drifted to Star Island on the breeze.

Ned Bunterman saw the lettering painted on the transom and felt a melancholy twinge beneath his breastbone: *Sweet Dreams* was the name of the yacht. It was registered in Copenhagen.

"Start at fifty grand," suggested Lucy Lark. "See what she says."

"That's a lot of money," Cherry's mother remarked unhappily.

Lila fired up another cigarette. "It's a bloody bargain, Janet."

"All right, then, how high would you go?"

The twins made eye contact with each other, as they often did before dispensing advice. "What's your comfort level?" Lucy asked Cherry's parents.

Again Ned Bunterman said, "Let's talk to Maury."

It made sense to him that the promoter should pony up the hush money. No one other than the Buntermans had more to lose than Maury Lykes if the new album flopped and the tour bombed, which was a real possibility if Ann popped up and started giving interviews about Cherry's dope binges and lip-synching lessons.

Janet Bunterman said, "If I could see her again one-on-one, even for just a few minutes, I could straighten this whole thing out. Annie's a decent soul. She *likes* me."

The Larks, who had no patience for mawkish nonsense, stood up and excused themselves from the garden party. "Call us when you hear from her," said Lila.

"But what if we don't?" asked Cherry's father.

"Then we move ahead. Stick to the plan, eyes wide open." This was Lucy. "When can we see the new photographs?"

"Tonight." Janet Bunterman said Chemo would be returning to the Stefano not only with Abbott's cameras but also with a signed release for all the pictures of Cherry.

"And the faux junkie shots of Ann? The toilet-bowl sequence?"

"Deleted. Chemo promised to supervise personally." Cherry's mother didn't know what methods the bodyguard would use to secure the paparazzo's cooperation, but she assumed that the weed whacker would come into play. She found it reassuring that Chemo had displayed no concern whatsoever about Abbott's handgun.

"We'll be waiting at the hotel. Try the spa first," said Lila

Lark, and walked off side by side with her sister. To Ned Bunterman there was something paramilitary about their stride and bearing, and he couldn't for a moment imagine sleeping with either (or both) of them, despite their finely crafted features.

He walked down to Julio's dock to have a look at the water, which was milky but nonetheless lulling. Soon his wife joined him, shielding her extravagantly shaded eyes against the morning glare.

"Wonder how it's going over there," Janet Bunterman said, looking off toward the big Spanish-style house where their daughter was posing for a creep, thinking she would be gracing the cover of *Vanity Fair*.

"Janet, how the hell did it come to this?" Her husband wasn't talking about the marriage; he was talking about the business.

"Cherry's a free spirit, Ned."

"No, she's a dolt. Harsh but true, and we both know it. What in the world are we gonna do if this doesn't work?"

His wife said, "That's the difference between you and me. I'm all about positive energy."

They were interrupted by a burst of sharp pops coming from the direction of Tanner Dane Keefe's rented mansion.

Cherry's mother flinched and moved behind her husband. "Firecrackers?"

"Gunshots," Ned Bunterman said. "You want positive, Janet? I'm fucking positive that was a gun."

24

 Blondell Wayne Tatum, also known as Chemo, knew something about dysfunctional families. His own parents had been members of a radical sect that renounced red meat, monogamy and income taxes, and they died in an inept shootout with federal agents outside a North Dakota post office. Young Blondell, only six at the time, went to live with an aunt and uncle who were themselves fugitives from felony mail-fraud charges, and had been masquerading with moderate success as Amish wheat farmers. It was no surprise that, in the absence of upright role models, Chemo had turned early to the criminal way.

Having seen the Buntermans up close, the bodyguard wasn't entirely unsympathetic to their famous daughter. With Ned and Janet at the wheel, Cherry never had a chance. While Chemo was pleased by how quickly she'd tidied her speech patterns under the cattle proddings, he planned no further outreach. He wasn't in the bimbo-salvaging business; his charity extended to not murdering Cherry, nothing more.

Her singing, however, stirred the homicidal impulse.

I need a jealous bone, jealous bo-ooooone
In my body.
It's been too long, I've been so wronnnngg
To hold out.
So, boy, don't talk, just take a waaaaalk
To my party.
They don't need to know, need to kno-ooooow
What's goin' on.
I need a jealous bone, jealous bo-ooooone,
In my body.
Want your jealous bone, jealous bo-oooone
So come on!

It was a caterwaul, off-key and glottal.

Chemo stepped up to Cherry Pye and said, "Shut it down."

Bang Abbott sidled around him, continuing to snap photos. "You kiddin' me? That's a great cut."

"It's the new single," Cherry said to Chemo. "God, what's your problem?"

She was straddling the back of the chair, and still wearing

Ann's little black dress. Her thong panties were the same color.

"The video seriously kills," she said, and defiantly resumed the song. Chemo clamped his hand over her mouth.

The paparazzo set down his camera and from his dingy pants pulled the Colt .38. Chemo saw rounds in the cylinder and he wondered when the sneaky shit had reloaded.

"Let go of her," Bang Abbott said with a twitch. His middle finger, not the bandaged one, was inchworming toward the trigger.

"Sure," Chemo said. As he backed away from Cherry, he pivoted and with the shoulder of his truncated left arm swung the weed whacker in the upward trajectory of a fungo bat. Although the golf-bag cover offered a bit of padding at impact, Bang Abbott nevertheless took a painful blow to the gourd. He toppled, snorting like a dazed warthog.

Chemo picked up the .38 from the polished maple floor and emptied all but one round into the watercolor of a circus clown that hung over the useless fireplace. He knew the clown painting couldn't be very valuable if the owner of the house had left it up on the wall, especially after renting to an actor. It would be worth even less with bullet holes.

"You killed Claude, you fucker!" Cherry bayed at Chemo.

"Claude should know better than to play with guns."

The photographer hauled himself to his feet, steadying himself against the mantel. Seconds later, the Buntermans burst into the room, Cherry's father armed with a Swiffer sweeper that he'd grabbed from the kitchen. It was no match for a motorized shrub shredder; Chemo had to smile.

"What happened here?" cried Janet Bunterman, rushing to her daughter's side. "Are you all right?"

"I hate him! He hurt Claude!"

"What for?" asked Cherry's father, hovering at what he perceived to be a safe distance.

"Fuckhead pointed a loaded weapon at me. Not acceptable," Chemo explained.

Ned Bunterman was proud of himself for having properly identified the loud noises as gunfire. If his wife was impressed, she didn't let on. Chemo handed her the Colt and told her to put it away before somebody got killed. Nervously she crammed it barrel-first into her purse.

Bang Abbott was fingering a pink knot on the side of his head. His crimped baseball cap was deftly Swiffered off the floor and returned to him by Cherry's father.

"I got some really good stuff. She's doing great," the paparazzo said.

"He's right, Mom, I look so freaking awe—" Cherry halted herself, remembering Chemo's forbidden-word list, and shot the bodyguard a septic glare. "Amazing. *Super*-amazing. Claude showed me the pictures."

Janet Bunterman said, "I told you, sweetie, he's an artist."

"I already know which one I want for the cover!"

His ears still ringing, Bang Abbott picked up a Nikon and fiddled with the f-stop. "Hell, we're just gettin' started," he said. "Aren't we, Cherish?"

Janet Bunterman told her husband to fetch some ice for Mr. Abbott's lump.

"No, no, I'm good," said the paparazzo, who'd been somewhat anesthetized by the intensity of his fixation.

Cherry's father asked, "Can we sneak a peek at the pics?"

"Maybe. After I'm done." Bang Abbott raised his head and peered up at the wall. "Jesus, I just got a smokin' hot idea. You folks can go now—everything's under control."

He took down the painting and placed it on the floor in front of the chair. He told Cherry to insert her fingers through the bullet holes in the clown's eyes, then wiggle the tips provocatively for the camera.

"Killer," she said. "I love it."

Chemo escorted the Buntermans to the foyer. He told them to hang around out front for a little while, in case the neighbors had called the cops about the gunshots.

"We'll tell them it was fireworks," Janet Bunterman suggested daringly.

"Brilliant."

Ned Bunterman propped the sweeper in a corner. "What do we do with the gun, Mr. Chemo? I mean, good Lord, this is out of our bailiwick."

"Leave it under the Denali."

"Is that safe?"

Chemo said, "Sure. There's no crime on Star Island." He smiled tightly as he let the Buntermans out.

Walking back to the photo set, he was thinking what a

pain in the ass these people were, every damn one of them, and how he couldn't wait to finish the job and split.

This time, Cherry stopped singing the moment he entered the room.

Jackie Sebago waddled to the bathroom and gingerly hoisted his bloated scrotum up on the vanity for self-inspection. He'd been reading all about spiny sea urchins on the Internet. The infection was being stubborn. Jackie couldn't fit his junk into his Jockey shorts, much less a pair of pants, so he was basically trapped indoors.

Earlier in the morning, after receiving the call from the Monroe County Building Department, the developer had furiously thrown on a robe and set out toward the residence of D. T. Maltby to ascertain why, after all the payoffs and chicanery, the Sebago project had abruptly been red-tagged. Jackie's labored stride and rumpled appearance attracted the attention of an Ocean Reef security guard, who placed the developer in a golf cart and drove him back to the borrowed condominium where he had been recuperating.

Being a mere guest and not a member, Jackie Sebago hadn't fully familiarized himself with Ocean Reef's dress code. At the very least, he should have cinched the bathrobe more snugly. His dour outlook did not improve when the security guard informed him that a chartered aircraft carrying Mr. Maltby had only minutes earlier departed from the club's private runway, destination undisclosed.

Alone at the condo, Jackie sagged into a leather recliner and spread wide his spindly legs to ease the pressure. The obstetrical pose was all the more apt because his grotesquely engorged nut sack resembled nothing so much as the slimy, purple-veined crown of an emerging newborn. He fanned his crotch and seethed, thinking about the ranting one-eyed stranger who had victimized him so sadistically. The crime reaffirmed his generic contempt for environmentalists—such fucking drama over a few town houses! The greatest country in the world, he huffed to himself, the shining goddamn beacon of capitalism—yet a respectable entrepreneur such as himself could be ambushed, hog-tied and sexually disfigured by a deranged crackpot with a political agenda. It was an outrage.

His cell phone rang. Jackie Sebago recognized the 401 area code.

"Shit," he murmured.

The caller was Shea, his least-favorite investor. Shea had learned about the red-tagging when he'd contacted the building department to find out if the plumbing permits had been pulled. The prick was always calling Key West behind Jackie's back, just so he could bust his chops about one chickenshit thing or the other. Shea had texted a half dozen times within the hour, but Jackie hadn't bothered to read any of them.

Now the guy was bellowing into the phone: "What the fuck, man? They shut down the project! What the fuck?"

"I'm on it," said Jackie.

But he wasn't on it, not really. The whole point of hiring

a "consultant" such as D. T. Maltby was to remain safely above all the prosaic little acts of corruption. Being kept in the dark was part of Jackie's system. He didn't know who had been bribed, or how much they'd been paid—but he definitely wanted to know why they'd suddenly reneged.

"What the hell happened? What did you do?" Shea demanded. "Know what? Never mind. Just wire my money back. I'm done."

"Slow down, Billy. I'll have all this shit smoothed out by tomorrow. Wednesday at the latest." There was little chance of that, Jackie knew, not with Maltby dodging him. "I gotta take care of some folks, that's all," he said to Shea. "You know, spread a little sunshine."

"I thought you already did."

"Me, too. But, hey, it's Florida."

"Guess what? You can have it," Shea said. "I want my fucking money. Tomorrow, nine sharp, I'm calling my bank. It better be there, all eight fifty."

Jackie Sebago couldn't possibly return Billy Shea's $850,000 investment because he'd already spent it on either a hydrofoil franchise in Crete or junk bonds. He couldn't remember. After purchasing the lots for Sebago Isle, he'd still had five million bucks to play with. To Jackie it all sort of poured together, like a tropical waterfall.

In the interest of harmony, he had allowed Shea and the other investors to think their funds were safe in an escrow account. Jackie Sebago believed escrow was for pussies. He preferred a more dynamic wealth strategy.

"Come on, Billy, lighten up. I'm still wiped out from what happened last week, what that damn maniac did to me."

From the other end, no sympathy: "You can still dial the motherfucking phone, no? Wire me the balance, Jackie. *Today.*"

The developer once heard that Shea had heavy mob connections up in Rhode Island, but he'd brushed it off as a rumor. Shea was always suing somebody, and wise guys generally avoided courtrooms. Jackie Sebago anticipated that the man's next step would be to have his lawyer write a menacing letter, and then maybe file a lawsuit. By the time the case wound its way through Florida's glacial court system, the real-estate market would have bounced back with a bang, the units at Sebago Isle would be presold, and there'd be plenty of cash with which to repay Mr. William Shea, with interest, if the dipshit still wanted out of the deal.

"Jackie, am I even making a dent?" Shea asked acerbically. "You *do* hear what I'm saying, right? This whole Key Largo thing has been a fuck story from day one, and now I want my eight fifty back."

"You're just frustrated, Billy, and so am I. Don't worry—I'll get the red tag lifted pronto and off we go," said the developer. "It's just a mistake is all."

"No, the mistake? For you to keep on bullshitting me. That's the mistake, you lying little cumwad."

The line went dead. Jackie Sebago tossed the phone, thinking: *That's one cold dude. He didn't even ask about my nuts.*

*

Ann DeLusia got a room at the Loft Hotel and Skink curled up on the floor. She made a call to his friend, the motorcycle man, who showed up ninety minutes later. Ann met him in the lobby, and they went down the street for coffee. He told her the whole story. She felt bad for not believing Skink when he'd said he was once the governor.

"He doesn't share that with everybody," Jim Tile said.

"And one day he just quit? How wild."

"It was either that or go off like a cluster bomb."

"So, what's your connection?" Ann asked.

"I worked for him back in the Tallahassee days. I'm the one who helped him disappear."

"It probably saved his life."

"Or somebody else's. He wasn't equipped for politics, trust me."

"Well, he's definitely not equipped for South Beach. You should take him back to the Keys."

Jim Tile said, "He won't go yet. No point in asking—the man won't go."

"What are you saying?" Ann saw that Skink's friend wore a rueful expression. She said, "Oh no. This I don't need."

"He'll head home when he thinks you're safe."

"I *am* safe . . . now. Totally safe."

"Don't be so certain," said Jim Tile. She had told him her story, too.

He added: "The governor might look shaky, but his survival instincts are superb. Listen to what he tells you."

"But he's a whack job, no offense. Scottish poetry! And

what's with that song—'Run Through the Jungle'? He snatched up some blond rollerblader and sang it to her belly button, for heaven's sake."

Jim Tile shrugged. "He loves Creedence. Says that's what got him through Nam."

"Take him with you. Please?"

"He won't hurt you."

"Yes, I know."

"More important: He won't let anyone else hurt you."

Ann said, "What are you talking about? Nobody wants to hurt me."

As they walked back to the hotel, Jim Tile asked about the shotgun. Ann told him where Skink had hidden it.

"You're gonna go get it, right?" she asked. "So he can't."

"Let's see—large black dude carrying a sawed-off on a motorcycle through the Magic City in broad daylight. No, dear, I don't think so."

"You're a big help."

"Hang on to my number," said Jim Tile.

She told him thanks a bunch, and took the stairs up to the room. Skink was still sleeping, his head sandwiched in a stack of pillows. She took a long, hot shower. The water felt heavenly; she closed her eyes and let the spray pulse against her cheeks. She wasn't sure whether or not she wanted the governor to be gone when she got out.

Ann's experience with damaged men was limited; for some reason, possibly her looks, she tended to attract the cocky and self-absorbed. The wounded ones were more interesting, according to her girlfriends, although they were lots of work. Ann wondered if her father had been such a man. When she was little she often asked her mother about him, but no distinct portrait was presented. "A worthless loser," her mom would say one day. Another time he might be an "irresponsible fool," or a "misguided schmo," or simply "nobody worth thinking about." The one that had sort of intrigued Ann was "mixed-up dreamer."

All she actually knew about her dad was that his name was Gil, he was two years younger than her mother, and he'd moved out of the apartment shortly before she was born. It was never made clear if the decision to leave was his, but Ann doubted it. Her mom was a relentless ballbuster. Before marrying the professional bowler she'd had a dozen other colorless but compliant suitors who dutifully converted to veganism, accompanied her to Bible readings and set aside their Saturdays for lawn work. All ended up being dumped for minor infractions, and Ann always felt sorry for them. She didn't miss her mom very much but she assumed they'd reconnect one day, probably at the bowler's funeral.

Skink was awake, buffing his glass eye, when she came out of the bathroom. He didn't seem to notice she had a towel on her head and another wrapped around her body.

"I'm going back to Star Island," he said, "to settle up with Abbott."

"You'll do no such thing." Ann sat beside him on the edge of the bed. "What do you plan to do—beat him to a pulp? Kill him? Don't expect me to be impressed."

He re-set the glass eye in its socket and blinked it into position. "What he did was wrong. He should be held to account."

"Why do you like to be called 'captain'?"

"That was my rank in the army. Maybe I should let it go." He started to rise, but Ann grabbed his arm.

"Did you ever have kids?" she asked.

"No children. No wives."

"And no regrets, I bet."

"Many," he said. "A shitload."

"Then forget about Claude and stay here with me. I need to tell you everything about what happened, and why," she said. "I also need to tell you about my ridiculous job."

"You're an actress. That's not altogether ridiculous."

"No, captain, I'm talking about *this* job—the one that got me in all this trouble."

"Will I become disillusioned?"

"Then afterward I'm going to ask you," she said, "for a really big favor."

"Whatever you want."

"Even if it involves shopping?"

Skink laughed. "Anything for you, fair Annie."

25

 Bang Abbott wasn't a big drinker but Cherry had found a bottle of Grey Goose, so he agreed to join her for martinis in the kitchen during their lunch break. She was getting pretty loose, which boded well for the afternoon photo session and also for his chances of getting some action. He was aware of his repellent effect on women; even the hookers he hired usually needed a stiff shot or two before getting down to business.

Despite the gunplay and baleful rumblings from Chemo, Bang Abbott was feeling good about the shoot. The photographs he'd taken so far were, in his own slanted view, gems. Cherry had never looked so beautiful and teasing and reckless and haunted . . .

Bang Abbott's sappy enchantment would have baffled his

fellow paparazzi, among whom he was regarded as coarse and heartless. But none of those jackoffs had ever spent what—three hours, now?—alone with one of their glam-nymph targets.

Getting flashed, flipped off, mooned, and serenaded. She'd even told a dirty joke, Cherry had, about a man with three testicles. Complete with visuals.

Teddy Loo, eat your fucking heart out.

Bang Abbott fixed a third martini and scrolled through the photos, basking in his own genius.

"Claude, I gotta go tinkle," Cherry said. "Is that a picture?"

"Not for *Vanity Fair*, darling." He directed her toward the bathroom. "Make it fast."

The format of the portrait book was taking shape in his mind—but, no, first an exhibit. At the National Portrait Gallery in Washington! Better still, a traveling exhibition, then afterward bring out the book, a masterpiece portfolio.

Upon returning, Cherry chirped, "Look what I found in the medicine chest!" She opened her hand to reveal three cocoa-colored pills.

"What are those?" Bang Abbott asked.

"Who cares."

"Hey, don't!" Chemo put down his sandwich and moved toward Cherry, but she was too quick. She swallowed the tablets in one gulp, then smacked her lips for the body-guard's benefit.

"Whatcha gonna do now?" she taunted.

"Those were heartworm pills," Chemo informed her, "for a dog. I wondered how long it would take you to find 'em."

"Asshole! I hate your guts!" Cherry screamed.

Bang Abbott told her to calm down—doggy meds wouldn't hurt her.

"But, goddammit, Claude, I wanna get high!" She lunged once more for the vodka. Bang Abbott, who himself was feeling buzzed, fished a fresh olive from the jar and plopped it into his glass.

Chemo clicked his grungy nubs in mock disapproval and returned to his pastrami on rye. He honestly didn't care if the two of them got bombed. The first forty grand from Maury Lykes was hidden securely in the jack compartment of his Denali, and the rest of the cash soon would be in his hands. By this time tomorrow, Abbott would be a nonfactor and the girl would be somebody else's headache.

After lunch he followed them upstairs, where Cherry shadowed her eyelids with dark purple crescents and shed the cocktail dress. She put on a long-sleeved polo shirt, open to her navel, and a pair of Tanner Dane Keefe's boxer shorts which had a dorky frog pattern.

Then Bang Abbott handcuffed her to the wrought-iron rail of a veranda overlooking the swimming pool. He said, "You get the concept, right? It's like you're a prisoner of fame."

Cherry seemed to twinkle and blush. "Claude, that is *so* freakin' heavy."

For Chemo, the interaction was nauseating to observe.

Remorseless by nature, he nevertheless found himself thinking of all the poor fuckers he'd conned into buying ARMs—now shattered and broke, their only sin trying to score a decent house for their families. The all-American dream! And here's some dumb chick with a voice that sounds like a sackful of starving kittens—filthy rich, and about to get richer. *So much for divine order*, Chemo thought bitterly.

"*Now* what's your problem?" Cherry snapped.

The bodyguard entertained the thought of taking the weed whacker to her god-awful tattoo, mulching the bestial rendition to an oozing scarlet pulp. Instead he went inside and settled down with a *National Geographic*, which in prison had become his favorite periodical. This particular issue featured an article about cosmetic microsurgery, a subject of keen personal interest to him. He'd had lousy luck with doctors, but now that he was coming into serious money, perhaps he could find a first-rate surgeon to de-corrugate his face.

After a while, Bang Abbott walked in from the veranda. On a wobbly track he approached Chemo and said, with a frat-boy leer, "Hey, can you give us an hour alone? Me and the tartlet?"

"You're kidding."

"No, man, I'm definitely feeling it. She's, uh, in major need."

"I got orders from Mr. Lykes not to let her outta my sight."

"Just wait outside the door, 'kay? Hell, you can *listen* if you want." Bang Abbott was perspiring more copiously than usual, and his brow felt as clammy as a mackerel. He was aware that the window of carnal opportunity with Cherry Pye could slam shut at any instant.

"Come on," he begged the bodyguard. "Give a brother a break."

Chemo said, "You're trashed."

"Just a little."

"Don't call me 'brother.'"

"What is it?" the paparazzo said. "You can't believe she'd ball a guy like me, right?"

"Oh, I believe it. Two nights ago I caught her grinding on her iPhone. She'd left it on vibrate, so every time a text or a call came in . . . Anyway, yeah, I believe you." Chemo stood up and tucked the magazine under his prosthesis.

"You got thirty minutes," he said to Bang Abbott.

Fremont Spores got interested in police scanners after his wife, Lenore, succumbed to lung cancer. She had never smoked, but living with Fremont, who was a human chimney, killed her. Lenore Spores had been in all ways a substantial presence, and her death left a sensory vacuum that Fremont needed to fill. After twenty-nine years of noise, he couldn't cope with a silent apartment. The scanners brought the place back to life; like Lenore, they never shut up.

At first, listening to the law-enforcement frequencies was

only a hobby. There was so much gore and mayhem in South Florida that Fremont Spores spent hours on end hunkered at the machines, enthralled by their static-filled bulletins—car wrecks, shoot-outs, home invasions, gang fights, cockfights, murder-suicides, drug busts, ODs, floaters, indecent exposures, cats up trees, pythons in swimming pools. Fremont became so fervidly immersed in cop-radio chatter that sometimes he wouldn't leave his post for the whole day, skipping meals and urinating into a Clorox bottle.

Then the landlord jacked up the rent and Fremont found himself strapped for dough. He was living on Social Security and a modest retirement from the *Florida Times-Union*, where he'd worked as a press mechanic before retiring to Miami Beach. The newspaper pension, which had barely covered Fremont's monthly tab for parakeet seed and Winston Lights, was now needed to augment the rent. So suddenly he faced the twin tragedies of forsaking cigarettes and also saying good-bye to Mr. Peeps, his mute but beloved English budgie.

One day, while browsing at the scanner shop, Fremont Spores struck up a conversation with a crusty character who'd brought in an old Uniden Bearcat for repair. The man confided to Fremont that he made a couple hundred bucks a week monitoring the police channels, feeding tips to local TV news and radio stations, and on occasion to the tabloids. South Beach had caught fire as a winter watering hole for supermodels, musicians and show-business phonies, and there was good cash to be made when even a D-list celebrity got arrested for a bar fight or drunk driving. The man generously cut Fremont in on the action, and even more generously keeled over from a brain aneurysm six months later.

Fremont took over the operation and soon developed into a virtuoso scanner fiend. He could simultaneously eavesdrop on twenty-two different police and fire departments, from Palmetto Bay to Palm Beach, as well as the state marine patrol, U.S. Coast Guard, DEA, even Fish and Wildlife. As Fremont's reputation grew, his client list expanded beyond reporters and camera crews, who were always chasing after the cops, to those who were always dodging them—dopers, gunrunners, street racers, livestock rustlers and migrant smugglers. Fremont wasn't selective. Whoever purchased his information could be confident it was solid, and fresh.

Most customers were good about the money, except for a few itinerant paparazzi. They'd swoop into town and immediately contact Fremont, promising beaucoup dollars if he'd steer them to the scene of some spaced-out starlet or wasted jock in the back of a squad car—or, better yet, an ambulance. Fremont's rates were fair, and he expected to be paid promptly for productive tips. Chasing down a deadbeat shooter took valuable time away from his scanning duties, but it was a matter of principle. More than anything, Fremont Spores hated being jerked around.

He called Bang Abbott's number again. The same flat voice answered as before—Fremont suspected it was Abbott himself, pretending to be someone else. Or maybe he had a cold.

"This is Spores. I want my two hundred bucks."

"For what? Remind me."

"For Larissa's DUI, asshole. The Idol?"

"No problem."

"I heard that before. Tomorrow morning. Nine sharp, the usual place."

"Which is?"

"Don't pull this shit with me, Claudius. I ain't got the patience," said Fremont. "I told you, there's a man in Bogotá said I can call him for a favor anytime. Is that how you want to play?"

"See you tomorrow."

"That's more like it." Fremont hung up, thinking: *He better show up*.

At the other end of the line, a person who was not Bang Abbott smiled as he pocketed the tangerine BlackBerry. Chemo had no intention of meeting with Fremont Spores. To ease his boredom, the bodyguard had been answering Abbott's calls, listening to the tipsters' hype and then casually agreeing to whatever fee they demanded. It was an amusing window into a realm of specialized bottom-feeding that was unfamiliar to Chemo. He saw no point in offering up the photographer's new cell number because, after tonight, the greedy sleazeball would be permanently out of business.

Turning back to his *National Geographic*, Chemo got

immersed in the surgery article and lost track of time. An hour slipped away before he remembered that he'd left Abbott and Cherry alone in a bedroom. They were still there, passed out in the sack, when Chemo charged through the door.

The corpulent paparazzo lay facedown and nude, except for his baseball cap and Bluetooth earpiece. The Nikons hung from their straps on the bedpost. The former Cheryl Gail Bunterman was wearing a jade-green kimono and one snakeskin cowboy boot. The bodyguard took a wrist and felt for a pulse. She stirred, blinked her eyes and lifted her head.

"Not you," she mumbled.

Chemo said, "Congratulations. A new low."

"Like I'd seriously do Claude again. No way." She cast a drowsy smirk at her snoring bedmate. "What a freakin' lightweight," she said.

Chemo jerked his thumb toward the bathroom. "Go clean up."

"Yo, I didn't even blow the dude. I swear!"

Yo? Chemo had forgotten to put that one on the cattle-prod list.

Cherry sat up and yawned with a simian grimace. "God, my hair's a disaster."

"Not compared to the rest of you."

"By the way—Tanny's 'happy pills'? I snuck down the hall and found 'em," she said smugly. "So there."

"How many did you feed Abbott?"

Cherry smiled to herself. "Three or four. I dunno."

"Great. I'll be here all goddamn night." Chemo used the sheathed head of his lawn trimmer to jostle the inert photographer, who snuffled but did not awaken.

From the folds of the bedcovers Cherry uncovered the bottle of Grey Goose, which was empty. She was too woozy to whine about it. Chemo watched her gimp in the oversized boot toward the john. She closed the door and vigorously commenced to vomit, ripe woofs echoing off the Italian marble.

Chemo took out Abbott's BlackBerry and punched in Janet Bunterman's number.

"We're done here," he said.

"Already?"

"Way done. Come get her."

The combination of alcohol, olives and pills adversely affected Bang Abbott's sleep pattern. He dreamed that a shark was chewing his ass off. A flurry of young women on the beach were cheering and taking pictures. They all wore little black dresses. Bang Abbott was struggling frantically to get out of the water but the shark wouldn't let go of his butt cheeks—a grisly replay of the attack on Terence Hughes, the unlucky tourist who'd unwittingly waded into Bang Abbott's chum slick at Clearwater Beach all those years ago. Hughes had wound up with 179 stitches and Abbott got a Pulitzer.

The paparazzo didn't often suffer nightmares, and this

one was vivid. The fiery, coiling pain he experienced seemed authentic, and largely unbuffered by the Lortabs that he'd gobbled idiotically on a dare from Cherry Pye. When he twisted around to punch the dogged shark with both fists, that hurt, too. Hurt like a mother.

Help me! Bang Abbott cried out in his sleep.

But the babes on shore just kept laughing and snapping photos with their candy-colored cell phones. Meanwhile, the shark made a high-pitched humming sound as it munched his salty flesh.

I'm bleeding! wailed the photographer.

And he was.

"Wake up, Slim. Let's get this over with."

Bang Abbott opened one sticky eyelid and saw Chemo looming like a scabrous buzzard. The rotor stem of the weed whacker was still spinning. Bang Abbott saw that his own knuckles were skinned, and a crimson saucer-sized wound glistened on the vast jellied slope of his right buttock. With a moan he rolled over on his back and yanked the bedcovers up to his neck. The Bluetooth fell out on the pillow.

"Why'd you slice me?" he bleated.

"'Cause you tried to ace me out of the action." Chemo propped the motorized yard tool on the headboard. In his good hand rested Bang Abbott's Colt .38.

"What the hell's going on? Where's Cherry?" the paparazzo asked. He had no memory of getting laid but he was reluctant to rule out the possibility. Why else would he have removed his clothes?

"She's back at the hotel with mummy and daddy," the bodyguard said.

Bang Abbott fought to clear his senses. He correctly perceived that his bold scheme was in jeopardy.

"Anything bad happens to me," he warned, "Cherry's done."

Chemo gave him that basilisk stare. "Nice try, dickbrain."

The photographer sat up, bracing on his elbows. His head felt like a cracked cinder block. "Those toilet shots I took of her double—with the needle? Anything happens to me, those pictures are all over the fucking Internet. Cherry is *finito*."

Chemo put the gun under his good arm and from his shirt pocket took out Abbott's replacement cell phone, the one that had been used to photograph Ann DeLusia holding the dirty hypodermic at the Marriott.

"You mean *these* pictures?" the bodyguard said.

Bang Abbott sagged. The bastard had gone through his pants while he was passed out.

"You keep losin' your phones," said Chemo. "That gets expensive."

The photographer hastily composed himself. "You can toss that stupid thing in the ocean, for all I care. I already e-mailed the junkie shots to my laptop, which is back in L.A. There's an editor at the *Eye*, he doesn't hear from me by noon tomorrow, he's sending a guy out to my apartment."

Chemo didn't seem concerned. He appeared to be thinking. He tucked away Abbott's cell and again drew out the pistol.

"I got two sets of orders," he said. "First: The Lark sisters, they're gonna put out a PR story saying it was Cherry—not the actress—who got snatched by a maniac and held prisoner while he made kinky pictures. The stuff you took today, they're gonna leak a few choice shots just in time for the tour. The idea, I'm guessin', is to juice ticket sales. And if you don't shut up and get on board, the Buntermans run to the cops and have you busted for kidnapping. Then, while you're sittin' in jail, they sue your fat ass in civil court."

Bang Abbott could scarcely absorb what he was hearing.

Chemo went on: "But Mr. Lykes, he's got a different plan. He wants me to kill you."

"No! What?"

"I'm supposed to make it look like a suicide. The way it'll come out, Cherry escaped from your hideout and ran away. You knew the law was gonna track you down and lock you up for a thousand years, so—*pow!*—you capped yourself. Remember that fuckwit who murdered Versace? That's how he bought it, shot himself dead while the cops were closing in," Chemo said. "Only yours would be what they call 'assisted.'"

"I don't believe this." Bang Abbott was trembling. His eyes cut to the handgun—he was fairly sure the bodyguard had emptied all the bullets into the clown painting.

Chemo delivered another hair-raising smile. "No, Slim, I saved one round for you."

"Big mistake!" The photographer jabbed the air with his

bandaged twig of a forefinger. "You kill me, all those junkie shots go viral and Cherry's new album is DOA. The tour? What motherfucking tour? Don't you get it?"

"You're the one doesn't get it," said the bodyguard.

At that moment, his brain fog cleared and Bang Abbott realized that Chemo was pure criminal, a freelancer who couldn't care less what happened to Cherry Pye's career. Bang Abbott believed he might save his own hide if he could just get the man invested.

"How much is Lykes paying you?"

Chemo said, "Eighty grand."

"Get serious." Bang Abbott squirmed; the bloody laceration on his rear end was starting to stick to the sheets. "I'm worth twice as much to you alive. Three times as much."

"This oughta be good. Keep talkin'."

"You see the pictures? They're amazing," Bang Abbott said. "Take a look."

Chemo stuck the gun in his belt. He grabbed one of Abbott's Nikons and sat down in a high-backed chair to scope out the lowlife's work. He was surprised by how good the shots had turned out—even those with the perforated clown painting. Through the eye of Abbott's camera, Cherry looked infinitely more interesting than she really was. Someone who'd never spent any time with her might conclude from the photographs that she was actually deep and mysterious.

"I'll be damned," Chemo said.

Bang Abbott's hopes skied. He was fully committed to talking his way out of being executed.

"*Lost Angel.* What do you think?" he asked the bodyguard. "For the title, I mean."

"Title of what?"

"My book of Cherry's portraits—*Lost Angel.* Or maybe *Doomed Angel.*"

Chemo looked doubtful. "You got enough of her to fill a whole book?"

"Plenty," said Bang Abbott. What he didn't have was a publisher—yet. "First I'll sell a couple of the shots to some upmarket rag like *Maxim* or maybe *W.* You know, just to give the world a taste. Then, soon as things heat up, I'll put the book project out for bids in New York."

"Tell me again why I shouldn't just shoot you and get the money from Mr. Lykes."

"Because I'll cut you in for forty percent of whatever I make, and I intend to make a bundle."

Chemo said, "I can see you never had a partner like me before."

"Fine. Fifty-fifty."

"Or I could just whack you anyway and sell the pictures myself."

Bang Abbott produced a trenchant laugh, which wasn't easy because he was terrified. His sphincter had puckered to the size of a tick.

To the bodyguard he said, "You wouldn't know where to start. They'd rip you off big-time, I mean you'd be screwed blue and tattooed. Man, there is zero honor in my business."

"Really? I used to be in the mortgage trade." Chemo peeled a cracker-sized flake of skin from his jawline. "Nothing but saints and choirboys there."

Bang Abbott watched the feathery slough flutter to the floor. "It would be a major collection, a big coffee-table book," he added, squaring his hands to illustrate the impressive dimensions.

"How much would it sell for?" Chemo asked.

"Thirty-nine, forty bucks."

"You're nuts, Slim. Nobody's gonna pay that much to see pictures of some messed-up ho that can't even sing."

"Oh yes, they will," Bang Abbott said, "after she's dead."

Chemo thought the book idea was ludicrous, but he believed the individual photos could be valuable under the right circumstances. Unfortunately, Abbott was correct about one thing: Chemo didn't know shit about dealing with magazines and tabloids. For that he would need the paparazzo.

He craned closer to inspect the image in the camera's viewfinder—Cherry wearing the unbuttoned polo shirt and frog boxers on the veranda, looking out across Biscayne Bay toward the Miami skyline. The gnawed fingernails of one hand were lightly tracing the zebra portion of her tattoo, while the other hand—the one cuffed to the rail—clutched a disposable lighter. She wore an expression that someone who didn't know her might mistake for one of turbulent rumination, but Chemo could tell she was just jonesing for another smoke.

"I got a better plan than yours," he said.

Bang Abbott swallowed an olive-tinged burp. "Can I hear it?"

"You get to live," Chemo told him. "That's all you need to know."

26

The tantalizing tweets had already begun. Cherry's ghostwritten blog entry was polished and ready to go. So was the press release describing her fictitious abduction, sordid imprisonment and daring escape. Producers from *Showbiz Tonight*, *Extra* and *ET* had been alerted to expect a blockbuster tip. All that remained to be done—before launching the bogus story—was to secure Ann DeLusia's silence.

At least that's what the Larks thought.

"Annie left the hotel," Janet Bunterman was saying. "Took all her stuff."

"Oh, she'll call," said Lucy.

"The girl's not stupid," her sister added.

Maury Lykes removed the celery stalk from his Bloody Mary and chomped off the head. "Let me get this straight: We've lost the actress *again*?"

"Temporarily," said Cherry's mother.

"The one person who can blow the whole deal wide open—your daughter's double."

"She's not a double, Maury, she's just a stand-in."

"More like a crawl-in." The promoter crunched loudly on the celery. "This is unfuckingbelievable. You people said you could handle her."

The Larks would have frowned, if they could. Ann DeLusia wasn't their responsibility.

Janet Bunterman said, "She's been through a lot. I'm sure she'll come around."

Maury Lykes spat a mulched gob of green fiber into his cocktail napkin. "Aren't we missing a key member of the brain trust?"

"Ned's with Cherry. Her costume fitter's stopping by after dinner."

"Jesus, I'm not talking about Ned. I'm talking about Chemo," Maury Lykes said.

He speared a scallop off a platter of finger food, checked his Rolex and wondered if something had gone wrong on Star Island. It seemed unlikely that the humongous bodyguard could have been outwitted or overpowered by the dumpy likes of Claude Abbott, but show business had taught Maury Lykes that nothing was a lock. Arranging the murder of a paparazzo wasn't the worst thing the promoter had ever done on behalf of a star, but it carried some uncommon risks.

"This," he said, gnawing on the scallop, "tastes like a broiled tumor."

"Try it with the ponzu sauce," Janet Bunterman suggested.

Lucy Lark said, "What if Abbott doesn't cave? The needle shots he took of Ann are bad. With that horrid tattoo, she looks just like Cherry."

"Those pictures'll never get out," asserted Maury Lykes. "They can't."

"Even if they do, it's not the end of the world." This from Lila, catching even her sister by surprise. "No, seriously, I've been thinking about it. Handcuffing a young woman to a toilet and forcing her to shoot up—it would show what a total ghoul he was, wouldn't it? And how gutsy Cherry was for fighting back and making her escape?"

Lucy sat forward intently. "She's right. We can run with that."

"If we have to," said Lila. "Whatever's in that syringe doesn't have to be heroin or meth. We can always say it was—"

"Coke," her sister proposed.

"Sure. Or maybe ketamine."

Maury Lykes rubbed the bridge of his nose. "Gee, I feel *so* much better."

"Can we please change the subject?" Cherry's mother said.

There was a rapping at the door. One of the twins got up and let Chemo in. He sat down on the couch between Janet Bunterman and Maury Lykes. To make room for his legs, he kicked the coffee table away.

"Well, we've all been waiting patiently," the promoter said. "How was the prom?"

Chemo adjusted his hairpiece. He asked for a Diet Pepsi, and Lucy brought him one.

"What happened with Abbott?" Maury Lykes pressed. "Is he cool, or not?"

That was the code word he and Chemo had agreed upon—*cool* meant "dead."

"Change of plans," Chemo said.

"What's *that* mean?" asked Janet Bunterman. "Where are Cherry's pictures?"

Maury Lykes noticed his own feet twitching, a symptom of high anxiety. Evidently the photographer was still alive, and the potential complications were ugly to contemplate.

Chemo took off his Palin frames and cleaned the lenses with the corner of a napkin. "I got both of the man's cameras. The pictures are stored on the memory sticks."

"Thank God," sighed Cherry's mother.

"So, where are they?" Lila said.

"Yes, we'll need to see them ASAP," her sister emphasized.

Chemo put the glasses back on and said, "Here's the deal. The cameras, they're in a safe place."

"I knew it," said Maury Lykes.

"That's right. They're mine now."

"Let me guess: You and Abbott came to an agreement."

Chemo shrugged. "His options were limited."

Janet Bunterman looked lost. The twins, who hadn't seen this scheming side of the bodyguard's personality, were simultaneously alarmed and intrigued. But, once again, they were ignored.

When Maury Lykes asked Chemo how much money he wanted for the photographs, he laughed and said, "Get in line."

"What the hell are you talkin' about?"

"Abbott has the primo connections."

Lucy Lark said, "Hold on. Are you talking about the tabloids? Because we can't make our kidnap story work for Cherry if we don't control these pictures. Nobody's going to believe her without photos."

"Even then, it won't be an easy sell," noted Lila.

Chemo pinched a loose tassel of dead skin from his brow. "Maybe I can spare one or two shots. Say fifty grand each."

Janet Bunterman gasped. "Are you insane?" A hundred thousand dollars was way beyond the budget discussed by her and Ned. She turned to Maury Lykes and said, "What's happening here? Can't you do something?"

The promoter was trying to maintain his poise. Instead of killing the paparazzo, Chemo had conscripted the sonofabitch and confiscated the goods. Maury Lykes, who hadn't seen it coming, grudgingly admired the pock-faced brute. By his own devious maneuvering, Chemo was no longer just a contract worker; he was a player.

"Let's think about this," said Maury Lykes, "in a way that would be mutually beneficial to everyone."

"What for?" The bodyguard scrutinized the hors d'oeuvres. "I got the photos. You got jack." He passed on the scallops and selected a Cajun-fried shrimp.

Maury Lykes turned to Cherry's mother and said, "I need to speak to him alone." Then, to the Larks: "Don't make another move until you hear from me."

The twins followed Janet Bunterman out of the suite. As soon as the door closed, Maury Lykes said, "Hey, what the fuck? We had a deal."

"Opportunity knocked," said Chemo.

"How much do you think those bimbette pictures are really worth? Seriously."

"Guess we'll find out."

The promoter presented a theory that the market value of Abbott's Star Island collection would be basically chump change unless *Skantily Klad* became a commercial smash. "You need this album to go big," he advised Chemo. "You need Cherry Pye's name back on the charts—if you're interested in the major bucks, that is."

The thought had occurred to Chemo, as well. A hit CD and a sold-out tour would make Abbott's moody portraits a much hotter commodity when Cherry finally overdosed. The bodyguard understood that he now had a stake in keeping the stoned nitwit breathing for at least the next two months.

"The tour opens where?" he asked.

"Right here in Miami," said Maury Lykes. "Then we take it to Orlando, Charlotte and so on up the coast."

Chemo hated to fly, not because he was afraid but because his extreme height made the seating miserable.

Maury Lykes laughed. "She goes private, man. You'll have tons of legroom."

"Plus, I'm keepin' that forty grand you gave me. For the hit." Chemo intended to live on the cash until Cherry punched out.

"I'm glad you brought that up." Maury Lykes slid closer and dropped his voice. "The other forty thousand, the second half, it's still out there."

Chemo grabbed some curly hairs on the promoter's neck and twisted hard. "I told you, I'm not gonna whack the fat boy. He's got ace connections for brokering those pictures."

The jerking of Maury Lykes's head caused something to pop in his neck. "Stop!" he yipped. "It's not Abbott who needs to be killed. It's somebody else."

"Who?" Chemo demanded. "What's his name?"

"It's a her, not a him."

"Jesus Horatio Christ." The bodyguard let go of the promoter's hair and shoved him to the floor.

"Just hear me out," said Maury Lykes.

For all his character defects, Bang Abbott wasn't prone to self-pity. He regarded himself as a seasoned street warrior—the job of hounding celebrities was mined with disappointments, deceits and humiliations. In Bang Abbott's lowly league of paparazzi, a good day was one in which you weren't spat upon or kneed in the groin. Still, reflecting upon the past week, he found it difficult not to feel snakebit. His expensive Nikons had been stolen by a starlet, recovered, then stolen again. He had mistakenly carjacked the starlet's double, who then somehow shot off his trigger finger. Then, just as things were finally looking up, he was assaulted by a double-crossing one-armed bodyguard who sadistically weed-whacked his ass flab. Most dispiritingly, Bang Abbott's ambitious plan for exploiting the inevitable self-destruction of Cherry Pye was in ruins. The *Lost Angel* portraits he'd taken of the singer at Star Island—in his opinion, the finest work of his career—were in the clutches of the seven-foot, pizza-faced Chemo, who had promised him only a photo credit and some vague overspill of the profits.

And now Peter Cartwill was on the line, spoiling Bang Abbott's dinner. The photographer had been relaxing outdoors at the News Café, inhaling a couple of cheeseburgers while watching all the gorgeous zombies stroll by on Ocean Drive. He'd called the editor of the *Eye* to say he was all right, and that there was no need to retrieve his laptop from the apartment in Los Angeles.

"Too late. Our guy fetched it yesterday and it arrived by FedEx this morning," Cartwill said. "Your screen saver, by the way, is disgusting."

"But I told you guys to wait till tomorrow!" Bang Abbott protested. "And only if I didn't call by noon."

"Really, Claude. That's sort of sad."

Cartwill was right. Bang Abbott knew better than to trust a tabloid editor.

"You're not thinking straight," Cartwill observed. "I'm worried about you."

"It's been a rough stretch."

"These pictures, Claude, I must say . . ."

"So you found 'em?"

Cartwill's chuckle had a fluttering quality. "The file was marked 'Toilet Art.' Somehow our IT lads managed to crack the code. What's she shooting up, by the way—smack?"

Bang Abbott swigged a gulp of warm Pellegrino and almost choked on a lemon rind. If those pictures leaked out now, Cherry Pye's tour would be doomed, the Star Island portfolio would be worthless and, worst of all, Chemo would hunt him down with that goddamn lawn trimmer and chop him into two hundred pounds of steaming slaw.

"You can't publish those shots, Peter."

"And why would that be?"

"It's complicated," Bang Abbott said.

"Actually, it's not. You remember the last conversation we had? About the picture you took of Cherry outside the Viper Room? The one we paid six grand for?"

"I remember."

"Except Cherry was actually in the ER at Cedars that night."

Bang Abbott said hotly, "You believe that stupid nurse and not me?"

Cartwill's tone made it clear that he did. "The woman

handcuffed to the toilet in these photographs—tell me the truth. Is that really Cherry?"

"Ha! Check out the freaky tatt."

"We have, Claude. Our guys in Digital enlarged the images. They say it looks like a henna."

Bang Abbott's Bluetooth fell off his head and landed in a glop of catsup. He wiped down the earpiece and, after two false stabs, re-inserted it.

"She's also missing a freckle," Cartwill was saying, "on her left wrist."

"Are you fucking serious?"

"The truth, Claude, or we'll never touch your stuff again," Cartwill warned. "Once the word gets out, you'll be shooting cruises and bar mitzvahs the rest of your life."

It was a hollow threat; Bang Abbott was confident that he'd always be able to peddle his celebrity candids somewhere. The market was bottomless in the purest sense of the word. However, considering the hefty lease on his Mercedes, he couldn't afford to be banned from top-paying magazines and tabloids such as the *Eye*, fussy as they might be about the authenticity of their art.

"Okay, Peter, you got me. It's not Cherry in those shots."

"Ah." Cartwill sounded no more superior than usual. "She's pretty. Who is it?"

"Long story," Bang Abbott said.

"What's in the spike?"

"Tap water."

"Claude, this is so disappointing."

"But, listen, the picture outside the Viper Room after the Emmys, the girl in the leather mini—that was an honest mistake." Bang Abbott wasn't about to sit mute while his reputation was shredded. He was good at what he did, even if most people considered what he did to be despicable.

"Cherry's people sometimes use a double," he informed Cartwill, "to throw us off."

"Maybe that's who balled you on the Gulfstream."

"I'm serious. They've got this chick on the payroll, some nobody actress."

Cartwill said, "I'm about to do you a huge professional favor, Claude. I'm going to delete these dreadful images from your laptop. Come by the office and fetch it before you fly back to L.A. And don't ever pull another shitwhistle stunt like this again. Are we clear?"

"Crystal," said Bang Abbott, buoyant with relief. "Hey, I'm still down on South Beach. Is anything happening?"

"Not much. Hasselhoff's shooting a German aftershave commercial by the pool at the Delano, and Megan Fox is in town for a club party."

"Yeah? Where?"

Cartwill said, "No worries, mate. We've got it covered." Then he hung up.

Bang Abbott ordered an eggplant and a side of fries. For a man whose lofty dreams had been stomped to tatters, he maintained his usual robust appetite. He wasn't sure that the spooky bodyguard's plan was going to work, but it wasn't like he had a vote. The man was a killer. If he happened to make some dough off the Star Island photos and dribble a few bucks to Bang Abbott, hey, it was better than nothing. And sure as hell better than being dead.

At the very least, Bang Abbott had successfully contrived to spend a whole day with Cherry, ending in a tangle of sheets. Although it now seemed unlikely that sex had occurred, the time wasn't wasted. Something big had happened. That last boozy hour with the young singer had served to dissolve the warped and misbegotten fascination that had overpowered Bang Abbott in recent days. Cherry was truly the simplest of souls, as vacant as she was beautiful. It was no act.

The conversation had been excruciating. Granted, the woman was only twenty-two, but she'd been a star for almost half her life. Surely something interesting must have happened along the way. *Of course she stayed high all the time*, Bang Abbott thought. *That's what boring people do.*

No, he was cured of his Cherry fixation. Eventually he might have come to enjoy being a serious portrait photographer with a respectable oeuvre, a mercurial artiste sought out by troubled divas. But Bang Abbott was at heart a denizen of the streets—studio settings were too tidy and sterile for his style. He preferred the challenge of an openly hostile work environment where daily he was cursed, loathed, snubbed and evaded. Bang Abbott loved the chill, and he loved the chase.

Among paparazzi, only the most resilient and remorseless

could thrive. Hell, this thing with Cherry Pye was just one more crappy gig. Bang Abbott had felt worse about himself after Charlie Sheen urinated in his ear.

Oddly, of his two most recent female subjects it was Cherry's decoy who had made the greater impression. She was scrappy and funny and proud, a different sort of handful. In the aftermath Bang Abbott found himself thinking more frequently of Ann, and he remained convinced that someday she'd be famous for something.

Packing his cheeks with curly fries, the photographer was feeling increasingly upbeat about his own prospects. Although the mutant bodyguard had impounded his expensive Nikons, Bang Abbott still had the secondhand Pentax that he'd bought, along with the cheap cell phone, at the Hialeah pawnshop. What other survival tools would he possibly need?

Unfortunately, the contact numbers for his best sources were programmed into his lost BlackBerry, so Bang Abbott was working from a reconstructed roster of tipsters. But he wasn't worried; he'd started from scratch before.

"Well, lookie who's here!" A man nearly as unkempt as himself stood with a shit-eating grin beside the table. He had three nice Leicas strung around his neck.

"My lucky day," Bang Abbott said.

"Dog, ain't you even gone ask me to sit down?" It was Teddy Loo. He took a seat anyway.

"Do have a fry," Bang Abbott offered sullenly.

Teddy Loo had a pipe-stem neck, a wide slice of a mouth

and gleaming, bugged-out eyeballs. He looked like an anorexic bullfrog. He said, "How's it hangin', Claude?"

"Long and strong. Same as always."

"You here for Megan Fox?"

"Oh, you bet," Bang Abbott lied.

"I heard she's stayin' at the Standard."

"Ha! Who fed you that shit?"

"Why? What'd you hear, dog?" Teddy Loo wrinkled his nose and hunched forward.

"The Clevelander is what I heard," Bang Abbott said. He was totally winging it.

"What the fuck is that smell? God."

"You don't like eggplant?" Bang Abbott wasn't about to admit that he'd spritzed his pits and crevices with a product called Axe "body spray." Ann's sharp comments during her captivity had caused him to rethink his libertarian outlook on hygiene.

Teddy Loo said, "The Clevelander—you sure 'bout that?"

"Rock solid."

"Cool. And the party's still Wednesday night, right?"

"Absolutely."

"At Pubes is what they said."

"I heard the Mondrian, but that's spongy." Bang Abbott winked. This was going to be fun. "Are you shootin' for the *Eye*?" he asked Teddy Loo.

"Good guess. How 'bout you?"

"The *Globe*."

"Yechh."

"Tell me about it." Bang Abbott stood up and slapped a fifty on the table. "See you in the trenches," he said to Teddy Loo.

"Yeah, dog. Thanks for the intel."

"Anytime." Bang Abbott was smiling as he walked down Ocean Drive. It was second nature to him, working these fools.

Like riding a bicycle.

27

Before being snatched by Bang Abbott, the worst thing that had happened to Ann DeLusia while acting as Cherry Pye's double was the funeral of Nils Creosoto, a Formula 1 driver and international playboy with whom Cherry had been romantically linked, meaning she had slept with him more than once.

As sometimes happened in the celebrity world, the circumstances of Nils Creosoto's death were more mundane than the tabloid media would have wished: He was run over while jay-walking in broad daylight on Bleecker Street down in the Village. Worse, he was stone sober and fully clothed at the time. The motorist who flattened Nils Creosoto wasn't a disgruntled ex-girlfriend or an envious racing rival, but rather an innocent Nigerian immigrant who'd been driving yellow cabs for eleven years with a spotless record.

Police determined Nils Creosoto was entirely to blame for the accident. As he stepped from the curb into traffic, he was fatally engrossed in a newspaper—specifically, the *New York Post*, which was scattered like pigeon feathers upon impact. It was later speculated (by the *Post*, naturally) that Nils Creosoto had been reading a Page Six item about himself at the time he was struck and killed. The gossip nugget, accompanied by a photograph of him and Cherry Pye leaving the Morgan Hotel, read as follows:

Hunky Swedish–Greco racing ace **Nils Creosoto** is no longer spinning his wheels with pouty **Mary-Kate Olsen**. Last night he steered new flame **Cherry Pye** to the **Yanni** concert at the Garden, then back to his ultra-cozy suite for a victory lap.

Confides a Creosoto pal: "It's getting pretty serious. I haven't seen him this happy in a long time." **Lucy and Lila Lark**, high-powered spokespersons for Cherry Pye, say the troubled pop star is "healthy, whole and enjoying life. She's very fond of Nils."

Time will tell whether he really turns out to be Le Man, or just another quick pit stop for wild-child Cherry.

The former Cheryl Gail Bunterman was saddened though not incapacitated by the unexpected death of Nils Creosoto. They had been out on exactly three dates. Contrary to the media speculation, there was nothing serious about the relationship. Auto racing bored Cherry to tears, and Nils had a disconcerting tendency to double-clutch during sex. Their last outing had been a let-down because Cherry had gone to Madison Square Garden expecting to see an exotic magic act. She'd had no idea that Yanni was a musician.

Shortly after Nils Creosoto got thumped by the taxi, the Larks mass-emailed a somber press release announcing that Cherry was "shocked and devastated" by the tragic news. She was, in fact, on her way to Steamboat Springs with an adult-film star named Rod Harder. A few days later, when the schedule of memorial services for Nils Creosoto was announced, the twins told the Buntermans that Cherry should attend. They said the funerals presented an opportunity to display her sensitive, compassionate side. Appearing as the grief-stricken girlfriend could only improve her image—it was the next best thing to being a widow, the Larks explained.

But Cherry was in no condition to go. So while she was being escorted back to Los Angeles for her semiannual septum reconstruction, Ann DeLusia was boarding a plane for Europe. Her first stop was Gothenburg and then Athens. Half of Nils Creosoto's ashes were scattered from a speeding Ferrari in each city, following lugubrious church ceremonies in which Ann convincingly sobbed and shuddered in the front pew. That was awful enough. Worse were all the consoling hugs from the race driver's heartsick relatives, who (thanks to global media saturation by the Larks) had been led to believe that Cherry was his fiancée, the light of his life. The Swedes were stolid mourners but the Greeks wept deliriously. By the end of the trip, Ann had become dangerously depressed.

"As I recall, we let you keep the funeral dress," Cherry's mother said.

"I gave it to Goodwill," said Ann.

"But that was Vera Wang!"

"See, Janet, this is the problem."

Both sides had agreed to meet at Dinner Key aboard a yacht owned by a producer friend of Maury Lykes. The Buntermans were accompanied by Chemo, garbed in corduroys, vintage Beatle boots, tan beret, his red Sarah Palins and a loose leather jacket that concealed the sheath of his ominous prosthesis. Ann brought Skink, refashioned in a tailored suit by Ermenegildo Zegna, blue pinstripes with a matching eye patch. She had persuaded him to lose the lopsided though festive braids, and his hairless, sun-cured dome glowed like burnished teak. The sawed-off Remington was stowed in a Converse gym bag that sat on the deck between the governor's new size-thirteen Kenneth Coles. The incongruously uptown look kindled Janet Bunterman's secret attraction, although Ann's companion displayed no interest in anyone other than her.

Even Chemo was initially taken aback. He hadn't expected the actress to show up with a jumbo bodyguard of her own, and he felt somewhat underdressed.

"Annie, you've been a real lifesaver for us," Cherry's

mother was saying. "The Creosoto gig—like you said, above and beyond the call. Time after time, you've come through for our Cherry when the chips were down."

"You mean when *she* was down," Ann said.

Chemo smiled to himself. This chick was a pisser.

Ned Bunterman cleared his throat. "We're prepared to offer you fifty thousand."

Ann wrinkled her brow in feigned disbelief. "For being kidnapped, drugged and humiliated? Did I mention that the guy took a three-minute pee while I was handcuffed to the damn toilet? Try to put a price tag on a moment like that."

Cherry's father reddened. Chemo said to Janet Bunterman: "Tell her the plan."

"Yes, please do," said Ann. "Hang on—I forgot to introduce my friend. This is the governor."

Skink, who was picking his teeth with a desiccated mockingbird beak, said nothing. The Zegna threads had put him in a ruminative frame of mind; it had been decades since he'd worn a suit and proper shoes. The outfit stirred fractured memories of Tallahassee.

Cherry's mother sat forward. "All right, here's the play: In a few days we'll give out a story saying our daughter was abducted and held captive by a deviate fan who was posing as a paparazzo. Abbott won't be mentioned by name, but a couple of the photos he took of Cherry on Star Island will be strategically leaked to create, you know, maximum buzz."

Ann, who had bought a strapless sundress and new sandals

for the meeting, folded her arms and said, "But it happened to *me*."

"Posing as her," Ned Bunterman noted. His left ear was still sore from where she'd whacked him with the spatula.

"So this fifty grand, it wouldn't be compensation for pain and suffering. It would be hush money, a good-bye kiss." Ann turned to Skink. "What do you make of these people, captain?"

He slipped one callused finger beneath the pinstriped eye patch and scratched at the empty ocular socket, which was itching. His good eye fixed on a flock of terns circling high above the yacht.

Chemo said, "What's with 'captain'? You said governor."

Ann signaled for him to hush. The Buntermans fidgeted like incontinent geezers in their canvas deck chairs.

Skink repositioned his patch and said, "'Hustlers of the world, there is one Mark you cannot beat: the Mark Inside.' That's William S. Burroughs."

"Oh, I like it," Ann remarked.

Chemo thought William Burroughs was the guy who wrote the Tarzan books he'd seen in the prison library, although the governor's quotation didn't seem to fit a jungle story.

"Back to business," Ned Bunterman said.

His wife added: "Nobody here has anything to gain from the destruction of Cherry's career. Can we at least agree on that?"

Chemo glanced across at Ann's bodyguard, who was

regarding him with neutral curiosity. "Sir, what's your stake in this clusterfuck?" the man inquired.

"I got all the goddamn pictures," Chemo replied, "and I also got a leash on Abbott."

Ann seemed impressed. "Well, good for you," she said, reaching across to pat one of Chemo's scaffold-sized legs.

He thought: *Screw Maury. No way can I kill this girl.*

Skink took the shotgun out of the gym bag and placed it across his lap. To the Buntermans he said: "You like the Stones? Because it feels like we're all in 'Memo from Turner.'"

"Good track," Cherry's father offered feebly.

Ann said, "No, Ned, it's a *great* fucking track."

Chemo stared at the Remington, which trumped his weed whacker big-time. Seventeen years of incarceration had sharpened his skills at threat assessment, and he pegged the one-eyed man as the real deal. Fearless and unbalanced was a formidable combination of traits.

"How much cash are you carrying?" Ann sprung on Ned Bunterman.

"What?"

"You heard me, big boy. Out with the wallet. You, too, Janet, open your purse."

Together Cherry's parents came up with $1,461.

Ann folded it into a wad and said, "That'll do. But you're also going to pay for the captain's new suit. I mean, does he not look hot?"

Skink told Chemo that the eye patch alone cost three bills.

"Are you shittin' me? Is it silk or somethin'?"

"Wool blend, swear to God," Skink said. "For three hundred dollars I could buy a whole goddamn sheep and train it to sit on my face."

Everyone laughed except Janet Bunterman. Her husband got on the phone and gave his AmEx number to the Zegna store in Bal Harbour. Ann made sure he instructed the clerk to tear up the sales slip for her credit card, the limits of which had been breached by the purchase of the governor's new wardrobe.

A young man in a white ship's uniform brought up rum drinks, lobster salad and a sterling-silver platter of tuna tataki, which was a bit too rare for Chemo but he ate it anyway.

As soon as the server departed, Ann said: "I don't want your fifty thousand dollars, Janet. Fourteen hundred is plenty to get me back to California."

Ever the bean counter, Ned Bunterman tried to conceal his elation, which his wife didn't share. She knew that Maury Lykes would be equally dismayed because Annie was essentially cutting herself loose from the team—and nobody who turned down fifty grand could be trusted.

Janet Bunterman said, "For heaven's sake, Annie, take the money. You earned it."

"And more," said Ann.

"Then what are you trying to prove?"

"Look, she's made up her mind," Cherry's father interjected. "We should respect her wishes."

Chemo himself was puzzled by Ann's move, but he felt no urge to talk her out of it. The fifty thousand she was rejecting could be put to good use by the whining Buntermans as a purchase price for one of the juicier Star Island portraits.

Again Cherry's mother said, "Take the fifty, Annie."

"No, I'm good." She stood to leave. Skink returned the shotgun to the Converse bag. When he rose from his chair, he cast a shadow like a cypress tree over the Buntermans.

"So where does this leave us?" Cherry's father asked with a larval wriggle.

Ann sighed. "You haven't been listening, have you? I'm done, Ned."

"Yes, but—"

"By the way? Your daughter's totally off the tracks. She's gonna kill herself."

"Oh, please," said Janet Bunterman.

"She won't make it through the tour alive," Ann said, "not the way she parties."

Ned Bunterman was looking straight at Chemo when he said, "We've got that situation buttoned down solid. It's a whole new program, right?"

"Yeah, mon," Chemo said with a reptilian blink.

"Don't ever call me again," Ann told Cherry's parents, "no matter what happens. I don't care if she's in a frigging coma."

Janet Bunterman was flustered and unmoored. "What—so this is it? For real?"

Chemo couldn't stand to be around such people. He envied the young actress for bailing out.

"Nobody dies from gastritis!" said Cherry's mother. "You've got some nerve, Annie."

Ned Bunterman, who was eager to seal the deal and save the family fifty thousand bucks, chose the amenable approach. "Don't worry, we're going to take super-good care of Cherry on the road. Mr. Chemo will be watching her like a hawk."

"Uh-oh. I hope he does a better job than the night he was watching me."

The dig by Ann caused Chemo to reconsider his decision not to murder her, but then she nudged him playfully with her foot. "It was your first carjacking," she teased. "You're forgiven."

They all got up and followed Skink and Ann down to the main deck, the yacht rocking gently from the wake of a passing tour boat. Standing at the gangplank, the governor asked about Chemo's arm. The bodyguard removed the Cobra Golf bag cover and demonstrated the motorized weed trimmer by shredding the colorful insignia of the Coral Gables Yacht Club, which had been flapping gaily from the stern.

"Fantastic!" Skink roared, his thousand-watt smile causing Janet Bunterman to tingle self-consciously.

Chemo had always felt more comfortable discussing his disability with somebody who had one of their own—in this case, a missing eye. "Battery's in a holster," he explained, patting his side.

"Pure genius!" Few men were tall enough to whisper in Chemo's ear, but the governor leaned in and said,

"Regardless of your loyalties, nothing must happen to fair Annie."

"I like her," Chemo conceded, "but she's the only one of this bunch."

Skink nodded and followed Ann down the gangplank.

"Take care of yourself now," Ned Bunterman sang out lamely.

"I am *so* touched," Ann said over her shoulder. "Toodle-oo!"

Cherry's mother grabbed the rail and squinted fretfully into the sun. "What is it you want from us, Annie? Don't play games."

Ann had to laugh. "Good luck with your 'maximum buzz'!" she shouted. Then she took Skink's arm and whispered, "Poor Janet."

"Hold up, captain!" It was Chemo, reaching into his trousers.

On the dock, Skink stepped in front of Ann just as the one-armed bodyguard lobbed something down from the yacht. Skink caught the small object and looked it over.

"Gimme," said Ann.

It was a BlackBerry phone with a tangerine-colored shell.

Chemo called out: "Fucking thing never shuts up."

Ann smiled and slipped the device into her handbag.

As they strolled off toward the Grove, she heard the governor grumble, "This damn shirt is too tight."

"It's Hermès, old man. Suck it up."

*

They identified Jackie Sebago's body by the swollen balls. Turkey vultures had already gnawed off the face.

"That's definitely him," Detective Reilly said to Corporal Valdez.

"Who uses a speargun?"

"Sends a message," Reilly said. "Also, it's quieter than a pistol."

The state trooper whistled. "These real-estate guys," he said.

"Yeah, what a shitty racket."

Valdez had been called to help secure the scene, which was unnecessary because the location of the homicide was so remote. He and Reilly positioned themselves upwind from the corpse, which had been discovered by a butterfly collector in some woods half a mile off of County Road 905, a short haul from the Ocean Reef Club. Somebody had shot Jackie Sebago in the heart with a Hawaiian sling, a light-weight apparatus popular with skin divers and lobster poachers. The spear had been discharged with such force that it had passed through the developer's chest, pinning him upright to a gumbo-limbo tree which had soon filled with the hungry buzzards.

Reilly said, "Could be our sea-urchin dude who did it."

Valdez was skeptical. "Half the people on that hijacked bus were ready to strangle this jerk."

"Yeah, but still." The detective paused to watch the crime-scene investigators measure the portion of the fish spear that was protruding from the remains of the developer. "They found a campsite near here," he said. "We took a fingerprint off a plastic water bottle, got a match with an individual named Clinton Tyree."

"So he's got a record," Valdez said.

"Naw, he's clean. The army had his prints on file—the guy did three tours in Nam."

That would explain how he survives in a crocodile preserve, the trooper thought. *If it's the same man.*

Reilly wasn't done. "Guess what else? He was the governor of Florida for about fifteen minutes. *The* governor."

"You're kidding," Valdez said, playing it close.

"It was back before you were born, and I was still sleeping with a Binky. One day he just disappeared off the planet. Mental breakdown, according to the newspapers."

The trooper listened. The Keys was a relatively laid-back place, and detectives such as Reilly had limited experience with flamboyant Miami-style homicides. However, as a road officer, Valdez knew better than to volunteer an opinion about anything more exotic than a DUI.

"The go-fast that was stolen at Ocean Reef, it turned up in South Beach," Reilly was saying. "I mean, literally up on the damn beach. Empty except for a few beer bottles."

"Any latents?"

"None," said the detective. "But the very next night, not far from where the boat came ashore, some loon matching Tyree's description torched a lady's suitcase and ran off with her dog. This is in the lobby of a Marriott."

"Big dude with a fake eyeball?" Valdez asked.

"Yup. There were other sightings, too."

"Weird." The trooper wondered why the volcanic hermit had left the safety of his swamp for the clamor of Miami Beach. And why would he return to Key Largo on a mission to murder Jackie Sebago? The man had graphically made his point with the developer—and he could have offed him during the bus hijacking, if he'd wanted.

"When did Sebago die?" Valdez asked.

"Last night. Maybe early this morning." Reilly knew what the trooper was thinking. He said, "It's not a long ride from South Beach to here. Ninety minutes in traffic."

"So you think he came back to the island."

"If not, somebody else committed this murder."

Valdez didn't believe that the ranting man who had diapered a sea urchin to Jackie Sebago was the same individual who'd killed him, but the guy was impossible to ignore.

"You check his camp?" Valdez asked.

"No signs of life. So tomorrow I've gotta drive up to the beach, interview these witnesses." Reilly chuckled ruefully. "I don't even have a recent picture of the sonofabitch to show 'em. He hasn't had a driver's license in thirty years."

The crime-scene technicians had finished taking photos of Jackie Sebago's body, which was now being strapped in a black bag to a stretcher. A bulge the size of a Kona pineapple delineated the victim's engorged testicles.

"I bet he didn't do it. I bet it was somebody else," Valdez said at last. He couldn't stop himself.

The detective received the comment thoughtfully. "You

might be right but, either way, the dude seriously needs to be taken off the streets. Did you know he took a dump in some rich guy's washing machine?"

"Get out."

"Oh yeah," Reilly said. "It happened up at Ocean Reef."

Valdez was still laughing when he got in his patrol car.

I hope they never catch him, he thought, but this he would never say aloud.

28

The former Cheryl Gail Bunterman had flashes of self-awareness that stopped just shy of introspection. She knew she wasn't the most talented blond singer in the world, but she was happy to play the part. Vanity, petulance and tardiness were expected, and she delivered. As for the partying, it wasn't a desperate cry for help; it was fun. Cherry hooted every time a blogger theorized she was subconsciously rebelling against her parents, or lashing out at Maury Lykes. She loved being a star and moreover was equipped for no other role. Her ambitions fully realized, coasting was all that remained. The possibility of losing her fame never occurred to her. She wouldn't have known how to live a private life, although occasionally she imagined it might be cool to work as a croupier on a Caribbean cruise ship.

Cherry seldom pondered the erratic arc of her singing career, but she recognized a shrinking entourage as a sign of hard times. Having only one bodyguard—and an untouchable one, at that—was humiliating, although Maury had promised that another would be added for the *Skantily Klad* tour. Cherry was lobbying her parents to hire an ex-middleweight boxer who'd formerly worked for Mary J. Blige and was rumored to be hung like a range bull.

"I'm on the case, sweetie," Janet Bunterman said.

She and her husband had stopped by the Fillmore, where their daughter was rehearsing. Cherry stood before the mirror in her dressing room, examining the Axl Rose tattoo. "You think it needs a butt?" she asked. "The zebra part, I mean. Maybe I should go back and ask the dude to finish."

Trying not to sound mortified, Ned Bunterman said, "No, baby, that's plenty."

Cherry was in full costume—ruby spandex capris, four-inch stilettos and a neoprene bustier threaded with neon tubing that pulsed electric blue. The hair was Greta Garbo from *Grand Hotel*, the makeup was Alice Cooper from his python period. Cherry's father had long ago given up on offering style suggestions.

He said, "Have a seat, honey."

"What for?"

"We've got a bit of news," Janet Bunterman said.

Cherry covered her ears. "No freakin' thanks. Not today."

"Sweetie, please."

"Why do you always do this to me? God!" Cherry popped open a Red Bull and flung herself on the couch.

"Promise you won't get upset," her mother began. "It's about the *Vanity Fair* cover."

"Yeah?"

"Well . . . it's not happening."

Ned Bunterman flinched when Cherry hurled the can against the wall. The spray caught his wife flush in the face.

"Now, settle down," he said to his daughter. "You've still got *Us Weekly*."

He hadn't the nerve to tell her that she'd been demoted from the front to an inside feature, due to late-breaking news about the late Anna Nicole Smith. According to the Larks, being bumped from a magazine cover by a dead actress was only slightly less tragic than being bumped by a live one.

"I hate you both! You are the *worst* humans ever!" Cherry screeched at her parents.

"That's enough."

"What about *Esquire*? Scarlett got the front of *Esquire* last Christmas."

"Please listen," said her father.

"*Details*? *Marie Claire*? God, what are you saying?" Cherry yanked off her spiked heels and threw those against the wall, too. While browsing through drugstores she always checked out the magazine racks to see which female entertainers were getting face exposure.

She said, "Mom, tell me what happened right this minute! I'm not kidding!"

After toweling off, Janet Bunterman laid out the situation. Eventually Cherry quit fuming and struggled to sort out the facts.

"So Claude wasn't really working for *VF*?"

"It's complicated. He was trying to blackmail us," Ned Bunterman said.

"Wow. We're talkin' about the same Claude, right?" Cherry could hardly believe it. "Who came up with this bizarro kidnap story? Was it Lucy or Lila?"

"Group effort," her mother said.

"And how long was I a hostage? For when people ask, I mean."

"Just say a couple of days. The Star Island pictures turned out amazing, by the way. Right, Ned?"

"Spectacular," agreed Cherry's father, who like his wife hadn't seen a single frame. "They'll be huge. Epic. We're going to blame the kidnapper for leaking them to the tabloids."

"This is after I supposedly escaped," said Cherry.

"Exactly."

"And how'd I pull *that* off?"

"Squeezed through a basement window and ran off into the swamp," Janet Bunterman said.

Cherry perked up. "That's pretty awesome. Was there, like, alligators and bears and stuff?"

"Sweetie, if you play this right, the new album shoots straight to number one and the tour sells out in a day. That's where we're at."

"Cool. But what about the police?"

Ned Bunterman clicked his jaw. "You'll have to tell them a little story, I'm afraid. You never saw the guy before. Don't know his name. Didn't get a good look at his face. You have no clue where he was holding you prisoner. It was dark outside when you got away. You just kept running and running. Think you can handle that?"

"So what happens to Claude?" she said. "Like I really care."

"He'll stay out of the way. He's totally down with this." Janet Bunterman saw no need to mention that Chemo had seized Abbott's photographs. Stripped of product, the paparazzo was no longer a factor.

Cherry was warming to the scam. "This is crazy sick," she said.

"And it'll work," her father asserted, "if we all stay on the same page."

"The twins are psyched," Janet Bunterman added.

"Can I tell Tanny?"

"Absolutely not. You can't talk to a soul about this."

"That sucks!"

Ned Bunterman said, "Remember, honey, you're supposed to be recovering from a horribly traumatic crime. You can't go out for a while, okay? You're damaged. You're scared. You cannot be seen running all over South Beach, having a big old time. You're a *victim*, Cherry."

"Trust us on this one," her mother added.

"Yeah, yeah." Cherry got up and took a Gatorade bottle

from the refrigerator. She had mixed in the Stoli earlier, after her parents had gone off to some business meeting. "So when does the story hit?" she asked.

"The Larks want to launch this weekend," Janet Bunterman said.

"Oh wow."

Ned Bunterman said they were waiting for Maury to sign off.

"Saturday or Sunday?" Cherry took a slug from the bottle. Vodka was clean and sneaky; that's what she liked about it.

"Saturday morning," her mother said, "right before CNN's ten a.m. newsbreak."

Not much time left to play, Cherry thought. She would make the best of it.

Billy Shea was double-bogeying the fifth hole at Metacomet when his cell phone rang, violating a strict club rule that he routinely ignored. The man on the other end of the line was waiting at Miami International for a nonstop to Las Vegas.

"They got me in coach," the man complained. "You promised first class."

"Did I?"

"If the job got done, yeah. You said I could fly back in first."

Shea sighed. "My travel agent, he's a moron."

"Can't you make some calls?"

"Man, I'm stuck on the golf course. How was the trip?"

"It went fine. Maybe you should cash in some frequent-flyer miles, get me an upgrade?"

Shea said, "Didn't I tell you the Keys was nice? The water down there, it's so fucking blue."

"Yeah, Billy, I speared me an eel."

"Excellent."

"A big sucker," the man said. "Now call your travel agent and get my ass bumped to first class. They board in twenty minutes."

Once Shea had concluded that no portion of his $850,000 would be returned in the foreseeable future, and that Jackie Sebago had spent most of the money before a single condo was built at Sebago Isle, he reached out to an acquaintance in the Providence underworld, who then put him in touch with a professional killer.

The killer normally used a .22, but Shea insisted on something special for Jackie Sebago, something that would give pause to other low-life Florida hustlers who preyed on earnest out-of-state investors. Shea was hoping for the murder to make a splash on TV, so he wanted it exceptionally messy, yet with a tropical touch befitting the locale. The Hawaiian sling was the killer's idea. He said he would practice on coconuts.

"I heard they get a Vince Vaughn movie in first class," the man was saying.

"Okay, let me see what I can do." Shea motioned for his golf partners to play on ahead. He told them he'd catch up on the next fairway.

"A promise is a promise," said the granite voice on the phone.

"Man, you're absolutely right."

Shea had no desire to end a murder-for-hire deal with hard feelings. The killer deserved to sit in the front of the airplane and watch a Vince Vaughn flick and order a Beefeater martini, whatever the fuck he wanted. Jackie Sebago was deceased, with an exclamation point, and would never again enjoy the fruits of deceit. Shea knew a law firm that would chase down the shithead's assets and tie up probate for years.

He dialed his travel agent and said, "Drop everything."

The local police were harried but helpful. They gave Detective Reilly a street map and a stack of recent incident reports deemed unusual even for Miami Beach. He culled out the three most promising sightings and set out to find the witnesses.

Unfortunately, the desk clerk at the Marriott had a memory as vexing as his accent. He squirmed under questioning, and his description of the intruder who'd set fire to Marian DeGregorio's luggage and stolen her Maltese changed repeatedly, until the suspect bore only a shaky resemblance to the Key Largo gypsy who was Reilly's main suspect. The detective's next stop was the duplex of a cocktail waitress who'd been rescued from a sexual assault on the beach; an anonymous Good Samaritan had put her would-be attackers into body casts. The victim told Reilly that her raging rescuer had a shaved head and wore a trench coat. It was the best she could do—she'd been drinking that night, and the scene of the attack had been very dark. Finally, Reilly attempted to interview a Haitian cabdriver who'd reported being carjacked by a tall, walleyed derelict, but the meeting was unproductive. The driver insisted he'd made a mistake; the crime had never happened. "He's still afraid of being deported," a Miami Beach detective explained to Reilly, "after twenty-seven years."

The two cops were eating Cuban sandwiches when a disturbance call came over the Miami Beach detective's handheld. Some big bald guy was going nuts down on Collins. Reilly figured it was too good to be true, but what the hell. They rushed to a small hotel called the Loft and made their way through a crowd of amused onlookers gathered out front. The man prancing around a palm tree at the center of the commotion wasn't the one whom Reilly was hunting. The prancer was somewhat tall and definitely bald, but he was also flabby, pale as a flounder and the owner of two functional though inflamed eyeballs.

Having worked the vice detail in Key West, a nightly festival of foolish behavior, Reilly was unfazed by the South Beach freak parade. That's why he wouldn't have been flabbergasted to learn that the shirtless man twirling and whooping near the hotel canopy was a well-respected podiatrist, Little League coach and church elder from Greenville, South Carolina. Evidently the fellow had been improperly briefed on the optimum dosages when mixing street MDMA with Xanax and mojitos. His Florida vacation had taken a turn for the worse.

As uniformed officers chased him in circles, the impaired tourist randomly snatched from the grass what appeared to be two multicolored cables, which he began slashing noisily back and forth over his head. "I'll save you, Rapunzel!" he crowed up at the building. "Wait for me, my princess!"

The crowd laughed, though Reilly didn't. He got a good look at what the man was whipping through the air: two silvery ropes of hair, strung with old shotgun shells. The cops tazed the wayward foot doctor, pried the pigtails from his fists and tossed them in the shrubs. Reilly waited until the man was hauled away and the gawkers dispersed before he retrieved the funky plaits, which appeared to have been freshly shorn at their roots.

The detective stepped back and looked up at the facing windows of the hotel. He saw only one that was open.

Ann DeLusia purchased a charger for the tangerine BlackBerry and, with trepidation, a pair of sea-green contact lenses. Then she went to see the henna artist.

"Why still on your neck this horrible thing?" Sasha demanded. "You promised to scrub off."

"Soon," Ann said. "But first I need a touch-up."

"No, is too ugly. Who this angry face would be?"

"A famous rock singer. Please, Sasha, I'll pay you a hundred dollars."

"From band Kiss this singer? Tell his name to me. Or Jam Pearl?"

"No, it's Axl Rose. The group is Guns N' Roses."

"And he paints up himself, this man, like wild zebra?" Sasha aimed the drawing lamp at Ann's tattoo and went to work with her pens. "This time no penis," she said firmly. "It for you is very wrong."

"Fine," said Ann. "No penis."

Refusing the Buntermans' money had been easier than she thought. She knew the fifty grand wouldn't have liberated her—just the opposite. After what had happened with the photographer, Ann needed a clean, irreparable break from Cherry's parents. From their laggard response to her kidnapping it was plain they wouldn't exactly have been crushed with grief had she wound up dead or permanently missing. Ann wasn't the vengeful sort but she had a mischievous streak and a flair for the ironic. She also believed that Cherry Pye would accidentally kill herself soon if nobody slammed on the brakes. Ann figured she might as well be the one.

"You don't have to stay for this," she'd told the governor.

"Of course I do," he'd said, and then crawled beneath the bed to hide from the housekeeping staff. She had left him there when she headed out to the henna parlor.

Inside her handbag, the BlackBerry chirped constantly with calls and texts and voice mails. That's how Ann had learned it belonged to Claude, although she wasn't clear on how Cherry's bodyguard had gained possession of it, or why he'd passed it along to her.

Up until then, Ann had never understood how the paparazzi always happened to be in the right place at the right time. Judging by the traffic lighting up Claude's smart phone, his network of scurrilous snoops and informants was far-reaching and vigilant. While the henna artist reluctantly freshened her tatt, Ann scrolled through the latest spate of messages, which offered an up-to-the-moment snapshot of celebrity activity from coast to coast. It reminded her of those flight-tracking Web sites that used real-time radar to show every jetliner in the air.

In New York, Kate and A-Rod were snuggling in a booth at the Gramercy Tavern.

In Las Vegas, Becks and Posh were quarreling in the lobby of the Bellagio.

In Santa Monica, Tom and Gisele were jogging on the beach with a rottweiler named Ludwig.

In Chicago, Jennifer Lopez was refusing to go on the Oprah show unless she could bring her Zumba instructor.

And in Miami Beach, Tanner Dane Keefe was sneaking through a backstage door of the Fillmore at the Gleason for a midday tryst with Cherry Pye, who was rehearsing for another comeback tour.

"Amazing," said Ann, clicking away. Each nugget arrived with the name (or nickname) of the tipster. When there was more than one, the details of the sightings often varied. One guy had Khloe and Lamar checking into the National, while another placed them at the Metropole.

Sasha looked up from her ink tracing and said, "Is only gossip, no?"

"This stuff?" Ann tapped the face of Claude's phone. "Yes, it's pretty dreadful."

"Do you know who is Matt Damon?"

"Sure."

"Does your BlackBerry know where is he? Someday I would like to meet."

"I'm afraid he's married," Ann said.

"Shit," said Sasha. "Then can you look up for me Owen Wilson?"

The phone began to ring. Ann usually let Claude's voice mail pick up, but she felt inspired by Sasha, who said, "You answer. I take a break."

On the other end, a gruff man demanded money.

"This is Fremont Spores. Where the hell's Abbott?"

Ann said, "He's not available right now. I'm his assistant— can I help you?"

"His assistant. That's a good one." Fremont Spores sounded crusty and perturbed. "Yeah, you can ask Claudius where was he yesterday. How come he didn't show up like he said."

In her most soothing PA imitation, Ann said, "I'm so sorry. Did you two have an appointment?"

"The Mickey D's on Lincoln, same as always. Only he blew me off."

"Well, Mr. Abbott's had a very hectic week."

Fremont said, "Who *are* you? That greasy A-hole owes me two hundred bucks."

Ann was thinking about how Claude had locked her in the

trunk of the car; she still had marks on her knuckles from trying to slug her way out. The handcuffing, too—completely unacceptable.

She said, "I wouldn't get your hopes too high, Mr. Spores."

"What?"

"About getting your money. Claude's not the most honorable person."

"Look, I always been straight with him. Now he fucks me over for two lousy C-notes?"

"For what it's worth," said Ann, "he owes me, too."

"How much?"

"Three days of my life."

Fremont said, "Lady, it ain't no joke. This is how I pay the rent."

"Hey, I've got something you might be interested in." Ann told him about a text message that had arrived an hour earlier: party tonite @ pubes. megan fox. lil wayne. u pay for more? word is lindsay mite crash it.

She said, "If Claude hears about this, he'll be there."

Fremont knew the girl was right. They'd all be there, the whole maggot mob. "Tonight, you said. Okay then."

"Maybe you'll get your money after all."

"Somethin' like that."

"Oh, one more thing." Ann could feel Sasha the henna artist pinching her elbow.

"Make it fast," said Fremont.

"You wouldn't happen to know if Owen Wilson was in town."

"I will if he gets busted, or maybe totals a car. That happens, you want a call? It's on me."

Sasha overheard and was nodding excitedly.

"You're a prince," Ann said to Fremont Spores, who grunted dubiously.

She added, "You got the name of the club, right? It's Pubes."

"Oh, I got it. Don't worry."

29

Chemo informed Maury Lykes that he'd decided not to kill the actress.

"Keep your damn money," he told the promoter.

"That's the same thing *she* said. Is it something in the fuckin' water?"

Maury Lykes was worried; he could not imagine Ann DeLusia fading quietly from the scene. "I'm starting to wonder about you," he said irritably to the bodyguard. "First you pass on Abbott, and now the girl."

"Abbott I can use. The actress, her I like."

They were sitting across from each other in the back of Maury Lykes's limousine, idling in the driveway of the Stefano.

"But she can wreck everything," the promoter said.

"Leave her alone." Chemo wasn't sure why, but he didn't want Maury Lykes hiring another hit man to go after Ann. He felt strongly about this.

"Anything happens to her," he said, "I'll hunt you down and chop your little monkey cock to the nub." To help Maury Lykes visualize, Chemo pressed the covered rotor of the weed whacker into the Y of the promoter's crotch, which was already chafed from a carpet romp with the Czech gymnasts.

"Okay, I get it!" Maury Lykes pushed the prosthesis away. The limo driver's eyes were as wide as a doll's in the rearview mirror. "Who's baby-sitting Cherry?"

"Mom and dad," said Chemo.

"What's on tap for her later?"

"Big night. Room service and Pay-per-View."

"And no actors!"

"Don't worry, Maury."

The promoter's phone began to ring, so Chemo got out of the car. He was approaching the lobby doors when he heard Maury Lykes shout his name.

What now? Chemo thought. He turned and walked back to the limo.

"That was Janet! You won't believe this," the promoter steamed.

"Let me guess."

"She said they left her alone for ten minutes and now she's gone. These people, they're goddamn idiots!" Maury Lykes was an unhealthy shade of purple. "Morons! Boobs!"

Chemo didn't disagree. The genetic proof was Cherry herself.

"I'll check the service exit," he said.

The woman who answered the door was blond and good-looking. She wore a hotel robe. Her coral toenails were freshly painted. When Detective Reilly flashed his badge, she invited him to come in. The room was small and furnished in trendy Caribbean; white drapes, ceiling fans and lots of tropical hardwood. The four-poster bed was made.

"My name's Ann," the woman said.

"Ann what?" Reilly asked.

"DeLusia. With a capital *L*."

"Are you alone?"

She pointed at the bathroom door. "I'm with a friend. He's in there."

"I'm looking for an individual," the detective said, "for questioning."

He told her the suspect's name was Clinton Tyree, and provided a short, graphic description. "I believe these belonged to him." Reilly held up the shotgun-shell braids. "I found them outside on the ground beneath your window."

The woman named Ann examined the plaits and said, "Wild." Then she knocked on the bathroom door. "Captain, you busy?"

Reilly was caught off guard by what happened next. A

large man stalked out of the bathroom singing, "Good Lord, I feel like I'm dyin'!"

He wore an expensive-looking blue suit and a matching eye patch. His sun-bronzed head was decorated with mystic-looking slashes and symbols, drawn with what appeared to be dark lipstick. Around his neck was a string bolo tie, cinched with the desiccated beak of a dead bird.

"Are you Governor Tyree?" the detective asked.

"'The strongest man on earth is he who stands most alone.'"

"Excuse me?"

"That's Ibsen. Another gloomy Nord, but palatable in small doses."

The woman named Ann said, "You two chat. I've gotta go get beautiful." She went into the bathroom, leaving the door ajar.

Reilly didn't sit down because he felt intimidated; the one-eyed man already towered over him. "Are these yours?" he asked, displaying the braids.

The suspect laughed. He had to be well into his sixties, yet he looked uncommonly fit. His fists hung at his sides like dented cowbells. "You seem like a decent sort," he said to the detective. "Kindly get to the point. The winsome Ann and I are preparing for an event."

Reilly asked him first about the bus hijacking and the sadistic assault on Jackie Sebago. "You match the description of the suspect—except for those expensive threads."

"You think it's too much?" The one-eyed man pinched the

pleats of his pant legs. "The things we do to please the ladies, no?"

"We found a campsite not far from the crime scene."

"Boy Scouts would be my guess. A radical cell."

The man was admitting nothing, and there wasn't much Reilly could do. He didn't have a speck of physical evidence connecting this character to the crime—one lousy fingerprint on a water bottle found far in the boonies, which proved nothing.

The detective said, "Sebago turned up dead yesterday in the crocodile refuge. Shot through the heart with a speargun."

"My, my." The big man cocked his illustrated head. He looked authentically surprised.

"Do you know anything about it?" Reilly asked.

"This murder, or death in general?"

Ann came out of the bathroom and said, "The captain was here with me all day yesterday, Detective. And the day before that and the day before that." She was putting on silver hoop earrings. "I need to get dressed, if you don't mind."

Reilly knew they didn't have to speak to him at all. He also knew he could call in one of the Beach cops and they'd haul the one-eyed guy down to the station and bust his balls for not having any ID, some bullshit like that. No actual crime solving would be achieved, and Reilly would end up spending an extra night in the city, which would piss off his lieutenant when he got the per diem voucher.

"Do you own a sawed-off shotgun?" Reilly asked the man.

"I'm not a hunter in the traditional sense. I prefer to eat what's already dead."

The detective patiently turned to Ann. "The passengers on the bus said the hijacker had a woman with him. Possibly a captive."

She smiled and nodded toward her companion. "He's *my* captive. Does he not look absolutely killer in pinstripes?"

Reilly, who'd seen many improbable couples in Key West, did not comment on the gaping and somewhat creepy age difference. "Why does she call you 'captain'?" he asked the man.

"I was in the army."

"Vietnam, right? And you came home and got elected governor."

The man turned his back on the detective and walked to the window.

Ann led Reilly to the door. "Sorry we weren't more helpful," she said. "He can be quite the scamp."

"His name is Clint Tyree, isn't it? You can tell me."

"Truly I don't know."

Reilly doubted that the one-eyed man had raced back to Monroe County just to shoot a fishing spear into Jackie Sebago. As for the earlier twisted mischief on Key Largo, Reilly had an equally strong feeling that he was looking at the culprit. They could stick the man in a lineup, just to rattle him, but then they'd have to fly in the eyewitnesses, a budget-busting gamble that Reilly's superiors were unlikely to approve. The passengers from the hijacked bus were scattered all over the country. Even if Reilly could get them back to the Keys, the suspect himself would be practically unrecognizable after his fresh grooming and dapper remake.

Still, the detective went ahead and told Ann that he might need to talk to both of them again. "It would be a more formal type of interview," he added for weight, "at the sheriff's office down in Marathon."

"Of course," she said pleasantly, and gave him a cell number. "This is my first time being somebody's alibi. It's kind of exciting."

Reilly took the stairwell down, the braided gun shells clicking like castanets. He was sure that a DNA test on the silver hair would lead back to the man he'd just met, but it was hardly enough on which to hang a criminal prosecution. There were plenty of bad Rasta jobs wandering around South Florida. His lieutenant wouldn't be impressed.

A larger question in Reilly's mind was what would be accomplished by locking up Tyree, if that's who it really was. The guy gave prime years to his country, won a boxful of combat medals—if he wants to grow old alone and whacked-out in crocodile country, who cares? He seemed to pose no threat to the innocent, only to scoundrels and fools who crossed his path.

Outside the hotel, the detective paused briefly, trying to recall where along Collins Avenue he'd parked his car. He didn't relish the long southbound drive to the Keys at rush hour. Somebody whistled, and he looked up. Framed in

Ann DeLusia's window was the man who might or might not have been governor in another life. He grinned down at Reilly and snapped the elastic band on his designer eye patch.

"I wish I were riding with you," he called out. "Two ghosts on a cloud!"

Reilly offered a small salute and said, "G'night, captain."

The former Cheryl Gail Bunterman snuck out of the Stefano when her parents went to the Larks' suite to preview the fabricated account of their daughter's "kidnapping," in advance of its Internet release. Cherry, who'd previously packed an outfit for the evening, took a service elevator to the first floor and then grabbed a cab to Star Island.

Tanner Dane Keefe was in a forlorn state, having sniffed out a rumor that Quentin Tarantino was cutting some of the actor's best scenes from his upcoming shocker, a blood-drenched takeoff of the beach-blanket films of the sixties. Evidently the director had been persuaded by the studio's marketing department to rethink the importance of the necrophiliac-surfer role to the script's core message. Key distributors in Japan, India and parts of the Mideast had emphatically stated they weren't interested in selling a movie in which drowned tourists were sodomized to the tunes of Frankie Avalon under the pier at Newport Beach. It was the prevailing sentiment that some foreign audiences would be confused, and possibly provoked to riot.

"Quentin won't even text me back," Tanner Dane Keefe lamented, "the cowardly prick."

Cherry was of course more interested in the actor's stash than in his career travails. She shamelessly sucked on his fingers while groping chimplike through the pockets of his jeans. "Baby, where are my vikes?" she cooed. "Tell momma now."

"Do we have to go out tonight?" grumped Tanner Dane Keefe.

"Most definitely. And we gotta make it crazy good," Cherry said, "'cause after tomorrow I turn into, like, a freakin' nun."

"What're you talkin' about?"

"You'll find out." She located a bottle of hydrocodone and washed down two pills with a slug of Bombay Sapphire. "No more parties for a while," she announced.

"Yeah, I'm so sure."

"Seriously, Tanny. This is huge." She just had to tell him all about it.

Afterward he said, "Cherry, that's fucking insane."

She giggled. "Isn't it?"

"No, I mean, like, insane in a really bad way. Who's gonna believe you got kidnapped?"

"Just wait. I'm makin' a police report and everything. Mom and Dad are totally down with this," said Cherry, "and so are the Larks—they do all my blogging and tweeting."

"No shit?" Tanner Dane Keefe had once tried to hire the twins as his publicists but they'd declined, saying he wasn't sufficiently famous or fucked-up.

"Maury says I can't be a kidnap victim and party, too. That's why tonight you and me are gonna take no prisoners." Cherry goosed him with a thumb. "Now, go put on something super-hot. Know what would rock? Those black Prada stretch pants I bought for you."

"Done," he said.

She rolled over on her tummy and belched into a pillow. "Am I the best, or what?"

Ann studied her face in the mirror and found no lingering marks of the car accident, or of Claude bonking her in the nose. The retouched henna tatt was tastelessly eye-catching, and she looked forward to scrubbing off the stupid thing the next morning. Her immediate challenge was fitting on the green contact lenses; Ann couldn't tolerate the sensation of foreign objects attached to her eyeballs. She kept tugging at her lids and blinking like a stone tweaker. Eventually one of the contacts dropped into the sink and rode a water droplet down the drain.

"To hell with it," she muttered, and tucked a pair of Tom Ford shades into her purse.

The new sleeveless dress she'd bought was candy red and way short; the matching strappy heels had an agonizing arch but they looked sexy. Lawrence the philandering flutist would have approved. Ann was jazzed about going out—it felt liberating not to have the Buntermans around, critiquing her choice of fashions.

Skink was pacing the hotel room, humming a melody that she recognized from a bank commercial but that was allegedly a rock anthem back in the sixties. Earlier he'd threatened to shoot out the flat-screen TV during a program featuring morbidly obese people who were competing to lose weight. One of the contestants had been reduced to tears by her buff, toothsome trainer. The scene had greatly upset the governor, who'd snatched the shotgun from the gym bag and was inserting a shell in the chamber before Ann managed to calm him.

He was such an interesting and complicated character that she decided to imagine, at least for tonight, that he was her secret lover. It was important to feel reckless and unbound when she made her entrance, and such a bold fantasy would put her in the proper spirit. She knew that nothing physical would ever happen between them, but she was flattered that he insisted on sleeping under the bed, presumably to avoid temptation.

After she emerged from the bathroom, Skink stopped pacing and said, "Tonight I'm not at my best."

Ann spun around gaily. "Whatcha think of the dress?"

"I think I was born too soon."

"Stash the gun," said Ann.

"Have you read Nietzsche? Of course you have."

"Look, I know this isn't easy for you."

Skink looked somber. "I can't promise civil comportment. Anything happens, say you never saw me before."

"For heaven's sake, it's just a nightclub." Ann stood on

tiptoes and kissed him lightly on one cheek, careful not to smear the tribal markings he had etched with lipstick. Earlier she'd asked if the dramatic pattern painted on his head was Mayan in origin. He had said it was a Calusa ceremonial mask, drawn from his memory of a museum piece in Fort Myers. The Calusas, he'd added, were badass magnificent. They decapitated their enemies and also invented the custom of mooning, which was first used to insult Spanish missionaries.

"If I make it through tonight," Skink said, "I'm taking off for the Keys tomorrow."

"And I'll be on a flight to L.A. So there."

Finally he smiled. "Annie the actress."

"You're a champ for doing this," she said. "We'll make some memories."

"I don't dance," Skink said.

"But you have a certain presence. I see epic fun in our future."

"Put on your shoes."

"Panties first." Ann pulled a sheer tan thong from a shopping bag and twirled it on her pinkie, causing him to sigh.

She said, "You've gotta promise me something."

"Now what?"

"Promise you'll keep the Zegna suit. After I'm gone? In case we hook up again someday."

He laughed thunderously. "Annie, don't push your luck."

*

Bang Abbott comfortably reverted to beast mode. He spent the night in the rental car and the morning at the topless beach, scouting for semi-famous breasts. The European tabloids were insatiable, though slow to pay. He'd picked up a few leads that didn't pan out: a Lohan sighting at the Delano, Daisy Fuentes playing volleyball at Lummus Park, Paris sneaking out of a collagen clinic on Lincoln Road.

All bogus, but that's how the game was played. Some days you ran your ass off and came up empty-handed.

Bang Abbott recalled what Peter Cartwill had told him when he'd tried to peddle his mile-high Cherry Pye story to the *National Eye*—that even the tabs were hot for street video these days. *Yeah, mate, we're paying good money. Check out our Web postings.*

Well, screw that. Bang Abbott didn't want to roll with a crew, and he definitely didn't want to lug a bulky Betacam. Besides, there was no strategic challenge in video pursuit; the pack swarmed in unison, baboons on autofocus. Bang Abbott enjoyed shooting stills on the fly because it required a creative engagement of the brain. And as long as American newsstands were such celebrity crapfests, he could make a damn good living. Headlines sold magazines, but photos sold the headlines.

He wondered what Cherry's bodyguard had done with his Nikons. The homicidal beanpole wasn't returning his calls, but Bang Abbott didn't want to seem pushy—he could get by with the old Pentax for now. Despite the collapse of his fatuous Star Island scheme, he remained optimistic that he'd eventually see some cash from the Cherry Pye pictures. He had urged Chemo to download the images from the cameras' memory cards, as a backup save, but the bodyguard didn't own a personal computer and trusted none of his associates who did. As long as that spooky freak was running the show, Bang Abbott could do little but hope for the best. Meanwhile there was rent to be paid, not to mention the car lease.

Most of his afternoon was wasted in Surfside staking out a Catholic church, of all places. A sixty-one-year-old priest was known to be having a fiery affair with the twenty-five-year-old star of a popular Cuban-American soap opera called *Amor y Lágrimas*. An Italian newspaper that feasted on Vatican discomfort was offering two thousand for a photo of the furtive couple holding hands, six grand for a lip-lock. Bang Abbott's tipster had neglected to say whether the young *telenovela* star was male or female, a detail that mattered more to the Church than to the paparazzo. He didn't care if the priest was boinking a llama.

For more than three hours Bang Abbott hugged the branches of an ant-infested banyan tree overlooking the rectory, but Father Franco and his mystery lover never emerged. Full concealment was unachievable for the photographer due to his corpulence and the low height of his perch; at one point a nun came out, rolling a wheelbarrow across the courtyard, and Bang Abbott was fairly sure that she flipped him the finger.

At dusk he descended, returned to South Beach and began

his crepuscular preparations for the party at Pubes. It was sure to be a cluster, but he'd make some dough. Every celeb hanging in Miami was supposed to show up. As usual, Bang Abbott planned to ignore the velvet-rope scene; the money shots always presented themselves later, at the back-door exits, when the action was winding down and the stars lurched out wasted and goofy.

As he cleaned the camera lenses, tested the flash units and recharged the battery packs, Bang Abbott's thoughts turned not once to Fremont Spores. He had practically forgotten the conversation in which Chemo informed him that he owed Fremont two hundred bucks for the solid tip about the drunken American Idol. Even had he remembered the debt, Bang Abbott wouldn't have paid the shriveled old wanker a nickel, since the information had gone unused.

He would be astounded to learn how miffed Fremont was.

30

Pubes was owned by an ambitious young Russian who'd gotten rich selling bootleg colonoscopes and recycled cardiac stents. He had purchased the nightclub for money-laundering purposes and gotten carried away with the theme, suggested by his stripper girlfriend. All the bartenders and wait staff wore V-cut vinyl pants that exposed tufts of their short-and-curlies, dyed luminescently. Even classier was the main dance floor, which featured nine hundred square feet of synthetic bush, black shag pile that mapped a heart-shaped pattern upon a sculpted mound of flashing flesh-tone fiberglass.

Chemo was immune to the dubious motif; to him, all these joints were the same—dark, loud and manic. The roid-head minding the door had confiscated his electric cattle prod and given him grief about his mechanical prosthesis, which Chemo refused to detach. A junior manager had been summoned and Chemo somewhat balefully recited his rights as a handicapped person in the state of Florida, and also the legal consequences for any establishment that was found to discriminate. Now he sat unbothered at the bar, sipping a diet Sprite and waiting for Cherry Pye to show up with Tanner Dane Keefe. The actor's personal assistant had helpfully set Chemo on their trail after Chemo had interrupted a genuflectional encounter between her and the pharmacy delivery boy beneath a pool-side gazebo at the mansion.

The club filled quickly. Chemo suppressed his bouncer instincts and kept his back to the door, because he knew Cherry would be on the lookout for him. He had ditched the skinny Palins in favor of black Ray-Bans. The look was completed by a raspberry beret and the calfskin bomber jacket with extra-baggy arms to accommodate the weed whacker, which was now propped on the pleather bar. Hunkered in the shadows, away from the throbbing lights, Chemo hoped that his igneous complexion and NBA altitude would go unnoticed—at least until he had to make a move. The beveled mirror behind the bar offered a champagne-glass view of the main room, and although he didn't recognize anyone, he assumed from the presence of so many leeches, bimbos and minders that some of the partyers were famous. A call girl sitting two bar stools away leaned over and said a singer named Pink was in the VIP room.

"Is she any relation to Dried Up?" Chemo said, causing the prostitute to grab her handbag and swirl away.

The music was blaring and boring, as melodic as a dental drill. World beat, trance, techno, electro, house funk—Chemo didn't care to know the difference. He reflexively tuned it all out, a survival skill he'd refined during long gigs as house muscle. The only alternative was to strangle the deejay, in this case a hyper little scarecrow who called himself Ricky Joy-Boy and wore a sleeveless kangaroo vest to show off the crucifixion ink on his stringy biceps.

As the bartender delivered another Sprite, Chemo glanced in the mirror and stiffened. Standing behind him was a slender blonde in a short dress and round lavender shades. Screaming in Technicolor from her neck was a familiar truncated zebra.

"Hey, you," the woman said playfully.

Chemo spun around slowly on the bar stool. After a hard look he realized it wasn't Cherry; it was the actress. The man she called "captain" loomed nearby, wearing the blue pinstriped suit, a bird-beak bolo tie and an expression of aching melancholy. His hairless orb was boldly streaked with primitive markings.

"Nice dress," Chemo said to Ann DeLusia.

"You really like it?"

The one-eyed man began to rumble. "This place is toxic."

"Oh, get a grip," Ann said, spearing him with an elbow. Then she smiled at the bartender and ordered two margaritas.

*

Cherry Pye and Tanner Dane Keefe were smoking a joint in the back of an Escalade outside the club. She had on a flimsy silk top, black pumps and four-hundred-dollar jeans. She would've worn her new Max & Cleo but she'd been too stoned to shave her legs.

"Ever been married?" Tanner Dane Keefe asked.

"Nah, but I was engaged two different times."

Cherry's first fiancé was the road manager for either Phish or Rusted Root—she often got the groups confused. She and Eric broke up when he refused to ask the band to let her sing on its next album. Her second fiancé, also named Eric, was a professional skateboarder whom she'd met at the X Games; he listened only to reggae and insisted on wearing his elbow pads to bed. Both engagements were brief, and Cherry never even got a rock out of the deal. Having the attention span of a gerbil, she never gave her infatuations enough time to bloom into love. Already she was growing weary of Tanny.

"I am totally into being free," she asserted thickly.

"Free is good." As Tanner Dane Keefe finished off the doob, he noticed a billowy entourage being led past the velvet rope. He pointed and said, "Look. Kardashians."

Cherry cheered. "They dance like freakin' buffaloes! Hurry, let's go."

The actor helped her out of the SUV and they locked arms before unsteadily making their way across the street. A couple of paparazzi shouted Cherry's name but she pretended not to hear.

She hustled her date to the front of the line, but the pinheaded simian at the door appraised them skeptically. After rechecking the list, he said, "I already let you in."

"Funny-funny-funny," said Cherry.

The no-neck shrugged. "Like an hour ago. See? 'Cherry Pye.' I already marked the name."

"It wasn't me, asshole. Here, you want some DNA?" She was preparing to spit on the man's clipboard when Tanner Dane Keefe stepped forward and said, "She's cool."

The security guy, who miraculously recognized the actor, lifted the rope. Roused by the affront, Cherry stormed into the club and beelined for the ladies' room.

Tanner Dane Keefe went to the bar. A longhaired Turk sat down beside him and grumbled, "This is no good. Music sucks pole."

The actor was distressed for another reason. He patted his pockets and said, "I think that crazy bitch jacked my meds."

Skink downed the margarita in two gulps. Chemo said he wasn't drinking. Ann was already on the dance floor, ripping it up.

"The fellow who kidnapped her, that so-called photographer," Skink said, "I'd like a word with him."

Chemo said it could be arranged. "But you can't kill the fucker yet." From his jacket he took out two plastic chips, which he explained were the memory cards from Abbott's cameras. "This is my 401k right here. I need that douche bag to help me sell these pictures."

Skink leaned closer. "Pictures of whom? Not Annie, I hope."

"No, man. These are the ones Abbott took of Cherry." Chemo had removed the stamp-sized cartridges before pawning the paparazzo's Nikons at a shop on Biscayne Boulevard.

"And when will this pricey auction take place?"

"After the tour," Chemo said, "when she overdoses. Abbott says it's a sure thing. Then people'll go fucking nuts over her, just like they did for Michael Jackson."

Skink fingered his eye patch. He was unaware of Jackson's death, or of the media convulsion that followed. That was one of the benefits of living in a crocodile swamp.

"What'd he do to her, anyway? The actress, I mean," said Chemo, "besides the handcuffs and all. He didn't try to—"

"She says no."

"'Cause if he did, I'd say go ahead and waste the bastard." Chemo put the memory cards away. In the mirror he was watching Ann dance. "I told him not to hurt her," he added.

Skink asked, "So where's *your* girl?"

"I expect her any minute."

Although Cherry's one-armed bodyguard and the ornate hermit didn't exactly blend with the sleek clientele, the club's rainbow strobing provided a measure of cover. In addition, the mutant factor at Pubes was high; they weren't the only ones drawing stares.

"How'd it happen?" Chemo pointed to Skink's eye patch.

"Got kicked with a boot. You?" Skink tapped the shaft of the weed whacker.

"Barracuda," Chemo said.

The governor whistled sympathetically.

Each of the men couldn't help but wonder about the other's backstory, but they let it be. The only thing that mattered was how the night would play out, and where the boundaries lay. Some of this would be decided by the two unpredictable women who were the subjects of their supervision.

Skink pressed a knuckle to his forehead. The bass line that blasted from the ceiling amps was stamping bruises on his brain. "I've been thinking about what you said—you really want your girl to OD? Son, that's pretty damn cold."

Chemo tweezed an itchy lesion on his nose. "Wanna trade? I'll take the actress, you take the train wreck." He wiped his fingers on a cocktail napkin and said, "Cherry croaks, I won't be the only one makin' money. Every damn magazine on the planet will paste her face on the cover. And all those fuckwits outside with their cameras—you don't think they'll be crashing the funeral?"

Skink turned away from the mirror. The reflection of himself dressed in a tailored suit was unnerving. "I just want to go home," he said.

Although Annie *was* a vision on the dance floor.

A waitress breezed past, handing out tubular glow-stick necklaces. The governor broke open a green one and smeared the luminous ooze all over his cheeks.

Chemo frowned. "You got good skin. You should take care of it."

Skink had his broad back to the bar. He said, "Well, sir, they *do* look alike!"

"Who?" Chemo whirled to see. "Jesus Henry Christ."

Cherry Pye had appeared, dancing on the bushy end of the floor with the triple-named actor. Of course she was already toasted.

Chemo stood up. "Here goes," he said.

The governor put a hand on his shoulder. "Let's give it a minute." He was smiling.

Cherry's bodyguard shrugged. "Sure. What the hell." Then he asked the bartender for a tall glass of gin, straight up with a twist of lime.

Ann spotted Cherry first and practically skipped across the dance floor. The singer was oblivious, fuzzily scouting the premises for Jay-Z or Lil Wayne or even Justin—anybody with a name, really. *Anybody.*

Tanner Dane Keefe recognized Ann as the photographer's assistant at the Star Island photo shoot. When he reintroduced himself, she dispensed air-kisses and never missed a beat, never stopped working it. This was her night to play; no pizza and cable movies in the manager's office. Ann told Tanner Dane Keefe that her name was Cheryl Gail. He offered a hit of X and she said, "No thanks, baby."

"Baby" usually worked on the young ones.

Tanner Dane Keefe was smiling. "So, Cheryl, what do I have to do to get on the cover of *Vanity Fair*?"

"Dance with me," Ann said.

"Hey, I'm serious." Then he actually winked. "Can't you make some calls?"

She thought: *Why burst his bubble?* "Okay, but it'll cost ya."

"Sweet," said the actor, fogbound as ever.

Nearby, Cherry Pye was listlessly shaking her hair to the music, still scanning the crowd. Her feet were moving, though it was more of a nursing-home shuffle than a techno dance move. Ann got right up beside her and said, "I really like your shoes."

Tanner Dane Keefe noticed Ann's tattoo and gleefully pointed it out to Cherry, who wasn't amused. She slapped a hand to her neck, blurting: "I thought I had the only one!"

Ann whispered, "I copied *you*."

"Really?" Cherry chose to be flattered. Besides the Axl tatt, she didn't pick up on the resemblance between herself and this unknown club tramp.

Tanner Dane Keefe did—the two hot long-legged blondes, shimmering side by side in designer shades.

"Outrageous," he said. "You're, like, two mirrors!"

Ann laughed. "Isn't it wild?"

The actor whipped out his cell phone and snapped a picture of the women and showed it to Cherry, who took several moments to focus. Then she wheeled angrily on Ann: "Are you some kinda freakin' wannabe, or stalker, or what? Get the fuck outta here—Tanny, go find a bouncer!"

Ann kicked it up a notch. She grabbed Cherry's hands and said, "Come on."

The singer tried to pull away but Ann was stronger and had the added advantage of not being loaded on weed, vodka and a ten-milligram diazepam scored off some fag hag in the john. Cherry had no choice but to dance.

"Who *are* you?" she demanded, jaws grinding.

"I'm you, Cheryl Gail."

"That's not my freaking name!"

Other partyers had stopped to watch the sloppy tango. Tanner Dane Keefe was snapping more photos with his cell.

"Seriously. I *am* you." Ann tugged Cherry closer. "That was my job—playing you. Is that pathetic or what? Ask your mom and dad, you don't believe me. I was you when you were too wrecked to be you."

Someone in the crowd called Cherry's name. Ann raised one arm and made a slinky lariat-twirling motion, which drew cheers and whoops.

The next moment she was down, pinned beneath the real Cheryl Gail Bunterman, who was punching at her wildly. Now lots of people had their phones out, taking pictures of the tangle. Not wishing to flash the whole world, Ann endeavored to keep her knees pressed together. She'd anticipated an awkward moment but not a full-on fistfight, though Cherry's blows were so feeble that it was sad, in a way.

"You—rotten—whore!" the singer grunted with each blow. "Who—are—you—whore?"

"I'm only trying to end it," Ann said, "for both of us."

"I hate you!"

"Otherwise you're gonna kill yourself."

"No—that's—you!" Cherry rasped. "You're—gonna—die—whore. One phone call."

"Okay, fine."

"One—phone—call—and—you're—freaking—dead!"

"Geez, are you done?" Ann pushed Cherry off and sat up. She saw Skink and Cherry's bodyguard advancing across the room, waving off the security goons.

"I guess we've been bad girls," she said to Cherry, who wobbled to her feet and tried to run. Chemo hooked her by the waist and flung her over a shoulder. A tipsy fan latched on and found himself flat on his back, staring at the business end of a motorized yard trimmer.

Chemo stepped over the mewling dork and made for the back exit. He was intercepted by Maury Lykes, accompanied by two females on the statutory cusp who'd been coached to introduce themselves as his nieces. The promoter was discomposed by the spectacle of Cherry, spitting and thrashing in Chemo's grasp.

"What the hell's she doing here?" he snapped. "Besides fucking up."

"It's not good," the bodyguard conceded.

"I mean, fucking up *everything*. Get her out!"

"That's Cherry Pye!" squeaked one of Maury's dates. "She's my ringtone!"

By the time Chemo emerged with Cherry from Pubes, she had gone limp. With elongated strides he crossed toward the Escalade; to clear a swath through the paparazzi, he kept the weed whacker buzzing. The singer dangled as deadweight, facedown against his chest. Her hair, shining like a flaxen pelt, cascaded below Chemo's belt buckle. He was fixed so intently on navigating a getaway that he didn't notice her vomiting quietly into the right pocket of his bomber jacket, the same pocket where he'd stashed the memory cards from Bang Abbott's Nikons.

The Star Island portfolio, no longer priceless, was afloat in puke.

Bang Abbott was so flustered to see Chemo carrying Cherry out of the club that he missed the damn picture.

Why is she here? the paparazzo wondered. *How could that seven-foot maniac let her come out and get wasted?*

Now the bogus kidnap story would never get traction. Her new CD was sure to bomb and the tour would fizzle and all those artful photographs he'd taken were doomed to be sold as agency stock, unless Cherry was considerate enough to die pretty soon.

Like maybe tonight.

But why would my luck change now? Bang Abbott mused bitterly.

He didn't even lift the Pentax to take aim—he just stood there like he was nailed to the sidewalk while Chemo stalked through the mob, swinging that goddamn lawn chopper. Moments later, the black Escalade peeled out.

Teddy Loo got the shot, of course. So did all the video crews, including Slyke, that rodent from TMZ. The only ones who missed out were Bang Abbott and some slippery geek he'd never seen before—lean, clean-cut, dressed sharp. The guy looked like a footwear salesman at Neiman's, not a shooter. The Canons hanging from his neck were shiny and unscuffed; clearly the kid was an amateur. While the rest of the maggots chased after Cherry, he hung back near Bang Abbott, who ignored him.

Silvio was his name. He worked for a man named Necker, who worked for a man named Smith, who worked for a man named Restrepo from Bogotá, Colombia. Silvio's assignment on South Beach had been set in motion by a phone call from Fremont Spores to Mr. Restrepo, who prized Fremont's police-scanning skills and was unhappy to hear him so agitated.

It was true that Silvio didn't know much about cameras, but he wasn't there to shoot pictures. Before long, he sidled away from Bang Abbott and eased himself into the swelling clot of paparazzi, who were returning to their lurking positions outside Pubes.

Cell phones tinkled and pinged, delivering news of Cherry's meltdown, including splotchy backlit snapshots taken inside the club. Bang Abbott groaned when he heard she'd tackled a woman on the dance floor, a headline that would not improve the market for a book of pensive portraiture. He resolved to put the empty-headed tartlet out of his mind and focus instead on the predatory task at hand.

Somebody famous was bound to come staggering out of the club any minute. It was time to feed the machine.

A back door opened and there was a starburst of camera flashes. Then in unison the paparazzi quit shooting, a battery-conserving reflex that kicked in as soon as they determined that the person emerging from Pubes was a mere civilian.

He was strapping and bald, his cheeks smeared with green Day-Glo goo. He wore a classy dark suit and a matching eye patch but otherwise appeared raw and unreliable. The photographers thought he was too old to be a bodyguard although he moved athletically, and with a forward sense of mission.

On instinct Bang Abbott scuttled closer, and he was rewarded. An attractive young woman materialized at the painted man's side. She wore here-I-am sunglasses, silver hoop earrings and a smoking red dress—Bang Abbott recognized her instantly.

"Ann!" he shouted excitedly. "Hey, over here!"

She peered into the oily throng. "Claude?"

Skink began guiding her across the street, where a man on a motorcycle waited.

"Ann, how 'bout a big smile?" Bang Abbott yelled, and started snapping pictures. The other paparazzi joined in, surging after them.

Ann DeLusia removed her sunglasses and stood for a pose. She had to laugh, it was all so ludicrous. There was Claude with his bandaged nubbin of a trigger finger, firing away. He hovered so close that she could smell the fresh drenching of Axe body spray, bless his lizardly heart.

"Hey, didn't I call it?" he shouted gleefully. "Wasn't I dead-on?"

"Yes, Claude. You're so wise, it's eerie."

One of the other shooters, probably Teddy Loo, called out, "Yo, sugar, who *are* you?"

"Oh, I'm nobody," said Ann.

"Not anymore!" crowed Bang Abbott.

Then Silvio, standing directly behind him, pulled out a gun.

When the 911 call came, Jimmy Campo and his partner were at Collins and Thirty-sixth, taping the ankle of a jogger who'd tripped over a stray Maltese. The paramedics raced down to Pubes and found bedlam. People were streaming out of the club, their bodyguards shoving and kicking at the swarm of photographers. Kanye, Lindsay, Wayne, Khloe, Fergie—yo, there's Megan Fox! Jimmy Campo knew who they were only because his girlfriend had started buying the *Eye*.

The street was so jammed with black SUVs that the cops had to clear a path for the ambulance. Lying in a sweaty heap on the sidewalk was an overweight white male suffering from a gunshot wound to his lower torso. Jimmy Campo recognized the prone man as the same toad who ten days earlier had paid him a grand for a stretcher photo in an alley behind the Stefano. *The guy's wallet might be worth checking*, Jimmy Campo thought, *if he passes out*.

Kneeling by the victim and holding his hand was a cute blonde in a short red dress who looked familiar. Jimmy Campo thought she couldn't possibly be the man's girlfriend, not if there was a God in heaven. The woman, who had dark glasses and a sketchy tatt on her neck, said the injured man's name was Claude. Standing beside her was an uncommonly large individual wearing a pinstriped eye patch and a bolo tie. His shaved head was marked with bold Indian symbols, and his face was striped with phosphorescent gunk.

It was in all respects a routine South Beach emergency call—until the one-eyed Samaritan peeled down the victim's pants to reveal a bloody perforation deep in the hairy cellulitic chasm of his scabbed buttocks.

"Behold!" the painted man boomed at the fallen paparazzo. "Somebody shot you a new asshole!"

Jimmy Campo stepped in and said, "Sir, we'll take it from here."

The bald man lifted the woman in red to his shoulders and carried her through the tumult. Jimmy Campo and his partner quickly began tending their new patient, who was pallid and clammy though still conscious.

The other photographers were more interested in chasing the spooked celebrities than consoling their stricken colleague; only Teddy Loo hung around to watch him hoisted on a stretcher.

"Does it hurt bad, bro?"

Bang Abbott shook off the oxygen mask and glared. "There's a bullet up my butt crack, you dumb sonofabitch."

"Yo, listen, before you go—who was the babe with the sick tatt?"

"What?"

"The one we just shot. That hot ringer for Cherry."

"You don't even know? Unfuckingbelievable."

"Don't be that way, bro. Share the love."

"Bite me, Teddy."

As the paramedics briskly rolled the stretcher toward the ambulance, Teddy Loo scurried to keep pace. He lifted one of his cameras and took aim.

Bang Abbott raised his head miserably. "Are you serious?"

Epilogue

CHERYL GAIL BUNTERMAN spent seven weeks at a rehab facility on St. Barts that specializes in holistic pomegranate cleansings. The concert tour was canceled and her album *Skantily Klad* sold poorly. *Rolling Stone* called it "wretchedly overproduced and underperformed" but praised the backup singer whose voice covered most of the tracks. The single "Jealous Bone" proved to be a modest success, selling 79,312 downloads after being plugged by Howard Stern on his radio program. Following her return from the Caribbean, Cheryl Bunterman announced she was changing her name from Cherry Pye to Chairish, the common spelling having been claimed by the Hasbro Company for a new self-wetting doll. Chairish's first post-rehab CD, a collection of Christian verses set to Bahamian junkanoo tunes, was never released.

She briefly joined the Church of Scientology but was expelled when a bong fell out of her handbag during an "introspection rundown." Currently, she lives in Los Angeles, where she's taping a reality show for TLC called *Almost Sober*. In the first episode, she persuades a reluctant neighbor to help her remove an unsightly tattoo.

Following the flop of *Skantily Klad*, NED and JANET BUNTERMAN separated. Ned partnered with the Jorgensens to purchase a thirty-acre vineyard in Mendocino County, while Janet moved in with her tennis instructor. The Buntermans continue to jointly manage their daughter's career, such as it is, and will make occasional paid appearances on her television show.

MAURY LYKES was indicted for income-tax evasion and fled to Bangkok, where he purchased a popular tourist hotel and introduced topless karaoke. He was later attacked and dismembered in his fern garden by the enraged father of a young cabaret singer named Linga Li. The savage crime received so much publicity that an enterprising Chinese music producer signed Linga to a long-term recording contract. Her first album, to be released throughout Asia on her eighteenth birthday, will be dedicated to "my dear Uncle Maury."

After the incident at Pubes, LUCY and LILA LARK terminated their association with Cherry Pye and the Bunterman family. The twins' publicity firm continues to thrive, rejecting all but the most recklessly unspooled celebrities. Most recently, the Larks have consented to represent a well-known star of action films who nearly garroted himself during a vigorous act of autoeroticism on the D train in midtown Manhattan. The sisters are said to have scored an exclusive interview for their client on an upcoming edition of *60 Minutes*, when he will reveal to Lesley Stahl a dark, gut-wrenching childhood secret that the Larks are now composing, and tweaking for maximum buzz.

The part of the deviant surfer was completely edited from the final cut of Quentin Tarantino's much-anticipated *Blister Beach*. Infuriated, TANNER DANE KEEFE fired his manager and legally changed the sequence of his name to DANE KEEFE TANNER. After their calamitous date at Pubes, he never contacted Cherry Pye again. On the advice of a barmaid, he switched chemical dependencies from hydrocodone to oxycodone, and took up free weights. He is now working on a Showtime miniseries about the Battle of the Little Bighorn in which he plays the role of Kyle, General Custer's loyal but headstrong groom.

After failing nine consecutive urine screens, METHANE DRUDGE was fired by the Poon Pilots and replaced on tour by the longtime drummer from the heavy-metal Canker Crew. Frantic to salvage his rock career, Drudge pleaded with the Lark sisters to become his publicists, but they turned him down. He fled the L.A. scene to join an obscure peyote cult, and was later found dead and half-eaten by coyotes in a homemade sweat lodge on the outskirts of Las Cruces, New Mexico.

The man who killed JACKIE SEBAGO was apprehended after the unusual murder weapon was traced to a Miami dive shop equipped with video cameras in the parking lot. A surveillance tape revealed the license number of the hit man's rental car, and the Avis Company helpfully supplied his driver's license information. Upon his arrest, the killer immediately ratted out WILLIAM SHEA, the person who'd hired him, and whose travel agent had failed to get him an upgrade from coach to first class. While Shea currently awaits trial for Sebago's murder, he and the other investors are aggressively suing the dead developer's estate to recover their stake in the Key Largo town-house project, which remains red-tagged and abandoned to this day.

After solving the Sebago homicide, DETECTIVE ROB REILLY received a commendation and a handsome glass paperweight from the Monroe County Sheriff's Office. He has kept an open file on the person he believes to be CLINTON TYREE, a former governor of Florida, and has returned several times to the remote campsite on North Key Largo. There is no sign of recent habitation.

Asserting that its home-owner policies don't cover bacterial contamination of household appliances, the Gulfstream Insurance Co. refused to buy a new washing machine for D. T. MALTBY. The ex–lieutenant governor of Florida eventually lost his house at the Ocean Reef Club to his fourth wife, who divorced him in favor of a local fishing guide. Maltby moved back to Tallahassee, slipped into renal failure and on his deathbed told friends about the harrowing visitation by Clinton Tyree. They all thought he was delirious.

RUBEN "WHADDUP" COYLE was cut from the Miami Heat after wrecking another leased Jaguar convertible. Unable to find work in the NBA, he moved to Athens and is now playing point guard for Olympiacos, one of the top basketball teams in Greece. He is not allowed to drive a car, or drink ouzo on game nights.

The memory cards containing the Star Island photographs of Cherry Pye were ruined by her own vomit, and in any event had attracted no interest from book publishers. BLONDELL WAYNE TATUM, also known as Chemo, gave up bodyguarding celebrities after that chaotic night on South Beach. The money paid to him by Maury Lykes was misspent on a series of experimental dermatological procedures that failed to improve his tragic facial appearance. Afterward, the doctor who performed the technique—known as "extreme laser brasion"—vanished from his Coconut Grove clinic and was never found. Chemo worked as an eviction specialist for several Florida banks until the real-estate market turned around, when he returned full-time to the home mortgage business.

Police never found out who shot BANG ABBOTT, or why. A photograph of the wounded paparazzo being borne away on a stretcher was published on page three of the *National Eye*, accompanied by a caption reading: **CATFIGHT CASUALTY—*Photog felled by sniper after Cherry's wild SoBe slapdown.*** Abbott underwent five hours of emergency surgery to repair bullet damage in his lower intestinal tract. Because of its problematic location, the entry wound was left open and a tube was inserted to serve indefinitely as a drain. Two days after the shooting, while still in the ICU, Abbott scribbled out a personal check to FREMONT SPORES for the sum of two hundred dollars, which was handdelivered by TEDDY LOO. Abbott recovered from his injuries, although it was many months before he again picked up a camera. Today he rents a small studio in Culver City, where he specializes in portraits of toddlers, prom couples and small pets. He is also available for corporate functions.

ANN DELUSIA became a star, though on her own terms. She chose *People* over *Us Weekly*, *Details* over *Vanity Fair*, Larry King over Mario Lopez, Ellen over Tyra, Kimmel over Leno, Tribeca over Sundance, ICM over CAA, and Revlon over Garnier. She still doesn't employ a stylist, publicist or bodyguard. In interviews she speaks pensively of her time as Cherry Pye's secret double, and always expresses compassion for the troubled singer. Ann steadfastly refuses to discuss what occurred while she was held captive by a "deeply disturbed fan" who'd mistaken her for the pop singer. She never brought criminal charges against Claude Abbott, and never publicly identified him. Three book publishers offered contracts in the mid-six figures, but Ann turned them down because they all insisted on pairing her with a ghostwriter. She also declined promising roles in films by Judd Apatow and the Coen brothers because she'd previously committed to appear in a Pedro Almodóvar project about three women hang gliders who become stranded on Gibraltar during a tsunami. She hasn't seen Skink since their motorcycle ride on the night Abbott was shot, although she occasionally speaks with JIM TILE, who reports that the former governor is in a good place.

BAD MONKEY

Carl Hiaasen

When a severed arm is discovered by a couple on honeymoon in the Florida Keys, former police detective – now reluctant restaurant inspector – Andrew Yancy senses that something doesn't add up. Determined to get his badge back, he undertakes an unofficial investigation of his own.

Yancy's search for the truth takes him to the Bahamas, where a local man, with the help of a very bad monkey (who allegedly worked on the Pirates of the Caribbean movies) is doing everything in his power to prevent a developer from building a new tourist resort on the island, with deadly consequences . . .

Outrageous, hilarious and addictive, this is the unique Carl Hiaasen at his absolute best. *Bad Monkey* will have you on the edge of your seat and laughing out loud.